The White Pig

A True History in Eight Books

The White Pig

A True History in Eight Books

**Nel Mezzo
della Vita**

Nel Mezzo della Vita Press

Copyright © 2007 Rob Swigart

ISBN 978-0-6151-4541-9

Family matters:

Cover and book design by Saramanda Penfield
Author photo by Tessa Swigart

These are signs you need to know:
When in your desperation
You come across a giant snow-white sow
lolling under oaks beside a hidden stream,
And she nurses a litter of piglets white as snow,
On that place you must build your town,
Safe harbor after all your strife.

—*The Aeneid*

BOOK THE FIRST: MARSHA, 1957

Chapter 1. In Which the Hero Visits the Zoo and Confronts His Simian Ancestry

This was a beginning: now the dead would rise from their graves, ghosts would roam the tormented night, and the pale hog-shape, resurrected, would drift among forest trees, huge and elusive and terrible. He couldn't be certain, because some things, many things, were yet in his future, but Cory Depew was about to exhume his family from an unmarked pauper's grave; he would turn up brittle bones, the faintest of outlines drawn in dust.

A pale shape, god of the great American Midwest, an indolent, lolling, smug, self-satisfied pig of a god, a huge hog-god, head sprawled, opened its eyes, snorts moving foul and damp through a rubber snout. It looked down now on this Cold Warrior, returned to Valhalla after three years in Thule, Greenland, where nothing existed but snow and fog and Mozart. It was the summer of 1957, and *Tammy*, sung by Debbie Reynolds, was Number One on the hit parade. The sounds of it buzzed in his ears.

Tammy, Tammy, Tammy's in love.

He walked aimlessly between the cages. The sun was high in a sky swept clean and blue. The humidity had risen, as always in summer when the river surrendered its vapors to the heat. Yet that was an autumn sky up there, above the Valhalla Zoo, above the gorilla, strangely pale, bleached by too much sunshine, too much rain.

Something profound was about to happen, though he could not say exactly what; something visceral and prophetic. Something *existential*.

He lingered by the gorilla cage with a small crowd of gawkers.

The gorilla, a sad, overweight, lugubrious Judge of a beast, sat gazing at the crowd with eyes that were tiny and

3

sly. Whatever his verdict, he did not pass it on, but returned to languid exploration of his chest.

From time to time some delectable flake — a bit of dead skin or small crawling thing — provoked a grunt, followed by a delicate and precise gesture as the gorilla plucked it from between thumb and forefinger with rubber lips.

"This the one?" someone said.

"Yeah," a boy said. "Watch."

The gorilla looked up again. Children called down the winding concrete aisles, through the decorative shrubbery, voices a shrill and distant happy summer sound. More Sunday customers strolled up to lean lazily against the rail.

The radio playing *Tammy* faded away. Although the day was sunny and hot and ordinary there was a sudden suspension of motion, a pause of collective indrawn breath. The ape was about to do something.

He did it.

He stood and turned to the crowd. He stretched his arms out toward the bars, reaching through with long fingers, and wrapped them around the metal one at a time, with an amazing deliberation. Still looking at the people on the other side of the bars, people who could see in those small brown eyes not only an extraordinary intelligence, but a haunted, chilling despair, he leaned back until those arms seemed to be stretched out longer than arms should be.

He paused. His legs were spread apart, his feet planted firmly on the bare cement littered with the rinds of previous meals. There was, in a momentary, almost subliminal undulation of his hips and in the apparent readiness of his now-obvious genitals beneath a sagging belly, something obscene and horrific.

Then he squeezed his eyes shut, hunched his head down, and with an intense though constrained violence, smashed the top of his head against the bars between his hands.

He looked at the crowd again. His loose lips were turned down in a frown of pain. A trickle of crimson blood

4

crawled down between his eyes. Then he turned away, loped to the back of the cage, sat for a moment, brushing the floor with the backs of his knuckles, and climbed to a wooden platform near the back of the cage.

The crowd was appalled. "Someone call a keeper! Someone! Get help!"

There was no help. No one appeared to soothe and reassure. The young man looked up at the pale sky neatly framed by the rich foliage of the zoo's sycamores and elms. The bars of the gorilla's roofless cage made straight, sharp lines; in either direction the walk curved away.

The gorilla, crouched on his platform, reached out for the rope dangling to the floor of his cage. He inspected the crowd adhered to the railing. No one could tear away. More and more ordinary Midwestern families, moms and pops and kiddies with dreams and desires, with diapers and secret despairs, were drawn into the hypnotic orbit swirling around the gorilla, under a swept blue sky above a Midwestern city beside a mighty river.

Behind the young man the press of people grew, gathering in density.

"Whadidedo?" someone asked behind him.

"Looked like he tried to kill hisself."

"Oh."

"You kidding?"

"Nope. Banged his head on the bars. Weird."

The gorilla looked up at this exchange, as though the conversation were familiar; were, in fact, a signal of some sort.

He cocked his head, eyes swiveled sideways toward his enthralled audience; he observed them all, the little boy pointing past Cory's elbow for his father, a couple relating events for others further back, where the language changed. "Gorilla tried to commit suicide," someone said.

"What, he sick?"

The gorilla seemed, uncannily, to smile.

He tossed the rope expertly into a single loop, twisted it cunningly into a knot, dropped the loop over his head, and

5

without once releasing the people at the railing from that terrible eye contact, launched himself into the air.

The rope snapped taut, and the gorilla hung, bouncing at the end of the rope, his arms and legs gesticulating wildly, his now swollen genitals obscene and distended, swaying. His eyes popped wildly, his tongue lolled from his loose mouth. All around him the young man heard shouts for keepers and help.

Then the knot slipped away and abruptly dropped the gorilla, who landed on the floor of the cage with a strange grace of legs bending at the knees and gentle knuckles brushing the cement as he turned slowly, with his shoulders slumped in sadness and failure, to vanish through a small door at the back of the cage.

The crowd, now solemn and hushed, broke up, its Sunday a ruin.

Chapter 2. In Which the Hero Returns Home and Sees a Friend

He paused a moment to look down the northern slopes of Mount Worthy at the city of Valhalla spread like blood pudding on sour rye; he looked at the river beyond, and beyond the river at the states of Ohio and Indiana. Deep green vegetation hid their towns — Lynnhaven, Sandy Harbor, Mayfield, Central City, Roseville.

He mouthed the names of those towns without saying them aloud.

Then he mouthed his own name. Cornelius Hauser Depew. Empty syllables, without meaning, without shape or form or substance, as ghostly and evanescent as the fogs of Thule blown across the glacier and down the rock slopes to the gray and oily sea. Cory Depew, a desolate young man.

While Cory contemplated the river, the gorilla's strange suicidal ritual glowing in afterimage, Hackamore Ovandrill was driving to the offices of Spiro Thanatopoulos, the Smyrna doctor, to consult with him about a small blastula sprouting in her womb, consequence of her very unsatisfactory liaison with the very Beat poet Gabriel Flagg. But Cory didn't know Hackamore Ovandrill, not yet.

His ancient DeSoto rusted on the cracked parking lot. A cloud of blue smoke erupted from the exhaust when he started it. Bald tires slipped, then caught. He cruised down Midgard Avenue through slanting gold light, turned right on Celestial Street. His left hand gripped the outside mirror while his right steered the car by means of a small knob attached to the steering wheel. The knob was designed to allow a driver to steer with his left hand leaving the right free to fondle a passenger. Cory had no passenger and was

7

inexperienced at fondling. He drove with his right hand so he could drape his left biceps over the windowsill, giving it the appearance of added bulk. He had bought this car from Vincent Black Shadow Lavere before he went to Thule; Vincent had always needed such a knob. Cory was sure of that.

Vincent was waiting outside his building. "How, kemosabe," Vincent said. Vincent claimed to be an Indian.

"Hey," Cory said.

"This your new place, eh, kemosabe?"

"Ugh," Cory said.

"Who's gonna believe it? 1001 Celestial Street. Nobody."

Cory shrugged. "I wish you wouldn't call me kemosabe all the time."

Vincent Black Shadow ran his hand through his spiky black hair. "It means good friend in the tongue of my people," Vincent informed him. "Are you not my good friend?"

"Not really your people," Cory said, but he said it to himself. Vincent liked the fiction and everyone pretended so hard to believe him that the story became true. He opened the door. Vincent winked at the huge Slyville Sinker hex sign the artist upstairs had painted over the entrance. The hex sign protected the building from evil cruising the streets of Valhalla. Vincent knew where Slyville was.

"Wow!" the Indian exclaimed, watching silverfish and roaches scatter. "This is some place. Two rooms! Tell me, kemosabe, do they share the rent?" He waved at the insects.

"Ha ha." Cory turned on the radio.

The radio told him of opportunities available, opportunities missed. Cory lived in the land of opportunity. Opportunity would come knocking. He should open up.

Vincent Black Shadow Lavere knocked on the kitchen table. Dust flew, roaches ran. "Wow," Black Shadow breathed.

"Baby, let me be," the radio crooned with Elvis' voice.

"Your lovin' Teddy Bear." Cory was nobody's Teddy Bear, but briefly sly gorilla eyes glittered in the insect dust.

"Nobody's gonna deliver mail to 1001 Celestial Street. I doubt if the Post Office believes in it. Your mail is going to go the same place as Santa's." Vincent scuffed his engineer boots through vast populations in the kitchenette.

Cory turned off the radio. Elvis died. "So what?" he said. "I don't get any mail anyway."

"How much you pay for this dump?" Vincent asked. The dump was an ancient mansion converted to two-room flats.

"Sixty-five a month, but that includes utilities."

Vincent thought that was robbery.

"It's what I can afford. I have to get a job. Nobody wants to hire an ex-radar technician with three years' experience peeling potatoes in Thule, Greenland, though." Across the street a rhythmic shattering sound began: Smash, pause. Smash, pause.

"What's that?"

"Something called karate," Cory said. "He breaks boards."

"No shit?"

"No. No shit."

"I have a lead for you," the Black Shadow told him a moment later. "A perfect job for the Masked Man. Schachter's Landing Rangers. Get it, Lone Ranger? Someone has to watch those big houses built on top of the Serpent Mound, you see. Indians are buried there. They need a Champion of Justice..."

"No, thanks."

"Come on, kemosabe. You're just afflicted with Eisenhower despair. You need something to take your mind off the existential dilemma, as Withrow would say."

"No, thanks."

"I have it on good authority there will soon be an opening. And you get silver bullets."

"What good authority?"

"I'm quitting."

9

"Oh. I didn't know you worked there."

"Weekends, eight to twelve pee-em. Doesn't pay much, but it's easy. Big tips, and if Christmas falls on a weekend, you get a nice glass of wine."

"Okay, Tonto, I'll think about it."

"He'll think about it," Vincent told the ceiling. The ceiling responded with a wet stain which gathered in the center and began, slowly, to drip onto Cory's bed.

"Do you know any girls?" Cory asked. He gazed sadly at a damp circle growing on his bed.

"Girls?" The Black Shadow gave an evil chuckle.

Chapter 3. In Which, After Some False Starts, He Sets Forth on His Quest, Takes a Side Trip Down Memory Lane, and Is, to His Regret, Successful

"The Silver Spoon out on the Louisville Highway," Vincent Black Shadow told him. "Beyond the Kernel Korn's. Lots of girls there, lots of them, hungry for your young body, kemosabe, and not a one of them will you know from high school, so don't worry. I promise, you'll be well laid. I do. But go early, the place is always crowded."

He roared away on his Vincent Black Shadow, the motorcycle after which he had named himself.

He was wrong, though. There were no girls at the Silver Spoon. So Cory went to Kernel Korn's, sat in his DeSoto and ate two deep-fried corn fritters on a double-deck bun and drank Coke from a cardboard cup which sat on a tray affixed to his window ledge, and saw no one to remind him of high school, though the lot was filled with enormous automobiles endlessly circling. Over his car radio the Everly Brothers sang *Bye-Bye, Love*. At that moment Cory did not think about the fat god of the midwest, the plump, indolent shufflebutt swine called time. At that moment Cory did not know that Hackamore Ovandrill had finished having her young womb scraped, the uterine curettage of Gabriel Flagg's implanted blastula, and was herself driving through these desolate streets as well.

All Cory knew was that the Everly Brothers were saying *Bye-bye* to happiness, and he was too.

As he drove back to the Silver Spoon he thought, as he often did when he was depressed, of the final movement *allegro assai* of Mozart's G-minor symphony, Number 40, Kochel 550.

11

He sat at the bar and stared at a glittery waterfall ashimmer with light. The waterfall was a replica of the spill from Lake Drowning Sow near Slyville into the Little Hawking River, but Cory did not recognize it. He did recognize the beer this waterfall was advertising, for he was sipping at it: Odrerir ("Say 'Oh-*dray*-rear'"). It was made with pure Little Hawking River water, in defiance, or in ignorance, of the virulent Schachter's Worm abreeding in those waters.

Behind the waterfall was a mirror, and in the mirror a stranger faced him.

"Who is that?" Cory asked, and the stranger said, "Who am I?"

Cornelius Hauser Depew, desperate for love. "Let me tell you about my family," Cory told the stranger.

"What's that?" the bartender said.

"Nothing," Cory muttered. "Talking to myself."

The bartender nodded, moved away.

"It's like this," Cory whispered, gazing around the nearly empty bar. A girl with red hair sat at the bar around the bend. Was she pretty? Cory could not tell. He turned back to the stranger. "When I was a kid it was Christmas. The terrible time of year." The stranger in the mirror nodded sympathetically.

Pine resins filled the living room, brownish yellow snow on the lawn, and the Philco brought news of war, rationing, fireside chats, so Cory was eight, and so was his twin sister Peggy who now lived with her husband who was a Negro named Withrow Duquesne and who had a baby and who was never mentioned at home. Despite the snow, new bikes sprouted in the streets, their fat tires sibilant on the damp pavement, sounding like the draft beer machine drawing another Odrerir. He could hardly sleep on Christmas Eve, because tomorrow he would get a new bike too.

"Ha ha," the stranger in the mirror laughed, and Cory laughed too, "Ha ha." When he did fall asleep that Christmas Eve, there were Negroes in his sleep who lived around the stadium, home of the Warriors who fell further and further behind in the race for the pennant. Negroes were exotic in those wartime days, and all the Negroes in his dream rode on bright red Schwinns.

"What do you want for Christmas, then?" his father asked, and Cory always said a Schwinn.

Peggy got a Schwinn. Cory got a wool suit.

Cory's mother Belle, whose father had once been physician to the Mayor of Valhalla, had her hair tied back. On Christmas she wore a veil over her face. "You look handsome in navy blue, Cory. Very handsome. Here, let me straighten your tie."

She straightened his tie. She kissed him through her veil, pressing tiny squares against his cheek. His face went numb.

He felt like he had been out in the snow melting on the street where his twin sister Peggy swerved and figure-eighted, but he had not been outside at all. He stood at the window in his new wool suit and watched Peggy on her girl's bike. He stood behind the straight-backed easy chair and pressed his face against the lace curtains and the cold glass and watched, and when he came away he had a delicate pattern of whorls and loops pushed into his forehead and cheek, almost like the pattern of his mother's veil, the lacy shapes of snowflakes.

It was three days before he could feel anything in his face, though his nose dripped continually onto his new lapels.

"Nice suit," daddy said. "We're proud of you, son. Aren't we proud of him, Belle?"

"Yes, Grouper, we're proud," Belle said with tight lips. She hadn't particularly liked *her* presents either, though God knows she did her best not to show it.

"I guess you want another," the bartender said, indicating the nickel beside Cory's glass. Cory nodded. "Name's Doc," the bartender said, setting the glass down again.

"Hi, Doc," Cory said. "What's up?" Beyond the

13

waterfall was Lake Drowning Sow, and beside the lake was Slyville where the Sinker's had established a utopia that had flourished and sunk a hundred years ago.

Cory saw crimson nails on the bar beside him. Long, plump, delicate fingers. A black turtleneck sweater, black leotards, dark secrets. A husky voice asked, "What's happening?"

"Huh?"

"What's happening? I said, what's happening?"

He looked at soft lips, long lashes, green eyes. Someone played *Tammy* on the jukebox, A-7, but she did not look like Debbie Reynolds.

"Oh," he mumbled.

"Well?" she persisted.

"Well, what?" Something in his beer intrigued him.

"What's happening?" She wasn't really interested, he could tell, despite her persistence. She looked sad.

"I don't know," he admitted. "What is happening?"

"I've just been to the doctor," she said. "It's just an office visit, that's all. Dr. Thanatopoulos, you know."

"I can't say I do." He ate his words. Was he going to get laid?

"Sure," she said. "Easy for you to say." She sounded bitter, sucking on a crimson nail. His heart leaped with fear, but she was looking around the room. "Excuse me," she said. "I think I see someone I know." Cory watched her black sweater go through the door into the night, where there was no one anybody knew.

He looked in the mirror; the stranger was gone. "That's funny," he said.

"Not it ain't. It ain't funny at all."

"What?"

Doc leaned toward him, blocking the mirror. Doc had once run over a North Korean soldier backing his halftrack out of a tight spot during a retreat. It was an accident for which he had been given a cluster of metal leaves to wear on his uniform.

"It ain't funny. I kilt a gook once, you know. In Korea.

14

It ain't funny, killing. Serious business. You been inna army?"

A cigarette was set into the corner of his mouth, LSMFT, a Lucky Strike, which meant fine tobacco; the long ash at the end sagged without falling. When he spoke, the cigarette remained motionless. Smoke rose straight from the red coal buried inside. At the ceiling the smoke flattened and spread.

"Three years," Cory answered, looking down the bar at the redhead. She was looking back, curiously. I'm going to get laid, Cory thought.

"Ya look young for the army. Peacetime. Pah!"

Even when he spit, the Lucky Strike did not quiver.

"You an oddball?" Doc asked him suddenly. His eyes were keen.

"I don't think so."

"Don't think so?" Doc turned to the redhead. "You hear that? He don't think so."

"Who was that girl?" Cory asked him, holding out his empty glass for another. "The one in the black turtleneck."

Doc tossed his head sideways toward the Nehi Orange sign on the door. "Her? Ovandrill girl. Funny name, that. Comes in here from time to time." He shook his head. "No good."

The girl around the bend in the bar was looking at him. His eyes faltered, lowered. He took a drink and looked again. Her eyes lowered. He could see her lashes.

"Whadidyado? Inna army?" Doc asked.

"KP, mostly."

"Cook, huh?"

"Radar tech."

"Oh. Oddball," Doc murmured. He had lost interest. He was a combat vet.

The girl around the bend of the bar raised her glass to Cory. He raised his. They drank to one another silently. Cory was a virgin.

"Nother beer," he croaked. Doc pulled the beer, set it down. The ash chose that moment to detach and fall. It

15

tumbled twice in neat loops end over end into the foam on Cory's draft Odrerir. First it was a heap, then a dark stain spreading, an evenly distributed rug of gray among the bubbles.

Before Cory could protest, Doc was gone. Cory looked up at the girl. She smiled.

He smiled back, raised his glass, gazed into it. The gray appeared to be gone. He wondered if it had ever been there.

"Something wrong?" Doc asked.

"No. Oh, no, no." Cory closed his eyes and gulped the beer. He set the glass down. Doc was watching him closely, so Cory smiled. "Perfect," he said. "Just perfect."

Doc nodded. His ash was exactly the same length it had been before. "Want another?" he asked.

Cory nodded. Soon he would be able to talk to her. One more beer. He looked over at her. Her eyelid drooped, and for a moment Cory thought she had an affliction. Then he realized it was a wink. He winked back.

"So where ya from?" Doc asked amiably.

Cory snatched his new beer out from under Doc's Lucky. "I grew up near Schachter's Landing. Now I live in Mount Worthy."

"Yeah?" Doc swirled his damp rag around the bar.

She wiped her tongue across the foam gathered on her upper lip, and Cory thought of the gorilla.

"What parta Mount Worthy?" Doc asked.

"Celestial Street."

"Oh. Got any Negroes out there yet?" He pronounced it knee-grows, like everyone else.

"No. No Negroes."

"Good," Doc said. "Getting to be a problem, them kneegrows. Pretty soon they're gonna wanna marry your sister."

She put her glass down very carefully. A hyperbola of foam sank down both sides of the glass.

"Did," Cory said, watching her glass.

She smiled at Cory in the silence; an open invitation to carnal bliss.

16

"I don't get it," Doc said. "Did what?"

"Marry my sister. A Negro."

He didn't notice when Doc left. The girl was about to slip down off her bar stool. She was going to come around to talk to him. He watched as she moved forward, thought with incoherent lust of that pelvic thrust, stared as she dropped from the edge of the stool.

She was gone. Plummeted utterly from sight.

Then she waddled around the end of the bar and approached him, a dwarf as tall as his knee.

"What's happening?" she asked.

Chapter 4. In Which He Comes Close

Fear rode Cornelius Hauser Depew all the way to the men's room, a profound dwarf-fear, dread of the diminutive, terror of the tiny. He'd fallen from his stool slack-kneed, mumbled "Excuse me," and stumbled from the nearly deserted Silver Spoon bar.

He stood in the baroque roadside lavatory and told himself that after all, he had consumed approximately 56 ounces of Odrerir Beer, made from pure Little Hawking River water (wherein Schachter's Worm wiggled out its life, over-nourished by industrial pollutants soon enough), and would have had to go soon anyway. Yet there lingered in his mind the bewildered dwarf-look following closely on her cheery "What's happening?"

So he drifted amid graffiti in an existential calm, relieved but not pardoned. Phone numbers beckoned with promises of what he had, after all, come to the Silver Spoon to find. Drawings diagrammed for him, though in admittedly sparse detail, some of the activities in which he could be expected to engage.

Beyond the last stall he found an elegant derivation of the Reimann-Papperitz second-order linear differential equation. It meant nothing to him. Just beneath it, however, someone had written, "Existence precedes essence." It reminded him of his brother-in-law Withrow Duquesne.

Cory read everything in the room twice. He examined the insides of the doors of all three stalls. He examined the minutiae of each declaration above the urinals. He measured the window four times, hoping it would in truth be large enough to allow his body to pass. It remained implacably small. He counted the flickers of the fluorescent light, measured against the second hand of his watch. On top of the 60-cycle flicker, there was a heterodyne beat, twelve times a minute. He began to work out the ratios in his head, but soon lost track. Math was not Cory's strong point.

He tried humming the first movement of *Eine Kleine Nachtmusik*, but had to stop when the door opened and Doc came in.

"She's gone," Doc said.

"Who?" Cory asked, all innocence.

"The dwarf."

"Oh." Cory went back to the bar.

She was gone, departed into that desolate abandoned night where small people are avoided because they are small, and big people fear them because they are not large. Cory did not know why he feared the dwarf. He only knew that cold moisture still clung to his forehead, his hair still stuck in damp spikes along his temples, and the thumping of his heart had not subsided. But there was someone else on the stool beside his own, someone with extraordinary pale hair and dark glasses, and she was tall and slender and belted into a trench coat and for a moment he thought it must be Lauren Bacall.

It was not Lauren Bacall. It was Marsha Willoughby.

"Hyall, honeysuck," she said. "Marsha Willoughby, wantchercock." She seemed to be introducing herself. Her lips were a pale pink, her skin the clearest white he had ever seen, and her small teeth behind her perfect lips were lovely, sharp and strong, and Cory was a man, though a virgin, who knew teeth. His father was in the business. And Marsha Willoughby, Cory could see, had perfect teeth.

"You have lovely teeth, Marsha Willoughby," he said. It was Odrerir talking then, the many ounces of alcohol abandoned in his bloodstream.

"Rally," she said. "Whah fuckyall gobble."

"Tell me," Cory spoke to her very seriously, leaning forward in a kind of desperation born of lust. "Are you from Slyville?"

"Whah, howjewall know that? Yuh mussbe uh minereader, darlin."

"You should get more sun," Cory observed. He

19

wondered what color her eyes were.

She laughed then such a throaty chuckle of libidinous promise, such ripe, tender, lubricated arpeggios of silvery mirth that Cory was reminded of the obbligato oboe of the *allegro* first movement of the Quartet in F, K. 370. Cheery, concupiscent and free. His own loins melted toward liberation.

"Do you like Mozart?" he asked.

"Whuh, honey, I lahkscrew everone, but I don't blow him yet. And honey fukaint stahnd the sun."

"Can I buy you a beer. Or something."

"Doc, I'll have me anothah boilahmahkah."

Doc smacked the shot glass of bourbon and the draft beer down in front of Marsha Willoughby with a small mordant ta-tum. Before the echoes died she had gulped the bourbon and slapped the empty shot glass on the bar and was swilling with lovely, round, alarming bobs of her slender neck the Odrerir draft, leaving behind the faint residues of thirst.

Then she put her hand on Cory's thigh. She was no longer Lauren Bacall, she was, oh, who, Marilyn Monroe, she was page 164 of *Battle Cry* by Leon Uris, she was that new *Playboy* magazine, large of breast and generous as all the natural world. She had perfect teeth. But, Cory knew, people from Slyville had bad teeth, bad habits of work and hygiene, bad ancestry and bad reputations.

He found her irresistible.

It seemed she might be speaking another language. He had terrific difficulty understanding what she was saying. She seemed to say, "Djall lahksex?"

Imagine Cory's beer, just at his lips then, flowing back to rejoin the image of the headwaters of the Little Hawking River there across the way from him. That would surely have happened if Cory had been drinking then.

"Let me get this right," he said after a pause, one, two, three. "Did you ask me if I *liked sex?*"

He couldn't see her eyes behind the darkness of her glass, but a certain recklessness had overtaken him.

And her hand did remain on his thigh. In fact, it moved there in a gentle, sinuous rhythmic circle, smoothing him, soothing him, stroking and stroking. Perhaps he should put his hand on her thigh too.

"Said djall lahk sexsuckfuck?

Cory shook his head. He could not be hearing correctly.

Her hand reached toward the zipper of his tan chinos. No, yes, he must be hearing correctly.

"Pussydew," he said, experimentally. "Yes, I do."

She smiled, showing him her two rows of perfect small teeth.

Down at the other end of the bar, Doc was masturbating the air and grinning. Beneath the blinking word Odrerir water poured from Lake Drowning Sow in increasing volume with a roar he hadn't heard before, a roar that swelled and fell like the opening of Mozart's *Haffner* symphony. Cory feared he was going to faint.

Marsha Willoughby had found what she was seeking, and stroked until it blew up beneath her hand, the stain spreading across the front of Cory's pants like the stain spreading earlier that night on his ceiling. She kept her hand there until it was cool, then with incredible lasciviousness she lifted her hand and licked her palm. She leaned toward him, bit his earlobe and breathed, in completely comprehensible English, "Let'sgo to your place and try again, shall we?"

Chapter 5. In Which He and Buddy Holly Slip Together into Existential Dread

Midges filled the air, but Cory didn't notice. Mosquitoes swooped through the gloom, alighted to extract a drop or two and took off unsteadily for their homes in the Little Hawking backwaters. Fat insect spirals swirled around the street lamp and the Silver Spoon's neon sign.

Beside him Marsha Willoughby hugged his arm, breathed in his ear, made steamy improbable suggestions he could neither comprehend nor contemplate. With difficulty he found his DeSoto, with greater difficulty he found his keys, which he surrendered to her.

She drove expertly, her left hand on the necker's knob, her right inside his shirt, where fingers twirled and tweaked his flesh as his head rested uneasily in her slender lap. Unfamiliar odors arose from that lap, odors of terrible havoc, intense chemical reactions between sexual pheromones and molecules of ethyl alcohol. Randy Cory rose again.

His head lay on the buckle of Marsha's trench coat belt, and from his perspective the spinning rear-view mirror was hypnotic and faintly nauseating, and quickly Cory spoke:

"Let me tell you about my family," he said to the undersides of Marsha Willoughby's firm breasts nested in her trench coat. Her very pale fingers tugged acquiescence, so he thought.

"My father's name is Farley," he crooned, trying to ignore the stiffening of his trousers, where a powerful erection encountered the dried evidence of earlier transient joy. "And my mother's name is Belle. My father's from Valhalla and my mother comes from...Well, my father's name is Farley, toodle-oo."

Marsha found rib and stroked between slender bones.

Cory shivered.

"No but seriously, everyone calls my father Grouper. Did you know that? Of course you didn't know that, you're from Slyville where the Sinkers stank, sank. What's that smell, well well." Cory didn't seem to notice that Marsha was saying nothing, though her fingers had found the olive drab waistband of his army issue boxer shorts. He had turned his face toward the dash in order to inhale more deeply of those troubling odors. Marsha's thighs separated slightly, just enough for Cory's ear to drop into a newly-formed hollow, the leg-pudendum intersection.

Cory groaned. He stared intently at the volume knob of his AM radio. Inside that radio would be Buddy Holly and The Crickets singing *That'll Be the Day*. Street light winked off the volume knob, obscene, concupiscent and depraved. Cory looked at the other knob; it winked at him. He looked up at Marsha Willoughby, but all he could see was the gentle swell of the undersides of breasts imagined in her coat.

"They call him Grouper," Cory told her solemnly, "because he is a hearty man, a cheerful man, a good-natured man. Everyone likes him, absolutely everyone. You'll like him, I feel sure, if you ever have the misfortune to meet him."

"Shewah, shewgah," Marsha said soothingly, fingers working beneath his waistband.

"Problem is," Cory told the pushbuttons of his radio, "that he says, 'Come on, group,' all the time."

Deep down and far away, his earthward ear heard sounds that sang like the odors, tiny fluid gurgles and slurps, and then Marsha found the soft flesh of his flank. Cory was listening to the sounds of organic lubrication and feeling the sinuous caress along his thigh, the painful pressures against the inside of his fly, and found it difficult to stay focused on Grouper's outrageous falseness and Belle's disdain. Somewhere in the past his wool suit itched.

His hand reached out and turned on the radio. Sure enough, Buddy Holly and the Crickets were singing number three.

That'll be the day-hay-hay/ that I die, they told him.

Cory turned away from the song, the dreadful words, and his nose plunged into the thickening atmosphere of Marsha Willoughby's lap. This was not what he had in mind, but he found it difficult to concentrate on what he actually did have in mind, so seized and taken away was his breath; and the spinning speeded up. Marsha Willoughby drove on through the warm August Valhalla night with the steamy odors of summer rank in her nostrils, and her own rank odors thick in Cory's, and it was as if she really did know the way, and that that'll be the day-hay-hay.

She did drive; and she knew the way; and Cory, carried along, realized much, much later, when he finally took possession of a pamphlet once passed through a coach window to Baxter Peabody one hundred years before, that he, Cory, was tracing in reverse a part of the route Baxter had taken up to Slyville, and he (Cory) was accompanied by a citizen of that peculiar place, and so Cory sang a little song to Marsha then, "So you're from Slyville where the Sinkers sank," and she had to content herself with his flank because his body, awkwardly turned on the DeSoto seat, did not allow her access to his virgin parts. She looked down at him instead just as he looked up at her, and she gazed deep into his swimming eyes and he gazed into the reflections of taillights and streetlamps and even, once, the spatter of mashed bugs on his windshield when a passing car's headlights glanced off her dark glasses.

"Yall said Slesstchull, nibblechew?" she seemed to ask, and Cory, seeing a sly askance prurient look of that zoo gorilla fooling him, leading him along, deceiving him, felt a stab of wormfear too. Obscurely he wondered what color her eyes might be, but saw instead as she gazed down at him the small even row of her upper teeth and was reminded of Grouper Depew, whose artificial smile was a product of his very own factory, and whose heartiness and good cheer had always caused Cory as much pain as his mother Belle's sarcastic rage. All in that moment, Cory's

24

iron hard-on melted away to a simulation of Schachter's Worm larva, small and curled and red, and he coughed in embarrassment.

The cough jiggled the pointy bone of his occiput against Marsha's soft-firm pudencum, though, and she mistook his meaning enough to do two things at once, for she did wriggle then that very mound against Cory's head and broke through with her ferret fingers to Cory's private parts, which immediately went public in a way that astounded even him, whose acquaintance with their little ways was as profound as nine years of diligent self-abuse could make it.

"Right," he gagged. "Celestial!"

"Why Shewgah, yall home!" Marsha exclaimed, intense delight in her aspect and her face as the DeSoto died with a rattle and a cough.

"That'll be the day-hay-hay," Buddy assured him.

Chapter 6. In Which Cory Arrives at a Beginning of His Troubles

"I gnawtricks," Marsha Willoughby breathed in Cory's ear. "Yall like me, doncha Barry?" She chewed his lobe, leading him from the car to the door of his building.

She paused to stare. The light thrown across the façade cast the blended shadows of a No Parking sign and the bent antenna of his DeSoto into a slavering carnivore on his building's wall.

But she wasn't looking at the animal, she was looking up at the Sinker hex sign, dark glasses fathomless. Then she made a rude gesture, and was just turning back to Cory when behind them wood splintered, preceded by a wordless cry, "Hi-YAH!"

It was only 10:25, barely dark at all. Wilmer Dougherty was practicing his karate in the front yard of his small cottage across the street.

"Never mind him," Cory said. "A crazy person."

"Shewah, shewgah," Marsha said. "Gwin sucker gock, crazy person."

The hex sign was spinning. The shadows were leaping with menace out of the wall, bared teeth and long claws. Lust swept terrible tides. He fumbled at the door lock with trembling fingers. Gently Marsha Willoughby took the keys from him for the second time, opened the front door, and asked him distinctly which was his apartment. He nodded to the right, and there was a person standing there, looking at his door.

"Oh," said the person, turning around. "Listen, is this your place? I'm so sorry. Really I am. I live upstairs, you know."

"No," he said.

"I just wanted to apologize for the water. Golly, you

26

see, I was doing laundry in my sink, and the phone rang, and well, the water was still running. I hope it didn't do any damage."

"I have no idea what you're talking about," he said carefully.

She was relieved. "Oh, good," she said, and patted him on the shoulder as she bounded up the stairs. "I'm so glad," she shouted down to him. He shrugged and opened his door.

Then he knew what she was talking about.

His ceiling was still dripping into the pool in the middle of his bed. His heart sank with every drop.

Marsha Willoughby, behind him, slipped her arms around his waist, reached under his shirt, put her chin on his shoulder, gazed through her dark glasses at his damp bed, smiled through her thin pink lips and said, very softly, "Oh, goody, wetfuck."

Then she took off Cory's clothes. "Boy, Cary, yall gotta beautiful rod."

"This couldn't be happening," he told her. She didn't answer, busy with the belt of her trench coat. She opened it, let it slide to the floor, and stood ghost-pale and absolutely naked beside him.

"This isn't happening," he repeated. "That's all you're wearing? Boots and a trench coat? And sun glasses?"

She ignored him. The room was beginning to move, a gathering of momentum to the right, in time to the beat of drops falling onto his bed, each tiny splat a subtle bell-rhythm that obscurely reminded him, combined as it was with the distant lentissimo crack of Wilmer Dougherty's lumber, of Mozart's Adagio and Rondo for Glass-harmonica, Flute, Oboe, Viola and Violoncello (K. 617), written for Marianne Kirchgassner's glass harmonica, invented, Cory remembered, by Benjamin Franklin. Marianne was a blind virtuoso who had great success with this instrumental counterpart, as Albert Einstein stated, to the *Ave Verum*, a piece of unearthly beauty.

There was an unearthly beauty to the percussive tinkle

27

of falling water, with its background beat of the shattering boards, and the heavy syncopation of Cory's heart.

He turned to look full at Marsha Willoughby, and she looked full at him, wearing only her dark glasses.

"Boy, you really ought to get more sun," he said. "You're the palest person I ever saw."

Marsha Willoughby sucked her lower lip between her teeth; she let the flesh of her lip slide back out from between those perfectly even rows, and when the lip had withdrawn completely, it was followed by the small pink nose of her tongue, questing between those lips toward Cory. A shudder ran through him.

"Jingles yoah dingle, Barney," Marsha Willoughby said softly, looking down.

"You know," Cory said in a rush of earnestness. "The dripping of that water reminds me of Mozart's Adagio and Rondo for glass-harmonica, an instrument invented by Benjamin Franklin. Especially the rondo."

"Rally?" Marsha breathed, moving closer to him. The points of her breasts were fractions of millimeters from Cory's chest. He reached up to grasp them, almost to keep them away. Marsha Willoughby laughed. "Oh, no," she said, taking his hands.

"No?"

"Nosah, fahkah, mah mammy said nevah let a mahyan touch mah tits, Barry." Still holding his hands, she pushed one of them violently between her legs, clasping it with iron thighs.

"Yes," Cory said briskly, as though briskness alone might halt the disturbing motion of the room. "Yes. Right. The introduction to the adagio portion is in the minor, and has an unearthly beauty, according to Einstein. Why don't you take off your dark glasses?"

Marsha pressed her chest against him and her breasts were full and firm and quite as sharply nippled as Cory had imagined them to be, and had thrust the prominent bone of her pubis against the edge of his hand, and the room was moving now in a stately minuet; soon, he feared, it would

28

become a waltz, and the waltz came too late for Mozart, too late by far.

She raised his other hand to her neck, where she left it. Her hair was extremely fine in texture, and as close to white in color as he had seen in someone her age. It felt unspeakably smooth to his fingers, and a panic began to rise in him when he thought about the pool of water in the middle of his bed, the swarms of roaches and silverfish on his floor, and the absence of any other usable furniture in this apartment. Marsha now had one free hand on the small of his back, and the other on his elbow. He considered their position awkward and unproductive, and tried to extract the hand between her thighs. He discovered he could not move it. By then her head was tilted back, her lips were parted, and her tongue was licking toward his lips. The hand on his elbow snapped to the back of his head and pulled him down, and the tongue achieved its goal, surpassed it, was deep in his mouth, swishing around in there like all the imagined pornography in his innocent mind.

He had never been naked with a female before. He had never seen a naked female (well, almost naked; she still had her glasses on). He knew this was supposed to go in there (near where his hand was trapped), he had a dim knowledge of the moves, and intense fantasies developed from reading *All About Sex and Love for Teenagers* when he was fourteen, but now, presented with the reality, his knowledge, even his fantasies, fled.

There was a knock on the door.

He stopped breathing. Marsha, tongue deep in his mouth, did not appear to notice. Her thighs did not give up their hold on his hand, and a muscle began to jump in his forearm. There was another knock. His mother Belle was calling to him. "Cory! Cory, are you in there?"

Of course she could see his DeSoto parked in the street in a No Parking zone, the doors open in the urgency of his need for Marsha Willoughby, pale body now glued to him, his stained chinos crumpled on the floor, her trench coat carelessly tangled, his bed drenched with laundry water, roaches and silverfish aswirm on his floors.

"I know you're in there," he heard her say.

Could he hide in the bathroom?

What would he do with Marsha, who even now had begun to rotate her pelvis, oblivious to the harsh demands of the virgin's mom?

"Cory, open up," she called.

"No!" He tried to shout, but his mouth was full, and no sound emerged. It was then he felt the first premonitory twitchings of pain along his hairline and under his chin.

"Come along, dear," Cory's father said. "He's probably down the street somewhere visiting."

"That man across the street, Grouper, said that Cory came home just a few minutes ago."

"Come along, dear," Grouper said. Cory's wide eyes, staring at his apartment door, which was very clearly not locked, wilted in relief when he heard the footsteps moving away, the front door close, a car door slam, engine start and drive away.

"Whah, whatsamattah, shewgah, donchall like me?" Marsha had stepped back, and was looking down, it seemed, with profound disappointment at his obvious lack of interest.

Cory groaned aloud.

Chapter 7. In Which He Gets a Neighborly Call

Cory stared down at his bed. Marsha stared at him. Water dripped from the ceiling.

Pling.

Pling.

Pling.

"Hi-yaah!" *Crinch*!

What vast silences, cold winds, empty spaces filled him: the vast silences, cold winds and empty spaces of Thule, Greenland.

Desire gone with hope, and his two-room apartment at 1001 Celestial Street in the city of Valhalla going around and around, Cornelius Hauser Depew was on a collision course with his fatal flaws — loaded with Odrerir draft, graduate of Valhalla Prep, a corporal in the U. S. Army (Ret.), of uncertain ancestry, son of the president and sole owner of a closely-held family corporation called the Rasmussen Dental Fabrication Works and the daughter of Dr. Hauser, a virgin on the very verge of a change in status, going all the way, getting it — had the flare of panic all around his face.

Overtaken by a memory then.

He never knew why he was standing out there in the hall looking up at the frosted glass door to his kindergarten room at the top of three short steps, three impossibly high steps, three steps away from warmth and companionship, from friends and hearthglow. Everyone else must have been in there, singing the rounds of *Frère Jacques* or *Row, Row, Row Your Boat*, but he, tiny Cory Depew, was here, in the corner, beside a table in the angle of two walls, staring at the lovely prismatic colors his tears made of that frosty glass.

Even without the tears, he would have been unable to see the strange, forbidding rites taking place inside.

31

Heavy steps ascended, and he blinked the tears away. A grown-up was coming up the stairs, and it became terribly important for him to be out here, in this otherwise deserted hallway, at the bottom of those three impossible steps to the frosted glass door, of his own absolutely free will. He knew in his five-year-old soul this was a transcendent metaphysical event; he knew it obscurely, intuitively, but with absolute certainty. No explanation presented itself why this knowledge was so important then, with the strains of *Frère Jacques* drifting beneath the wooden bottom half of that door and down those three steps.

A large woman whose head floated on a raft of dead fox appeared on the landing. An intricate hat was balanced atop her massive hair, a hat which anticipated a kind of metal sculpture popular almost forty years later in fashionable art boutiques — birds with welded wingspans and burned metal bodies. The difference was that this hat, or bird of prey, had a black veil depending from it, a veil effectively concealing the woman's eyes.

"Hello," she said, amiably enough.

"Hello, I'm here because I want to be," Cory told her hurriedly.

"Really?" she said without interest. She sat heavily in the chair at the other end of the table and let out a long sigh. With that sigh, Cory's heart fell.

It was a great falling, that heartsink, from which at times he felt he had never really recovered, not years later when he went into the army and discovered that the profession of warrior was not for him, nor later yet, when he moved into this apartment on Celestial Street and realized this was the real world. As if anything called Celestial Street could exist in the real world. As if he, Cornelius Hauser Depew could live on such a street, in a city with such an improbable name as Valhalla populated by the dim descendents of legendary, if somewhat gloomy heroes of the eastern arc of a gloomy Europe.

His heart was sinking in exactly that same way. But Marsha Willloughby put her sympathetic hand on his shoulder and he realized that the dripping on the bed was matched by a dripping of his eyes. He shook his head to steady the room, turned back to her, this pale slender naked woman form beside him, and saw, reflected in the dark lenses of her sun glasses his own face about to burst into flame, a prismatic flare of color around its perimeter. So he decided then and there to get a grip on himself. After all, he was about to get laid.

Thoughtlessly he reached up to touch her breast once more. And once again she laughed a splintery tinkle of laughs and grasped his reaching hand. "Come'ere," she said softly. "Gorchuck yerprick, Gary."

What?

She sat on the edge of the bed. Cory backed away. She was wearing dark glasses. She was nude, and desirable, and he was a five-year-old kindergartner guilty of obscure crimes. It seemed as if her eyes behind their dark lenses belonged to some dim vast bird of prey. So he reached out and removed her glasses.

He shouldn't have done that. She gave a startled little cry of alarm. She dropped his other hand to reach for the one with the glasses, but too late, too late. Behind her the water continued to pling onto the puddle on the bed.

Her eyes were, of course, pink. She squinted against the harsh ceiling light.

"The light hurts my eyes," she said quite clearly and distinctly. "I'm an albino."

"You're an albino!" Cory blurted. Shame filled him.

"Yes," she said with contagious shame. "I'm an albino."

"Pale," Cory muttered. "Pink eyes."

"There are a lot of us in Slyville," she said, sad, downcast, drained of her unintelligible lusts. Cory sat beside her on the bed, shriveled himself.

"It's all right," he said, not looking at her. "I don't mind."

"Really?" she said, not looking at him. "You really don't mind?"

"No, really," he said. "I don't mind."

"Really?" She sounded a little more hopeful.

"Really," he said. "I mean it."

Pling.

Pling.

Pling.

"Come here," she said. "Sickle bitcherfuck." She lapsed once more into her incomprehensible sexual dialect, and Cory turned to her. There she was, reaching for him. Would, he wondered, anything at all happen?

Something did, indeed, happen.

He rose, as it were, to meet the occasion. Obscure terrors flowed through him on tides of hormone as Marsha Willoughby leaned down. What was she going to do?

In the American Midwest in 1957 there was scarcely such a thing as oral sex. Nor was Marsha Willoughby about to demonstrate it, whatever her knowledge.

She was, however, quite interested in his apparatus, inspecting it closely. Perhaps she was troubled by something about it, some malformation in its shape or size, some evidence of disease of which he was unaware. He blushed under this intense inspection, began to wilt, but then she gave it a vigorous rub, and smiled up at him.

"Oh," he said. "Here." He realized he was still holding her dark glasses.

"Whah," she said, taking them and putting them back on. "Thankyall."

Then she took him firmly in hand and pulled him back into the cold puddle of soapy water.

Before the shock of cold could dampen him, there was yet another knock on the door.

He sat up in alarm. This was too damn much.

"Too damn much," he said.

"Halloo," the voice of the girl upstairs called through his door, which then swung open before her push. She came into the room. "Halloo," she said again. "Oh, there you are. Listen, I really am sorry about the water. I know it's still coming down, because there's some kind of leak in the pipes under my sink, and even though it was overflowing when I did the laundry, it still is absolutely pouring out of this leak. And I was wondering if you knew anything about plumbing, because my boyfriend works nights and can't come over, and there doesn't seem to be anyone else in the building just now. I see that you're busy and all, but that dripping from your ceiling isn't going to stop until the leak is fixed, so could you please come up and do something about it?"

"Uh," Cory said to the ceiling. "I don't know. I'm a radar technician. I don't know much about plumbing."

In the spreading damp stain of his ceiling he saw, as clearly as if squatting in flesh before him, the gorilla staring at him. He knew the gorilla was about to jump in suicidal dismay, so it was no surprise at all when a large section of the ceiling detached itself and fell on him with the wet splintering sound of rotten plaster.

Chapter 8. In Which Cory Attempts Plumbing, Among Other Things

He squatted on the peeled linoleum floor of the apartment above his own, gazing at ruptured pipes in a sea of desolation. Eternal tides of warm water were all flowing over his penny loafers toward the corner of the kitchenette and on to the middle of the bedroom floor, where the torrent disappeared down some invisible sinkhole in the structure; down below it was pouring now from his ceiling onto his bed, where pale, pink-eyed Marsha Willoughby wallowed.

"I don't know anything about plumbing," he complained. A roach, swimming for survival, was swept over his foot; it seized hold of the leather notch on the tongue of his shoe and pulled itself to apparent safety. He kicked the insect back into the flow of water and it vanished spinning around the doorjamb into the bedroom.

"I don't either." She was all demure helplessness. "I really appreciate this, I really do, my name's Suzy, what's yours?"

"Cory. Do you have a wrench?"

She found a small crescent wrench and handed it to him. Opened all the way it just made it around the pipe. There did appear to be a nut of some kind there, so Cory gave it a tentative twist; greasy water shot forth over his hands.

"Try it the other way," Suzy suggested.

"Thanks, oh, thanks a lot," Cory said, but he tried it. The flow reduced to a trickle.

"Would you like to see what I'm giving my boyfriend for his birthday?" she asked suddenly. Before Cory could rise to his feet out of the linoleum floodplain, she had vanished into the other room.

"Not really," he told his wet shoes.

"Here." With an ear-splitting whistle and crack she demonstrated a black leather whip.

"Wonderful," Cory said. What else could he say?

"Last week he gave me a black eye, my boyfriend. He's a really keen guy, I mean, very exciting."

"I can imagine," Cory assured her. "But I'd better get back. I have a, uh, date downstairs, you know, and probably she's...."

"Oh, sure," she laughed. "I guess I did sort of interrupt something. You know, it looked kind of like fun. I wish my boyfriend liked to do it naked like that." Her high, pure voice was wistful.

"I'll just be going," he said, edging toward the door. "You might want to get him a pipe wrench instead of that whip, though."

She smiled sweetly, and he realized that she was wearing only a black lace bra and panties, and that she had large breasts of a shape and color very similar to the July playmate. He had perused that issue very carefully while waiting for his transport out of Thule, Greenland. He'd been listening to the Mozart B-minor *Adagio* for piano, K. 540, as he studied the contours of the playmate's breasts; he would always associate that music with the desperation of impossible lust. Downstairs his first successful pickup was waiting (he did not count the dwarf), and she was hot, and so he fled.

On the dark carpet of the stairway he remembered the job he was going to have to get. Vincent Black Shadow was no doubt just turning in his resignation, and Cory Depew would probably become a Lone Ranger. It hadn't struck him before that he, Cory Depew, a man always guilty of obscure, unnamed crimes for which he was always punished, would become an officer of the law. Humiliated, cast out, sent away to Thule, Greenland, the most forsaken, dismal, ultimate place in the known world, where there was nothing to do but listen to the phonograph, and read books at the Base library, and gaze with awful yearning on the bared bosoms of airbrushed centerfolds. He was never allowed to service radar antennas, the job for which he had been trained. The Base was overstaffed with radar technicians.

The carpet under his soggy loafers was gray, with a raised, vaguely floral pattern worn threadbare by a hundred years of feet, happy feet, some of them, dancing feet, feet with purpose to their tread, feet sullen and feet spry, yellow geriatric feet and pink baby feet acrawl on the pattern which seemed itself to crawl like injured worms in the gloomy landing. The dim bulb in the ceiling too crawled with electric life.

At the bottom of the stairway his door glowed; frosted glass filled the top half: his kindergarten classroom, up three short steps, the glass fractured by his tears — Rage? Fear? Pain? Certainly he had perpetrated some terrible insult against the awesome Miss Buford, there could be no doubt about that. Here he was, in exile, a fitting punishment for offenders against her fiefdom's laws.

It seemed that the glass of his kindergarten door was shattering behind those tears, that the glass was erupting into a spray of shards, tiny malevolent and cruelly sharp weapons that would slice Miss Buford to ribbons. Perhaps that was his crime, he had killed Miss Buford, his kindergarten teacher!

And now he, killer of helpless teachers, window-breaker, mischief maker, raper and ripper, would take Tonto's place on the front lines, become a Champion of Justice. It was not possible. Cory Depew did not belong on the frontier as a defender of law and order, with a gun and a badge and a belt full of silver bullets.

He stood outside his door for a long time, staring at the yellow rectangle of frosted glass, and felt a flare of heat flash around the perimeter of his face. It was so intense that for a moment he squeezed his eyes shut tight, and pretty stars popped out all across the field of his vision, phosphenes of geometric ribbons and concentric circles. He shook his head, opened his eyes and then his door.

Marsha Willoughby was gone. Her naked body had left a damp outline in the center of his bed, but she was nowhere to be seen.

Then he heard the shower; he closed and locked his door very carefully. He did not want Suzy's boyfriend, or his mother Belle, or Vincent Black Shadow Lavere, or Wilmer Dougherty across the street (who had stopped cracking his boards, apparently retired for the night), or anyone else, for that matter, to interrupt what was well begun but not nearly finished.

He did not want to be interrupted again. It was, as he had said, too damn much.

"Barry!" Marsha called. "Barry, izzit chall?"

He tiptoed to the bathroom and looked in. She had not bothered with the shower curtain, and water was sluicing down her, flowing with sudsy lather. Her breasts were pointed and pouted, languorous, melonlike, and of a ghostly whiteness that reminded him of the great white whale breaching off the bow of the *Pequod*. Her waist was narrow and her navel deeply dimpled. Cory felt a rush of incoherence seize him. He hardly dared to look lower, but it was certainly true that her hair was very light all over her body, and that it had flowed together into a pale arrowhead between her legs.

"It's me," he shouted, and Marsha jumped.

She squinted out from the running water. "Oh," she said. "I guess it gobblechew. Why are you dressed? Come on in."

She wanted him in the shower with her! His heart leaped into his throat and remained. Such a large object prevented respiration.

"Rally!" She was smacking him on the back. "Cary, I'm worried about you, rally yam. You a virgin or somethin, you seem so nervous?"

His coughing grew worse, but Marsha was peeling off his clothes by then; she could see that it was going to take a lot of coaxing to get him back into the mood.

Cory was coming down with something, a fever of

39

some kind; his forehead was on fire, his cheeks burned, his hands were shaking, the Odrerir draft sloshed in his belly like liquid fire. His best laid plans were all going astray. The Lone Ranger was trapped in the canyon ambush, bullets flying all around, the sound of radio ricochets whined in his ears, the *William Tell Overture* trumpeted loud and clear.

Saturday morning was drenched with that sound, that deep voice, those hoofbeats and that cloud of dust. Cory huddled by the Philco, desperate for every sound, every word, hoping for an Indian companion. And now he had Vincent Black Shadow and a Negro brother-in-law who was an existentialist. Life was strange. *Toot-te-toot-te-to-to-to-to- to-to-to-to-to-to*.

It was the radio, of course. Marsha had turned it on while Cory was lying on his soggy bathmat staring into the ceiling light.

The light was a badge, a Ranger's badge. Its edges flared with silver light, winked through the rainbow spectrum, aglow with frontier virtues, the virtues of honesty and sincerity, of righteousness and revenge.

He sat up. "Revenge!" he shouted.

"What's that?" Marsha called from the bedroom.

"Revenge. Someone's getting revenge. The sins of the fathers."

"Oh. Suckon tweakertits," Marsha called.

That's it, Cory thought. I am the object of someone's revenge. But what did I do, or was it my father? Or his father?

Even his brother-in-law Withrow Duquesne would be able to cast a little light of his own on Cory's life, certainly more light than the ceiling was shedding at that moment. But he too was away this night, doing a gig at the Telltale Heart with Cory's twin sister Peggy, so Cory must lie on his back on the damp bath mat and stare at a glistening ceiling light and listen to the *William Tell Overture* and wonder.

The radio faded out; it was an advertisement for cheese

spread. Cory didn't notice. He spoke softly instead, to the dim mists of his bathroom ceiling.

"Come back with us now," Cory said. "To those thrilling days of yesteryear. Back with us now."

He galloped across the plains, dust kicked high from the heels of his mighty white stallion. Intricate red mesas — layered, hard-edged and clean — rose around him. The trail wound through dry gullies, arroyos, cacti. Wind blew past his ears and whipped his hair. He was strong and clean and filled with the hot wires of righteous anger. Innocent people were threatened by evil men who hid their faces behind masks.

And yet Paul Anka was deeply committed to a girl named Diana. "Oh, oh oh, Diana," Paul Anka moaned. His voice throbbed. Cory rolled his eyes to the right. There was the open door to his bathroom. Beyond it he could see his couch, a red mesa in Monument Valley. The stagecoach rumbled, hoofbeats clattered on the hard earth, dust rose in his bathroom. Paul Anka was heartsick.

"Oh, oh, oh," he sang. "Diana."

"Oh, oh," Cory said. He closed his eyes. Where was his faithful Indian companion? Where were the thrilling days of yesteryear? Where was justice?

"Rally? Cuncher fahkme?"

Cory opened his eyes once more. He stared upward. Marsha's pubic arrow was winging toward his heart. Her hands rested on her hips, the dimple of her navel was out of sight around the curve of her belly, her thighs were ajar. A sharp, fierce stab of fear ricocheted through Cory's prairie home.

Marsha Willoughby, albino hillbilly harlot, rotated her hips over his spinning head. Her small perfect teeth nibbled at light pink lower lip, her eyes were hidden behind dark glasses, her white flesh gleamed in streaks beneath the steamy ceiling light.

Cory turned his head away to stare at the lip of his shower stall. A black, rubbery substance peeled away from the tin threshold. The end curled toward him. He could see

41

stripes on the tin where the glue had dried, turned to brittle dust and fallen away. Gravity pulled the rubber down, was pulling at him, pinning him to this damp bathmat. The bathmat was damp from Marsha's recent shower. Marsha. He turned his head back. The pale arrow still flew down. It would spear him through, pin him to the floor. He should get up.

"I should get up," he said.

"Morey, yall limprick," Marsha told him. Slowly, with an almost painfully exquisite display of muscular control, she squatted beside him. He could see individual muscle groups and tendons, tender flesh tauten and relax inside her thighs beside her genital pout. His eyes dropped closed again. He could not look. There were teeth in the night.

Paul Anka throbbed with yearning; Cory throbbed. Marsha had reached out for him, had taken him into her thin fingers, so he lay inside their curl, and the fingers were trembling ever so slightly, a tiny vibration like the 25-cent units on some motel beds.

"Honeysuckle," Marsha said. At least, that's what he thought she said. But she was not about to invent anything that perverse. "Handzhob," she said, stroking.

The effect was electric. He sat bolt upright, and his forehead collided with her cheek.

"Oh, god," he groaned. "Oh, god, I'm sorry." She had dropped him to rub her cheek. Oh, the smart there. Oh, oh Diana.

"Sawright lover, yalla virgin, Ah cuntell." She grinned a wry grin, but he could see her patience was growing short.

"Listen, maybe we could talk, you know? Get to know each other. A little."

"Little lover," she smiled down at his littleness.

Poor Cory tried again. "No, what do you do? I mean, do you have work you do?"

She shifted from squatting spreadlegged to kneeling the same on his bathroom floor, one white knee against his armpit, the other at his hip. She took his hand and put it on

42

her pout. "There," she said, damp as his bathmat.

Oh, oh. Diana. Paul Anka sobbed and died away. Where had he gone. Silver hooves pounded the dust. Bullets flew into the dust, into the walls, into the air. Cory shot guns from the hands of every bad man in town. The guns they flew away from stinging hands. Where was his hand? It was there, beneath her arrow, the arrow's point was bent and blunt. A hair-row, ha ha.

Cory tried to think of Mozart. Mozart played lewd games with his cousin when he was young. Mozart knew what to do. Amorous music, clamorous music. Mozart would have sneered at Paul Anka and his simple passion. But this was 1957 in America. There was no room for Mozart in America in 1957. Even if he did die young.

Cory's forehead hurt, but the pain did not stay in one place. It moved around his face like his old Lionel electric train around the circle of track, which was all the further he got in building it because Grouper was not very interested in electric trains, and never helped Cory install the little stations and crossings and houses, the little mountains and tunnels and lakes and waterfalls, the miniature landscapes that other kids had on Ping-Pong tables. The pain went round and round, the train went round and round, his brain went round and round. He didn't even have an oval, just a simple circle. Like a wheel. Perry Como. Round and Round. Number ten on the hit parade for the year 1957 in America. Like a wheel.

The little train of pain, little pain train went round and round. Cory stood slowly, Marsha kneeled, and he had to turn away lest she see. She saw anyway.

"Cmon Cary, the dripping's stopped," she said distinctly.

He nodded. "Yeah, right. Right. Stopped. Right. Yeah." Cory worried about the dripping, the many drippings of his life right now.

He nodded all the way to the bed. The piano Adagio drifted like a huge white pig through his head. Could it compete with Buddy Holly, who now was telling him once more *That'll Be the Day*? It could not. He turned off the radio. The evening was a mess and the night was the color of winter in Thule, Greenland.

"No really, I mean it, do you have a job of some kind? I mean, what's your life like?"

"Listen, Barry, want some gum?" she asked him. Her purse was on the table. His bed squished when she sat on it, rummaging. "Here." Juicy Fruit. He shook his head.

"Do you go to the Silver Spoon often?" Cory jigged now from foot to foot, felt beneath his bare soles the grime of his carpet, feared for crushed bugs ascuttle there. Even now he felt the roach from upstairs was probably hanging desperately to the shattered plaster of his ceiling, ready to drop.

His floor would be a city, and he would be the great god of it, a vast and imponderable source of crumbfood and waterspill. Roaches would have a religious revival now he had come into this apartment, there would be endless chants rising up to him in tiny roach tongue, chants of thanksgiving and praise and supplication.

Marsha snapped her gum. "Shewah," she told him. Bits of broken plaster were sticking to her pale bottom and long white flanks.

"Oh, Jesus," Cory said. "Here, let's clean this up." A frenzy of brushing. He ripped the spread off his bed, and plaster showered in a circle around his room. Underneath, the sheets were wet. Pulling the spread away had raised a soapy bubble in the very exact center of the bed. He stared down at it as if it could somehow show him what to do next.

Marsha didn't move, though, and he gave up, let the spread drop to the floor in a sticky heap. Sat beside her in despair, all frenzied energy gone. "I don't want to be a virgin forever," he said.

Snap, crack, Marsha's Juicy Fruit answered, no less juicy than words.

"I mean, that's why I went there. To the Silver Spoon. Because I don't want to be a virgin forever." Flaming

44

cheeks sank into trembling palms. Marsha's gum cracked beside him. She put her slender arms around his shoulder and pulled him to her tenderly, and he put his head gently onto her albino shoulder and stared at his own splayed toes amid the powder and damp plaster. He wiggled his toes, and outside 1001 Celestial Street was no breath of air, only an indrawn hush in the steamy damp heat, a suspension.

He stared disconsolately at the untouchable pink nipples of his pink-eyed girl and held, deep inside his own trembling body, the breath of fear, the breath of lust, the breath of guilt.

"Yabble snarchew, Carny," Marsha Willoughby said, twisting around to pull him down atop her in the soapy damp, where she pulled his earlobe between her pale lips and chewed softly, and filled his terrible night with sharp devouring teeth.

Chapter 9. Resurrection

Cory risen. Cory flashed white teeth in semi-dark, thin lips and bright hazel eyes glistening. Cory gleamed, a halo of fire around his face aglow with supernatural flame. His chin ablaze, his cheeks spouting auroras and coruscations of foxfire, witchfire, his pale body lambent with despairing lusts.

Cory embarrassed. Cory twisted into knots of humiliation. He writhed, he squirmed. Now on the brink, poised at the lip, ready to plunge, and he wanted out. He did not want to go on with it, to enter the dreaded places, to become one of the boys, to dip his pen in the inkwell, to loose his arrow from the bow, to impale this albino wanton on his eager sword, to spear her through, to skewer her, plank her, lay, screw, boff, bang, ball, frig, diddle, mount or serve, hump or jump her. He no longer desired to shoot his wad in her honeypot, get off, lose his cherry, not one bit. He wanted to go home, to curl up and hide.

But of course he *was* home. He was aquiver at her gate, the twitchy tip of his very third, or fifth, or twelfth erection of the evening pressing even as he thought of flight between the soft blonde labes of his Slyville babe. Her head was back in musty rut and he was sure her eyes were closed, her neck curved away, tendons standing like Doric columns beside the ridged portico of her larynx, her pale cheeks cheesy smooth in the wretched light from his bedside lamp. And above his head, reflected in her dark lenses, were the exposed floor joists of Suzy's apartment, all plaster gone from his ceiling in a huge irregular map of one of those new African nations he could never name or some distorted animal shape. When he was lying on his back, just moments ago, looking past her shoulder as she rolled her slinky length, her silken skin, her soft bones against him, he felt he might be falling down through an

46

open floor to some depth of doom far beyond Thule, Greenland.

The joists were dark wood, the planks of the floor above were dark, and vast populations of interstitial creatures scuttled from the light flooding there. Rats retreated, screeching. Roaches moved in phalanxes and formations, silverfish darted and spiders folded up their webs and moved away. Cory had never seen a naked ceiling, and this was an old, old house, its construction that of a more leisurely, more permanent day. The building was solid, and a century had made it available for settlement by those who sought homes in the small dark places.

Now, though, Cory was poised at the dark home he thought he wanted, and he did not want it.

Too late, too late. Her long thin fingers were clutching at his nakedness, her blunt nails seeking his soft flesh; she was tugging gently at him, pulling him in.

He was awkward, his thighs were trembling from the strain of supporting his weight, his elbows, locked in an oblique angle beside her shoulders, hurt. He stared at her upturned neck, a vulnerable pulse beating beside her throat, her curiously tiny ears showing where white hair had fallen back onto his wet pillow. Marsha's right hand was creeping around his hip toward his bouncing baby bean liplocked at her entryway.

He was afraid he was going to hurt her, for one thing.

"Barry, yall gotchersef one big limber member; put 'er in and hump you bastard!"

Her voice was a whisper, a whine, soft sibilance and caress of liquid trailing down his back, the soft fall of a plumber's helper, obscene and corrosive. One limber member, he thought, what a curious phrase.

"Stuff me full, yercubblefuck," Marsha Willoughby said, her head now lifted from his tangled pillow so her dark lenses stared at him with the vacant, tormented glare of lickerish lust. Her hand had found his hard stick softening and had started to reel it in like fire hose when the water has been shut off though not so long by far.

47

"No, I." He got no further with his words, for she had by now reeled him fully in, and that was that, it was too late. Too late by far. There were no teeth in there, no teeth, but an indescribable creaminess and small gummy nibbles. And suddenly he thought despite himself: I'm getting laid. I'm one of the boys. Pen in the inkwell, and etcetera. Pat Boone, son of Daniel, where are you now? Where is my faithful Indian companion, Tonto, where are Buddy Holly, Paul Anka, Debbie Reynolds? Where are Dobie Gillis and David and Ricky? Beaver Cleaver? Where is Beaver Cleaver?

He is here, a voice answered in his head, the beaver cleaver is here, cleaving the beaver. O my O my, the army locker rooms did loom in memory then. He was Mammy Sly's ole rockin chair just arockin and arockin, and Marsha Willoughby's long long ghostlegs twined around his calves, his knees so buckled weak, his muscled thighs, her heels began to drum against his bottom, and he knew that Ozzie did not approve, that Harriet would turn away, that even Paul Anka pining for Diana would not have done what he was doing, because he didn't know this person underneath him, didn't know where she had come from, where she had been, what her habits were, whether she was clean (she had taken a shower though, he did know that, could smell the Dial soap on her shoulder and in her ears). He could hear his mother Belle gasp in horror, he could hear her then, banging at his door, "I know you're in there, Cory Depew, open the door this instant," but of course that was a memory from before he went into the army and locked himself in the bathroom from time to time, not from now when he was rockin and rollin around the clock, around the world atop Marsha Willoughby who had bourbon on her breath, he noticed for the first time, all those, what had she called them, boilermakers downed down at the Silver Spoon.

There was no way he could stop now. Too late, too late, he was gliding in and out just as he had imagined it a trillion times after reading *Sex and Love for Teenagers* and had found out that was what you did for sure, and not just as a nasty rumor passed on to him by his sexy sister Peggy who lived with a Negro and had a small son named Buster who was cute and chocolatey and illegit-imate, though he had been made legit in secret.

"Buster!" Cory shouted, and Marsha gasped, "Oh yes, yes, Buster."

She pushed soft pubes hard against him and began to quiver with something like revenge, and Cory discovered suddenly that he had entered into a vastly mysterious and mythical realm. Later he would learn it was what was known as the female orgasm, but for now it was so odd and frightening that he tried to draw back, pull out, pack up and leave, decamp, depart, undeploy. And found he could not.

"Stuck!" he shouted.

And Marsha answered, "Yes! Ogodyes, stick, stick, stuck, ungh ungh, gah."

"Gah?" His answering grunt had the interrogative intonation of surprise, for he was so suddenly released from her demonic grip, he flipped back and out. Marsha pressed her thighs together for a moment, then looked up at him with a quizzical expression.

"Boy, yaller good!" she said. Cory flushed with pleasure, then realized she was about to get up. "But I," he started, as he had so many times.

She laughed, a tinkly little sound, and said Oh yes, and took him in hand and rubbed him briskly once or twice, and he popped into her hand. Then she said goodbye.

"Goodbye?"

"Shewah, shewgah. I do have to get mah ayass on home, Big Mike, mah husband'll be waitin foah me. Yaller a nice boy, though, Cary. Now you gotta drive me back."

"Oh. Yes. Cory. My name. It's Cory. I'll drive you back, I guess. Back. Yes."

"Shewah Shewgah," Marsha Willoughby said with a gentle smile. "That was nice, though. Ah thought yall'd be the death of me, rally ah did."

"The death of you," Cory said. Flame seared around his

49

face; was it the flame of shame, her kiss of fire, or just the shrimp boats a-coming?

Chapter 10. In Which Cory Loses Face

Cory had never seen anyone clean up and dress so rapidly. But then all she had to do was wipe her hands on his sheet, pull on her boots and buckle her coat. He was still hopping around the room, one leg stuck into his stiff damp chinos when she was standing calmly by his door, exasperation in her white face, her booted toe in silent tapping on his threadbare carpet, scattering insects.

Hopping, he thought of Suzy, upstairs in black lacy bra and panties, the whistle of her whip, the enormous boy friend he imagined for her handing out a little punishment for love. Suzy was pretty and helpless and hopelessly sick, and so he sighed. All doors were closed. Perhaps he should take up that karate, smash boards, toughen his hands to lethal weapons, wander around like Richard (not Pat or Daniel) Boone, the Paladin who had a gun and would travel. A champion of justice, sweating under the torment of his horny gynecomania, the lubricious itchy heat of all adolescent dissatisfactions.

Marsha Willoughby tapping her toes by the door, chewing her underlip, might never have been long and naked under him, might never have fretted his dongle in her slender hand, have caught his doughy fizz. She might have been a building inspector, or Valhalla Gas and Electric clerk come to read the meter, an official come to check his plumbing, conduct a survey of television habits, sell him brushes for his buggy kitchen. She was the perfect stranger at his door, waiting for him to show her out.

Show her out he did, in fear and trembling, to his rusted auto, and turn on the radio he also did, to drown his sorrow and his trouble, and who should be there for him but The Coasters singing *Searchin'*, and that was perhaps his fate and doom.

The night was hot and filled with mists. He drove

through them, out Midgard, onto a short spur of the Louisa May Alcott Expressway and off again on the Louisville Highway, past the Kernel Korn's Drive-in Restaurant where he had eaten his solitary dinner so long ago that very night, and into the parking lot of the Silver Spoon, where shameful cowardice rose in his heart like the head of the Midgard Serpent rising to devour the world.

Her car was parked there, a Nash Rambler with a deeply rusted fender. Next to it was a Ford pickup truck with a gun rack in the back window. The gun rack held two guns. Otherwise the lot was empty, though the neon sign still crackled in the heat. Cory imagined Doc inside, hunched over his bar, drawing drinks for the huge man who hunkered there waiting for his wife.

His worst fears were realized when Marsha said cheerily, "Why that's mah husband's truck, Suckscrew buggerbut."

"Oh," Cory said softly. The serpent uncoiled and looked out through his eyes at a seriously disordered world. "Perhaps I should just let you out here."

"Aw, shewgah, come'on in an meet Mike. Yall'd lahk him."

"No, really, I guess I'd rather not."

Sheets of flame raced one another around his face, the flame of shame, the flame of fear, the flame of sick despair. And was that the Bobbettes singing about *Mr. Lee*? Should he get out his side, walk around the old DeSoto, open Marsha's door and lead her into the Silver Spoon where a thorough stomping surely waited for him, and he not ever having broken a board with his bare hand in his life, wanting more than anything at this moment to be good friends with Wilmer Dougherty who lived on the other side of Celestial Street, and who even now was no doubt sleeping the sleep of the just and happy while Cory faced a dismal end on a dusty bar-room floor.

Marsha Willoughby smiled what was surely a smile of vast derision, and even though she was the end product of a hundred years of intensive inbreeding and a profound gathering of recessive genes. Cory was small and insignificant beneath that glare. He ducked his head, felt the fire, stared with burning eyes at his plastic steering wheel, the little plastic knob for lovers he didn't get to use.

A figure appeared in the screen door of the Silver Spoon behind the Nehi sign. The screen door swung open. Cory prepared himself for death, resignation married cowardice in a quick civil ceremony, but it was Doc at the door, Doc who threw a pail of sudsy water off the step toward the DeSoto. More derision. Marsha opened her own door.

She leaned toward him, one boot extended out, and whispered in his ear. "One limber member, Cary, but not so stiff as Big Mike. Yaller nice boy, though, goodbye."

She stepped saucily toward the step, where Doc gave her a wave and opened up the door, and Cory wasted so little time moving his DeSoto he left twelve months or 15,000 miles (whichever comes first) worth of tire behind him on the parking lot of the Silver Spoon.

He drove alone through that late Valhalla night, and it was fate coming down on him, imponderable and fat. Jerry Lee Lewis told him there was a whole lotta shakin goin on, but Cory didn't care, for he could feel, all around his face, a sinister loosening, a smacking terror. Along his cheek the skin did itch, then burn, then fell away, separated from the teguments of fascia and bone. It shot, this pain, along his hairline, down beside his ears and underneath his chin. There was that sound, the sound of loose lips smacking with some unnamed but depraved hunger, a wet, obscene sound heard distinctly above the raucous shakin which preoccupied Jerry Lee Lewis just then.

His face was a pancake, sliding down the bony front of his skull; if he could tilt his head back, so, he could slide it back onto his facial griddle. He reached up and held the skin of his forehead against the bones, felt as if the face hung from the pressure of his forefinger and thumb. He would indeed be the Lone Ranger, shaded eyes ascan the limitless horizons of that internal west Despair, keen in the search for lurking hostiles, cursed and hopeless.

He felt the stringy tendon and gray damp coils of connective tissue with a deepening dread. He leaned his head against the seat back and gazed down through lowered eyes at roads unwinding before him, streetlights alternating his dark and light; he thought of social diseases: They showed us movies, that albino gave me clap, and that is why my face is falling off.

But as he thought it, he knew it was not true. Obscurely he felt there must be some deeper disease of the soul afflicting him here.

The pain increased, the fire and fear, and he considered options as Jerry Lee Lewis faded out. He descended the long curve of Mount Worthy's nether flank, aware he could not stop at home, his soggy bed, his plaster cataclysm, he must find, at this late hour, a doctor to bind up his falling face. He drove on, descending, descending, down toward Niffelheim and the bottoms, the downtown of Valhalla, the waterfront beneath the Cliffside hills where the University was, beyond the baseball stadium in the middle of the Niffelheim ghetto.

He drove through Heimdall Square beneath the towering hulk of Conrad and Busby's Department Store, past the enormous rococo bronze fountain that graced its center. Atop the broad (but now dry) waterfalls a mighty oak of bronze sheltered an enormous sow, her sides and belly polished bright by thousands of hands. She was suckling a human infant with a curiously grown-up face, the face, they said, of Valhalla's founder, Dudley Worthington Depew the First, progenitor of that mighty line.

He passed beyond the square, moving restlessly and at random. The street lights cast over him the endless repeated striations of panic. His head tilted back, steering with his lover's knob, body drained so completely of any of his lusts he might be a eunuch guarding the Seraglio of Thule, Greenland.

Downtown, adrift in the deserted streets in search of

healing, he thought abruptly of the dark existential girl who had spoken to him at the Silver Spoon, the Ovandrill girl Doc had called her, and for some reason Cory remembered the desolate look of her, the distracted air, the haze of sadness.

She had been to the doctor that very day.

Her husky voice had spoken out of her own private gloom. She had plump, delicate fingers and was dressed in black. She had asked him what was happening, and then he would have answered that nothing was happening and that was his problem, but now his answer would be very different. Too much was happening.

"Thanatopsis," Cory spoke his anguish to the sports announcer. "No. Something like that. Greek. Thanatopoulos, that's it. She had been to Dr. Thanatopoulos, an office visit. I need an office visit."

The sports announcer assured him that though the Valhalla Warriors were in last place, they had an even shot at seventh before the season ended.

"I need an office visit," Cory said, holding his face. "I need."

In search of a doctor, he drove then up Midgard Avenue again through the evening heat, toward a time in another century when insects buzzed and whirled, dove and devoured, and pursuit was always a way of life. He drove up into the past.

BOOK THE SECOND:
BAXTER, 1857

Chapter 1. In Which One Baxter Peabody Enters into Another Beginning

It was 1857, and the August evening steeped in heat. Mosquito clouds swirled in the gaslight. A miasma rises from the rivers this time of year, from the broad Ohio and the narrower, swifter Little Hawking; their valleys exhale fetid vapors into the ague-locked joints of the dwellers in the bottom lands. Dense cloud glowers over cliffs to the south, held back by the pressure of those mephitic vapors.

There was about this man an air of desperation as he walked up Midgard Avenue, boots scuffling the brown dust. His mind was turning ponderously, almost visibly, like a locomotive attempting a steep grade. He didn't notice the small herd of sanitation swine muttering in the gutters until he came upon them and was forced to go around. The sounds of their munching faded as he moved on toward the Museum of Western Oddities, one step ahead of his twin brother Norman.

He knew Norman had inquired at the hotel for him; he could see it in the desk clerk's face. Norman had preceded him at McCauley's Tavern. Norman dogged his footsteps; that was Norman a block below in the evening dust, Norman's conspiratorial tread, that distant creak of boot leather.

Baxter's hand left its absent-minded stroking of his fine whiskers to swipe at a mosquito. His hand passed through the cloud without diminishing its ferocity.

"I need time," he said aloud. The mosquitoes paid no more attention than the grunting swine downhill. The garbage in the middle of the road reeked of time at its patient work.

"Norman!" Baxter Peabody shouted suddenly. The hogs looked up and grunted, turned back to cleaning up the street.

There was no reply, not even an echo in this thick, humid, darkening air. Baxter trudged on. "The bastard," he exclaimed beneath his breath. "I hate you, Norman," he shouted softly. "Tyrant! Ah, but there is something about Norman, isn't there?" he asked himself. "He's a cunning bastard."

Here in Valhalla there was opportunity everywhere for refugee scoundrels like Norman and Baxter Peabody. Opportunity shuffled up the street with a bag full of trinkets, jars of unguents, lotions, potions, remedies and notions, lamp oil, snake oil, hair oil, powders for aches of tooth and lower back, instant education, memory improvement, potency and fertility, con and contraception, more powerful vocabulary or more powerful biceps, mesmerism self-taught, heart's desire, characterological analysis, phrenological road maps to the future. Opportunity knocked at every door, had a smile and handshake for all, a wink and a twinkle of the eye, full set of dazzling white teeth broadly grinning.

Teeth.

Baxter smacked his cheek and squashed a critter flat within his whisker forest, leaving a smear of blood. His tongue probed thoughtfully at his left canine, left bicuspid.

Teeth.

There was money in teeth. Opportunity came in many guises, many forms. "Opportunity, you bastard," Baxter said aloud, momentarily confusing opportunity with Norman. Then he said: "Teeth."

Teeth could well be one of opportunity's strange disguises. And what would Norman, Caliban twin, know of teeth? As much as Baxter knew, fully as much.

"All over this fertile valley are rotten teeth, crying, wailing, shrieking and gnashing for relief," Baxter told the mosquitoes. "Relief, or replacement."

Baxter struck again atop his wrist between cuff and the buttons of his glove. An uncertain insect shape, surely monstrous large, evaded him with irritating ease; behind him footfalls grew loud.

It is said that genius may flourish in the world, but more often than not it fails to find the light of history and like the past is buried, though (like the past) never dead. Genius, caught in a matrix of time and place, has its own motives, which may push the ordinary, or the less than ordinary, into the sublime, the transcendent. Baxter Peabody may have been one of those unsung geniuses of an age, forced by circumstances, or by needs, desires, or ambitions more obscure than any of these, to exceed himself. That his particular accomplishments fell into obscurity, leaving only dry bones buried in time's dry soils, was one of those casual accidents of history.

Ahead of him Midgard Avenue rose, lofted a bluff, settled for a stretch or two, dipped softly parallel to the river along Mount Worthy, curled a low ridge and rose once more. Paved street had ended where the hills began to pile up southward, and the horse trolley lines had dwindled away soon after. The inclined railroad was years in the future. Norman's footsteps plodded in the past after him.

Baxter looked northward. He could see the city, the docks, the black curve of the river. Valhalla spread out at his feet, flickering with gaslight. Near the docks the district of Niffelheim snaked along the river, its three- and four-story buildings constructed of porous, insubstantial "Valhalla brick." Stacks spewed dark smoke into the air. He could make out, in a clear space where the public square left room, a line of paddlewheelers lashed along the levee, although the one on which he had arrived, the Simon Girty, had long since returned to Memphis.

Two riverboats jockeyed for a landing. Spires from a dozen churches thrust skyward, although the magnificent cathedral of St. Credula the Ulcerated Martyr of Shköder had yet to crown Mount Worthy to the west. She would be built in the seventies by the small but devout wave of Albanian refugees to arrive in that decade.

There was no sign of Norman. Footfalls had ceased. Only the distant chuff of the boats, the babble of the Front Street market, the slurping of the swine and the mosquito whine broke the silence. Darkness gathered toward him, ominous and bleak. Dust settled as the vapors rose. Baxter clenched his teeth.

He was alone. Ahead of him the Museum of Western Oddities commanded a spectacular view of the Niffelheim industrial and commercial center — Niffelheim, named after the vaporous home of the Teutonic dead.

The museum was gargantuan, crenellated, cupolaed, rotundaed, pilastered, colonnaded, swirling unhygienic scoop of pistachio plaster, gimmicky, awkward, grotesque and useless; the architectural nightmare of Mrs. Arlene Wilberforce, home and platform of the Invisible Girl.

Arlene waited within, seated amid her ample skirts, bounteous and available derrière spread on an imported horsehair ottoman, smiling with a relish as imperfect as her teeth at the success of this recent venture, this snatching of fiscal victory from the jaws of bankruptcy. She had plunged her life savings, accrued with varying degrees of legality, into its construction, intending it for a shopping arena, a many-tiered, faceted and, as one Valhalla newspaper termed it, outrageous department store.

Unfortunately she knew little of psychology, less of commerce, and nothing whatsoever of architecture. She bought cheap real estate too far from town, remote and inaccessible to shoppers, and the stock the late Reggie Wilberforce had ordered for her from the finest Paris suppliers just prior to his untimely apoplectic demise in the parlor of a Pigalle brothel was inferior in quality and excessive in price when compared to what was available in the markets downtown; her imported goods failed to excite a lust of ownership in these provincials.

But the brick had been purchased, the pipe fitters and gas fixtures contracted, the limestone facing quarried from Aristera County, Indiana, ferried across and paid for on delivery; the curlicues had been designed, the entire hodgepodge contraption, this whole and total blend of Egyptian, Armenian, Turkish, Frankish, English Gothic, Tudor, Queen Anne, Greek, French Academic, Italianate

61

and Chinese architectural features had been transferred from paper to stone and plaster; hard cash up front had gone for minarets and balconies, for the gilt rotunda dome, for the molded plaster of the Adam's ceiling in the ballroom, and it was quite simply too late to opt for disaster.

So the Museum of Western Oddities was born, rising Phoenix-like from the ashes of Arlene's financial folly. Not the least odd of all the oddities was this building itself.

The people of Valhalla loved it. They were flocking to her exhibits, first the Indian skulls dug from the Serpent Mound out near Schachter's Landing; then the procession of two-headed pigs and six-legged sheep, the jar of Schachter's Worm larvae so red and awful in sluggish fluids, all these now stored in a back room. Lately it was the waxworks that brought them in — for a time the horrors of what she called "Indian Massacre," a depiction in lifelike wax of a scalp being severed from a fair lady's head by savage painted redskins with all the details of ligament and blood. Horrors were what they had wanted, and horrors were what they got. Arlene had risen to that particular challenge.

Alas, eventually even horrors palled, and so she had invented the Oracle of the Invisible Girl, an inspiration of an afternoon's nap over the newly popular works of Edgar Allan Poe, whose works she had looted for ideas before.

Today the Museum had been packed, the entrance too narrow to accommodate them all; now evening, insects and heat had leached the visitors away, and she was about to close. So the Invisible Girl was at this very moment probing a wide left nostril while waiting. It seemed unlikely there would be another seeker today; yet at that very moment Baxter Peabody was staring up at the building which beckoned him to enter, while behind him Norman pressed hard.

The building was vast and dark and remote and gloomy, but the entrance lured him with the cheery blue flickering of gaslight, a visual oasis in this waste of dreadful architecture. Behind, Norman's footfalls were hurrying near, and he needed time to consider teeth and evade his twin, trying even then to recruit him into a mad conspiracy to dethrone Queen Victoria.

He reached out and seized the handle as if it might save his life.

Chapter 2. The Museum

"Who's there?" Arlene Wilberforce asked. Gaslights smoked with untrimmed mantles. Arlene Bethany Rasmussen Wilberforce, thrice widowed genius behind the Museum of Western Oddities, had sensed a need for her dramatic flare, her taste for the gothic, as long as these could coincide with the demands of profit.

"A gentleman," Baxter Peabody lied.

"Even gentlemen pay twenty-five cents," she told him coyly. The eldritch flicker of the lamps, actinic and murky, gave ersatz life to a wax figure of Leda seized by the swan, though gentility and decorum softened that rough rape as Victoria's age demanded. Baxter fished in his pocket. The lights flickered on the waxy columns of the Temple of Apollo at Delphi as recreated in Arlene's fertile, if inaccurate, imagination. Beyond, a frolic of satyrs and centaurs was half-hidden in gloom against a back wall.

Baxter looked around at the complex display: an iron grill barred his approach to the Invisible Girl, identified by a sign affixed to a gate. Suppliants or the merely curious would have to remain outside. Her sculpture was barely discernible in this quarter-light, for the intervening space was occupied by a profusely smoking bronze tripod. A tiny core of crimson flared dangerously in the heart of thick smoke, and the glossy cheeks and eyewhites of the statue were given spurious motion.

"What the hell's that?" Baxter asked. An ungentlemanly question.

"Twenty-five cents." Arlene held out her hand.

Baxter's jaw ached from grinding his teeth out there in the mosquito-riddled dusk. His twin brother Norman pursued, and Norman was a dog who hounded, beagled, spanieled and terriered, yapped and snapped at Baxter's heels, and frayed his cuffs and nerves. He had little choice, yet he held back. "What for?" he asked.

"For a session with the Invisible Girl, of course. What else? She is the greatest mantic prognosticator since Tiresius. Answers to all your questions, personal or professional. All your questions. Guidance. Counsel. Illumination from Beyond the Veil of Mystery."

"All that for only twenty-five cents?"

Even irony as clumsy as Baxter's was lost on Arlene Wilberforce. She nodded without expression, plump chin swelling and shrinking with the nod.

Baxter's quarter winked goodbye into her palm. She nodded toward the entrance of the inner temple where Baxter should pass.

His eyes adjusted to the darkness and he smiled, thinking of Norman out there slapping insects. He turned toward the Oracle, seated beyond the flickering tripod.

Behind his screen the Invisible Girl wheezed softly into a damp palm. The torch flared, enhancing mystery. The Invisible Girl was quelling an asthma attack, however, and when the oracular question finally emerged, it was through stifled larynx and constricted adenoids, an effect not unlike sand running through a meat grinder.

"What?" Baxter had to ask. He was looking around for the source of this sound, which might have been language of some sort.

"What is your question?" the voice intoned, attack over for the moment, in a strangled falsetto.

"Ah." Baxter couldn't find the source. "Ah?"

Silence. Along the wall Leda struggled in vain against the lubricious depredations of the god-swan. Baxter could almost hear the wings beating: Norman, overhead.

"Has not Thomas Fuller said," the Invisible Girl spoke, husky falsetto become utterly weird as asthma evolved into a wheeze, a long despairing outblow of breath without end, "Heeeeeeeew."

"I don't...," Baxter began, but the wheeze ended, and the Invisible Girl continued as if nothing had happened.

"He was one of 'lean body and visage, as if his eager

65

soul, biting for anger at the dog of his body, desired to fret a passage through it?'"

"Biting?" Baxter asked. "At the dog of his body? My brother Norman out there, his teeth?"

"Yes," the Invisible Girl intoned. "Thy brother Norman. For the Holy Prophet Zoroaster has said, 'The Lord who made thy teeth shall give thee bread.'"

Baxter was startled. "What?" he asked. "What was that?" His own voice rose, a cockateel imitating dread.

"'The Lord who made thy teeth shall give thee bread,'" The Invisible Girl sounded puzzled. "'The Lord who made thy teeth shall give thee bread.' Zoroaster. I thought I said that. The Holy Prophet Zoroaster."

"What the Invisible Girl means," Arlene quickly interposed behind him, "is that your brother Norman..."

Baxter waved her aside without looking back. "No. Teeth, she said. Make teeth. Get bread. Incredible!" He apparently hadn't noticed the Invisible Girl's querulous lapse. Arlene left well enough alone. "'The Lord who made thy teeth shall give me bread.' Amazing."

"That's what I said," the Invisible Girl complained, and fell into such a fit of wheezing near to strangulation Arlene rose up in alarm at the same moment that Baxter, seized by peculiar dread, turned to flee the temple. They collided violently in the gate and fell together in a heap.

"Well," she said, skirts flounced over him, her breath a little short and hot in his ear. "Questions answered?"

"Answered?" he repeated stupidly as Arlene's pouty mound pressed his thigh through her skirts and petticoats. "Yes, answered." He tried to rise, but her weight was on him, and his struggle only seemed to bring her breathing faster.

"Don't you want to see the exhibits?" she asked softly, her hands moving against his chest, pressing him back to the floor. In the background, the Invisible Girl continued that violent wheeze, but Arlene had forgotten her alarm.

"No. What? Exhibits? No." Again he struggled to

stand, but suddenly Norman seemed to be calling for him out there on Midgard Avenue. "Bax-ter-r-r-r," Norman called. "Victoria must be deposed, Bax-ter-r-r. The Cabal need you, Baxter."

"Yes!" he shouted. "The exhibits." Norman was desiring to fret a passage through the dog of his body. "Nice!" he shouted, not knowing if what was under discussion were the exhibits or Arlene's hips rotating against him.

"Twenty-five cents," she said, holding out her palm. Arlene never lost her head.

"I'm sorry," Baxter said, climbing to his feet. "I don't have it."

Arlene gave him a curious look, and he wondered if he had misinterpreted her actions on the floor. She might have been trying to get at his wallet, which was, as usual, empty.

"I'm temporarily out of funds," he confessed.

"Oh." Was she disappointed? But her small, round, intelligent face peered up at him. Her eyes glittered. "You're a well set up man," she observed quaintly.

Baxter didn't understand.

"I'm getting on," she said. "Not as young as I used to be." Her gloved hand drifted over to rest on his biceps. It slid down his arm, light as feathers, floated near his trouser pocket as though seeking small change. There was a curious glitter in her eye, a trick of the gaslight, no doubt. "I have needs," she breathed, stroking him. "I'm forty-three years old."

He wanted to rush out into the street, but Norman was out there. Behind Arlene, Leda struggled with the swan in decorous rape. Teeth gleamed in his head.

"I need love," Arlene whispered in his ear, leaning toward him. Her hand had found his crotch.

"No, I..."

Norman's hyena grin, his jackal prowl; and not since the river boat had Baxter himself had love.

"In here," she said, tugging at his swelling member

67

through his pants. He followed, her grip growing painful; she backed through another doorway, not into the Oracle, but another door, a room filled with bottles, jars, stuffed owls, white-tailed deer, squirrels, hares and hounds. A six-legged sheep, a two-headed pig. A room of monstrosities.

An Ohio buzzard suspended by wires from the ceiling circled the walls, eye cocked for carcasses. Baxter, lying in the August sun, rotted there. He turned. A wolf leered at him with gleaming teeth, eyes red in the light falling across this dusty storeroom from the doorway. He turned again, trapped.

A bear stood seven feet tall, claws outstretched. Toward him.

Baxter saw stares returning his all around the room. Beasts skulked, prey was ripped asunder, long teeth devoured, sharp teeth, teeth that tore and teeth that rent. Through the dog of his body. Fret a passage. His eager soul.

"What about the, er, Invisible Girl?" His hands groped blindly for her protective whalebones.

"Oh," she answered, hands button-busy, voice matter-of-fact. "Never mind about him."

Baxter blinked. Him?

The Lord who made thy teeth shall give thee bread.

Baxter fell then atop Arlene Wilberforce whose skirts had floated mysteriously up around her dense waist, another mystery in a world of mysteries, and he found himself within a deep and seething warmth that pulled from him all that is sacred of the flesh; her legs were clamped behind his naked knees above his crumpled trouser legs, she found his liberated organ with her gloved hands and guided him into that oracular temple where the ancient rhythms could carry him away to a world of teeth and wings.

Later she showed him the bottles and jars. Schachter's Worm was a red curl made lavender by actinic gaslight — small, fetal, monstrous.

Chapter 3. In Which the Invisible Girl Makes An Appearance

"What's happening?"

The Invisible Girl was agitated. Amid the dusty stuffed animals, the bears and buzzards, the terrible jars of Schachter's Worm larvae, the tangle on the floor writhed.

"Go away, dear," Arlene grunted sweetly.

"Mpphh," Baxter Peabody tried to speak. Somewhere in the rumple of skirt and trouser, petticoat and whalebone, Baxter's pelvis thrusted, severed from his brain, a rampant boar set loose in his spinal column. "Gnk gnk," he said, troubled by the Invisible Girl's presence.

"Not again!" the Invisible Girl exclaimed, and fell to such a wheezing fit that Baxter could almost hear the red facial flush, strangled on exasperation.

"Go away," Arlene implored, to no avail.

"I'm going...to..." Baxter huffed.

"Oh, do!" Arlene exclaimed.

He did. She didn't.

"Never mind," she said. "Women aren't supposed to enjoy it anyway, although God knows something happens. Usually." She brushed her skirt down. "I suppose I'd better find Henry. This sort of thing always upsets him."

"Upsets him," Baxter repeated stupidly. "Henry?"

"Why, yes. He's a delicate boy, and not too bright, I'm afraid. He failed in school, you know, in England. Remembers a lot of things from school, but can't make any sense of it. That's why I created the Invisible Girl. All Henry can do is repeat things at random — Cicero, Tacitus, bits and pieces of Herodotus and Sappho, Aeschylus and Homer, little smidgens of Milton, morsels of Shakespeare. Sometimes he says, 'Omnia Gallia in tres partes divisa est.' Then I have to interpret." Arlene sighed, her magnificent

69

bosoms heaving deeply. Baxter, fluids drained, did not fail to notice their depth, fullness, peachy softness, their smooth texture visible above her bodice.

He ground his teeth.

"Don't do that," Arlene said.

"Do that?"

"Don't grind your teeth. Dear." She put her soft gloved hand on his arm again.

"Teeth!" he shouted. "I must tell you about teeth. The Invisible...your son, Henry, he said that about teeth. I've been thinking about teeth."

Arlene was resourceful. Baxter could see that. She had a foothold here in Valhalla. She knew the territory. She would keep him safe from Norman. He could tell her about teeth.

So he told her about teeth. About their propensity toward decay, about foul odors and racking pain, the desperation engendered of teeth. Before he was run out of Memphis, he had been in the tooth business.

Arlene listened, Henry's wheezing in the next room unnoticed. She was interested in teeth now, in their shapes and textures, their malformations and proclivities, the possibilities they might offer for profit.

For 200 years, Baxter told her, people had been willing to pay good money for powders or tinctures that promised to prevent decay, restore fragrant breath, keep dentition white and sound. In Memphis he had promoted a substance known as Baxter's Botanic Tooth Powder which would, he said, cure the scurvy in the gums, prevent rheum and defluxions, kill worms at the root, fasten those which are loose, preserve them from rotting and decay, act as an antidote for gum-boils, swelled face, the excruciating pain of toothache; also it was safe for infants to swallow.

"All that?" Arlene breathed.

"And more," Baxter boasted. "But Norman wants to steal my secrets. He's trying to depose Queen Victoria, you see, and needs funds to finance the cabal. He's willing to do anything in pursuit of this mad obsession. He's a

70

dangerous man."

"I can imagine," Arlene said, thinking of Baxter's Botanic Tooth Powder, made from salt and alum, coral and pumice.

Yet she knew of numbers of other tinctures on sale in the Valhalla stores, products with names like Sozodont and Russell's Dandelion Dentifrice. Surely there was a new territory here, an arena in which her fervent imagination might exercise itself.

"I think," she said softly, her hand in absent-minded stroking of Baxter's trousers, "that you and I may be able to do great things together. Business, yes." The thought of business moved through her loins, and that lovely mound Baxter had so recently left began to strain toward him once more, unfulfilled as it was. "Shake," she said.

Baxter jumped. "What?"

His Lazarus loins risen again, her hand, having abandoned his trousers, was held out to seal a bargain he didn't know he'd made. Yet their pelvic yearning continued unabated, a yeasty swelling toward one another.

"Er," he said. But he shook her hand. In the other room, Henry had stopped wheezing, and had his head cocked alertly to one side, straining for the musical rhythms of lust. He was a retarded lad, but not without his own primitive juices, stirred by sounds from the abandoned animal room, a room in which the teeth gleamed and winked in all their whites and yellows, lips curled back from them, and in Arlene's fevered brain teeth gleamed and winked also, row upon row, smiling with profit, for the valley was filled with suffering people yearning to bite free. And out in the dark, fireflies blinked their own mating signs, deceiving and deceiving, trapping, tripping, mating and devouring. And out there, too, Baxter knew, Norman the dog was fretting him, and while Baxter didn't like queen Victoria and all she represented, he had no desire to join a Cabal to unseat her, for he had (his trousers falling a second time to his boot tops) other, more pressing demands on his attention.

71

Not least among them the demands of profit and loss. Most especially loss; loss was a small wail amid desolation, for he could hear, seemingly from just the next room, the sounds of sanitation swine grunting with rude pleasures, sharp snorts and lustful squeaks.

The sounds filled him with an obscure fear that drove his engine harder; Arlene breathed, "Yes, harder," in his ear, and a tide rose to obscure all but the most brilliant gleams of incisors, bicuspids and canines in his mind. The gleams of terror.

Chapter 4. In Which Baxter, Grown Querulous, Takes a Journey

"I wish he wouldn't wear that dress all the time. People are talking, you know." Baxter complained and complained.

"Henry," Arlene told her son, "Baxter doesn't like it that you wear that dress all the time."

Henry replied, as always, with a flounce of his plump hips and a swish of taffeta or crinoline, "Bugger Baxter, I'm the Invisible Girl, ain't I? So I should wear what's right."

To which Arlene had no further comment, growing ever more inward at 43, with this late bloom in her womb, and Henry had a point: people still poured through the doors of the Museum of Western Oddities for prognostications of all future courses, and Henry in his dress dispensed what literary tags occurred to him, will-he nill-he, and all departed satisfied.

Thus Arlene, large with child, paid Baxter ever-decreasing heed until at last she sent him up to Slyville for a talk with Mammy Sly. Mammy Sly was a crone, but she was as well an expert on the mouth and all its parts and workings and she felt perhaps Baxter could make himself a little bit useful.

Baxter departed mystified. He did not understand why he was going up to Slyville; he did not know what Slyville was, nor what Arlene had up her sleeve, so secretive had she grown. All he really knew was that Norman had not found him, and with the growth of his personal safety grew also gratitude.

The stagecoach rattled off through a late October calm, colorful ripe leaves decorously splashed across the hillsides, the deep blue sky thrilling with electric health, negative ions, the lush pulsations of a positively sexual autumn energy.

Baxter stared gloomily out the window at this passing scenery. His coach rattled and jounced along the rutted tracks. Dust boiled up behind, choking the occasional cow languishing beside a small homestead. The weather was so good, the air so clean and tangy, the land so robust and prosperous that Baxter knew he was in for a very bad time.

They clattered into the tiny village of Schachter's Landing on the Little Hawking River. The road agent handed Baxter a pamphlet through the window while the stage dropped off supplies, took on other cargo, and changed horses. The pamphlet was called The Strange Origins and Historical Development of Schachter's Landing.

The Little Hawking River had acquired this name, it seemed, only last spring, when old Dr. Heinrick Schachter had succumbed to the Worm to which he had devoted the final years of his life. Until then his village of Schachter's Landing had languished on the banks of the Mumaway; but then he died, and the river's name was changed. So it was Baxter learned that Heinrick Schachter's pretty young bride, Alicia Petrale (the first white woman to be born in July in the Niffelheim River Bottoms where Valhalla now blossomed) had remarked — when her husband, locally famed naturalist, died of pleurisy brought on by a combination of the virulent depredations of the Worm in his kidneys and the miasmas of the river valley — that the sounds he made as he expired had resembled "a little hawking," a linguistic neologism meant to convey by imitation the unsuccessful throat-clearing in which he indulged: "Hawk! Hawk!"

This was a fact about which Baxter could well have remained in ignorance; yet the expression was one which would disappear from American argot for another cycle of the Worm's life at least.

It was true, the pamphlet told him, that the sounds were dreadful — harsh, rapid and unintelligible. But more

74

recent research (the pamphlet informed him) revealed that the professor had been talking, dictating his all-important dying notes on the life cycle of the worm with which he had been obsessed, some said, and to which he had given his name; a parasite with a complex and fascinating life cycle, no doubt about that. The pamphlet contained a sequence of drawings depicting the monstrous worm with row upon concentric row of sharp, barbed teeth, spiky outgrowths of various sorts, and repellent sexual parts disguised as organs of defense or aggression.

Unfortunately, Baxter learned, even had Alicia been proficient in German, which she most certainly was not, having only indifferent Italian outside her English, she would have had difficulty understanding what her husband was saying, so clogged was his dictation with gasps, coughs, and guttural wheezes bringing up an awful greenish spittle the color and consistency of the algae-choked backwaters of the river itself. Thus his notes were lost forever, all the knowledge he had gained about this strange phenomenon coughed away.

The drawings in the pamphlet in no way resembled the actual worm larvae that drifted in sluggish currents of preservative in a jar in the back room of the Museum of Western Oddities, though that object certainly had once qualified as a western oddity. But the actual worm was much smaller, red and invasive, with a taste for the flesh of the human kidney. Eventually, despite steady attrition among the inhabitants of Schachter's Landing, the worm was a forgotten bit of local folklore. Even the jar containing the specimen from the Museum would find itself, along with other archives and exhibits, stored in a back room of the Depew Memorial Art Museum in Eden Park, on the end of the ridge of Mount Worthy before it dipped westward toward the Serpent Mound. One hundred years later, there was only one person left in the entire tristate area who even knew of the existence of the worm, Dr. Spiro Thanatopoulos, a man with an antiquarian turn of mind, among other turns.

As the stage rattled out of Schachter's Landing, it carried a morose and pensive Baxter Peabody, a-brooding on the worm all afternoon. He brooded as well on his incipient parenthood, though Arlene had never indicated he should. He brooded on Henry flouncing in his dress about the apartments of the Museum of Western Oddities, increasingly flagrant in his defiance of convention with each passing day; and Baxter, who, like all dishonest men, had an exaggerated respect for convention, worried constantly about Henry and the impression he was making on the community. But as long as his well-being depended on Henry's peculiar mind, there was little he could do.

He tried to think about teeth instead. But they reminded him of the lurid drawings contained in the pamphlet on his lap, and once more he brooded on the worm. For a time he became morbidly, and incorrectly, convinced the worm was going to get him. Then the coach filled up with evening midges, and he was occupied with swatting.

At dusk the stage deposited him in Slyville and rattled off westward to Louisville, thirty miles on down the road.

"Yall must be Mist Peabody," a voice said out of the half-gloom of the hillbilly dusk.

Baxter looked around. A small herd of swine muttered in the gloom. In the background half-light he could see a shape, pale and vast and hugely tusked, a boar both vast and white. The animal seemed to watch him for a moment, then turn to vanish into the forest.

An ancient crone appeared at his side. She smiled at him, and he could see she had not a single tooth in her mouth. An intense if irrational fear of pigs shot through him.

Chapter 5. In Which Baxter, in the Mountains, Learns a Little History, Some Curious Customs and Not a Little Fear

"Welcome to my home," Mammy Sly said so graciously Baxter shuddered.

She was a courtly woman, Mammy Sly, bent, gnarled, wrinkled, foul-breathed, with a grip like a pipe wrench, but, withall, a delicate turn of phrase. Baxter, clutching his pamphlet as if it somehow might save his life, found her disconcerting.

"Thanks," he choked.

"Arlene tells me in her letter that you are considering the fabrication of teeth, is it not so?"

"Well," he began, but Mammy Sly was sitting down just then, and it was a process painful to watch: first a slow reaching behind with knotted hands, then a shuffle backwards until bent fingers touched the arms of the lopsided rocking chair beside the cinder-blackened hearth, then a wiggle of the jutting backside bones over the chairseat, accompanied by a low moan approaching groan, a sectional devolution of her spine as she lowered herself back so slowly, slowly, fingers gripped now around both arms of the chair so fiercely the swollen knuckles turned an alarming shade of yellowish white in the dim whale-oil light, and an expression of such agony twitching across her face Baxter half-rose from his bench in consternation before she fell with a sharp rattle onto the seat of the chair and her face fell into the placid, somewhat simple lines of relaxation and a gust of foul breath reached toward him across the tiny room of her shack, pushing him back into his own seat in dismay.

"...yes," he concluded weakly, fighting nausea.

Mammy Sly nodded to herself. The nod went on. And

77

on. Her ancient eyes drooped closed, and, still nodding, she began to snore. The snores rattled and rasped, her large beaky nose quivered, her lips hung slack. Baxter averted his eyes.

"So?" she said suddenly.

"Eh?"

Her beady eyes stared intently from a head cocked to one side.

"So? Teeth, boy. We were discussing teeth."

Baxter Peabody was 47 years old. It had been some time since anyone had called him boy. "Teeth," he repeated stupidly.

Mammy Sly abruptly threw her hands in the air with such vigor and such a harsh cry of exasperation that she rose from her chair and tottered two involuntary steps toward the fire before she could stop herself.

Baxter had had a difficult day. He'd been riding in a rattletrap stage since noon. He'd been to Schachter's Landing and read about the worm. His waking dreams were now filled with the grunting of swine, a huge white boar indistinctly seen, and his twin Norman.

It all caught up with him then, and he leaped back, seated though he was, as if bitten by a snake. Behind him the hut's stone wall remained imperturbable.

When he awoke from his brief unconsciousness, fire was blazing in his mouth and throat. Shadows leaped fitfully on the rude ceiling toward which he was staring with eyes which, as it was described in those days, started from his head.

"There, there," Mammy Sly crooned, pouring some foul liquid into his mouth. "There, there. We feel better now, don't we?"

"No," he said, coughing. "What is that?"

"We call it Sinker Sauce. I gave some to Dan'l Boone once. He had a lovely prick, did Dan'l Boone, a lovely lovely."

Baxter shook his head, not sure he had heard correctly; her accent had lapsed into some nearly impenetrable Balkan guttural.

"Teeth," he said softly, when his coughing had subsided. "We were to discuss teeth, you said."

"Well," Mammy Sly leaned back in her rocker once more, clasped her hands across her plump belly, cocked her head again slyly as befit her name, and prepared to tell a story.

"Dan'l Boone..." she began. Then she sighed. Baxter flinched as the air gusted past him. "Never mind that for now. Here, I can show you."

She creaked out of the chair, tottered into the other room, returned in a few moments with an object cupped in her hands. For a minute Baxter thought it was a frog.

She held it to his face, flicked her fingers back, and presented her guest with a smile of such bleak and dark perfection that for a moment he thought it was real, despite the fact that it gleamed through her splayed fingers.

"I've never seen anything like that," he told her truthfully.

"I don't suppose you have, sonny. I don't suppose you have. These here are teeth."

"Yes, I can see that."

"These here teeth were manufactured in 1729 in the country of France by Pierre Fauchard. As you can see, they are quite dark."

He could see.

"This is an effect of the port on ivory. Something George Washington The Father of Our Country needed to be constantly reminded of. He he he." She cackled then, a peculiar sound in this peculiar place. Baxter shuddered once more, a faint horripilation trickling his nape, a tenuous nausea knocking at his awareness, a distant fear darkening life's horizons.

"Port," he said.

"You don't think these here teeth were made for me, do you? Why, sonny, I wan't around in 1729 now was I? Near a hundred twenty years ago, that was, and I ain't that old, now." She was laughing. "Someone else was drinkin

79

all that port, sir, but then I come in possession of these ivory teeth, and very well made they are, too, even if they do look like spinet keys, and dark, too." She popped them into her mouth, and her face was suddenly transformed.

Her enunciation clarified with teeth. "When I was young, sir, I was a pretty lass, and a failure as a Sinker since I failed to sink, though there's many a lass didn't fail when it comes to that, gone now and saved for sure. But then Dan'l come into my life, and that was that, my reputation ruined forever. Because you see, it was my teeth he loved down there when all this was Indians and wildwood, to have them, even and white, chew gently on his limber member, ah." She sighed deeply, lost to him, gazing into her past as into a stereopticon. Seeing Dan'l's limber member there, swaying large and stiff before her.

Baxter Peabody was neither a modest man nor a prudent one. He'd left his share of undesired babies in the riverboats and hotels of his wanderings, breached his share of promises, gulled his share of pigeons, as he liked to put it. But he could not be sure who was the pigeon here, and wanted to put an end to the tenor of this discourse as quickly as he could.

So he introjected, "But Madame, it is teeth we came together to discuss, and while I am interested, personally, in this Mr. Boom, it is not, it seems to me, relevant to the subject at hand."

"Ah," sighed Mammy Sly again. "Boone, it is, not Boom, sir. And teeth are most relevant, for I do understand that it is the teeth you are planning on providing, and know nothing of, either the ways and whys, or the wherefores, or indeed the whats of the matter. And that is why Arlene, my friend, for friend she is to all who are interested, has asked you, — whose germy, shall we say, seminal," and here she winked most lewdly, "idea it is to provide the people of this cursed valley with teeth, is it not sir? — did ask you to come up and discuss this matter with me. So don't interrupt, sonny, when I'm talking about my Dan'l, for he did most lushly gush between my teeth, when I had 'em, and that's a fact. So teeth are important when it comes to fall-*at*-i-o, or what is known as the sucking. You likely would think an ignorant old woman like myself would know nothing of such things, and likely you would be right in that, if it hadn't been for Dan'l Boone, and of course my failure to sink." She smiled, and he realized that the smile was rather sweet, all in all, despite its dingy coloration, when she had her teeth in.

This was a long speech, and she needed a rest. Baxter squirmed on his bench, reached at last for the bottle of what she had referred to as Sinker Sauce, and had another mouthful. He was then incapable of speech, and Mammy Sly took advantage of his silence to continue.

"But the benefits of oral copulation are not what interest you, are they? Fact is, there is suffering aplenty down there in the valley, and plenty here in the hills, too, for that matter, what with bad water, and poor soil, and the disease and death and dust, not all that different from the homeland. And much of that suffering has to do with the inability to eat or to speak clearly. That is where teeth come in."

Baxter tried to protest that it was not teeth he was thinking of providing, after all, but tinctures and powders for their relief, but Mammy Sly raised her hand and stopped him. "I know, I know, you think there is profit in powders. I do know about Baxter's Botanic Balsam, or whatever it was. But my boy, you are not dreaming large enough, not large enough at all. Certainly not large enough for Arlene. She says to me in her letter, she says, Pull all the teeth, and let'sgive them new ones! That is where you must seek, sir."

"False teeth?" he asked, wondering.

"Yes! False teeth." She pulled her set from between her lips. She pointed at the cunning arrangement of springs and levers that held them fast to her gums. "'Eee, 'ere," she said. "'F'at, 'ack 'astening 'ings." She put them back in. "Flat back-fastening springs. New models are better. Coils at the sides. Oh, ask me, for I am an expert. We have skills, up here, secret skills. We don't use ivory, neither. Not any more. For one, it's hard on the elephants. For another, it do turn black from drinking the port. It rots. (Not these, of course, I take good care.) We have other methods. Methods Arlene thinks could be useful. And we will have an arrangement, you understand. I do not give this knowledge away, not at all. You'll have to pay."

Mammy Sly leered, and pigfear shot his groin. Then she was laughing, laughing so hard her lovely dark ivory teeth shot out of her mouth into the fireplace, and she leaped to her feet with an agility Baxter found quite incredible and tonged them from the smoky flames.

"Never you mind, deary duck," she said, to Baxter's vast relief. "I'm too old for Dan'l's tricks now."

Chapter 6. Teeth

Baxter groaned in dreams filled with the obscure and improbable sexual practices of degenerate mountain people. He tossed on the awkward rocking chair in Mammy Sly's house. It had come upon him with a kind of horror that he was going to have to remain here in Slyville for some time, and that his time here was going to be spent in arduous labor, not the serene contemplation of profit he had imagined; for Mammy Sly did indeed have secrets to teach.

His worst moment came when she arose at last from her rocker, walked to the rude door to her house, threw it open and shouted in a loud, crackled voice into the firefly-spattered darkness, "Norman! Norman, get your smelly ass in here!"

Yes, then Baxter Peabody did have his worst moment, thinking that he had escaped forever from his malevolent lunatic twin, yet here he was, as if he knew Baxter's every move before it was made, anticipating him, crouching here smugly in Slyville like the spider in his web awaiting fly Baxter.

His eyes darted about the tiny room frantic for concealment — a chest, a closet, perhaps, or under the fat feather bed in the other room. Norman was shuffling even then up the warped front steps, across the gray and weathered boards, untroubled by insect swarms.

Baxter half rose from his bench; his hands were raised to ward off his brother's approach. Incoherent, half-formed thoughts of Queen Victoria wafted through the fever of fear which had seized him. Was she secure on her throne? Could she be toppled?

Of course his twin image did not shamble through the door at all, but a large, round-edged, gap-toothed pale-skinned fellow with a simple grin.

"Norman, you half-wit," Mammy Sly said

83

affectionately, giving him a cuff on the neck with her callused hand. "I want you to take our guest down to the Mozart Cave tomorrow. This is our guest." She pointed a long twisted finger at trembling Baxter. "Baxter, this here's Norman Balshajt, my son-in-law, though a course there ain't nothing normal about him, he he he. But he do know the way to the cave, and the cave has the secrets to make us all rich in the world, he he."

Norman said, "Unh."

So Baxter Peabody, dizzy with relief, was given his food for thought. After Norman had shuffled off into the night once more, Mammy Sly had presented him with the rocker to sleep in for the night; tomorrow he would be fixed up with a permanent place of his own, perhaps the pig shed, eh? and could start right in learning some of those secrets.

Dreams tormented him, though. The rocking chair dug into his back, the thought of moving to the pig shed filled his gut with hot oil, mouths and genitals yawned, toothy with obscure hungers. Baxter did not like caves, either, dark holes in the earth filled with scuttling teeth, damp, leprous and obscene. And what could this dismal old hag know? Baxter had never considered knowledge of a subject any prerequisite for making a profit at it. What had he known when he devised Baxter's Botanical Tooth Balsam? Nothing. Just mingle a bunch of corrosives with some abrasives, add some lemon juice and away to market you went. It worked quite well, in fact, leaving teeth white and spotless. Of course, half an hour's vigorous rubbing was all that was needed to remove every shred of enamel on every visible tooth, but by that time Baxter was far upriver on the *Simon Girty*.

In his sleep he heard the thump-splash rhythm of the paddles as the rocking chair creaked back and forth in front of the now-cold fire. He saw in his vivid dream world the cruelly-shaped pelican used by the 'dentist' aboard the boat to extract one of Baxter's own painful teeth, and the leather straps that had bound him to his chair. This chair.

84

Baxter started up, stared wildly around the dark room. A moon hung somewhere outside, casting a pale frosty light through the cracked window. A light the color of tooth enamel.

Then he heard the grunting. Pigs in the pig shed.

His relief at the appearance of dawn was as great as his relief when he had discovered Norman Balshajt was not his twin. He rose and had a short shot of Sinker Sauce, which cleansed his mouth and stole his breath. Then he went outside in his shirt-sleeves and suspenders to stretch at the rising sun.

A voice beside him said, "Unh," and Norman Balshajt was there, fat tongue hanging through splayed and yellow teeth.

"Good morrow," Baxter said with all the friendliness he could muster. A smile spread across Norman's vacant face, a subtle shift in the shape of his mouth and a dry squinting at the corners of his pink eyes.

"Unh," he said.

"I see," Baxter assured him. "Well, good enough, then. What's for breakfast?"

Norman showed him. Baxter played with it for a while, then with desperate good cheer rose from the table, leaned forward, and accidentally placed the palm of his hand in the plate of gray substance. "Shall we go?" he asked, wiping his hand on the edge of the table.

"Unh."

They went.

The sun was high by the time they crashed through the final blackberry brambles and approached the mouth of the Mozart Cave, an irregular oblong twenty feet high and five or six feet wide. From deep inside, beyond the shrill drowse of insects, Baxter could hear the slow dripping of water, imagined cold and dank and in a darkness as total as death.

Mammy Sly was there before them, standing by a crude wooden table scattered with objects. To one side of the cave mouth a small fire crackled under what might have

85

been some kind of still or kiln.

"Hey, sonny," the old woman called. She had her teeth in today, and the words were clear. "Lookee here."

He looked. "So?" he said.

Small lumps of orange-ish gray stuff lay on the table.

She cocked her owlish head. "So?" she repeated. "So? Sonny, what does that look like to you?"

"Orange-gray stuff. Why?"

"Does it have a nice translucent quality to it, do you think?"

"Yeah. Maybe. Why?"

"Oh, you are a dense one, you are. If I didn't know better, I'd'a thought you were related to Norman here, half-wit that he is. But I know better. Don't I?"

Baxter squirmed. Forty-seven years old, and treated like a child. He was tempted to leave, but Arlene would never take him back if he did, and Norman was still down there in Valhalla somewhere waiting for him. So he shrugged. "I suppose," he said sullenly.

She snorted. "Of course I do. This here is the color of teeth, boy. New, fresh milky teeth, the kind of teeth I had when Dan'l Boone liked to slide the full handsome length of..."

Baxter held up his hand. "I know. Yes. It is the color of teeth. So what?"

"Lord, you are an ignorant one. So this stuff is what you are going to use to make your teeth from, boy. Don't you know nothing?"

The day was rapidly growing hotter than the one before; even October near the Ohio River Valley could be a killer this time of year. Ague rattled, seized, locked tight the joints, socked the sufferer with intolerable pain. Killed in three days or so as often as not. Did Baxter feel a sudden shot of that pain from knees and elbows just then, a sallow chill despite the intemperate sun overhead, the steaming humidity rising from the ground, the swamps, Lake Drowning Sow and the Little Hawking headwaters not ten miles from this spot? Was the ague going to carry him off before his time, as it had so very many others, as he had heard at McCauley's tavern. It was unseasonable, this heat, belonged to July or August, yet here it was. Something terrible was going to happen with the weather; Baxter hadn't lived here long, but he felt it. Blizzard, epidemic, plague, earthquake; locusts, for all he knew. He wiped his perspiring forehead with a kerchief.

"Know nothing," he repeated, to himself. "I do know nothing. Yes. We are going to make teeth from this stuff. So what is it?"

"Porcelain, boy. Good porcelain. Better than anywhere else. Something in the clay of this here cave. The Mozart Cave, it's called. Named after the man who found it. Died in there, he did. Bad story. Never mind, these here minerals make porcelain that looks just like teeth. That's our secret. Now you have to learn it. And there is one other tiny matter you're goin to have to take care of."

"Oh?"

"Pah! Look at it! This stuff is hard, fucking damn hard. Won't turn black with the porter, it won't. Won't chip, flake or peel like teeth made out of sea horses. Won't rot in the mouth. Problem is, it shrinks and changes shape when it's put in the kiln. A little thing, Baxter Peabody. Get to work on it."

"But I don't..."

"Norman," Mammy Sly called. "Baxter here is going to be working with the kiln over there. You understand? Pristine'll be along soon to help him out. Show him where everything is, and get him started. He's gonna learn how to make teeth."

"But I..." Baxter protested. Norman Balshajt looked at him. The look was unmistakable. It told Baxter he was going to stay down here in the heat and the flies and on into the winter weather until he learned how to make teeth.

87

Chapter 7. In Which the Sky Falls

He sweated beside the kiln in the strange October heat for a week, and sprawled exhausted with the pigs at night to sleep the dead sleep of righteous despair. The huge white boar he had glimpsed in the dusk at the edge of the woods was not among his nocturnal companions; he began to doubt he had ever seen it at all.

One morning he awoke in the dim false dawn to find the temperature had plummeted, and with the temperature, the sky was also falling, first freezing slush with a ghoulish touch to his neck and face, and later, as leaden clouds sank over Slyville and the bleak surface of Lake Drowning Sow froze to a crackled dull reflective finish, large, lazily spinning flakes of raw, gray snow.

Norman appeared at the pig shed at his usual time, oblivious to this depressing shift in the weather. He grunted his usual greeting, which appeared to Baxter, as it had every day, to mean something like, "Nice day."

So Baxter growled, "No!"

"Unh?" Norman said, adding for the first time, it seemed, some inflection to his grunt.

"No. It is not a nice day." Baxter's teeth clattered together in his mouth, his shoulders hunched against the cold, he held his collar closed ineffectually before his throat. "And I am not going to hike down to that goddam cave again."

"Unh," Norman said.

When they got to the cave, the table was covered with a thin layer of slick, greasy snow, and the fire in the kiln was out. Baxter probed the ashes with stiff fingers, and finally got a small flame going in the chill, wet mass.

Baxter had been learning, though. Pristine, a gangling pale adolescent with a perpetually running nose, and sour Norman, Baxter's age, were swift, efficient and taciturn.

They knew how to mix the mineral paste, how to prepare it for the fire, how to make the fire reach the desired temperatures.

Baxter learned. He experimented. He tried different mixes, and measured the shrinkage when fired. Tried lower temperatures, more of the purplish mineral, less of the purplish mineral; he tried grinding the stuff finer. Some things helped to lessen the shrinkage; others made it worse.

He kept notes. Arlene would never take him back unless he could produce workable teeth. Oddly, it did not bother him that their product might actually be a good one, that the false teeth they produced would be the best in the world. The thought never arose in his mind. He was too busy hating the swine-smell on his clothes, the rotten gray mush he had to eat, the miserable flies and heat and humidity, and now he had this terrible camp cold to curse.

"Well, well, boy," Mammy Sly hailed him, her breath pluming from her pink-gummed mouth in long, ovoid wraiths, the ghost of a full set of teeth on the frozen air. "I see you're here, ha ha." She removed her teeth from a reticule of frayed fishnet and popped them in her mouth. "Hell, it are brisk, an't? A day for hard work, boy."

"Hell," he began, but she laughed and held out her red-raw palm to him.

"Hell is right, boy. I recall a day like this back in '78, when Dan'l Boone ruled these parts and the wild pigs froze to the ground, even the great white one, some said, though no one ever knew that for sure, but easy pickings then it was. Now it is hell, for sure, no wild pigs left, hardly. But we're all going to make our fortunes, because no one puts a fast one over Mammy Sly, and that's a fact."

"You don't think I would..."

"Hoo, no, boy, not you, you're a smooth one, all right. You're silk, you are, and spices from Araby. You'd melt lard and love it, you would. But you make some progress on the porcelain, I hear tell from half-wit Norman here. So show it me."

He showed her, numb fingers holding out the cup-

89

shaped ovals of orange-gray ceramic, the outlines he had drawn on paper before and after firing. "Lower temperatures," he told her. "And some more of this stuff, that girl Pristine there calls it feldspar, though how she has got hold of all this scientific claptrap I will never understand."

Mammy Sly cocked her sharp face at him. "So you'd like to know that, would you. I'll tell 'ee, though all the good it'll do you. There was some years back, after Dan'l took his randy rod away from here, it was, a Chinee come through these parts, mostly savage and godless country then, and because I'd failed to sink and so was outcast, I took up with 'em, and that's a story you'll like to hear over some Sinker Sauce one of these nights if you can spare the time from them pigs, he he, cause the Chinee liked my teeth near as much as Dan'l did, and for similar reasons, mind, though I hadn't so many of 'em then as when Boone were here. All that heathen could do was make this stuff. Never knew it looked like teeth, he didn't; and I taught these two, Norman over there, and then later Pristine there when she come along, unwanted but welcome, worthless clods though they all are, but still my Norman's my son-in-law and she's my granddaughter."

"I didn't know that."

"So now you do." Flakes were piling up on her scrawny shoulders, turning to melt, running down her tattered coat. The fire sputtered and fizzed behind him. But the porcelain on the table before him was hard, and nearly the same size as his patterns on the paper, though its color was off what she showed him first, and not as successful an imitation of real teeth.

"This here feldspar, as it's called, or petuntse, is mingled with that there kaolin, the white clay. Now the Chinee, he did know how to make the stuff hard, real hard it was, not like city junk at all. I found if ye add a little bone ash — and there's plenty of that from all these Sinker funerals and all the brides that sunk and drowned and were saved — then it do firm up hard as stone. The secrets are all here, and all you must do is the cleaning up, and you're nearly done, I do see that."

Here she fell into such a fit of cackling giggles she doubled over breathless, and Norman had to smack her hard on the back, which projected her teeth out into the snow where gangly Pristine retrieved them and handed them back to the old woman, gasping with her hand against her bony chest.

A wonderful hope of release rose up in Baxter Peabody then, so he mixed with terrific vigor a new batch of his thick, hard, fine-ground paste, and molded it crudely and placed it in his kiln, where the fire emitted a soft simper in the falling snow.

He turned away, pulled the jug of Sinker Sauce over to him, sat heavily on his bench, and drank deeply, between draughts staring moodily off into the non-distance of falling precipitation. The day wore on as his porcelain fired, the gangly girl fell asleep with her mouth open, flakes melting on her bad teeth, and Norman sat still as a stone and stared into some private distance of his own.

The day grew darker. Mammy Sly had long turned her back on the group and trudged up to Slyville. To Baxter, the sound of grunting pigs was audible even at this distance. The only mercy was the absence of Indian summer's ubiquitous insect life.

Gloom gathered in the blackberry brambles. Snow mounded on the chimney of the kiln. No birds sang. The forest extended forever. The cave was filled with sleeping bats, with things that slithered and things that crawled.

Baxter drank some more. A mist began to fill his mind, and the mist was filled with teeth. They did not appear to be human teeth, but rather the sharp, yellow fangs and tusks of wild beasts, of bears and wolves and swine.

Pristine snored and snorted into the falling snow. Norman did not move. Baxter stared.

From time to time he had to drag himself away from his bench, bend his numb limbs to the task of feeding the fire. Then he would linger before the door of the kiln and

91

try to thaw his fingers, but such pain would rush into the joints that he would retreat to his bench again and the false warmth of the jug.

His boots froze to the ground, his coatsleeve froze to the table. He was alone and friendless in an endless hostile universe without meaning beyond survival. Pain crawled through his back, harsh carborundum rasped at his throat. He sneezed violently, and took another drink. Likely as not he would die out here in this godforsaken wilderness, far even from the gaslights of Valhalla glowing beside the river.

He propped his sad chin in his frozen hand and stared at his lumps of ragged pottery. He must be a fool, he thought, for being here, for imagining any profit to be had in teeth, for having a twin named Norman who dogged his feet and tried to fret through his dog of a body, even for falling into Arlene's clutches, who now would be collecting the quarters the Invisible Girl was bringing into the flickering warm depths of the Museum of Western Oddities. He must be a fool.

An orange-gray lump looked up at him and agreed.

Fingers touched his nape; warm breath blew across his cheek. He lifted his head into what charity might call a kiss. In moments he was on his back, unbuttoned and undone, looking past Pristine Balshajt's shoulder at the dark edge of the snowy wood, where a huge white shape witnessed through red eyes the crime they were committing; then when he was truly done, the great white hog vanished behind a swirl of falling snow, and a short, rapidly rising whistling sound, followed by a sharp staccato series of cracks, pierced his heart of snow as the kiln exploded with a tremendous sound, spraying the glade with shards of lovely translucent orange-gray porcelain the very shade and consistency of human teeth.

Pristine, her head arched back in frozen ecstasy, suffered severe lacerations of the face and neck. Baxter pinned beneath her and so protected, was unhurt. Sullen Norman remained unmoved. It wasn't until much later that the sharp glittering spear of lovely translucent porcelain shaped like a boar's tusk was found embedded in his jugular; he was accorded a proper Sinker funeral and his bones joined the next batch of hard-paste porcelain, the very batch that would establish the Rasmussen Dental Fabrication Works for all time.

Chapter 8. In Which a Curse is Made, and Baxter Returns to Carve His Small Place in History

When Baxter returned to the Museum, his fears had multiplied beyond counting: pig fear, lust fear, tooth fear, worm fear. He clutched the small pamphlet on Schachter's Landing and the Worm in his sweating hands and stared into the murky depths of the jar, chills coruscating down his spine before its evil colors, the menace of its nature, the insidious small parasitic comma poised cruelly to invade his kidneys. The bears and wolves, the buzzard circling forever, the family of wild pigs behind the bear, all gathered to watch the cough he had contracted at the kiln worsen as winter settled, damp and foul, on the city of Valhalla. All memories of Pristine Balshajt and her father Norman were drowned.

Thus the origins of a family history were lost for a time. After his departure from Slyville Mammy Sly frowned often at her daughter-in-law's growing belly and at her dead son, speared by ceramics.

When Pristine bloomed forth a girl-child the following August, Mammy Sly saw it was sturdy and dark, not pale and long, and she had Pristine name the girl child Narcissa, that evil seed engendered there; but now it was winter she worked her teeth and tongue, and spoke one fevered night to the wrack-torn sky and gathering yellow darkness over Lake Drowning Sow in a voice demonic and dull, with all the rage of her Gheg ancestry in the dark forests, harsh superstitious mountain fastnesses and flinty sullen soil of the Albanian uplands. Her reedy voice was torn from her mouth by the wind and carried northward toward Valhalla itself.

"All generations engendered from Baxter Peabody

unto the fourth from this moment henceforward save only this one alone, will be cursed and blighted," Mammy Sly chanted through her false and port-darkened teeth, pale sullen Pristine beside her holding the babe in her arm. "All seed shall be blasted, all shall come to naught. I call upon Allah and His attendant demons and gods, His sprites and spirits, ordinaries and extraordinaries. I call too upon Christ and Mohammed to come down and curse this man, this thief and liar, seducer and betrayer. to bring horror and despair upon Baxter and his spawn. I call upon the spirit of Skenderbeg himself to return for revenge, as he did once against the evil Turks. And I call finally upon the Great Swine of Diabolus, whose whiteness is Terror and whose Golden Tushes reek of Blood, to root him out, to trample him beneath his hooves, to crack his bones and the bones of all who follow!"

Then, in case the curse would not prove adequate to the task, she devoted the remainder of her life to assuring that Pristine's child Narcissa would carry forever a hatred for her natural father so intense as to animate her with the fevered energies of revenge alone.

And she had the curse written down and sent to Baxter so that the message would be known.

Baxter read the paper, and burned it secretly, thinking thus he could stave off the curse's dire effects, but even so he sank into fruitful fears as they multiplied beyond counting; he grew more inward and despairing, and a haunted look came into his eyes.

He sat in the dark. A set of porcelain teeth smiled beside a jar, the first set he made using the special processes, the unique clays and minerals of the Mozart Cave, the secrets of Mammy Sly and her brood. The teeth were extraordinary — crudely shaped, spatulate, demented. Their grin was the grin he imagined on the narrow heads of those minions of evil twisting in the sluggish currents of the jar.

Baxter seldom roused himself to satisfy either Arlene's lusts or her sporadic curiosity. She did not appear

95

to mind, so inward had she also grown. The doctor told her she was carrying twins, and on that news Baxter sank lower, now beneath the notice of his own twin brother Norman, out there in the awful winter waiting for him.

"I have something to show you, Baxter," Arlene said one afternoon. He did not turn. His gaze was fixed on the jar where small red spirals twined.

"Baxter, look up." She swatted him on the back of his head, where his once-elegant brown curls hung gray and listless.

"Hah?" he said.

"I have something to show you."

"La-la-la lala," the Invisible Girl sang, twirling before his altar in taffeta and lace. Young Henry's health seemed to be in remission of some kind, his own cough cured as Baxter's increased. His cheeks glowed with rouge and health, his eyes sparkled with the clarity of madness, his hands caressed his hips and belly as though he were the pregnant one and not his mother. "Lalala la-la," he trilled.

Baxter clapped his hands over his ears. The exertion seemed to tax him, and he fell into a paroxysm of coughing which showered droplets onto the jar of Schachter's Worms.

Arlene sniffed. "Really!" she exclaimed. "Can't you control yourself?"

"That boy...can't...stand it," Baxter wheezed. His dim eyes stared out under brows lower than the clouds over Valhalla.

"Look," she said, handing him a set of teeth.

He looked.

"These are good," he said in a feeble voice. "Very good."

"Well, they should be," she told him. "They're real."

"Hah?"

"Real. They are taken from dead soldiers at Waterloo. A full set of human teeth."

"That's disgusting," Baxter said without force. In the other room Henry waltzed around the statue of the Invisible

96

Girl, an imaginary partner cradled in his arms.

"It's not disgusting, it's competition. The only thing going for us is that these teeth are very expensive. Teams of so-called resurrectionists have to comb battlefields and tombs for these teeth. They are paid a lot for them. I imagine it's unpleasant work."

Baxter was looking up at his mistress in horror. "Unpleasant work," he murmured. Wonder crossed his face like a soldier crossing a battlefield. "Unpleasant?"

She slapped the set of teeth down next to the blunders he had made. "That is what you have to match. Henry will operate the kiln, and you are going to teach him how to mix the pastes. He's our hope for the future, even if he is the son of Arthur Rasmussen and an idiot like his father."

"Our hope for the future?" A vague impulse to flee this madhouse swept through Baxter and left desolation behind. He stared moodily at the worm as Arlene swirled from the room.

"Teeth from the battle of Waterloo," he said. "Waterloo teeth. Real teeth. I can't do that. I can't do that. Do that. What we need is a war. That's what we need. A war. Lots and lots of dead people. Dead people don't need teeth."

The worm did not answer, introspective in formaldehyde.

"No, no no," Baxter said. "Don't need their teeth." He gnashed his own, felt gaps where the dentist on the Simon Girty had pulled. He saw the pelican, the curved pliers the man had used. "The dead don't need their teeth. Ha ha."

Slowly he climbed to his feet and turned from the room. The worm writhed and glowed in afterimage. Beyond the windows a greasy snow swirled and fell, clung damply to the sills. He looked down at the street where the sanitation swine churned the snow to mud, rooting for offal. They were large, wide-bellied, dun-colored, serene and implacable, a small herd of grunting machines built for consumption, efficient as mechanical looms. He thought of the great white hog he'd glimpsed while Pristine Balshajt twirled atop him. He remembered curved tushes raking back under the hog's lip. He shrugged. The universe was filled with teeth, but now he was beyond fear. He pulled a small plaque of oak onto his knees, opened his pocket knife, and began slowly to carve into the dense, close-grained surface.

Outside, snow fell lazily, indifferently. It was piling up in the mountains of West Virginia, in the hills beyond Slyville, in Pennsylvania mining towns, preparing for spring melt, flood torrent, plague and death. This was not hard, clean, diamond snow, it was soft, dark bituminous snow, a gray, streaked, greasy snow pregnant with the twins: Disease and Despair. A snow that mingled with the sooty outpourings of those stacks along the waterfront and settled like the wings of an immense bird of prey over the city.

As the snow fell, so did the sun, a dim orange blur. Afternoon sagged into evening. Baxter carved intently on his oak panel. Downstairs Henry twirled with a swish of skirts, his plump hips swelling almost visibly, his delicate lips pursed. Strange hormones were at work in Henry, swellings of complex molecules secreted from hidden glands into his bloodstream, the estrogens of bizarre longings. He felt arise in him the secretive, inward tenderness of motherhood. Henry wanted to brood, to nest, to nurture and sustain.

Darkness fell. Valhalla smoked, dark fires guttering. The river was chunked with ice. No traffic moved on its surface. A dark dread seemed to fall. Old-timers predicted floods, or worse.

Summer heat and ague in the joints were gone. Mosquitoes and midges, flies and humidity were gone. What was left was chill, and damp, and breath harsh in the throat, clouds of virulent germs sneezed into the air, contagion and pallor and death.

Baxter carved on. The wood was hard and resisted the pressures of his knife. He paused from time to time to sharpen it, rubbing the blade carefully on a block of carborundum. He tested it with his thumb, the white skin peeling back before its fine edge. Not enough to draw blood, but thin translucent shavings close in color to his special porcelain. Henry entered once and caressed the back of Baxter's neck, but Baxter did not stir, his concentration unbroken.

"La la la," Henry hummed softly in Baxter's ear.

Baxter carved on.

"Well," Henry pouted. "Well."

"Leave him alone, Henry. He's busy."

Arlene did not particularly care what Baxter was doing. Clearly it had nothing to do with teeth, and she was imagining a dynasty founded on her porcelain teeth. For the first time in her life she was doing proper market research, analyzing the competition. A warm satisfaction spread through her. Waterloo teeth.

Baxter brushed away the final curls of wood and looked on his handiwork. It was elegant lettering, far better than he had education or skill to produce, yet produce it he had.

He grunted softly. "There."

"Well, what is it?" Arlene asked, looking up from her book, Thomas Berdmore's classic treatise on the teeth and gums.

Henry, nodding at the window sill, dreaming of babies, now waltzed sleepily over to gaze at Baxter's work.

The words were sharp and fine on the surface. All in all, it was a lovely plaque, one that would last a hundred years and more.

"Ah," Arlene whispered. "A family motto. Very nice, Baxter." She patted him on the back.

Henry giggled.

Baxter traced with a thin, trembling finger, very slowly, over the deep letters:

The Lord Who Made Thy Teeth Shall Give Thee Bread.

Chapter 9. In Which Baxter, for Reasons of His Own, Goes Out

Why did he step out into that dark night, midge-clouds of soft snow awhirl in the air around the gaslights? Why did he stumble down Midgard Avenue on Mount Worthy's slopes clutching to his chest the sacred tablet he had carved with words given him by the Invisible Girl: The Lord Who Made Thy Teeth Shall Give Thee Bread?

Was he seeking that bread on his own, no longer trusting to the clear cause and effect of teeth and sustenance, no longer certain of his place in this determined universe, where swine roamed the foul streets, seeking their own bread with their own teeth?

He could not have said, and there was no one else about who cared.

It is a matter of record, though, that the night was bald, wrinkled and arthritic, as nights are in Valhalla when they wither beyond winter, and that Baxter did go out into it. And did not return.

Despite the thin shrieking wheeze that rose from some forgotten country deep within, he was a man, so when he came to McCauley's Tavern he did what men do: he entered, and sat alone, and drank deeply and with great solemnity. Twin Norman had been here, there was that spoor, the trace of his depraved twin brother in the air. Baxter looked around him with fogged eyes. He saw nothing but smoke and strange immigrant faces. The languages of the place were strange too, despite the tavern's Scottish name. McCauley had been long replaced by a German named Hauser, a man whose arms were pastry dough squeezed from the cloth tube of his rolled sleeves. Those white, soft arms decorated the bar like a burgher wedding cake festooned with fat.

Baxter, booted feet crossed beneath the bar, his own arms supporting his chin, drank and drank and stared at the bartender.

A man sat beside. The man stared into Baxter's face, and the man's stare was the stare of the dead, and Baxter felt it upon him like the breath of fear, for that man was his twin, his brother, caught up with him at last. "Hello, Baxter," Norman said softly.

Baxter nodded, not trusting speech.

"So," Norman hissed to him, voice low and sibilant, as if he wanted no one else to hear him, no one else to see him. It was an alien tongue amid all these harsh guttural syllables, and hot as well, pouring forth a fantastic fire, dragon's breath, the breath of the Midgard Serpent wrapped, hissing and hot, around the world.

Midgard Avenue wound around the world, too. It was the Worm, the red twist in the bottle, illustrated raw and toothed in the pamphlet from Schachter's Landing. So Baxter said, perfectly reasonable, "You're from the Worm, aren't you."

Surprisingly, perhaps, Norman nodded with a sharp but civil smile. "I've come for you, Baxter."

Baxter nodded. His forehead flamed beneath lank gray hair. His cheeks flushed in the blue light of the tavern. He sat in the Asgard Hall and drank amid heroes, for the warriors of Valhalla all were ghosts, drinking and wenching in the night, fighting and dying every day, resurrected to fight and drink again.

The fat tender of the bar remained immobile, a plaster statue who stared at Baxter until he squirmed. Norman leaned toward him. "Come, Baxter. It is time. Queen Victoria is waiting. The others are waiting. It's time." He reached for Baxter's hand.

They stepped into the night.

"Ach!" A voice shouted behind them. Baxter did not turn. Rapid German and guttural Albanian syllables trailed behind him, sharp and hard-edged as porcelain teeth, as shards from the Mozart Cave. They told of cruel deeds and

101

mighty deaths. Baxter paid no heed. His brother Norman was leading him to the Cabal, the conspiracy of death. Behind him, in the warm gaslight glow of the Museum of Western Oddities, the Invisible Girl waltzed and Arlene Bethany Rasmussen Wilberforce knitted for the small bodies growing in her. Baxter would not be missed this March.

A small herd of swine grunted and rooted around his feet in the snow, overturning the chunked icy slush, the frozen mud. Bits of steam twisted from fresh garbage in the road, from the mounds of offal the pigs left behind as they roamed the street. Bristled bodies pushed against him as he tried to drag his feet through their massed legs, their thick trunks, their hard, questing snouts.

"Snrf, snrf, gurp gurp," they said to Baxter, pushing against his knees, his calves, his thighs. He tried to answer them, as though their utterances were as meaningful as those of the bartender, still standing in the lighted doorway, spitting harsh words into the cold night.

"Grph," Baxter said. "Schnarp grunt." He pulled cold, snow-shrouded air through his adenoids in a phlegmy snort, over and over until a pain high in his forehead compelled him to stop. Beneath his arm he held the tablet of his law. Suddenly he sat down. Norman sat beside him, and their heads were level with the swine milling around in search of food.

"I have come unto you," Baxter said, and the pigs ceased their grunting for a moment to look up. "I have come to bring you the word, the law." His words burned in his throat, but the swine watched him closely in silence, small eyes glittering beneath bristled brows.

In the front a huge white boar with golden tushes sat carefully on its haunches, ready and attentive, for it wanted to learn the law; it believed. Baxter saw belief in those small, intelligent eyes. He recognized the hog, the ghostly figure dimly seen in the hills, at the edge of the wood near Slyville so long ago. Warmth and fellow-feeling flooded Baxter, and so he began to speak.

102

He spoke to them first of the words he had received, the words of the great Zoroaster, who had told him that the Lord who made thy teeth shall give thee bread. He told them of the dog of his body, and the fretting thereof. Now all the swine were seated around him in the mud of the gutter, all now were watching him, heads tilted attentively, every word filled with precious meaning to them, to their lives and deaths, to their hungers.

Especially he spoke to their leader, to the great white Hog whose tusks gleamed in the lamplight, to the glitter of intelligence in his small eyes.

He told them of the making of the world, and how it depended on the sharp teeth and the blunt teeth. He told them that beneath the smile was the tooth, and that some teeth were for cutting and some teeth were for tearing and some teeth were for grinding, and they made small smacking noises with their loose lips, and small cluckings with their tongues, for they understood well what he was saying.

Norman sat beside him, and attended well, for the spirit was upon Baxter; his words were divinely inspired. He held up the plaque for the swine to see, and they saw and were made glad. He could tell they were glad, for their eyes were filled with tears of gladness, and their tongues lolled from their mouths beneath their snouts with happiness, and their small lower teeth were like ivory kernels in the darkness.

Baxter did not notice that a crowd had gathered behind him, spilled from the doorway of McCauley's Tavern to watch this man preaching to the pigs, and to jeer at him in harsh alien tongues. He did not notice when his twin brother Norman rose first to his feet and then into the air, gently wafted on the breezes of God into the dark swirl of the heavens, the thin sound of his voice telling Baxter that he was going now to fulfill his destiny, that Queen Victoria was uneasy on her throne, for the word of Baxter Peabody would reach the world, through these twelve disciples seated in a semicircle around their prophet Baxter,

103

holding the plaque up even now for them to see, to read the words carved deeply therein.

The cold drove the crowd back soon enough. They tired of watching this lunatic drunk sprawled in the gutter talking to pigs, and turned back to McCauley's Tavern, and the door closed, shutting them away in ignorance and fear. Baxter spoke on into the night, and the pigs listened.

"But the children of the kingdom shall be cast out into outer darkness," Baxter told them. "There shall be weeping and gnashing of teeth."

There was gnashing of teeth. He could hear the gnashing as he spoke, and it heartened him.

"The fathers," he said, "have eaten sour grapes, and the children's teeth are set on edge."

"Yea," answered the great white swine, and the others answered, speaking all together. "Yea, verily."

"For my brother is ascended unto heaven," Baxter said, waving his hand at the empty place where invisible Norman had been sitting. "While mine enemies that trouble me cast me in the teeth. I shall remain while he does get rewarded, for it is unto me to speak the words of the Lord. And those words are that teeth do make the universe, and teeth shall unmake it."

"Master," the white hog asked then. "Why is it that the world is filled with suffering, that there is sickness, and old age, and dying, and death? Why is it?"

Baxter thought hard then, to put his answer into the right words for his humble listeners. Then he spoke. "The world is suffering," he said. "For if there were not suffering, and old age, and dying, and death, there would be no bread, for even as the wheat must die to make the bread, so must the bread in turn be eaten."

At this there was muttering among the disciples, and more cries of "Why, why?" and Baxter scowled on them, and spoke sternly.

"There are teeth in the world," he told them. "And those teeth must cut and tear and grind, for that is their nature. And it is unto the lowly such as we to come

104

between those teeth, and to be cut, and torn, and ground, even as the wheat."

"Ah," said the twelve, as understanding came upon them. The great white boar edged closer and spoke, "Master, we understand. We do understand. You are right, the word you have given us is true, verily, and we shall heed."

Baxter nodded, for he too understood.

Chapter 10. In Which There is an Ending That is Also a Beginning

"You'll be the death of me, you foolish boy." Arlene was saying to daffy Henry as he danced. She said, "You'll never know what troubles I have had. This building cost me dear. They made mistakes, the builders. The gas pipes spouted smoke. Do you remember?" Henry danced and said, "La la."

Arlene knitted on, quick needles clicking as the long baby blanket raveled at her feet. The doctor had assured her the time would be on her in May when spring came to Valhalla and that there would be twins for sure, he could feel the tiny heads banging together inside her white belly.

Briefly she wondered where Baxter could have got to, and if his phantom twin would turn up to acknowledge his nephews or nieces. What was his name, the twin? Ah, Norman, lost in the city looking for conspirators. Arlene smiled. Queen Victoria on her throne, knitting.

This winter was the worst in living memory, the cold clamped down, snow falling late in the spring, so now, in March, it was deepest winter into which Baxter had roamed, an even deeper decay worrying at his lungs and a madness in his brain. He sat splayed on the street before McCauley's Tavern and spoke earnestly to the swine seated around him. They paid attention, all of them, for they knew he would be able to answer to their hungers. He brought them gifts of his prophecy and himself.

"Something is begun," he told them, his mantic trance still upon him. "Something great in this city is begun, and spring will see it abroad in the streets."

They grunted appreciation, their enormous white leader moving closer. Baxter was a great man, a man of vision. Baxter was bringing to this valley the comfort of teeth, the consolation of teeth; he was bringing to the people the ability to eat without fear, to speak with clarity, to smile unashamed. He was bringing joy and light into the world. He had a mission. So the hogs grunted.

"I've written the first advertisement for the newspapers of Valhalla. Would you like to hear it?"

They grunted, yes, yes, let us hear.

"Baxter's Beneficent Bite," he intoned, reading from a dirty scrap of paper he pulled from a pocket and spread with careful trembling fingers on the flat surface of his plaque. "Painless Dentistry! Artificial Teeth by Atmospheric Pressure. Mastication and Articulation Better than Nature can provide. An entirely new process has enabled the manufacturers of Baxter's Beneficent Bite to produce entire sets of teeth specially fitted to the individual mouth. Lifelike appearance, durability and extreme lightness make these the most painless and naturalistic teeth available to the public. No more suffering! No more pain! Away with foul breath and embarrassment!"

The street lamp guttered and smoked foul breath above his head, its actinic flame casting lurid shadows across the slushy road. The pigs were ecstatic. They grunted, "Oh, yes. Oh, yes, you are a great man, Baxter Peabody. A great benefactor." He looked up and saw the teeth and golden tushes glinting in the smile that wreathed the leader's face. He could see the others, too, their interested faces, the attention that twinkled in their eyes, showed in the set of their stout substantial bodies. They all applauded him mightily, and he smiled in return.

He put his hand on the paper and looked into their eyes. "You see," he said earnestly, "we will have testimonials from patients who have purchased our teeth. 'Allow me to express my sincere thanks for the skill and attention displayed in the construction of my Artificial Teeth,' and etcetera, and etcetera. We have the secrets of the Mozart Cave, the special processes. But I am not at liberty at this time to disclose more on this subject."

He gazed up at the darkening heavens where he saw,

transfigured, the spread-eagled form of Norman his twin drifting through the drifting snow, drifting toward him with arms spread wide as wings, banking on currents, tilting back and forward, spiraling down, a hawk of the wind and snow, the angel of God, to come close, and to turn upward at the last moment, and to fall, seated, upon the frozen mud of the road beside him. Brother Norman moved up close, laid his hand on Baxter's shoulder. "Ha ha ha," Norman laughed.

"Ha ha," Baxter chuckled happily. The night was fine, it was fine to have a twin like this, to have this attentive crowd to welcome him, applaud him, respect and admire him. He was the prophet of teeth, the savior of all who suffer in the mouth, those whose speech falters and fails, who must eat mush, whose breath offends and drives friends away, who are humiliated and despairing, old and sick and tired and afraid.

Even now he could feel breath in his face, the breath of his admirers, the breath of his brother against his cheek, his neck, his forehead. He flushed with pleasure, the beginnings of all madness and confusion, for he was here, in the warm center of things, admired, stroked, attended, and those teeth which once filled his nights and dreams with torment, all those sharp bicuspids and grinding molars and keen tusks, turned to friendly lamps, aglow in the peculiar prophetic night which enveloped him, leaving behind in his vision smears of light and movement, tears of bright hope. "Allow me to express," he said aloud to his twin brother Norman who had pressed close and vanished into his flesh as if he had never existed, "my sincere appreciation. Allow me to express." Norman did not reply, could not reply, would not reply, Norman was gone, dead as a babe, swept away by cholera in the cradle of their lives, and Baxter, baby Baxter would be told of it over and over, his mother crooning through his childhood. "You had a twin, Baby Baxter, you had a twin and he is gone, he died young. He died young, and you alone remained."

And for the second time Norman rose into the

heavens and left him, and Baxter fell over onto his right side, and spoke from there to his disciples, crowding around him now weeping and gnashing their teeth, wailing piteously, the great white leaning close, his breath hot and steaming.

"Behold," he said softly, and they did have to crowd him close then to hear, "there shall be a supper, and all shall be present at it, and you shall eat of my body and drink of my blood, for the Lord who made thy teeth shall give thee bread. So it is written, and so it shall be."

Baxter smiled gently up at the wise and wondering faces above him, and those faces smiled sadly back down at him, as though seeking from him his forgiveness, his blessing. He raised his hand, holding the plaque high for them to see, and they gazed upon it. "Master," the white boar said to him, and he nodded. "Master, you have spoken to us wisely, and we have heard. We have understood. Your sacrifice could not be greater. Surely you are God. We love you." Thus spake the pig whose tushes were of gold and whose body was white as alabaster, nearly invisible in the falling snow.

"And I love you," he told the swine. He thought of Mammy Sly, her ivory teeth, her failure to sink. The Sinkers were false prophets, he considered. He alone was true. It would be right, some day, to take from them what was now theirs, for their claim to it was false. Some day when he had written in his will and locked it carefully away at the Museum of Western Oddities, some day the Mozart Cave should be taken, and used as it was meant to be used, in the manufacture of superior teeth.

Some day, when the time was right.

It would happen as he had willed.

"I love you," he repeated, as the pigs closed about him, and snuffled against him, and began happily to chew, and rend, and cut, to tear and grind, and to consume him, and they did finish him completely, until there was nothing left but the plaque lying amid his bones before the door of McCauley's Tavern, for they were sanitation swine, and it

109

was their lot and task in life to clean up.

BOOK THE THIRD: HACKAMORE, 1957

Chapter 1. In Which the Hero is Introduced to Modern Medicine

Dr. Thanatopoulos, general practitioner and society abortionist, with offices in the old Rasmussen Building, was cleaning up. He was, in one sense, cleaning his instruments. Yet in another sense he was, he had to admit, *cleaning up.*

He had, for example, just that afternoon *cleaned up* the Ovandrill girl's uterus.

He kept late hours, so even at two in the morning Cory found a physician for his despair. Dr. T, napping on his couch, heard Cory's bell and leaped to his sink, his autoclave, and scrubbed away all signs of his last client. He'd turned, hands dripping, as Cory entered, and said, "Aha! I was just cleaning up."

Now he sat at his desk with his fingers tented and peered thoughtfully into the digital lattice at the patterns of shadow on his green blotter.

"Well?" Cory asked.

"Mmm," the doctor murmured. This was out of his line; his illegal but profitable expertise lay more in the directions of vitamin therapy or a standard D & C. "Curious," he said. "Were you ever in the military service?"

"Army."

"Speak up, son."

"Army. I was in the army."

Dr. Thanatopoulos nodded, flexing his fingers. The pointed top of his little tent bobbed up and down, altering the configuration of shadow on the meadow of his blotter. Nice. He pressed his fingertips together, bending back the top joint. It made his tent a bit more exotic. Arabic, perhaps. Or Persian. He thought about the Persians, invading his homeland, and ground his teeth. As bad as the

Turks, he thought. Almost. "Army," he said aloud. "Yes."

His fingers rustled against one another, intertwined, settled into the shallow depressions of his knuckles. He looked at his patient, slumped in a chair, fingers and thumb pressed to his forehead. "Did you see the movies?" he asked.

Cory pressed his palms against his cheeks. "Movies?" he asked through his hands.

"The...films!" The peculiar emphasis insinuated unspeakable things. Cory thought he knew what those things might be.

"Social disease," Dr. Thanatopoulos hissed. "The clap."

"It can't be that," Cory said weakly. "It can't be. No contact. Until tonight."

The doctor leaned back in his chair, hands clasped behind his neck. He stared at his high ceiling, eyes crinkled kindly. "No. I suppose not." he said quietly, tenderly, with a compassion limpid as the blue Aegean. "How long have I been your personal physician, son?"

"I don't know. Ten minutes?"

"Yes." Dr. Thanatopoulos pursed his lips, sucked them in, expelled air. "Just as I thought."

"Doctor," Cory pleaded. "There's something wrong with my face. It's falling off. Can't you examine me or something?"

"Oh, very well," the doctor said, suddenly irritable. He pushed back his chair and left the room without looking back, leaving the door open.

Buddy Holly spoke to Cory from the deserts of Texas. That'll be the day, he said.

"Well, come on!" the doctor called from the doorway.

Holding his face, Cory followed.

Wooden cases with glass doors crowded the examining room. Behind the glass were jars in which pale organic shapes floated, indefinite, barely formed: a fetal pig, an appendix, a section of transverse colon. A jar of Planter's Peanuts. The doctor waved at the jars. "Got some

114

from the Depew Museum. Any relation?"

"I don't know. I don't think so."

"Hah! You wouldn't believe what they have buried in the back of that place. *Christos anesti!* Jars and jars of stuff."

Another case held a few books, tilted against the side, cheap paperbacks already yellowing. *My Gun Is Quick, How To Win Friends and Influence People.*

"Take off your shirt."

The voice called him back from the bookcases. He considered the opening of the G-minor symphony, dadeda-dadeda-dadeda-DA, Oh Mozart. Melancholy filled him. "I don't think I can," he said.

"I haven't got all night," Dr. Thanatopoulos told him, sweeping his hand at the dark windows. Outside, Valhalla drowsed in August heat. Lights would twinkle out there along the waterfront.

His cheek was the linoleum in his kitchen peeling back from the flow of insect traffic. He fumbled with his buttons, protest squashed like a roach. It was his face that hurt.

"Hemorrhoids!"

"What?" Cory tried to look up, but it seemed the skin of his forehead flopped before his eyes.

"Hemorrhoids, I said. Hemorrhoids. You got 'em?"

"No."

"I do. Terrible. Swollen knots of them. They pulsate. Throb, you understand. Terrible. Itch something fierce, *skhata*! You wouldn't believe. Nothing you can do. Nothing." Dr. Thanatopoulos, who lapsed from time to time into Greek obscenities Cory did not understand, had an odd accent which became more pronounced whenever he discussed suffering, particularly his own.

Cory got his shirt off, one arm at a time, holding his face. It was numb now, all of it. No nose, eyelids, lips. His cheeks were cool slabs of pork fat, waxy to the touch.

"Where does it hurt?" Dr. Thanatopoulos drummed his fingers on a wooden cabinet, his back to the patient.

115

Inside, instruments danced and clattered with faint metallic sounds. On the wall danced what might have been a medical degree, but it was in another alphabet, another language.

"Negroes," the doctor continued without pause for answer.

"What?"

"Negroes are going to go to the schools. Don't you read the papers? There's going to be trouble, but then, I'm no stranger to trouble, am I? Four hundred years of slavery under the cursed Turks, the debacle at Smyrna. No stranger. And now Negroes."

"What are you talking about?" Cory cried. "I'm losing my face! You've got to do something!"

A long cold wind was blowing, winter on the way. Dr. Thanatopoulos was not going to help him. Cory's voice was slurred, his tongue was yesterday's waffle.

"Bah!" the doctor turned. He slapped his palm on the glass top of another case, and inside the jars jumped. "What do I care?" he shouted.

Cory was now stuck to the paper cover of the examining table. He lifted himself from it, felt his back peel away; his face slipped. He tilted his head back. "I don't understand," he told the ceiling.

"What do I care?" Dr. Thanatopoulos repeated, as though answering an unspoken query. "I've got my own problems. Hemorrhoids. They might not even want to go to school. I wouldn't, if I were them, the schools are terrible, especially further south. Bad enough here, *Theos xerei*, and this is practically the north. But I'm not them, of course. Of course. I'm getting old, you know that? You wouldn't believe." He held up his fingers for Cory to examine, fixing him with a penetrating glance. "Look at that," he said. "Swollen. The knuckles all swollen. Arthritis, my boy. You understand me?"

Spume flew from his mouth, fluorescing under the lights. "Painful, swollen joints," he continued. "And not only that. More, much more. The bathroom, you hear?

116

Hours without result. Spastic colon, that's my diagnosis. I've even been to a specialist, but what do they know? Less than I do. Nothing. Nothing at all. They went to school! What did school do? Nothing! Gives me hemorrhoids, though."

He paused, panting. Hairs sprouted from his nostrils, from his ears. His fingers were long and darkly furred, the joints swollen. As Cory watched the doctor's own face slipped, expanded, snapped back into place.

The doctor's voice dropped to a tremulous whisper. "I haven't been laid in years." For a moment Cory thought he was going to cry; his lips were trembling and a rheumy moisture had gathered in the corners of his eyes. "Years," he repeated. "I'm married, too."

He quivered with self-pity. That'll be the day. Here was the G-minor quintet, infinitely sad.

Instead the doctor was abruptly contemptuous. "Your face is falling off? Don't give me that crap, you're young yet. A randy young buck. Get laid all the time. Bowels regular. No hemorrhoids. No mortgage, no club dues; the club dues are killers, and in my business it's important to belong to the club, all those patients with enough money to pay their bills! No, you don't have to pay AMA membership fees, or malpractice insurance premiums. No payoffs to the cops. Abortions are illegal, you know that? But the demand. My god, the demand. I had a young woman in here today, just this afternoon...well, never mind that. No sniveling around people with influence trying to get them to pay their goddamn bills. Rich people, *po-po-po*!" — he shook his finger in the air — "never pay their bills, you know that? So I gotta belong to the club, sit in the bar with a Manhattan, eat those endless walnuts, pah! Casually, you know, but loud, I have to mention things.' Say, Charles, about that bill I sent you, remember, for your daughter's D & C?' And then does Charles go, 'Shhh,' and pay up, ha ha! You wouldn't know, though. You're young yet. No problems. No problems."

He leaned toward Cory. White whiskers sprouted

117

from enormous pores on the flare of his nostrils. It was as if the hairs inside his nose had some intelligence the body was dying and were trying to escape by the most direct route.

Up close, his breath was redolent of garlic and cucumbers.

"And you're worried about your face! Pah, what you need a face for, anyhow, hah?"

Chapter 2. In Which There is a Discussion of Matters Medical

Here on the fourth floor of the Rasmussen Building, a tottering brick structure nearly seventy years old, Cory listened to the dust of ancient plaster sift inside the walls as his face fell. Into his hands. Was it some genetic problem, some flawed chromosome in the family tree, some defect along the fault line of his personality where face and identity are joined, a tectonic eruption that would skin his head and expose the anonymous grinning skull beneath?

Or was the problem moral and historical, a family curse, penance for obscure kindergarten crimes, the terrible unnamed guilts he so often felt, since that haunted day outside Miss Buford's class?

Or was it only a matter of losing face? A misfired defloration, some seismic accident in the depths of his psychic geology?

"Vitamins," Dr. Thanatopoulos proposed. The doctor, whose origins were Levantine, was indifferent to the fat god of the Midwest, even now picking history's lint from its navel and dropping it with incomprehensible indolence into this very room, an evanescent dry tumbleweed, faint as the sift of plaster in the walls.

"Vitamins," Cory repeated into his fallen face.

"You need vitamins," the doctor assured him, busy with trays and needles. "B12 and K. Very good for the face, K. Keep the damn thing going a few more hours, anyway."

Furry arthritic fingers fumbled with the syringe. He squinted through heavy glasses at the tube, and a tiny fountain of pale yellow liquid squirted toward the ceiling lights and fell back to dew his hands. Quickly as the ape at the zoo that very afternoon, Dr. Thanatopoulos licked the residue off his hand. His expression was sly and uncanny as he looked at Cory.

119

Then he winked. Cory saw this wink, a conspiratorial, we're-in-this-together kind of wink.

"Take down your pants," the doctor ordered, as if the wink had never been.

Cory complied.

Dr. Thanatopoulos snorted.

"Ha!" He plunged the needle into Cory's left buttock, Mount Worthy on the map of his body.

Yes, this was the Rasmussen Building; the first two floors held the offices and workrooms of the Rasmussen Dental Fabrication Works, the largest producer of false teeth and dental accessories in the tri-state area, purveyors to a grateful Valley of the finest porcelain choppers around, and Grouper Depew, dear old affable dad of Cornelius Hauser Depew, was president and sole owner. This thought soared through Cory's mind with a tender, rather melancholy irony as the vitamins hit his system.

A rush of ethereal bliss swept through him.

Very gently his feet lifted from the floor and bobbed to the ceiling. The interior of the Rasmussen Building began to glow, then to pulsate like Dr. T's hemorrhoids. Cory's face grew warm, floated away from him. He giggled, reached out and recaptured it. He pushed his feet toward the floor with his other hand, but they resisted, slipped from his grasp and rose again. He held his face tightly to his bones.

"See?" Dr. Thanatopoulos gargled from very far away, bubbles in his voice. "Vitamins. Laced with methamphetamines, of course. Face feels better, doesn't it, son? Your problem is spiritual, after all. This needle holds solace for the spirit."

Cory tried to nod; the gesture seemed to send his face sailing across the office like a paper plate.

"He-he," Cory giggled again, adrift on the random air currents near the ceiling. Oh, the day was catching up with him. The day was filled with teeth.

"My daddy will bite you," he said. He had no particular reason for saying that. His daddy was amiable as a pig in fresh wallow. Everyone said so. Everyone loved Grouper Depew. Grouper never bit anyone.

"Ah!" Dr. Thanatopoulos exclaimed. Did he smack his palm to his forehead? Perhaps he did, perhaps he did. "You are the son of Grouper Depew. So. This is wonderful, quite wonderful. First I get the Reverend Ovandrill's daughter in today for a dusting and cleaning, a little bastard blastula as it were, and now the son of Grouper Depew in for some vitamins. Wonderful, wonderful."

"Why, what are you saying, doctor?" Cory asked. He should be alarmed, but the air was so radiant up here near the ceiling that he could only join in the doctor's delight and wonder.

"Look at it this way," the doctor said solemnly, seated behind his desk once more, hands clasped on the blotter before him. "When I was a student..." He gazed at the ceiling. He frowned. He pursed his lips. A faraway look appeared in his eyes. His ceiling had been darkened by years of tiny deaths: flies and nocturnal insects which favored high places and an inverted life, an inverted death.

"Yes?" Cory queried, afloat above his chair, face idly held in one drooping cluster of fingers.

"Well," the doctor cleared his throat. "I did come across one or two rather rare skin diseases. Skin diseases were quite shall we say popular in Constantinople when I was a student. Oh," he held up his hand, "I know. I know, the name has been changed." He lapsed into a swing version, "'It's Is-tan-bul, not Constant-inople.'" He paused and smiled. "Your Mr. Benny Goodman, you know. But I am old fashioned. For me it will always be the City of Constantine." He glared at Cory.

Cory squirmed. "Skin diseases," he repeated.

"Yes!" Dr. Thanatopoulos smacked his hand on the blotter. "Skin diseases. Not in the Greek community, of course, not in the Greek community. The Turks. *They* have skin diseases."

Cory attempted another nod.

"Now you do understand that these diseases are rare.

And while they are sometimes fatal, it is not likely in your case. Not likely at all. I can't even be certain you have one of these diseases. You have no visible symptoms. Medicine, you see, is an art, not a science. So much depends on intuition, hunch, inspiration. So, you must be patient."

Cory leaned into his hands which held his face. He giggled again.

"Don't you get it? Patient. You're my patient. Yes? Never mind." The doctor gazed at a ceiling painted with dead insects. "We have, for instance, *mycosis sungoides*. From the Greek. Normally this disease is terminal. There isn't a damned thing medical science — or should I say art? — can do about it. On the other hand it is manifested by small flakings of the skin until eventually the whole face has fallen off and the terminal infection sets in. Oh, we have that new penicillin, of course, but it is completely ineffective, as are the sulfas. Of no use whatever." He sighed deeply.

"I do recall one patient who suffered from this disease. All over his face. A guard at the Topkapi Museum. Eventually his appearance was so repulsive he lost his job. Only a prelude, of course, to losing his life. But then, perhaps you don't know the streets of Istanbul are filthy. Really filthy. Hygiene is not all it could be in that part of the world. Among the Turks. A nasty people, the Turks, on the whole. Don't get me wrong, some of my best friends are of Turkish descent, but on the whole they are brutal, squalid and mean-tempered. Four hundred years of slavery under the Turks has taught us Greeks a thing or two about Turkish temperament. They have none. So I was secretly delighted at the progress of this particular unpleasant fellow's *sungoides*. He came to a Greek doctor, you see. A delight, really, but he showed good sense. Turkish doctors are dreadful. Fortunately, however, there was absolutely nothing I could do for him, ha ha!"

It was a long speech, and appeared to both exhaust and exhilarate Dr. Thanatopoulos, who collapsed gently into a quiet reminiscent chuckle. Finally he looked up at Cory, slumped in his misery. "Don't you get it?" the doctor asked him. "The irony? Ah, well."

Cory said nothing. What was there to say?

"Okey-dokey," Dr. Thanatopoulos said. "In your case, I would be more inclined to suspect an *exfoliated erythroderma*. Just a suspicion, *katalaves*? Here the skin comes off in broad sheets. However, it's usually preceded by a reddening of the skin, and I must say that your skin appears quite healthy, even well-attached. So I think perhaps we should adopt a wait-and-see posture on this, what do you think? Or would you prefer surgery?"

Cory thought surgery would be fun, and so Dr. Thanatopoulos sewed his face back on for him, he was quite sure of that, and so quickly, too, his furry fingers swiftly flying (Cory thought) with the tiny motions of the needle, threading in and out under his jaw, up his cheeks, along the hairline, beside his ears, minute and complicated stitches like his mother used to make on the hems of her summer frocks because she didn't trust the maid Rebecca to sew them up properly. Little stitches like the lace curtains in the living room that once when he was young had pressed their tiny patterns into his numb cheek.

It happened so swiftly, the doctor ushered him to the door and told him not to worry. After all, his problem was a spiritual one. He'd only lost face. Nothing permanent in that. He'd get over it.

Chapter 3. In Which There Are Three Phone Calls

Cory asleep at 1001 Celestial Street. Cory dreaming of dark faces flowing across the Bifrost Bridge across the Ohio, dark faces staring at him, accusing. Boy Cory, you really did it this time.

Cory dreamed of Marsha Willoughby, long thighs open to him as ghastly pale as death. Cory in flight before the furious avengers, faceless and dreadful, wings beating slowly but very strong. Cory afraid.

It was a dismal morning in Valhalla. Wilmer was cracking boards, clouds had gathered with no promise of rain, the heat was intense and dense. The telephone rang, and even the ring sounded turgid with atmospheric moisture. "Hello," Cory said thickly. He was lying on his back.

"It is I," said Vincent Black Shadow, "your faithful Indian companion. Do not speak. Follow directions carefully. Do everything I say, and your future is assured."

"Oh. Shut up. Goodbye." Cory hung up. His face had slipped a little sideways as he leaned on one elbow to talk. So in fact Dr. Thanatopoulos had not sutured it back on. Dr. T had given him a shot of something, certainly; something which blended rather badly with 57 ounces of Odrerir draft.

He waited, hand poised over the receiver. When it rang, he seized it. "What?"

"Your fab DeSoto, kemosabe, was named after Hernando De Soto, the man who brought an even dozen hogs from the West Indies to Florida in 1539, and so introduced the European pig to the Indians. My people."

"What is all this? Pigs? You sound like a tour guide!" Cory was hooked.

"It's my new job, tours of Historic Valhalla, the City,

124

Her History and Her Peoples. From the Indians of the Serpent Mound to the Hog-butcher Burghers of Niffelheim, from the Albanian Ghegs and Sinkers of Slyville to the Albanian Tosks of Mount Worthy and the Monastery of St. Credula. You should come along some day, you'd be surprised. I always tell the ancient Indian legend of the Great White Hog. Remind me. Meantime, drive to Schachter's Landing. Talk to a man named Chasen Mason. He has a moustache which fails to conceal a hare lip badly repaired in his youth by a Dr. Mortimer Hauser, your maternal grandfather. Chasen Mason is 47 years old, and his brother is a minister in Schachter's Landing. He himself is the chief of the Schachter's Landing Rangers. You are going to be a Ranger, as I told you last night. By the way, Marsha Willoughby is one hot number. I trust you had fun."

"How did you know?"

"Ha ha ha and ho ho ho. The drums, my friend. The drums have been throbbing all morning. Did you?"

"Did I what?"

"Have fun."

"Go away. And I don't want to be a Ranger. My face is falling off." Cory fell back. His face rested quietly on its bones.

"Do as I say. And when you go, in exactly 94 minutes, you are not to wear Bermuda shorts. Chasen Mason hates Bermuda shorts. Especially on his officers."

"I never wear Bermuda shorts," Cory told the hole in his ceiling. The receiver happened to rest near his mouth, so Vincent heard him. "I don't wear Madras, either. I do not wear charcoal gray suits and pink shirts with black knit ties."

"Your mom gave you a whole wardrobe of Bermuda shorts, Core. And all that other stuff. Don't kid me."

"I don't wear them."

All he heard then was dial tone. He sighed. He looked into the irregular opening in his ceiling. He rolled over into crumbled damp plaster. When he locked upon his floor, he

125

saw it was scattered with the rubble of last night's desperation. His bedspread was there, and most of his ceiling. A thin film of Suzy's detergent covered everything. Cory's virginity was there. Perhaps.

He lay back and stared into the ceiling again. The shape was not so much a map this morning as the profile of a face. Not a human face, but something animal, totemic. Ah. A gorilla. A sly look in the gorilla's eyes, glancing sideways at him. Yes, that small scrap of — what? insulation? paper? — looked like the white of the gorilla's eye. And of course the mouth was ajar, slightly opened. The gorilla was about to...

The telephone rang again. "What?" said Cory.

"I hear you had a girl at your apartment last night," his mother told him. "A hillbilly. From Slyville."

"Unh." The accusation was an electrocuted starling hanging in the wires.

"We stopped by to visit last night, your father and I." Belle's voice was silken, but its color was bilious. Hints of antebellum south wafted through her words like the faintest scent of magnolia.

"Unh," Cory said again.

He was staring at the whites of the gorilla's eyes. It had reminded him that he had adhesive tape in his medicine cabinet. Perhaps he could tape up his face. Then he wondered whether the oil had been changed recently on his DeSoto. After all, his sister Peggy had been using it while he was in the army, and she affected bewilderment at the sight of machinery. She was an artist, a singer and musician. But Withrow should know about cars. Negroes loved automobiles.

"You didn't answer my knock," Belle continued. One accusation after another. "That stubby fellow across the street told us you were home."

"Unh."

"Your car was parked in front. Badly. A yard from the curb. You're lucky you didn't get a ticket. You didn't get a ticket, did you, Cory?"

126

"You tell me."

"Well." She sniffed. Cory's bad smell carried over the wires. "We are having your uncle Cornelius over for dinner tonight. You are to be here at six."

"I think I have a..."

"Six," she said. "Sharp."

"Unh," he told the dial tone.

Chapter 4. In Which Business Is Discussed

Belle smiled thinly at Cory, showing her teeth.

"What's all that tape on your face?" She could have sounded indignant, but Cory knew better. She was worried about the dinner. The veal birds would probably be overdone. They nearly always were when Rebecca cooked. Rebecca had been overcooking veal birds since 1932, four years before Cory was born.

"Funny, that's exactly what Chief Mason asked me," Cory said.

"What did you tell him, Dear?" She was fluttering.

"I told him that I cut myself shaving." It was six o'clock sharp, and he was still wearing his black Bermuda shorts, his Madras jacket and his pink shirt. "Tell me, was Grandfather Hauser really known as the Niffelheim Butcher?"

"Now where would you have heard something like that?" Cory suspected they were in for a bout of southern helplessness.

"Well, Chief Mason mentioned it."

"My father's family was in the pork sausage business in Niffelheim in the early part of the last century. That's all there is to it. The Chief is most likely unhappy. He has a habit of saying unpleasant things about people. I just simply don't know what it could be, really I don't, unless it has to do with his hare lip."

"Mph. Hello, Uncle Cornelius."

"Graff, son. Harbo?"

"I'm fine. How's about yourself?"

Belle wandered into the kitchen, where Cory could hear her remonstrating. That was her word; it went with her helplessness. She was always remonstrating. Usually it was Rebecca. Cory heard Rebecca say, "Well, shut mah mouf." She nearly always said that.

"Well, well, come on group," Grouper said heartily. He was mixing at the bar. He considered himself a master mixologist with a broad repertoire of exotic beverages. "What'll it be?"

"Graff," said Uncle Cornelius. "Watcha watcha?"

"A muggy day," Grouper answered. "Perhaps a DeWitt Cooler?"

Uncle Cornelius nodded. Cory said, "Bourbon for me."

"Fine, son. Fine. Water?" Grouper's disappointment was a tangible substance in the air of the bar, sticky and gray as the god of the Midwest's navel lint. "By the way, what's that tape on your face?"

"I cut myself shaving."

Belle came into the room. "On your forehead?" She continued the conversation as if she had never absented herself to the kitchen, where even now Rebecca was grumbling, "Well, shut mah mouf." It was no wonder to Cory that Peggy was living with a Negro.

"Razor slipped," he said.

"Oh. The veal birds are overcooked," Belle told everyone. "I am going to fire Rebecca."

"Yes, dear," Grouper said. "Have a DeWitt Cooler."

"What the hell is a DeWitt Cooler?" Belle demanded. She had forgotten already she was going to fire Rebecca.

"Dinnerzerved," Rebecca announced sullenly. They all went in to eat.

"Three jiggers of white Rum," Grouper explained. "One jigger of Angostura bitters, one jigger of peach brandy, soda water, crushed ice and three tablespoons of confectioner's sugar. Blend and serve with lemon wedge. I skip the lemon wedge."

"How come Peg and Withrow aren't here?" Cory asked Belle, just to make trouble. She gave him a hard look and sniffed.

Uncle Cornelius finished his DeWitt Cooler and asked for another. While Grouper was gone from the table, Belle said, "Tell us about your new job."

129

"I'm a Schachter's Landing Ranger. But Chief Mason asked me not to wear Bermuda shorts on the job, so I'll have to get some kind of uniform, a double-breasted blue blazer and charcoal gray slacks. With pleats, no buckle in the back. And I can't wear white buck shoes like Pat Boone."

"Ho ho," Grouper laughed as he returned bearing a new round of drinks. "Pat Boone. Went out and shot his breakfast, eh?"

"No. That was Daniel Boone." Cory swallowed a lump of veal bird and put down his fork. He chased the veal bird with the remainder of his bourbon.

Grouper said, "Another, son."

"No no," Cory waved him off. "I'll get it myself."

"Fine, son," Grouper told him. "We're all proud of you."

"What for?"

"Well, for all your fine work." Grouper really wasn't sure.

"Oh." Cory poured himself a second bourbon and began to feel better.

"I've been working on a new invention," Uncle Cornelius announced. He was approaching seventy but seemed older; his voice was his oldest feature by far. There were rumors of an unhappy childhood.

Inwardly Cory groaned. Uncle Cornelius' inventions were well known in the family.

"What's that, son?" Grouper asked.

"Nothing."

"That's nice," Belle said sweetly to Uncle Cornelius. Silence dropped, dead as the veal birds. Rebecca brought dessert. Cory's legs stuck to his chair just below the edge of his Bermuda shorts. The shorts were made of wool, and the itch grew ferocious. Cory needed anesthetic; instead dessert was slumping on his plate.

Finally everyone pushed away from the table with a relief as tangible as the effects of DeWitt's Coolers. Back at the bar Cory had another bourbon. He gazed fondly at the label: Snapdragon Reserve. It reminded him of Marsha Willoughby, pale and pink-eyed. Were there an Odrerir in the house he would have one and chase it with bourbon. Or was it the other way around. But Belle and Grouper did not drink beer. They dieted.

Cory leaned against the bar and read labels. The labels were quite pretty. They reminded him, somewhere beneath the bourbon, of Mozart's Divertimento Number 5 in C Major for two flutes, five trumpets and four kettledrums, K. 187. They were bright, cheerful and, of course, diverting.

"Uncle Cornelius," Cory asked suddenly. "Why is your last name Rasmussen, and our last name Depew, if you are Grouper's brother? I've always wondered."

"Graff," said Uncle Cornelius. "Gorblinder."

"I'm not sure I follow you." Cory told him. The Snapdragon bourbon was working faster than he had anticipated, and he was unprepared, after three years in Thule, Greenland, for serious drinking, an activity at which the Depews and the Rasmussens excelled.

"Half brothers," Grouper said. "Or is it step brothers? I'm never too clear on such things."

Grouper was considerably younger than Cornelius, but his indifference to family history was vast. "After dinner drinks," he proclaimed. The blending machine started up, and a greenish-pink liquid began to froth in the glass. "Blooming Bayous!"

"From New Orleans," Cornelius figured. "Oh, goody." He tapped the side of his head beside his ear. No one knew what that gesture meant, but it was a standard in Uncle Cornelius' rather limited stock.

It did, however, prompt Cory to ask, "What was the invention you were going to tell us about, Uncle Cornelius."

Uncle Cornelius came to life, a glimmer of excitement entering his dim, watery eyes. He shuffled from the room, and returned with a rumpled paper sack. "Here," he said, fishing inside. He pulled out a black plastic plaque

131

about three inches wide and a foot long.

"Oh!" Belle clapped her palms together and exclaimed. It was the South, expressing bewildered admiration.

"Mph," Grouper said without interest. The Blooming Bayous were almost ready, and there was something about the timing of their consistency that required the utmost concentration. The pink had to be swirled just so into the green.

"This should be more successful than the vegetable slicer," Uncle Cornelius assured them. The vegetable slicer had been powered by cylinders of compressed air, but it had failed to slice vegetables. Instead it had fired a circular blade across the kitchen and sliced the toaster cord, causing a short circuit. The electricity had been out for five hours.

"Or the plastic grocery carts," Cory said.

"The world wasn't ready for plastic grocery carts," Uncle Cornelius told him.

"Well, they were five times as expensive as the metal ones," Cory said.

"Shut up," Belle suggested. "You don't know anything about business."

Uncle Cornelius was holding his invention up for inspection. What appeared to be a plastic shepherdess was fixed to the top, and two metal tracks ran down the sides. Cory very carefully poured himself another drink. He had already surpassed the previous evening for alcohol consumption, but he had long ago discovered this was a survival tactic that nearly always worked and completely inconspicuous in this household.

He did, however, shut up. That left no one to ask Uncle Cornelius what his invention did. Belle had her hands clasped in front of her bosoms, the Oh! of admiration still fixed to her lips. Gouper was studying the aesthetic effect his Blooming Bayous created as he poured them into highball glasses.

"I could have gone into Real Estate," Uncle Cornelius said at last. He did, in fact, own large if nearly worthless holdings between Schachter's Landing and Slyville, but he had, it seemed, inherited them. "I aimed for Higher Things," he said. He waved the plastic stick in his hand. "This, for instance."

That did it. Someone had to speak. Cory had been silenced, however, and was not inclined to be the goat. Belle had it made, her long-held flutter doing stevedore service. Grouper could no longer gaze down into the filled glasses.

"What is it?" he asked innocently.

"Bow Keep!" Cornelius tilted his head, and all the wrinkles on his face seemed to slip to the down side, like a damaged freighter with badly shifted cargo.

Inadvertently Grouper broke the silence. "Hah?"

"Bow Keep!" Uncle Cornelius repeated, a little louder, as though speaking at a banquet for the hearing impaired. He looked around at the three of them, and for the first time Cory noticed that his lips had shriveled into his mouth. He had forgotten his lower teeth again. The veal birds were for Uncle Cornelius, because he often forgot his lower teeth and couldn't chew very well.

"Bow Keep?" Cory said. It was all right, since Grouper had broken the silence first.

"Yes. I thought perhaps the Rasmussen Dental Fabrication Works might be interested in manufacturing it." He looked hopefully at Grouper, who smiled noncommittally. The structure of the family business was a touchy, if obscure, subject.

"There are millions of clip-on bow ties out there," Uncle Cornelius pursued earnestly. "They have metal clips, don't they? These here are magnets. Bow Keep stands up on the dresser, or on store counters. The metal clips stick to the magnet. You can fit an even dozen clip-on bow ties on Bow Keep. The potential for this is enormous, boundless. Consider. I get a patent. We franchise national distribution. There are international sales, why even the French wear bow ties. Bow Keep is inexpensive to manufacture."

"Unlike the plastic grocery carts," Cory said. Belle

133

glared at him with her shut-up look. He poured himself another drink.

"You can't hang bow ties up in the closet like real ties. They clutter up dresser drawers, get lost, fall behind things. Bow Keep is the answer!"

Deep inside Cory wondered what the question might be.

Chapter 5. In Which Cory Makes a Mistake

Cory's DeSoto clattered, banged, wheezed, thumped, rasped and scraped down the main street of Schachter's Landing, past the shops, past Kernel Korn's, past the bank and the movie theater showing a film called *Rock Around the Clock*, with Bill Haley and His Comets, The Platters, Freddie Bell and His Bellboys, Alan Freed and Johnny Johnston. He clanked past the Little Hawking Yacht harbor where houseboats bobbed on the slight current. They had names like *Sans Souci, Care Free, Domingo, Holy Cow.*

A cloud of dark smoke puffed from his exhaust. The cloud was a signal, ancient Indian writing with a simple message if one knew the language. But only Vincent Black Shadow Lavere knew, and he was not present, although a number of his ancestors rested inside the Serpent Mound not far from here. Cory was reasonably certain now Peggy had not changed the oil in the three years she had been caring for his automobile.

He squealed to a halt in the Rangers' parking lot. He climbed out and straightened his blazer.

As a Ranger he was required to carry a gun.

"What do I need a gun for? I don't know how to shoot."

"It's your badge of office. Besides, you were in the army."

Chasen Mason gave him a map and a flashlight as well. "Here," Chase told him, pressing a blunt finger on the map, tracing Cory's beat. "Down this road. Turn here. Up the Mound. Go to it, boy."

Darkness was just squatting over the tri-state area when Cory wheeled his out-of-date patrol car out onto the country roads. With the darkness came the mist.

It rose from dips and hollows in shapes which writhed as they met overhead. He drove through a tunnel of ghosts dancing in the dark.

As the mist thickened, Cory reflected on his afternoon visiting with Peggy and Withrow at Stoop's Grocery. It was called a grocery, and indeed, it did sell food, but it had a back room where the local existentialists were permitted hang out. It was also near the stadium where the Valhalla Warriors struggled to move up to seventh place. This put Stoop's Grocery in the precise middle of the Cliffside Ghetto, beneath the raw hills atop which the University of Valhalla sprawled.

He turned on the wipers of his patrol car to wipe away the moisture dotted there. Only the one on the driver's side seemed to work.

Cory had asked Withrow, who was lean and dark and cultivated, a philosophy graduate of Ohio State University, why his face should be falling off like this. Withrow had replied that there might be something in the history of his family to account for it. "But as my main man, Jean-Paul would say..."

"John Paul?" Cory interrupted.

"Sartre, of course. Jean-Paul Sartre. My main man." Withrow was richly surprised.

"I don't know anything about him," Cory said. "I only know about Wolfgang Amadeus. I don't know about John Paul."

"Well." Withrow drawled it in his best Jack Benny impression, which was, in fact, quite good. He refused to do Rochester, but he was good on Jack. (Peggy always did Rochester — "Yassah, Mistah Benny.") "Well," Withrow repeated, "Jean-Paul says, 'How can I, who have not the strength to hold to my own past, hope to save the past of someone else?'"

"I don't understand," Cory told him. He was looking across the room at a large black man who was studiously reading a book called *No Exit*.

"OK," Withrow said, holding out a palm. "I'll look into it. I do know how to do research. You ought to get yourself some college, and learn something for a change yourself."

"I'm going to, I'm going to. In the fall. I thought I'd study animal husbandry."

"Sure, sure," Withrow agreed. "Animal husbandry. Anyway, if I were you, I'd consider it another example of the Absurd in the Human Condition. I can't promise anything. It isn't even clear to me, if you don't mind my saying so, that your face is, in fact, actually falling off, though of course, if you believe that it is, really believe it, then perhaps that in itself constitutes the reality in which you live."

"It sure feels like it is," Cory said. His sister looked at him hopelessly. She was tuning her Gibson and said nothing.

The man reading *No Exit* looked up. "You know what it says here?" he asked. "It says hell is other people. Ain't that something? Hell is other people. This here is one whitey on to something, for sure."

The mist around Cory's cruiser was thickening rapidly, and with the darkness, Cory was now in the center of a gray sphere. He could see, unreeling before him, two or three yellow dashes on the road. The wiper clacked against the bottom, then against the side, leaving a series of curved parallel streaks on the glass. They were rather pretty, symmetrical and clean.

Somewhere to the left, hidden in the dense vapors from the valley bottoms, Cory thought the Schachter's Landing Country Club must be filled with laughing, drinking, smoking, and chit-chat. Yes, for here was Asgard Road, which went to the left past the Country Club. After stopping to squint through the mist at the sign, he turned carefully and proceeded in an easterly direction along Asgard Road in pursuance of his duties.

He had a list of residents who were out of town; he was to check their houses three times during the night. The first house was number 47 Asgard Road. There were, however, no indications of house numbers visible on the road. Cory drove slowly, staring at the side of the road, but

137

all he could see there were a few feet along the edge, thickly choked by fog-drenched weeds, ghostly shapes which waved and bowed in the small breeze of his passage. They were souls damned to darkness, startled by his headlights.

The wiper began to develop an irregular rhythm, syncopated at peculiar intervals, slap, slap, slapslap...slap! The light condensation collected instantly after its passage. He had to open his window and lean out, shining the searchlight mounted beside him into the fog. It made a swirling shape in the mist but revealed nothing. He could no longer be sure this was Asgard Road.

While his head was out the window, moisture began to seep beneath the tape holding his face on. The tape began to peel, and he patted it absently as he stared into the mist.

Where was he? Where was he going? The questions were large ones. He was driving through a brilliant white mist, without form or dimension. He had to admit that he was lost. It did not appear on the map that Asgard Road made so many sinuous turns, and surely there were houses on it, with driveways and numbers.

But there were no driveways, no numbers, and many turns in this road, turns which went nowhere, revealed nothing. He stopped the car. He leaned his head back. He turned on the radio.

"Hello, loneliness," the Everly Brothers sang.

He turned off the radio.

He spread his map on the seat and looked at it hopelessly in the beam of his flash. Here was the Serpent Mound, a drop of moisture gathered on the head, right where the eye would be, glittering maliciously. Something wicked.

That was on the map. He was in a car, and he was nowhere on the map. Asgard Road, if he was on it still, or indeed ever had been, had long since wandered off the map flattened on his car seat. He had no idea where he was; he had no idea how to get back.

If he had a two-way radio, he could call in and ask for directions. But this ancient cruiser only had a one-way radio.

He opened his window again and leaned out into the fog. From somewhere nearby the sharp, acrid odor of dead skunk smacked him in the face. He pulled in and closed the window, drove on a little further, around turns amid the dark, brittle weeds. The fog had long since ceased being mere patches rising from hollows and dips in the road; it was no longer a tunnel arched over the car, no longer curtains sweeping across the meadows and woods. It was no longer even merely a fog that made the dark canopies of trees shadows in the white. Now it was a soft, tenuous, but crushing fist of cloud, which had carried him away from the world to a place from which there was truly no exit.

His cruiser coasted to a stop in what must be the middle of the street. Where was Asgard Avenue? Where was the Serpent Mound? Where were Schachter's Landing, the boats on the river, the houses, the people? All gone, lost, vanished, and no way back.

So Cory turned on the radio once more, searching for the lost souls of his world. What he got was The Bobbettes singing Mr. Lee, an up and comer on the top forty, next month it would be number eight.

"Where am I?" Cory asked the radio.

"Oooh, ooh, Mr. Lee," the Bobbettes told him. He turned the knob, changed the station. He found WVVU, the Wonderful Voice of Valhalla University, and what did that wonderful voice give him? Not Mr. Lee, surely? No. It gave him Mozart.

It gave him, to be precise, the first measures of the *Introit—Requiem aeternam dona eis, Domine* from the Requiem Mass, K. 626, the very last piece of music Mozart wrote, the unfinished Requiem Mozart felt was for himself, dying even then at thirty-six. Cory felt himself to be a very long way from the age of thirty-six; yet he listened intently to the pairs of basset horns and bassoons playing out feelings of mild resignation atop the strings until the words

139

"Exaudi orationem meam" turned the orchestra jagged and rough and rebellious. Cornelius Depew sat in a police cruiser in the middle of a nameless road in the land of lost souls and stared, dry-eyed and desperate, at the lighted dial of his radio, the one contact he maintained with a real world in which Wilmer Dougherty smashed boards, Suzy gave her boyfriend a whip for his birthday, and albinos and dwarfs roamed the night in search of love.

Some time passed. Cory was remembering that Mozart's composition student Sussmayr had completed the mass for the man who had commissioned it, Count Franz Walsegg zu Stuppach, a dilettante who wanted to claim it as his own; there were those who said that Sussmayr had completed the mass just as Mozart would have, had he lived, and that thereafter Sussmayr had vanished from the world of music.

The mass moved on toward the "Lux aeternae." Mozart rose to embrace his own end. He had written a letter describing death as a distant friend toward whom he was striving to come close.

The fog did not lift when the last chord had died away. Cory turned off the radio and stared at the damp windshield. Then he started the car once more and drove on slowly through the silence. Even the spiky weeds beside the road had been swallowed by the mist until Cory drove over them by mistake and the rasp of weeds underneath his tires guided him along the edge of this road.

"Ha ha." He laughed. Or barked. He pressed harder on the accelerator, crunching along the ditch-side. Nettles, thistles, horse parsnips fell before the onslaught of his behemoth machine. He was driving a 1956 Mercury sedan especially adapted for police work with a 525 horsepower engine, Merc-O-Matic transmission, special suspension, reinforced bumpers and a rotating red light on top. He turned on the light.

The effect was eerie, reminding him of accidents, mayhem and death. He turned the light off. Then he tried the siren. It sounded distant and shrill, detached and unhappy, the shriek of a damned soul. He turned it off.

Blacktop appeared to his right as the weeds abruptly ceased. Another road? He looked for a sign. He stopped, climbed out and walked a few steps, groping for some trace of civilization. The lights of his car nearly disappeared in the mist, and he quelled a shot of panic as he groped back to its comforting touch. He got back in and turned up this new, narrow, but reassuringly dark asphalt.

Once in the driver's seat, he could no longer see the road at all, hidden below his hood ornament. He squinted through the cloying damp, caught a fragmented glimpse of the roadside, and followed it. Sweat trickled his back. Atomic mutants swarmed in the dark mists after the Final War. Gigantic tarantulas, crabs, lizards, ants crawled in the mist, driven by insatiable hungers.

He considered his options. He must be somewhere, adrift in the wastelands that belonged to Uncle Cornelius, perhaps, somewhere between Schachter's Landing and Slyville. Had he gone uphill? He did not know. Were there tatters, shapes, monster wraiths in this fog?

There was a bump, and the car stopped.

"Uh-oh," he said. The right headlamp was out. Just in front of it was a post; atop the post, a mailbox.

On top of the mailbox was an ornate wrought-iron carriage with driver and footman. The carriage rolled smoothly, eternally, along the top of the mailbox toward what surely must be a house, invisible up the driveway. The carriage would never arrive at the house, of course, and by now was far too late, for the world itself had moved into another era, a more mechanized, less sedate and elegant, but perhaps more democratic time.

Cory backed away from the post and drove up the driveway. At least he could ask where he was. But the driveway extended into another dimension called forever, and fear was a cold hand reaching out of the dark.

The drive twisted and twined. Dark trees gathered on either side, huge insect shapes growing from the mist, stretching out dark limbs toward him, heavy and menacing, glowing a radioactive blue. With every beat of his heart his face throbbed and the tape loosened. He drove one handed, holding his forehead with the other hand. Atomic testing had done this. And then the mist thinned and he saw it.

Lights agleam through the mist, diffused by the fog, spraying in geometric patterns a lacy shape toward him. Behind, above, below and around those lights was a sense of the building itself, turrets, towers, bay windows, cupolas and pilasters. Gray slate roof slippery with moisture. And everywhere the play of yellow lights, not so much comforting by their presence as overwhelming with their sense of magic impossibility, a faery castle.

The house was huge, but its true size was lost in the ambiguity of mist and distance, where insets and buttresses created confusion of shape, where leaded panes in the windows cascaded dazzling diamonds into the night, where the mist itself swirled around dark shrubs, shrubs of juniper and boxwood that lurked like peepers, burglars, mutants intent with evil secrets.

Suddenly Cory wanted, with a desperation he had not felt since kindergarten, to be elsewhere. He slammed into reverse. He backed away from this glittering monstrosity down the curving driveway, away, away. He backed for a long, long time. He came once more to the mailbox, and stopped with a screech. There had been a name, hadn't there?

There was a name. The name was Ovandrill, wrought from iron under the wheels of the carriage. Cory slammed the squad car into gear once more, driving in a random panic back toward the house. Then he stopped again when the lights appeared, the Cyclops eye of his one headlamp gleaming. He threw the car into reverse again. He pressed the accelerator to the floor. He laughed wildly. He was a padiddle. If someone saw it, they were owed a kiss. Ha ha.

He was still laughing when he crashed. This time it was not a mere mailbox. This time, driving in reverse at high speed, he smashed into another automobile.

An absolute silence fell. A slow ticking began. Small

142

wisps of steam began to emerge from the radiator of the car behind him, a car which he recognized as a Cadillac Coupe de Ville. Both its headlights were out, but yellow fog lights gleamed in the steam. The ticking grew louder. There was a loud snap, and Cory's trunk lid popped up, obscuring the Cadillac. Then there was another loud crack, and the Cadillac's hood snapped up. A wheeze of hot steam, followed by a geyser of boiling water heavy with the smell of anti-freeze, shot into the air. The door of the Cadillac opened, and a portly man got out. He and Cory met half way. As the ghosts of steam rose in the peculiar red and yellow glow of tail and fog lights, the portly man, who had a very red face and a trickle of blood running down his temple, introduced himself to Cory.

"Good evening, young man," the portly man said, wiping at the blood. Cory noticed that he was wearing a reversed clerical collar. "I am Reverend Ovandrill. Now who the hell are you?"

It was a voice accustomed to thundering from a pulpit.

"I'm the Lone Ranger," Cory shouted wildly, drawing his gun. "And you're under arrest."

Chapter 6. In Which Some Things Come Clean

The machine's beat was rhythm and blues. Cory sat cross-legged on the linoleum floor and watched his blazer cartwheel behind the porthole. His gray trousers walked there too, striding along their own police beat as if he were in them and still employed.

It was quarter to three, and there was no one else in the place. "Except you and me," Cory told his clothes. How could he know that his new blue blazer was shrinking, the wool fibers shriveling before the humid tropical climate of this Norge? Soon it would fit the dwarf's daddy. Cory was not competent at such things. Belle handled his laundering until he went to Thule, Greenland, and there his Uncle Sam handled the laundry.

The radio in the Laundromat, through some serendipitous concatenation of event, matched the song perfectly to the rhythms of dirty clothes; Cory and his Ranger suit were treated to *Silhouettes*, by The Rays, wherein the singer has walked around the block and seen his girlfriend's shadow kissing someone else behind her shades. Heartbreak and the gurgle of soapy water.

"Silhouettes on the shade," lamented The Rays, trapped in illusion and existential paranoia.

Slursh-slop, his shirts and coat and trousers and army-issue olive-drab boxer shorts told him.

"What would Mozart do?" Cory wondered. He had to confess he didn't know, though he suspected that Mozart would have been able to carry off this awkward moment with elegance and aplomb, as he had with Constanze's sister Sophie when she was so shallow and cool toward him. But Cory did not have a girlfriend to mourn, only a fallen face.

The singer discovered with relief and some chagrin that he was on the wrong block, and this was someone

144

else's house. That a mistake like this could be made so easily was both a summary and indictment of certain Post-Korean war Eisenhower suburbs of Valhalla.

Cory did not hear the door open above the sound of Silhouettes, nor see the dark night swirling in. He didn't see it, because he was watching the silhouettes of laundry dancing behind thick glass.

"Harf," said the person who entered, apparently clearing his throat. Cory did hear that.

He turned. An old monk shuffled across the linoleum toward him. One gnarled hand clutched beads at his belt; the other was lifted, twisted forefinger quivering at Cory. Beneath the sooty explosions of his brows dark eyes glittered with malevolence. "Harf," he repeated.

A terrific fear electrocuted Cory. "What?" he yelled, but it came out a squeak. The monk ignored him. Instead he spoke, in words which were completely unintelligible and barely audible above the radio, where the last of the Silhouettes were fading away. In his panic Cory thought this must be an escapee of some kind, or a monk from the monastery attached to the Church of St. Credula the Ulcerated Martyr of Shköder, or both. What was he doing at three o'clock in the morning in mid-September? Cory had cowered in his room at 1001 Celestial Street for three and a half weeks now, feeding on Ritz crackers and Velveeta cheese and wondering what to do with his life. He was suffering from a battery of failures. Failure of battery, failure of nerve, failure of imagination, failure of spirit, an existential failure of Failure itself only laundry could soothe. He had only questions without answers.

"Vhat chew vhant?" the monk asked in a reedy voice atremble with righteous rage.

"Who?" Cory shrieked one of his questions. He was twisted awkwardly, still cross-legged and unable to get up without turning his back on what was apparently a dangerous religious fanatic.

"I," said the monk, pointing that lumpy forefinger at his own chest, "yam Brodder Grigory, sir-r-r. You

145

Cornelius Depew are." He rolled his Rs magnificently.

The malicious glitter in those old eyes was an effect of a wash of rheum reflecting the fluorescent light of the Laundromat. Yet Cory's fear remained, for this mad monk knew who he was.

Cory thought of himself as the completely disguised Claude Rains in The Invisible Man, but Brother Grigory pointed at the cloud of white gauze surrounding Cory's head, and repeated, "Vhat chew vhant?"

Cory put his hand to his bandaged cheek. "My face," he confessed in a rush. "I'm losing my face."

"Ooooh," Brother Grigory wailed; he lifted his hands in tremulous supplication to the fluorescent lamps in the ceiling and fell precipitously to his knees. "Ooo-ooh!"

The old eyes were raised blindly to the light, hands clasped together above his head. His long rope of beads clattered on the worn linoleum. He mumbled at length. Cory caught the words, *Christos anesti.*

"Are you the doctor's brother?" Cory asked in sudden inspiration.

The monk abruptly put his forefinger to his lips and gave Cory a fierce nod; then he shuffled toward him on his knees, fingering his beads and wagging his other hand in the air before him. He seized Cory by the shoulder. "Chew are soffrink, my child, hah?"

"Well, I..."

The monk's breath hissed in Cory's ear through the swathing of gauze. "Chew gnaw them truth, hah?"

"What? I..."

"Pah!" Brother Grigory released Cory's shoulder in disgust. "Chew dant gnaw truth. Chew dant gnaw nottink. Liff in house of zinfulness and wickedly."

"I live just down the street," Cory protested, though not without a nameless guilt. "1001 Celestial."

"Chew zee!" Brother Grigory said triumphantly. "Costa was right! Chew are zick with zin, child."

"I don't understand." Little Richard began to sing number 10, Keep A Knockin. Brother Grigory nodded

146

imperiously at the radio; Cory turned it off. In the sudden silence, the slursh of laundry was the only sound.

"Vill ex-plan." The monk whispered now, and Cory had to bend very near to hear. "Pappers. I have pappers." He flicked his eyes up, toward St. Credula where she towered atop the steeple, her ulcerated hands held out in supplication, or in blessing.

"Pappers?"

"Pah!" The monk spit again. "Four truths are there. Von is soffrink, chew gnaw? Two is soffrink has causings. Zo, vhat chew VHANT?"

He shouted the last word, deafening even through the gauze. His knotted dark hand was resting heavily on Cory's shoulder again, pinning his knees to the floor; Cory's head, bowed before the monk, looked like a pillow confessing sins while the fierce priest listened.

"Want?" Cory recoiled, ears ringing. "Want? I want my face. I want to know who I am. Why I am."

"*Stassou*! Stop. Enoff. Chew are foolish stupid boy vhant too moch. Chew should be talking to The Dead Man. Talk to The Dead Man, boy! He iss vary how do you say, wize? Zen I giff you pappers. Many pappers, vary important. The Pig! The Pig! Hah! First, be still. Listen."

Cory kneeled in silence, head bowed. He listened. The laundry went round and round with a quiet steady rhythm, slursh, slursh. Slursh, slop. He did not look up again until the door slammed shut.

Chapter 7. In Which Autumn Arrives and Cory Learns a Few Things

Withrow Duquesne was not pleased at all. "I did a little research," he said. "The results are perplexing. Quite perplexing."

Cory's face was lost in a mound of bandage. His eyes peered through curtains of gauze as if he were counting the house at the opening of an optimistic new musical doomed to close in two days. The eyes blinked. "Perplexing how?"

Golden sunlight splashed on Cory's white head, stippled him yellow and green, shadows of early autumn leaves waltzing in the ballroom of his brain. They were seated on the steps at the main entrance to Valhalla University, a swarm of students flowing around them, in and out of the shadows and light. Cory watched the shadow of a frown between his brother-in-law's black brows as they worked up and down.

"Well," Withrow drawled, leaning back on his straightened arms. He had arms long enough to earn him a basketball scholarship to Ohio State, which in turn had earned him a doctorate in philosophy and a nice job at the zoo. Sometimes Cory didn't know what he was talking about. "There are some records missing, for instance. It seems that oh, way back in 1890, there was some kind of disaster. Big disaster."

Cory pulled the collar of his red windbreaker together at his throat. Disaster he could understand. Ever since James Dean died, Cory understood disaster; that terrible day he had stared out at the white fog and desolation of the windswept glacier in Thule, Greenland, and mourned. James had the nickname "Little Bastard" on the back of his Silver Porche Spyder, and now he was buried over the River there in Fairmount, Indiana, somewhere between

Kokomo and Fort Wayne, and he never got to marry Pier Angeli, who married Vic Damone instead.

So he said, "Disaster," and held the collar of his Jimmie Dean jacket tight.

Withrow nodded. "Disaster," he repeated. The two of them sat on the steps and contemplated disaster. "As my man T. S. Eliot would say," Withrow went on, "'Human kind cannot bear very much reality.'"

"Oh."

"Hey!" They looked up to see a tall boy sporting a wild flattop with fenders, his dark hair combed back into an elaborate duckass, a pair of hockey skates hung over his shoulder by the laces.

"Yes?" Withrow inquired mildly, expecting remarks regarding his color.

"You guys ought to face it," the hockey player said. "We're all going to be blown up before long. The atom bomb, the hydro-gen bomb, the Russians. The Chinese, hell, the Chinese, there's millions of 'em, you know that?"

Disaster was in the air today; it hid in the sunlight dappling the campus greensward.

"Well," Cory said, "it's true there are a lot of them, but I don't know that we really have to worry about them just now."

"Didn't you hear? We're all going to get blown to hell and gone, Kingdom Come, clinkers. Nothing left but dry, fluffy ashes. So what are we doing here? What are we all doing here, anyway? Why go to college? What's the point, tell me that?" He glowered at Withrow.

"Despair is the Sickness Unto Death, according to Kierkegaard. Perhaps we're here to learn about that."

"Phah. Ashes. Dust. Death and destruction. Atomic waste. Mutants everywhere, like the ants in Them! There's no hope, already we're suffering the effects of fallout. You are anyway, right?" He pointed at Cory's bandages.

Cory nodded. "More or less," he agreed.

"Phah," the gloomy hockey player repeated. "Easy for you to say. I have to go. Hockey practice. I just don't know,

149

what's the point."

He trudged away in radiant gloom, sunlight all around.

"You know that gorilla in the zoo, the one that keeps trying to kill himself?" Cory asked.

Withrow nodded. "Kierkegaard," he said.

"Hm?"

"Kierkegaard. I call him Kierkegaard. The Sickness Unto Death."

"Oh. Well, my ceiling fell in a few weeks ago, and there's this hole in it shaped like that gorilla's head. Exposed beams and stuff up there. See the girl upstairs, Suzy, she gave her boyfriend a whip for his birthday, well, her laundry overflowed and it soaked through my ceiling."

"I know. You told me."

"Oh. Well, I lie in bed and see that gorilla looking down at me. He's very sly and sneaky looking. The white of his eye was bothering me for a long time. Especially after I lost my Ranger job and didn't have any money. Finally, last night, I climbed on a chair and looked closer at it. See they are going to replaster the ceiling today, so I thought if I was going to find out about it, I'd better do it now."

"You sure do have trouble getting to the point, boy."

Cory's balloon head bobbed. "Sorry. Anyway, it was a book stuck between the floors." He opened his bag, pulled out his copy of *Moby Dick*, his unopened text of *Liberal Arts Calculus*, rummaged through the mess inside, and pulled out a heap of yellow journal. "Here. It seems to be real old. But what is interesting is that Uncle Cornelius' name is in it. At least I think it's Uncle Cornelius' name. Cornelius Rasmussen."

"Looks like a diary," Withrow murmured. "Old, too. What you got here is history, boy."

"Hey, kemosabe, I thought I'd find you here."

Vincent Black Shadow Lavere stood against the sun, Indian outline on the ridge above Cory's despair. "Oh. Hi," Cory said.

150

"Kemosabe, what is ailing you? You seem down, man. Real down. Hey, I heard it didn't work out too well with the Rangers, eh? You arrested old Reverend Ovandrill. Not such a good move, kemosabe."

"I think it was the patrol car they were really angry about. At least that's what Chief Mason said. But then it was his cousin I arrested; that may have had something to do with it."

Vincent laughed; then he hollered, whooped, Indian on the warpath. "Something to do with it! Boy, kemosabe, you are a genuine wit, you are. Say, how's your love life?" Vincent changed subjects rapidly.

"It isn't."

Vincent Black Shadow grinned at him. "Did you see a guy with a flattop and fenders go by? Had a pair of hockey skates over his shoulder? Real gloomy?"

Cory stuck his thumb out in the direction of the gym. "Hockey practice, he said."

"Thanks. That's my cousin. He thinks we're all going to get blown up by the Chinese or something. A real racist, but his mother owns the tour company I work for."

Withrow waved to Vincent. "Sure."

"You were saying what I had here was history," Cory reminded him, tapping the papers.

"Yup. History. You know what Henry Ford said about history, eh? Bunk, he said. History is more or less bunk. So what? Plutarch tells a story about Iphicrates, a shoemaker's son who became a famous general later on. Iphicrates says to this other fellow, Harmodius, a man of very distinguished birth, he says, 'My family history begins with me, but yours ends with you.'"

Withrow was staring at him intently.

Cory didn't get it. "So? I don't get it," he said.

"Wonderful!" Withrow exclaimed, clapping his hands. "He don't get it. Lookee here, human kind can't bear too much reality. You have a family history, though. This could be part of it. Never mind. I'll try to figure out what all this is. But I was going to tell you about my

151

research. Disaster, remember."

"Sure." Cory looked up at the stately elms which lined the walk between Depew Hall and Loki Gym. They were probably a hundred years old, those elms. Their leaves stirred in the slight warm Indian Summer breeze. "Sure. Disaster."

"Records were destroyed," Withrow went on. "Lots of records. Paper burns." Suddenly he seemed gloomy himself, Withrow, usually so cheerful and sunny. Clouds crossed his dark face for a moment, then he smiled. "Never mind," he said. "Listen, why don't you come over to the Telltale Heart Saturday. Peggy and I are going to sing, and I might know a little more then. I can look this over, see. And I can tell you about the curse then, too."

"Curse?" Cory squeaked. "Curse? What curse? What are you talking about? God dammit, you can't do that. What curse?"

Lanky Withrow doubled over, hands clutching his belly. "Oh, oh," he laughed. "Oh, oh, oh. A family curse, Core. A family curse. Mammy Sly and the Great White Boar. History...." He trailed off. "It's OK, really it is. I'll be fine." He was gasping for breath.

"You'll be fine. What about me?"

"Hey." Withrow put his hand on Cory's arm. "In 1890 it was as if suddenly some new Depews appeared out of nowhere. Maybe related to the Depews," here he gestured toward the administration building, "who left their name all over Valhalla, maybe not. Anyway, they just suddenly appeared. Your family, yours and Peggy's. And that very year, you see, all the court records were destroyed. There was a big fire. The courthouse and City Hall burned to the ground."

152

Chapter 8. In Which Cory Develops a Relationship with Art

Cory sat alone. The surface of the table before him was covered with deep carving, chiseled since the Telltale Heart opened a few months before. The graffiti, intricate, subtle, occasionally profound, informed him. It informed him, for instance, that existence, contrary to popular opinion, preceded essence.

"Yes," Cory said aloud, his voice hollow in the depths of his wooly bandage. "I'm sure that's true. It said so at the Silver Spoon."

The table said: You may not wall your destined city until deadly famine, for this bloodshed has made you grind your table with your teeth.—The Aeneid.

Grind your table with your teeth?

Behind him two people sat by the window. One was Hackamore Ovandrill, young and round and sad and dressed in black. "Life is like a smell," she said softly. The person across from her was old. Very old and shrunken and gloomy. He stared into his coffee cup. He sucked on a pipe. It, like the coffee cup, was empty. On the other side of this vast square room, the coffee machine hissed, echoing the sound of his frail breath indrawn through the empty pipe.

"How's that?" he said at last. His voice was a ghost whispering in the steam. Behind him the window was opaque with condensation.

"Well," she explained, "it sort of drifts in, you know, and then, when you've gotten used to it, and don't notice it any more, it drifts away again."

The ancient swirled his coffee cup, but the brown stain in the bottom did not move. "I'm ninety-nine years old," he said finally. "So I wouldn't know. Is it a good smell?" he asked after a pause, in a sepulchral whine. "Or a

153

bad smell?"

"Oh," Hackamore said, feeling a cold wind herself. She always felt a cold wind when she talked to The Dead Man, but the chill was worse since her D and C. She liked The Dead Man. She was interested in him. But he was not one to offer any information, or even much conversation.

"It depends," she said with a sigh. "It depends on the nose. I suppose." After all, Hackamore Ovandrill was a poet.

Cory half-heard this strange conversation, but the carving on his table was warning him just then. "Beware the Teleological Suspension of the Ethical," the table chided. He vowed that he would try. The walls were plastered with posters of famous people. Vic Damone, spouse of James Dean's beloved Pier Angeli, was there: someone's idea of a joke, perhaps. Allen Ginsberg was pointing at a huge building, headquarters of Moloch, in the background, lit up at night, his clean young bespectacled face earnest, a howl on his lips. An enormous close-up poster of Albert Einstein hung above the small stage, his large hair backlit and wispy and all relative. And over there was Snooky Lanson, hero of the *American Hit Parade*, a smoker of Lucky Strikes, just like Doc, the bartender at the Silver Spoon. All were wary of the teleological suspension of the ethical.

Hackamore Ovandrill brushed past his table. He didn't notice. Behind him the old man said, to no one in particular, "I remember things. I remember many things. But I'm a Dead Man."

"What's that?" asked an old man at the next table. He had windswept hair and was playing chess with a pimpled junior high physics genius. "What's that you said?"

"Hackamore says life is a smell. Did you know that?" said The Dead Man.

"What are you talking about?" The old man with windswept hair snorted and turned back to his game. The Dead Man was a regular.

"I could tell you things," The Dead Man said softly.

154

"Really, I could tell you things. But I'm a Dead Man."

"Jees," said the old man at the next table, moving a rook.

Fuck the Atom Bomb, Cory's table told him. Underneath someone had emphatically written: And Vice Versa.

Vincent Black Shadow Lavere sat opposite him and hunched down inside a leather motorcycle jacket. His enormous bike would be parked in the street, glistening with the oils of power. "Hi-oh, Silver, kemosabe."

"Well," said Cory dully. "If it isn't my faithful Indian companion." His finger traced carving in the table.

"He he," chuckled his faithful Indian companion. "How ya doin, kemosabe?"

"Awful, you want to know. My face hurts all the time. I went back to Dr. Thanatopoulos and he told me it was all in my mind. He gave me another shot. Then the other night I was in a laundromat washing my clothes, which all shrank, and this mad monk came in. He turned out to be Dr. Thanatopoulos' brother. He told me to talk to The Dead Man, whoever that is. It was like when Count Franz Walsegg zu Stuppach sent his steward Leutgeb to commission Mozart to write a Requiem Mass. The count wanted to claim it as his own, so Leutgeb wouldn't tell Mozart who he was or who he was working for. And Mozart was sure it was a message from beyond the grave, commissioning him to write his own Requiem. Leutgeb was tall and pale and gray, like that monk. It gave me chills, I'll tell you. I mean, Mozart actually died before he could finish the mass, though it was one of his best works, took all his soul. I mean, The Dead Man. Pah."

Cory shrunk back into his bandages.

But Vincent Black Shadow was staring at him. "You're kidding," he said finally.

"Uh uh. Three o'clock in the morning, in an all-night laundromat. And now my Schachter's Landing blazer is just the right size for Howdy Doody."

"He told you to talk to The Dead Man?"

155

"Why, you know someone called that?" Cory's voice held no curiosity.

"He's sitting behind you."

"He's sitting behind me?"

Vincent nodded, his spiky black hair bobbing. "Yup."

Cory turned around. The Dead Man was staring at his cup again, frail old turtle-head bobbing like Vincent's hair. Cory shuddered and turned back. "Tell me," he whispered.

Vincent laughed, but he did lean forward to speak. "Well, he never says much. He sits there all the time chewing on his pipe. About the only person who finds him interesting is Hackamore Ovandrill, and she's a little strange."

"Hackamore Ovandrill? Pretty, sad girl in black? Doc said she was no good."

"Doc? Oh, right, the bartender at the Silver Spoon. Yeah, he would say that. Sure." Vincent nodded. "Well," he continued, "all The Dead Man ever says is, 'Don't talk to me.' He says it over and over, 'Don't talk to me. Won't do you no good, I'm a dead man. Don't know nuttin, I don't.'" Vincent shook his head. "Really strange, you know. Kind of a village idiot."

Vincent's voice must have gotten louder, because behind Cory The Dead Man spoke. "Don't talk to me," he said, echoing Vincent. "I been dead a long time. I remember Mayor Depew. I remember Norman. I remember the Worm. Flames, f-f-flames everywhere. Don't talk to me. Won't do no good, I won't talk. Nossir."

Cory turned around again, but he had lapsed into silence, staring into the bowl of his pipe.

Cory shuddered, despite the warmth of the Telltale Heart, the thick humid air, the layer of dark smoke beneath the sooty ceiling. Leutgeb approached Mozart on a cold summer day in Vienna.

"I have kind of a bad feeling, Vince. I've got the creeps. Where're Withrow and Peggy? They're going to sing, aren't they?"

"Take it easy, Core. Take it easy. They'll be here."

Vincent was gazing at the surface of the table before him with a bemused expression, a slight smile tugging at his mouth. "They'll be here. Let me tell you about the Great White Boar, who is crafty and swift, and is the Indian's enemy guardian, because he came with the white man to the forests of Kentucky.

"You see, the spirit of those betrayed and unavenged in life enter into the body of the White Boar in order to pursue their betrayers throughout their lifetimes. It is said of the great hunter Nesting Eagle that he soared above the forests for many years to scry the wandering path of the White Boar, and that his hunt was so all-consuming that he starved in the hunt. And that when he fell dead from the sky, the White Boar laughed, for it was Nesting Eagle who had betrayed his friend's gift."

While Vincent talked, Cory stared around the room. Could Albert Einstein help him, his cheerful face wreathed in wrinkles and smiles and hair and smoke? Could Snooky Lanson or Vic Damone? No one could help Cory Depew, whose face had fallen, whose heart had fallen, and who had himself now fallen into such fear and trembling. Neither the Great White Boar nor the ape in the zoo vomiting for the crowds could help him.

Nor The Dead Man behind him, for that matter, who never said anything.

"Look here," Vincent said, his legend finished.

"Where?"

"Here." He was running his fingertip around a carved notice.

Cory craned his neck to see.

The carving was minute but very precise: Marsha Willoughby Suck Cock.

Untrue, thought Cory. Untrue!

"Hey," said a voice behind him. A faintly familiar voice, throaty and sad.

"Yes?" Cory looked up at Hackamore Ovandrill with a quick fear but she didn't recognize him from their brief unsatisfactory encounter at the Silver Spoon these many weeks ago. Could she know that he had tried to arrest her father the Right Reverend Wallace Ovandrill?

"Can I write my name on your cast?" she asked.

"Cast?"

Vincent Black Shadow was laughing, pointing still at the carving in the table top. Cory gave him a hard stare.

"Yeah, cast. Isn't that a cast on your head?"

Chapter 9. In Which Hackamore Ovandrill Writes a Poem

The Telltale Heart filled rapidly with smoke. Cory's mind too filled with smoke that coiled, twisted and obscured. He gazed up at Hackamore Ovandrill and fell. In love.

"Cory bumped into the Reverend a while back," Vincent Black Shadow told her. Cory glowered through his gauze, but the Indian's spiky hair was facing him, his black eyes elsewhere.

Yet Hackamore gave a throaty laugh, a deep, rich, melodious laugh that reminded Cory of the "transparent sonority" of the solo instrument in the Adagio from the Clarinet Concerto in A, K. 622, the last concerto Mozart ever wrote. "Your laugh," he said impulsively. "It reminds me of the clarinet from Mozart's last Concerto. In A. Especially the Adagio."

She arched one brow finely, a plump and quirky smile. "Really? And you're the one who arrested Daddums?" She held out her hand. "I'm pleased to meet you. Can I write my name on your cast? Please?"

"It's not really a cast." Cory gazed up at her awkwardly, puppy love trapped in bandages. "But it would be nice if you wrote your name on it. And your phone number."

She drew out a lipstick and carefully printed on the ring of bandage around Cory's forehead, and just as she finished, Withrow and Peggy struck opening chords. Cory had not seen them come in. He had not heard them say hello. He had not noticed when they climbed onto the small stage in the corner of the room, where Withrow even now was sitting underneath a huge portrait of Werner Heisenberg, discoverer of the Uncertainty Principle and one

159

of the minor heroes of the Niffelheim Existentialists who met irregularly at Stoop's Grocery. Withrow was proud to sit under that portrait and sing with his creamy wife Peggy, Cory's twin.

They sang that he (Withrow) had followed the drinking gourd, they wailed for Barbry Allen, they chuffed along with Railroad Bill, they suggested that her mother was a truck driver, that Johnny had gone for a soldier, that they never would marry, that they took a walk down by the O-hi-o, there was betrayal and blood.

Then they took a break to tune their guitars, and Hack told Cory she was going to read some poems next, and she hoped he would stay to hear them. He told her that Withrow had told him that there was a curse on him.

"Me too," she said. "I have a curse too." That reminded her that she was no longer pregnant, and her mood turned momentarily gray. "I used to be pregnant," she whispered. "Does that upset you? I have to know."

"No," Cory lied. "It doesn't upset me." A touch of honesty crept in, and he added, "I don't think."

"He was a poet," she brightened a little. "Very famous. Gabriel Flagg. He wrote *Blow Job*."

Cory blushed, but how could she notice? He was swathed in clouds of white. "I don't know much about poetry," he admitted. "Is it good?"

Did he mean the poem?

"It's great, if he does it with the right group."

Cory grew increasingly confused. "He does it with a group?"

"Jazz," she said. "A jazz group. The poem is really just the word 'Suck' repeated about fifty times to jazz. It's very political. It's a satire on Eisenhower, though I don't think he knows about it." She looked thoughtful. "He plays quite a bit of golf. Eisenhower, I mean."

"It sounds...interesting," Cory said; thus love made a liar of him twice.

"Oh, yes," she said distantly, her gaze elsewhere for a long moment, while Cory's love leaped salmon-bright up

160

his rivers of blood. "Why does he have those bandages on, anyway?" she asked Vincent.

"Ugh," Vincent said enigmatically, scowling.

"My face is falling off," Cory told her.

She smiled absently. "Don't you think suffering is romantic?" she asked him, patting the top of his bandaged head softly.

"No."

"I'm going to write a poem for you. Right now." She sat at the table, pulled a small notebook and a stub of pencil from a large leather bag, and set to work. Cory gazed at the layers of smoke against the ceiling. For some reason the ceiling reminded him of the ceiling in Dr. Thanatopoulos' office, and that reminded him that Dr. Thanatopoulos had mentioned this plump girl sitting beside him.

"I'm going to call it 'Navel Lint,'" she said. A tiny point of tongue protruded from the very luscious corner of her plump lips. She was concentrating.

"I saw the face of my friend falling off," she said. Then she looked up at Cory. "Does that sound too much like Ginsberg's *Howl*? 'I saw the best minds of my generation...?' Never mind. I saw my friend's face falling..." she fell back to writing furiously. "A wounded veteran of the Asylum Wars. His naked penis was a purple heart on his groin, a sad song at the frontiers of rage, navel lint in the hollow tears of the electric rose of Sorrow."

Cory gazed stupidly at Hackamore Ovandrill in the throes of creation, and imagined loving her forever. She didn't seem to mind that he had wrecked her father's car and tried to arrest him, but then she was a rebel.

"A wart," she continued, "on the foreskin of despair, angry dripping in gnawed wires, in the radium rot, in the flaming potatoes of his face falling through the intestinal meadows of midnight. What do you think?"

Vincent was nodding appreciatively, but Cory found himself unable to move.

"Hey!" she said, punching him lightly on the biceps. "I said what do you think?"

161

"Oh. I'm sorry. I thought that was part of the poem. I don't know too much about poetry, I guess. English wasn't my good subject. I'm going to major in animal husbandry. It sounds very, uh, strong."

"Bet your ass it's strong. It's Beat. Very Beat. Gabriel Flagg taught me a lot about poetry, the bastard, when he was here giving a reading at the University. He's very famous, but I think underneath it all he's probably a homosexual. Or a sadist."

"Really?" Cory said, because he couldn't think of anything else to say.

"Is there much pain?" she asked, her face open and plump and concerned. "In your face, I mean."

"Yes," he said.

"Oh, good. I'm so glad. Suffering is romantic, you know. I'm not making fun of it, though. And it's all right if you don't know much about poetry. You seem to know a lot about music."

"Not really. Just Mozart. And that's sort of an accident."

She tilted her head. "An accident?"

"Yes. See, in Thule, Greenland," he began, but just then Peggy and Withrow strummed again, and silence had to fall as they sang *Muleskinner Blues*, and *Down in the Valley*, and *Willie the Weeper*, who had the hop habit and he had it bad, and then thunderous applause when they had finished drowned out Cory's story about Thule, Greenland, and he had to stop, at least for a time, because it was Hackamore Ovandrill's turn to read her poems, and she read the poem for Cory, which embarrassed him tremendously. When she came back to his table she said again that suffering was romantic, but that they should put some tea on his bandages because that would help his face which was falling off, and Cory realized she was the only person he had told who seemed to take his situation seriously, who accepted him at his word, and he felt very, very grateful.

"Tea?" he asked.

162

"Yes, it will soothe the pain. It's very good for sunburn, too. The tannic acid." She knew a lot of things.

Cory groaned.

She clapped her hands. "That groan is very good, just like The Dead Man. He groans like that."

"He does?"

She pointed at The Dead Man, who sat with his tattered shoulder against the T of Heart on the window writ backwards so the outside world would know. Cory felt a stab of old anxiety even though Peggy and Withrow were joining them at that moment, and Hack was on her way to the bar to get some tea for Cory's bandages. Was the outside world going to do something to him, or had it already done so? Cory's heart was beating hard, and he did not know why. Love or dread, he thought.

"Here," she said, and soaked his head. "You have been burned," she told him. "You are a victim of some secret weapon of the Military-Industrial Complex, as President Eisenhower has so aptly called it. Fallout from atomic testing makes the skin fall off. Tannic acid will help." His gauze turned damp and brown. "There. Feels better, doesn't it?"

"Not really."

"Sure it does," Withrow told him. "You're suffering from the Existential Dilemma, brother, proof that life is absurd. Hackamore's name looks pretty good up there on your bandages, especially now they are all soaked like that. Some day those bandages are going to be worth a fortune, signed by the poet."

"No need to get down," Vincent Black Shadow told him. "This sort of thing happens to lots of people, one way or another. It used to be scalps, you dig? Now it's your face. An inevitable development."

Hack smiled. She had a nice smile.

"You have a nice smile," Cory said. "Anyway."

"Thank you," she said. "Now here, smoke this."

"What is it?"

"Muggles. Gabriel Flagg gave it to me. It's really

163

good stuff. He got it in Mexico. Or maybe it was Chicago. Anyway it'll help your face, make it numb."

"My face is already numb," he protested. "It's all around my face that hurts."

She nodded, sucking the dope deep into her lungs. She handed the joint around, and Withrow and Peggy and Vincent Black Shadow did the same, and so Cory did too, coughing loud and long, and then he did it again, and yet again, and she was right, the pain in his face did seem to ease up a little, become a distant object of some curiosity but little else, and then his hair fell asleep, and St. Credula the Ulcerated Martyr of Shköder spoke to him and said from very far away that he had better go to the bathroom before he exploded because the coffee had worked its way through every system there, and there was a jiggling line outside the rest room doors where Cory had to wait and wait and finally go, so that he was back to his table and stoned cold clobbered when all the bad stuff from Heaven or the Avengers or City Hall came down on them all there at the Telltale Heart.

Chapter 10. In Which There is a Raid

The whole affair, it seemed, was carried out by a couple of aging uniforms on detached duty to the Bureau of Identification, located in the new City Hall, built after the fire some 67 years before. The boys, one bald, one not, were bored, stuck down there in the basement, and had plenty of time to cook up something. They had, as it were, heard the knock of Opportunity and had opened the door wide and let in Mr. O.

Valhalla, after all, was the City of Hope, Gateway to the South, Pride of the River, sister city to Porkopolis upstream. Opportunity was always welcome.

Around the Telltale Heart activities occurred which failed to meet with the approval of the boys from the B of I. Two tables away from Cory a girl with chalk-white skin and black clothing (for instance) was discussing abstract expressionism with a girl who had black skin and chalk-white clothing. This may be Valhalla, but it was still South of the Mason Dixon.

By the window the old man with windswept hair was hunched inside his ancient raincoat over a classic Maksutov opening. He had lost one game already, and the thin, beak-nosed and slightly exophthalmic physics wizard waited patiently to pounce with a Diego response as soon as the old man moved his bishop. Both were engaged in a suspiciously subversive activity involving foreign names, one Russian, the other Spanish.

Yet for Cory, looking around through a fog of marijuana, the room held naught but ghosts, hissing and clattering in the manner of ghosts. These were the sounds of coffee and china, but to Cory they belonged to this room's former incarnation as a garage and body shop: pneumatic lifts, an atmosphere of troubled transmissions, the sounds of dropped socket wrenches and the squeak of

165

dolly wheels seemed to fill the tiny interstices of silence which fell upon the room from time to time. Stains of oil and spilled brake fluid seeped beneath remnants from Carpet City Warehouse out near Alcott Pike, but Cory thought he could still see the sad hulks of diseased Henry Js and Hudsons drifting slowly through the air, seeking the solace of repair. Cups and saucers clattered like lugs and hubcaps spinning on bare cement.

Withrow tapped him on the knee, bringing him back from the past. "I read over that book you gave me," he said.

"Hah?"

"And I did a little more checking."

"Hah?"

"Your grandfather was adopted by a Depew. That's how your family got the name, it seems. It was Dudley's wife Francine who wrote all this down. She also tells where some other documents are hidden. She lived, or worked, or spent a lot of time, at 1001 Celestial Street, where you found the diary. I need to do some more checking. It isn't too clear, but 1001 Celestial Street might not have had a very good reputation."

"Hah."

A pale girl sat down at the next table. She had an iguana on a gold leash. The iguana crawled slowly and clumsily over the sugar bowl. "Excuse me," she said to Cory, leaning across the space between them. "Are you Snooky Lanson? From *Your Hit Parade*? I heard he was in a accident."

"No," Cory told her. "Actually I am Wernher von Braun. Of the Army Ballistic Missile Agency."

"Oh. Hi, Withrow. How ya doin?"

Withrow nodded. "Fine, fine. And you?"

"Godzilla!" the girl scolded. "Get out of the sugar." Godzilla's tongue was lapping the little cubes scattered across the table top. "You still at the zoo?" she asked Withrow.

"If you're a black existentialist in Valhalla, that's about the only place you can get a job. Despite the troops in

166

Little Rock."

"What do you do there, anyway?" Cory asked. "I never did know."

"Clean up. What you think, white boy?"

"Sounds shitty. Why don't you quit? Get a decent job."

"What?" Withrow drew back in mock alarm. "And give up show business."

"Ha ha. That's an old one."

"The Russians," Godzilla's pale owner said. "They sent up a satellite today, Sputnik. They'll send a dog into space next."

"Don't worry," Cory declared. "Our rockets will be working soon. I, Wernher von Braun, decree it. This is America. We have Yankee Ingenuity, and a general for President. How can we lose?"

"We can't," Hackamore said. "We also have rhythm and blues, Dick Clark, Pat Boone singing *April Love, Howdy Doody*, Milton Berle, *The Honeymooners, Ozzie and Harriet, Leave It to Beaver*, Mike Todd and Elizabeth Taylor, the hula hoop and Donna Reed."

Peggy took up the refrain. "'Sincerity is the quality that comes through on television,'" she said. "Vice President Richard Milhouse Nixon."

Hack continued. "The theme song from *The Blob*, by Burt Bacharach."

"We will bury you, by Nikita Khrushchev," Vincent Black Shadow put in.

"Merc-O-Matic," said the girl who owned Godzilla.

"What's green and jumps from bed to bed?" Peggy asked.

"Lizard Taylor," Withrow answered, and they clapped hands together.

A swarthy boy stopped to chuck the lizard under the chin. Godzilla gazed at him without interest. "Well, keep your finger up the social pulse," he told the pale girl.

"Up yours too," she said. Godzilla flicked his black tongue over her fingers.

167

"There's a lot of loose talk down in Niffelheim these days," Withrow said softly. "They plan to tear down the stadium in the ghetto and build a new one closer to the river. Get it away from the Negroes. That would be bad news for a lot of folks down there." He stretched his long legs out under the table. "Hey, who's that?"

A pale beaky man in a hat and raincoat let the front door swing shut behind him and stood beside it, gazing around the room through melodramatically narrowed eyes. It was possible he was trying to compensate for advanced myopia, but the effect was out of place in a room full of proto-beatniks. The windows had steamed solidly by now, and the gilt lettering, even the T in Heart, was invisible. Only a faint glow from the street lights filtered through.

"Don't know," Hackamore said, looking at the snap-brim hat the man was wearing, the gray trench coat. "Bogey?"

"Cagney," Vincent Black Shadow said firmly. "Looking for the garage that used to be here, the ghosts of the St. Valentine's Day Massacre."

The man shifted from foot to foot, apparently looking for someone he knew. Then he opened the front door once more to look up and down the street, closed it and walked with elaborate casualness to the back where the rest rooms were.

"Say," Vincent asked. "Does anyone know a person name of Marsha Willoughby?" He winked at Cory, who blushed inside his bandages.

"The albino?" Hackamore Ovandrill asked. "Everyone knows her. She is hot to trot."

Cory hated that phrase. He began falling out of love. The pain was worse than falling in.

"Now who's that?" Withrow asked. A balding man, also very pale, was standing by the front door mopping his forehead with a checkered handkerchief, as if it were extraordinarily hot outside. It was not hot, it was the fifth of October.

"It's another one," Cory said. "He looks nervous."

168

"Same raincoat," Vincent added. "You don't suppose they're cops, do you?"

Peggy snorted. "What would cops be doing in a place like this?"

"Dunno," Withrow shrugged. "Who do you think is going to win the Nobel Prize for Literature this year?"

"Camus," Vincent said. "Or Sartre."

"Two to one it's Camus," Withrow offered.

"Done," Vincent said. "How much?"

"All right, everybody, this is a raid," said the short bald man at the front door.

"Ten dollars," Withrow suggested.

"This is a raid! Nobody move!" the man at the door repeated.

"Ten dollars? Are you sure? That's a lot of money."

"Nobody move," the first man ordered from the back of the room.

"Aw, shut up and sit down," someone yelled.

"I'm sure," Withrow said. "Two to one." But he was watching the room. There were a lot of black faces here, and that could mean trouble if these really were police.

"Godammit, where are the uniforms? Where's Moose?" the man by the front door complained. The old man with windswept hair looked up and said, "Who cares? The war's over, you know. Your move," he told to the bulgy-eyed physics genius. Behind him The Dead Man sucked sorrow through his empty pipe.

"I don't think they'll give it to Camus," Vincent said. "For one thing he's too young, and too well-known. Besides, he hasn't written that much. Furthermore, he's outside the mainstream of Existentialist thought."

"Yup," said Withrow. "That's just why they'll give it to him."

"You don't suppose they really are cops, do you?" Peggy asked.

"Naw. Rednecks probably, out for cheap thrills. You know, scare the Bohemians. Just practical jokers." But Vincent was worried too. "What would the police want

169

here?"

The front door crashed open, frame splintered away from the hinges, latch sprung; the door slammed back against the wall and rebounded into the face of a uniformed policeman charging through with drawn gun. He stopped, pushed the door away viciously. It bounced again.

"Shit!" he yelled. In the sudden silence of the room the sound of splintering wood could be heard from the back door. The sound of an ax. There was a pause, then a screech as the metal bit was pulled from the wood. Another crack, pause, screech. And another.

Everyone in the room stared at the back. The rest room doors opened as the occupants peered out to see what the noise was all about. Even the two plainclothesmen stared. And Moose, the uniform at the door, with various kinds of smoke billowing past him into the night, was staring.

Conversation was suspended. The girls discussing Jackson Pollack were stopped in mid splash; The Dead Man was watching the Civil War again, as from an enormous distance, performed by Mickey Mouse and the Mouseketeers. The man with windswept hair was holding his queen over his opponent's knight. Time slowed to a halt, the sound of the ax deepened to a bass rumble, emerged through the door, pulled back to reveal the night outside.

Godzilla turned, mouth open, tongue extended. Grains of impossibly white sugar were stuck to his chin. It looked as if he were wearing a diamond choker.

A moon-faced man holding the handle of the espresso machine stood immobile as a continuous hiss of steam shot into a cup of milk which foamed up the sides in a cloud of vapor to obscure the ghosts of old Studebakers suspended in the air.

Steam hit his hand, he dropped the lever, more in surprise than pain, and the pale man beside Moose brought up his .38.

The moon-faced man opened his mouth. "It's not

locked," he said to the back door.

Cory stared at the men by the entrance. The plainclothesman was staring right at him.

"Shut up, you," Moose shouted, on the heels of the moon-faced man's protest. Beside him, the bald pale man's gun went off.

The sound was enormously loud. It seemed as if this room were an empty garage again, filled only with the huge, continuous echo of the shot rolling around the walls and ceiling and floor, a bowling ball looking for a home in God's own empty basement.

Then the sound did not die away, it suddenly stopped.

The cessation was as abrupt as the small, round, innocuous hole which appeared in the very center of the moon-faced man's forehead.

He stood there amid the final wisps of steam rising from the hot milk on the chrome grating under the spout and his face held an expression of utter and comic surprise. He stood a long time before toppling, and no one laughed, despite his expression.

Finally, when the moon-faced man had fallen behind the counter and even the sound of his fall had died away, the balding man beside the front door sighed wearily.

Cory rested his head on his table. He knew the bullet had been meant for him. As he fell forward into the well of the past, muffled words drifted after him.

"This is a raid," the man from the B of I said in a voice thick with fatigue. "Nobody move."

It was the last thing anyone considered doing. Cory faded out.

BOOK THE FOURTH: NORMAN, 1890

Chapter 1. In Which There Are Twins

The darkness was complete down the well of the past, a dense womb-dark, deep and tense. Yet there, dark as it was, the first fitful flames of the conflagration at City Hall were ignited in Arlene's twins, who were locked face to face in pre-natal struggle for first place. Their dispute made the birth extraordinarily difficult for the attending physician, more difficult still for Norman and Baxter, bear-hugging one another into the cervical foyer, but most difficult of all for their mother.

The contest continued for a day and a half of that lovely Valhalla spring in 1858. The dogwoods bloomed, lovely English and German flowers splashed color everywhere, the mists rising from the river were fragrant and tender, but those two boys would not give up their frozen waltz of refusal and antagonism. In the long run it could never be entirely certain whether they were fighting to be the first out, or fighting to remain inside. Appearances would always deceive.

Arlene thrashed in her bed, Henry la-la-ed about the ground floor of the Museum, gowns aswish around plump legs. He did not care for his mother's cries of agony and rage. Henry did not care for suffering in any form, and so he danced instead, a dreamy dance with some dashing imaginary gentleman of the ante-bellum south while his twin half-brothers wrestled one another to a standstill at the world's doorway.

Was Norman a little stronger, or did he merely have the advantage of position at the post, slightly twisted in the direction of the open air?

It could not matter, the twin called Norman won the battle, if not the war. So Baxter lost.

The biggest loser of all, of course, was Arlene: she died.

174

Henry was forced to attend the end. Pale, drenched with perspiration, Arlene reached feebly for feeble Henry's hand, clutched it in her expiring grip. "The first one's name is Norman," she said in a soft rasp. "The other is Baxter. You will care for them."

She fixed her eyes on the plaque, rescued from the street before McCauley's Tavern after the pigs moved on, returned to her by the barkeeper with a lopsided and faintly apologetic grin, for it seemed no one had heard the snuffling of the pigs as they devoured Baxter Peabody, though the herd had been seen snuffling off into the snow, led by a white boar of prodigious size. He felt vaguely responsible, though it was clearly not his fault. But after all, he reported, the swine had been eating near his very door, and when they left, one of his customers was gone forever into sow-belly, boar-belly, pork-belly heaven, and only this plaque remained, and so he returned it along with a clipping of the article in the Valhalla *Clarion*.

It would be, she told him, a family motto, a reminder, a bit of history, that plaque. The Lord Who Made Thy Teeth Shall Give Thee Bread. Henry would raise the twins to run the business she and Baxter had begun.

So Henry Rasmussen, a mother at seventeen, raised his boys, Norman the strong and Baxter the weak. And throughout the period of his strange motherhood, he maintained a hatred both obscure and intense toward that huge white hog and its band of followers. For many square blocks around the Museum, folks knew Henry feared and hated the White Hog, and faithfully they reported every sighting, real or imagined, and Henry flew to the spot, sniffed around the location, and questioned all witnesses intently. But always he returned home unsatisfied, his thirst for revenge on the eaters of the man who left him in this position of intolerable responsibility unsated.

At night, as the twins gurgled in their cradles, snuffled in their beds, groaned on the rack of puberty and otherwise grew up. Henry, whom everyone, including his twins, believed to be a perfect Mom and woman, told

175

stories of that killer hog and what it had done, and the twins grew with that same hatred and fear.

Eventually the miasmas of the river bottom, the weakness of his own lungs and the cholera epidemic of 1879 la-la-laed Henry out of the city of Valhalla and into the mythic Niffelheim whence no man returns. It was the end of the Invisible Girl.

Certainly it was not the end of Norman, or Baxter, though as twins they mirrored one another, face to face in life's little minuet. While Henry was alive the Rasmussen Dental Fabrication Works thrived and grew on the late Baxter Peabody's knowledge of ceramics, on the feldspar clays from the Mozart Cave (provided by those descendents of Mammy Sly who survived the kiln explosion), and on Henry's strange but effective conduct of the business, so much more reliable although perhaps less imaginative than his mother's.

So it was that years later, in the fall of 1890, 32-year-old Norman Rasmussen (oh, there was some confusion about names back then — should they be Peabodys, or Wilberforces, or Rasmussens? — but Henry, as sole guardian, solved the matter by decree, giving the twins his own surname) had, in a series of ruthless (Norman the Strong!) moves, become as close to being boss of the city of Valhalla as possible short of public office. Now it was toward public office that he was directing his attentions.

"How much?" he asked. He was frowning, but Baxter couldn't know that, for he had his back to Norman, and was staring out the window at the rain. On the other hand, Norman nearly always frowned, and Baxter almost always feared him and looked away.

A Bell Telephone Company instrument wagon creaked by, the horse's forehead down against the veils of rain. Wagon wheels spattered mud against the curb in front of McCauley's Tavern, but Baxter couldn't hear anything over the hiss of rain against the window. Not even the ghost echoes of long-dead swine grunting in pleasure as they devoured. The twins had been told little else of Baxter's life and had grown up thinking of Henry Rasmussen as their beloved Mamma, widowed by swine.

Finally Norman's twin meekly replied. "Nuttin," he said.

His brother's voice was silky behind him. "Nuttin?"

"That's what he said, Norm. Nuttin. He won't give nuttin. Ever since they found Willy's body stuffed up the chimney at the stables, he's got unreasonable. I tried, honest, but the whole council was there." Baxter was as big as his brother, and as powerfully built, but he was runner-up in life's race.

Behind him there was heard an elaborate sigh. "Must I do everything myself, Bax?"

"I wish Mamma was here," Baxter said. "She wunt let you be so mean."

"You do have a coozy brain, Bax. Mamma always let me do what I wanted to do. And now she's dead as Willy up the chimney. So you go back down there and tell His Honor that this is 1890, not 1790; it's no longer a lawless frontier here. There are rules. If he wants to stay in office, he's going to have to deliver. I have the votes, Baxter. You go back down there and tell him I have the votes."

"Okay, Norman." Baxter shoved a cap onto his thick head and went out into the rain.

Laughter filled the barroom behind him as he left, but the laughter was not for him. The Valhalla Berserkers baseball team liked to hang out at McCauley's Tavern, which Norman owned lock, stock, spittoons and barrels. So the fans liked to hang out there with them, too. The Berserkers were hard drinkers and very good for business, and good business was the one thing that could always make Norman smile. They were not a great team as teams went on those days, but they were excellent for business.

So Norman was smiling as he watched his twin brother trudge through the rain. When he smiled, he showed his teeth.

He grew thoughtful then, and when he grew thoughtful he tapped a front tooth with his fingernail. Then he shook his head, stood up, pulled on his own coat and went out through the back. Raucous Berserker laughter followed him.

As he walked up Midgard Avenue, he reflected with pleasure on the signs of prosperity around him. The avenue was paved despite the mud running in the gutters. At the corner, the old Museum of Western Oddities quietly decayed. He leaned against the façade of Aristera County granite while he waited for the trolley. At least it was relatively dry under the eaves of the western portico beside the Egyptian column under the rotunda. Impassively he watched the traffic clatter and splash before him. This building would have to be torn down soon. Not only was it an eyesore, it was losing money. The ballroom was the only section rented out — to the Sons of Western Temperance — and the temperance movement was drying up, as it were.

"Haha." Norman chuckled. "Drying up."

Torrents fell on the vast tracts of real estate he owned here on the slopes of Mount Worthy. Profit lurked in it somewhere. Perhaps he could sell it to the city, rid himself of this ailing monstrosity. Yet he should, in some way, be able to continue the fine traditions his grandmother Arlene had begun with her Museum. Traditions of public service, entertainment and delight.

Dimly outlined through the rain on the next rise was the spire of the Cathedral of St. Credula, the Ulcerated Martyr of Shköder. The whole goddam Mount Worthy was swarming with Albanians, a people with unpleasant habits of personal hygiene and no sense of humility. Unlike the cheerful Negro roustabouts by the river, the Albanians were sullen workers, superstitious, yet indifferent to religion, and possessed of a highly inflated self-pride. Norman wrinkled his nose as the trolley clattered toward him at last, the overhead wires ahum with power.

He owned a small piece of the inclined railway, and he thought bitterly as it clanked ponderously downhill that he could have owned more if he hadn't been so timid. So he began to scheme a way to acquire a larger share. If he

178

sold the Museum and the surrounding acres to the city, he could exchange the land for some more shares in the railway. The railway was profitable, no money would change hands, nothing illegal would happen, and cash would pour into his accounts.

His good humor returned as he contemplated this notion. He gazed fondly through the window at the sprawl of Niffelheim and the waterfront. Gusts of rain swept across the windows. Runnels of water ran down the brick buildings. Tatters of cloud drifted above the basin. Dark bituminous coal smoke poured into the air from the rows of tall stacks along the waterfront and on up Blood Gully and the Little Hawking Valley.

Breweries, Baxter thought. Booze. The mead of the gods in Valhalla. He owned considerable interest in breweries, and always laughed when he collected rent from the Sons of Western Temperance. Breweries, and sausage. Pork sausage.

The trolley continued from the bottom of the incline into the central downtown area and stopped before city hall. Baxter should be in there talking to the Mayor once again.

Norman turned up his coat collar and ran through the rain to his own building two blocks away. It was a new five-storey brick structure on prime downtown real estate: his own place, his base and his front. Inside three dozen workers ground and mixed and shaped and baked. Over the door was a wooden sign.

The Lord Who Made Thy Teeth Shall Give Thee Bread.

Norman rubbed his hands together and entered under that sign. All Valhalla was buying his teeth. Soon he would own all Valhalla.

The door to the Rasmussen Building closed behind him.

Chapter 2. In Which Norman Does Business

"I appreciate it. Really I do." Norman leaned on his ebony walking stick. Behind him huge wheels turned, broad belts rolled, machines whined. The air was filled with porcelain dust.

Norman was smiling. His teeth gleamed, and behind him ranks and rows, columns and stacks of teeth gleamed along with him.

"Thank you, sir." Alonzo Schmitzer rubbed his palms together with a dry, chalky sound. "I thought you would be interested, and I didn't want to talk about it over the telephone. Mr. Depew has friends at the Bell Company."

"Of course, Alonzo. You've done a fine job. The Mayor is a tiny reluctant, you see. This will be a great help. How was she, by the way?"

Alonzo was a large man, larger than Norman, larger than Baxter, larger perhaps than the two of them together. It was fat, however, which gave him his bulk, rings and rolls, layers and jiggling piles of fat depending from his large bones. His plump hands, rubbing briskly together, were soft and dry, powdered deeply with ceramic dusts. His leer emerged from the oily layers of his face like a weasel emerging from its lair, a small questing nose and bright malicious eyes.

"So-so," he replied. "She was just so-so. Too much hop, I spect — she's a sniffer. And a pig. No enthusiasm, if you understand me. No enthusiasm at all."

He winked. The wink was a reptile swallowing a beetle. Norman continued smiling with effort. "I understand you," he said. "Did you know," he added thoughtfully, looking around him, "that the word porcelain comes from the Italian porcella, meaning 'a little sow?'"

He walked then down the long rows between work tables, tapping his stick on the floor. He always left this

180

stick at the office, and when he made an inspection tour of the tooth factory, he carried the stick so he could tap the floor with it, and point delicately at objects and machines without getting porcelain dust on his gloves. The workers tipped their caps or saluted him as he strolled past them. He smiled and nodded.

The profit margin, though not broad, was fattened by other enterprises.

Alonzo shuffled along behind him, pointing out recent improvements, the latest additions in production machinery. Norman had little interest in teeth per se but they were necessary, so he nodded and smiled politely. There were the new electric lights, much needed on this dark gray day. "We fill orders faster than before," Alonzo assured him. "Production is up." He paused shyly, looked down at his high-topped shoes, and his eyes vanished for a moment. He cleared his throat. "I thought maybe we could come out with a line of off-the-shelf teeth. You know, standard sizes. Cheaper than the custom sets. We could produce them very cheap, hundreds of them. Put some salesmen out on the road. Some of those small towns have lots of people with no teeth. Hell, up in Slyville hardly anybody's got teeth."

"Not a bad idea, Alonzo. Not a bad idea at all. Go ahead. That reminds me of the other matter we have to discuss."

Alonzo nodded. It looked as if his chin were sinking in quicksand. "The Cave," he said. "I have a couple of people checking into it. Those are crafty people up there, though. All Albanians, originally. Very suspicious people. No morals, you know what I mean?"

"I do indeed, Alonzo. I do indeed. But those were orders from Grandfather Baxter. It is time we acquired the Cave. A needless drain on our profits, having them dig the stuff out and sell it to us. And I have other uses for it besides the feldspar."

"It shouldn't take long," Alonzo assured him.

They strolled back up the next row. Norman tapped

181

the table tops, greeted the workers.

"Baxter is down speaking with the His Honor," Norman told his supervisor when they were back in the office. "Most likely he'll get nowhere. The Depews do not seem to like the Rasmussens. But the Depews are Republicans. They live out toward Schachter's Landing, remote from the heartbeat of Valhalla, from the lives of the people. What you have discovered is most likely going to turn the tide, so to speak. We do have some other problems, however. Small things which require your organizational skills. I'm concerned about the rain, for one thing. The rain is going to be a problem. Tomorrow is election day. Rain is going to keep a number of people at home. We don't want that."

Alonzo shook his head. It was a porcupine trembling in a vat of yogurt. "We don't want that," he echoed.

"Rain is going to dampen things. We don't want that, either."

"We don't want that, either," Alonzo agreed. "But I don't know what to do about the rain. But we done a lot of preparation down to City Hall. It shouldn't be no problem."

"It had better be no problem." Norman showed his teeth. "This is the last election I am going to fool with. So I would like to run through it one last time."

"Sure, boss. One," Alonzo held up his forefinger, a bratwurst on a stick, "Schachter's Landing is resentful, most of it, because they dint want to be annexed, but they was annexed and that's too bad. All Republicans out there anyway, but they will vote. They can afford it. Now, Mount Worthy is ours, and Niffelheim, all of downtown, in fact. The Albanians up there're Tosks, they'll do anything for a couple of dollars. Not suspicious like them Ghegs up to Slyville."

Norman nodded. "Go on."

Alonzo raised a second wurst beside the first. "Your brother Baxter has access to the voting records, and the lists are there, in the safe." He pointed.

"I'd like to see them."

Alonzo squatted down; to Norman he looked like a wedding cake melting on the office floor. He opened the huge safe, and pulled from it a thick sheaf of papers with the official seal of the City of Valhalla on them. Voting rolls. The date at the top was 1864.

Norman looked them over, lips pursed. "How many died in the war?"

"Over half." Alonzo smiled.

"Good. Very good. They will all vote our way this time. Looks like Bax did a good job for a change."

"He did a swell job." Alonzo returned the lists to the safe, and spun the lock.

"What else?" Norman asked.

The third wurst joined the other two, a full meal of fingers. "City Hall's took care of. I got a man there already. Don't worry. He's from Slyville, fellow named Balshajt. Nobody knows him, and he's a little coozy in the head. He's gonna be fine. A real pyro."

"Fine, Alonzo, just fine. This is the year for reforms. The people want reforms, I want reforms. We all want reforms. The Depews are hoity-toity people, Alonzo, and they've lost touch. This past year there were 66,986 arrests for serious crimes in downtown Valhalla alone. Fifteen for malicious shooting, 64 for malicious cutting, 96 for cutting with intent to wound, 365 for shooting with intent to kill— that's one for very day of the year, as the Clarion so aptly pointed out. 1,146 arrests for carrying concealed weapons, 103 for murder and manslaughter. Public feeling is running high for reform."

"Very high," Alonzo agreed.

"Our party is the progressive party. Next spring we will point out that since we were in office, there were fifteen thousand, two hundred and six telephone poles installed in the city. We're going to string over seven thousand miles of wire. Sixteen miles of street will be lit by gas. Another five miles by electricity. We will own the Valhalla Gas and Electric Company by then. Dudley Depew is going to admit us as silent partners. After the election we may become vocal."

"It's all set."

"Fine, just fine. And now, where was that house you went to? I think perhaps I will pay the Mayor's pig wife a visit before going on to discuss the matter with his very temporary honor." Alonzo told him. 1001 Celestial Street.

Chapter 3. 1001 Celestial Street

"Evenin' sir. Nice to see you again." The policeman at the door tipped his cap politely. Norman had never been here before, but all the coppers in town knew the Boss's face. So this man tipped his cap, and Norman smiled and raised his ebony walking stick and brushed past him into the foyer.

The place was chosen for its address; it was indeed a celestial location, with a heavenly view, offering 1001 delights. Red brocade, horsehair plush, gas lamps and nudes in oils, a quiet piano in the corner, all promised a depth of sensuality, a breadth of diversity, an intimacy of delight unparalleled in Valhalla. Norman shuddered to think of Alonzo Schmitzer's enormous bulk squeezed into this close, hot place. Or worse, jiggling atop one of these close, hot women.

Madame was thin, and tough, and sharp, but she could be gracious, and Norman exuded power. "Good afternoon, sir. Welcome back to 1001 Celestial. We cater to all tastes. Take your time, have a drink on the house."

"Thanks. I've never been here before." Norman strolled over to the bar, shaking his head. Two or three men moved aside to make room for him, and he recognized by their clothing, their close-set eyes and furtive manner, that they were Albanians, refugees from both tomato blight and one of the most sullen cultures in the civilized world. Nor were they likely to have much in the way of money.

"Evnank," one of them said with a respectful but significant look.

"Alonzo sent you?" Norman guessed.

"Fa," the man said. He rolled his eyes toward the ceiling. "Dar she iss," he said. "Opstars."

Norman nodded. "Opstars," he repeated.

A barmaid in whalebones pressed a glass of

185

champagne into his hand. Norman took a sip, and set the glass down. "Hello, lover, back so soon?"

He turned. "What?" he asked the tall, long-faced woman standing behind him.

"Back so soon? You are a devil, aren't you? Or is it love?"

"I have no idea what you're talking about."

She laughed richly, a phlegmy catch trapped in her throat like a rodent snared in a Slyville basement. "Sure, lover. I understand. She's upstairs still; she's waiting for you, I expect. Why don't you go on up and get it up, eh?"

A dim light grew brighter in Norman's mind as he climbed the thickly carpeted stairs. It was a light from such an inconceivable source Norman had trouble crediting it: Baxter had preceded him here. This was the first time in his life Baxter had preceded him. It was a thorn stuck into the heel of his sense of well-being, and Norman began to worry at it.

But he forgot it all when he was ushered into the room where Francine Depew was waiting.

She may have been a sniffer; she might suck enormous mounds of powder in her nose, which was, on close inspection, rather pink; she may have no enthusiasm, no passion, no juice in her jelly-roll; she may have lean cheeks, sloe eyes, lips drenched vermilion and a haze of ill-health around her head; she may have been languorous by default, because otherwise Norman would have had to call her stumble-stupid; she may have been all that and more, but she was stunning beyond dream, beautiful past all believing, and Norman's little heart did beat like a bat in the soft spaces of its cage, crying little shrieks for freedom.

Downstairs the piano rippled and the professor wheedled, he did, as he diddled the black and whites, "I got a woman lives back of the jail," the professor sang, "She got a sign on her window — Pussy For Sale!"

"Hello," Norman said courteously, and she lifted her sloe eyes slow to his and smiled a long, wide, sad, unhappy smile at him from her little seat before her little table

186

covered with little bottles in front of a little mirror, where her naked back reflected and winky lights from cut glass glimmered. Did those deep hazel eyes leap with sudden recognition? Norman could not be sure. They were dense and dark and fathomless with snow, but they had smoky fires that caught him, and he burned.

"Hey, baby," she said, and her voice was deep in her throat, a little hoarse, frogged and warbled. "Welcome back."

Rage lolled its woofy head in Norman. Damn that Baxter, and double damn. Then rage fell back to drowsy sleep, for Francine lifted her long arms toward him, and her peignoir fell away, and her dense, contrite bosoms winked at him, and he fell upon them in a sudden access of desire with bristly lips, and her thighs sighed open, and Norman for once did not even consider that this was the mayor's wife he had fallen upon, nor what it was going to cost in the end.

In the beginning it was going to cost him fifty cents. Cast against her chest he murmured to her that this was double what it had cost a man thirty years ago to visit with his mother the Invisible Girl for prognostications and advice, to which Francine replied that these were inflationary times and the cost of love had risen.

So Norman asked what was her name, and she replied, "Lulu, of course, but you know that," and he only half wondered how.

She leaned up on one bare elbow to look at him, and her lovely bosoms leaned down to look at her sheets as though bashful before his brazen gaze; a puzzle twitched at the open space between her brows and she told him, "But you just were here, or was that a dream I had, I don't know any more. Maybe this is the dream," and she grew thoughtful and quiet. So did Norman Rasmussen, Boss of Valhalla.

"Maybe," he said at last. "Maybe this is a dream. Francine."

Her eyes widened then, he was sure of that. "How do

187

you know that name? That is not my name. How do you know it?"

Those wondrous breasts, their splendor dimmed by a subtle increase in distance, were looking at him now, but the look was snide and mean. Francine had pulled away. He tried to tear his own eyes away from the delicate nipple-whorls and could not; Dr. Mesmer went to work, and Norman lost track of time.

"How do I know it," he murmured. His risen lust pained him, and he scurried forward toward her. She reached out with a slim-fingered hand and seized him.

"Yes," she murmured back to him, squeezing. "How do you know it?"

Norman was palely loitering; sudden sweat had dewed his brow. Teeth clenched, he answered, "That hurts."

She smiled. "I know."

"You are Dudley Worthington Depew III's wife. He is the Mayor of Valhalla."

"Ah," she said, letting go. He fell back and throbbed with two kinds of pain, perhaps three. A catalog of agony unscrolled in his mind.

"Ah," he said.

She smiled at him. "Well, it can't be helped. Besides, I like you, so come on. Stick it in." There were dark smudges underneath her eyes, circles of fatigue or of despair. On her back now she let her thighs fall open, and Norman stared in fascination at what he had never really seen, not even from his furtive couplings with Mrs. Rasmussen, a colorless woman who even now was tending the brat Cornelius at home.

"Stick it in?" he said stupidly, staring.

Suddenly she yawned. Her mouth flew wide, her teeth glimmered in its depths, and Norman fell in love with her dentition. Raised as he had been with teeth, he knew a great deal more about their composition, structure, weaknesses and diseases than he ever would have cared to know, but never had he seen a set like Francine Depew's. They were pearled, clean, sharply delineated, and of absolute perfection. Her breath, despite the quantities of narcotic she inhaled or smoked, was fresh. Her pink, soft, tender and lubricious tongue curled in front of her incisors, twanging. He felt an uncontrollable impulse to suck it into his own mouth, but she was yawning so loudly, with such bone-cracking dimension, that he feared for her jaw.

Yet at the same moment she was reaching down, and once again with her delicate hand she seized and pulled him with an expert flick of her wrist into that fascinating dry jelly-roll, and he was the shortest hitter of the season but didn't care at all, love beached him dry and gasping on her long body, and he knew he had to have her for his very own. Wheels started to turn the ponderous machinery of his mind; he began to scheme.

Above the top of his head, Francine began to sniff, and as she did, her breasts bobbed beneath his ear. She was completely snowed in by the time he pulled himself from her bed to visit the Mayor of Valhalla, but his plans were laid, and all he had to do was follow through. Above Francine's head a small painting of a group of pale swine rooted in pre-Raphaelite woods, but Norman did not see, not then.

If he had noticed the painting, he probably would not have been smiling when he left, thin-lipped. The merest edges of his teeth showed in that smile. The professor waved at him as he left. Everyone thought he was a regular.

Chapter 4. In Which Norman Pays a Visit

Dudley Worthington Depew III knew the question he should ask, but a powerful constriction in his neck wattles prevented his asking it. Instead a large, knobbed vein pulsed vigorously in his temple.

Norman's walking stick was balanced carefully across his knees. A fresh rosebud graced his buttonhole. A fresh smile graced his lips, which somehow resembled the rose nestled amid his beardy briars. Fresh raindrops gleamed in his moustache, fresh mud graced his boots resting in small brown puddles on Dudley's carpet. None of this had escaped Dudley's notice, but he knew he could not call in his policeman to have this man removed.

"Look at it this way, Your Honor," Norman urged gently. "You want to stay in office, despite the fact that your only qualifications are family name and wealth. Now, I will support you in return for certain considerations."

The Mayor's eyes were swept under a wave of dismay: *certain considerations.*

A faint wheeze did escape him. Norman took it as a question, though it was not the question Dudley Worthington Depew III wanted so desperately to ask. The wheeze was a grating "What?" not unlike steam escaping from his radiator, and the rest of the question — "...the hell are you doing here in my offices?" — was lost, unasked, gone still-born and unbaptized to question heaven.

Norman gazed at his nails. He was not a malicious man. Not at all. He was a generous, warm-hearted, compassionate man who always held the best interests of others close to his heart. It happened that the best interests of others paralleled his own interests rather closely, certainly a pleasant but in no way remarkable coincidence.

"Baxter has spoken to you," he said softly. "Twice."

"Baxter?" The wheeze had gained no strength, though

the Mayor's confusion had.

"My brother."

"Brother?"

"My twin brother."

"Twin brother?"

"Twice."

"Twice?"

"Twice."

"Your brother?"

"Yes. Today. Baxter has been here twice. Today. He has spoken to you. You have remained unreasonable."

The Mayor, seated in a huge leather chair whose wings rose over his shoulders like the protective shadow of a black angel, managed to gasp out several words at once. "You have a twin brother? I thought." Breath failed him.

"Ah." Norman smiled, showing the lower edges of his teeth. "No, that was Baxter. You thought you had me cowed, didn't you? You thought you had won, because my brother Baxter left unsatisfied. But that was Baxter. Baxter is weak. Now you must deal with me, Norman Rasmussen. I have the central wards under control. I can deliver them to you, or I can deliver them...elsewhere. If I take my wards elsewhere, you too will be elsewhere."

"Get out," Dudley managed to say.

Norman held up his carefully manicured hand. He thought for a moment that Dudley might be able to catch the scent of his wife Francine Depew on it. "Hear me out, your honor." Norman grew increasingly polite. He could afford it, and besides, he was a gentleman, compassionate, benign, powerful. He had the election in his pocket. And he had something else. "There are one or two other things that Baxter may not have mentioned."

"Get...out."

"There is the matter, for example, of Mrs. Depew." The words floated across the Mayor's broad desk like dandelion fluff or fungus spores. They bobbed above the green, inviting blotter as above a meadow, floated downward, rose again, sought fertile ground in the Mayor's

191

ears, took root, grew with alarming rapidity into the poisonous puffs they were, flowered visibly in Dudley's face, bloomed crimson. "What about Mrs. Depew?" was the harvest reaped there.

But he knew what about Mrs. Depew.

Norman contemplated his nails again, his fine eyes hidden by modestly lowered lashes. "One thousand and one Celestial Street," he said softly, as if to himself.

Steam hissed from the radiator across the room. The potted palm on the round oak table there seemed to wilt in the heat. Rain sluiced down the Mayor's windows with a quiet hiss. Darkness was gathering outside. Tomorrow was election day.

"It is close in here, isn't it?" Norman said in response to the sounds coming from the Mayor of Valhalla, afflicted just then with shortness of breath. A consequence, possibly, of too rich a life.

Finally he whispered, "How do you know?"

Norman brushed the question aside. "Oh, well. Now, about tomorrow. I can deliver Mount Worthy, six Niffelheim wards, Pecan Heights and the east side. Sixty-seven percent of the vote, for certain. If you want to remain in office."

"What considerations?" The protecting angel hovering over the Mayor's shoulders had failed to act, and now it was too late. Far too late.

"I've been thinking about an appointment."

"Appointment?"

"Commissioner of Public Works. I've given it a great deal of thought."

"I couldn't do that! You're a *Democrat*!"

Norman smiled thinly, but said nothing.

"All right," Dudley sagged in his angel's arms.

"There are one or two other matters, although I suppose they could wait until day after tomorrow."

"You may as well tell me." The Mayor dipped snuff from a gold box, the only adornment on his vast desk aside from the blotter. It did not improve the sound of his

192

breathing. He then rose and went to a well-equipped bar, where he poured himself a large glass.

"I have considerable property up on Mount Worthy," Norman continued. "I would like to dispose of it. You, on the other hand, have a controlling interest in the Mount Worthy inclined railroad."

Norman left it at that. Dudley considered. They discussed the project. Norman wanted seventy percent, Dudley protested that would be a controlling interest. Norman agreed that indeed it would be. He mentioned the Mayor's wife, whose cocaine habit had driven her into such an unsavory profession, a profession of which Queen Victoria, for one, sharply disapproved. Dudley pointed out, irrelevantly of course, that Queen Victoria was not going to be around much longer. Norman replied that she might be around longer than anyone thought. She had survived quite a while. She might last, oh, another ten years. He suggested there were people who would like to see her gone. Dudley suggested that there were people who would like to see Norman gone. Norman pointed out that the Democrats would like to see Dudley gone. Dudley said he had the city council on his side, all of it. Norman pointed out that that made no particular difference, unless the Mayor wanted the city council to know about Francine. Dudley agreed that the city council made no particular difference.

Norman stood up to go. Dudley Worthington Depew stood up to say goodbye. Norman had been considering some resemblances between the Mayor and Alonzo Schmitzer, resemblances of bulk and girth, of a common porcine nature. But when the Mayor stood up, the resemblance ended, for the Mayor was not so tall. Certainly not tall enough for Francine.

Dudley waddled around his desk. Norman thought he was not going to last as long as Queen Victoria, not by a long shot. The knotted vein in his temple pounded relentlessly. "Goodbye," Dudley said. "I don't know how you have gotten all these votes, but for Francine's sake I have to do what you ask."

"Oh, not for Francine's sake, surely, your honor. For your sake. Surely just for your sake."

The beat in the Mayor's temple skipped, rippled, paradiddled, syncopated. It could have been a drumroll for an execution.

Chapter 5. In Which Baxter Doesn't Know

Baxter Rasmussen, dandling his little nephew Cornelius on his knee, was trying to find a way out of his difficulties. Cornelius gurgled like an infant, though he was five years old. He had not really conquered the art of human speech as yet; this suited Baxter just fine.

"Gneah," Cornelius said. Baxter smiled and repeated the noise. This sent Cornelius into gusts and hoots of a joy great enough to deposit a long silvery line of drool onto Baxter's trousers.

A number of problems thronged his mind, and he didn't notice the drool. There was Francine, for instance. He was powerfully attracted to Francine, but she thought he was Norman. Baxter had often posed as Norman; he was quite good at it. It wasn't difficult since they were identical. The problem was preventing Norman from finding out. And now it appeared that Norman had visited the Mayor's wife already, and was even now talking with Mayor Depew himself.

The situation could grow unpleasant.

Then there was the problem of his own failure with the Mayor. Norman was not going to be pleased about that. It was an instance where he had not convincingly posed as his brother. Everyone who knew he was Norman Rasmussen's twin laughed at Baxter. Norman was the strong one. Baxter was the weak one. Everyone laughed.

Cornelius laughed, showing snarled teeth. Spray shot from his mouth, falling lightly on his uncle's shirt front.

Somewhere in the house, colorless Mrs. Rasmussen was doing something colorless. Cleaning, perhaps, or cooking, though no odors came from the kitchen. But they never did. Her meals had no aroma.

Rainwater flowed down the windows. It roared in the gutters. It sluiced through the streets, it rolled and rumbled.

Baxter loved it. Even little Cornelius loved it. Norman always said he didn't have sense enough to come in out of it.

Norman would be back soon, and Baxter better have something ready. A distraction.

The front door banged open. Norman was whistling. That was a bad sign. It meant he had had a good day. Baxter thought of Francine. How had Norman found out about her?

"Jesus and Jehovah," Norman said, shaking water from his hat. It was a wet day for Baxter. "What the hell are you doing here?"

"Well, Norman, I thought you might like to hear about what I done. See, the Dead Men are all ready to go. You just say the word, Norm. Just say the word."

Norman cocked his head. "What word?"

Baxter swallowed. For some reason, Cornelius found this gesture utterly hilarious and fell down laughing.

"Hello, dear," Norman said to Mrs. Rasmussen. She was in the other room and Baxter couldn't see her.

"Did you have a nice day, honey?" she asked. Her voice was a ghost in the kitchen, a pale, indefinite kind of voice.

"What difference does it make?" Norman asked cheerfully.

Mrs. Rasmussen's voice vanished as well.

"So, Bax, I did want to speak with you." There was no diminishing Norman's good cheer, his irrepressible high spirits. Clearly his own interview with Mayor Depew had gone better than Baxter's had. "We have a few plans to polish up before tomorrow. You say the Dead Men are in place?"

"Right. I found some more files, too many to move. Way too many, even with help."

"Don't worry, Bax. Don't worry. It's all been arranged. It's time Valhalla had a new City Hall, anyway. But there are some other items on our list. The Cave, for one thing. The Cave must be handled carefully. That of

196

course is another matter, in another department. The Surveyor's office, the title department. It was in Grandfather's will that we get the Cave, and the time is now, while everything is in place for the election. After tomorrow.... Well, we need the proper documents tonight. You will see to it."

"Yes, Norman." Baxter's relief was tangible. Perhaps Norman had not discovered he had been to 1001 Celestial before him.

"Now, Bax," Norman said with a wide and wolfish grin so similar to the stuffed beasts in the back room of the Museum of Western Oddities. "You are a devil, aren't you? Sneaking off to Celestial Street. I had no idea you were interested in such things."

Was Norman giving him a special look to go with his special hand gestures, his special grin? Baxter grinned foolishly in return. It was always his last defense, that foolish grin. Baxter played the fool.

But Norman was on to other things. "What do you know about zoos, Baxter?" he asked.

"Zoose? I don't know nuttin about zoose. Is it a kind of chewing tobacco?"

"No, it is not a kind of chewing tobacco. That is snoose. I am talking about zoological gardens. A large park containing different kinds of animals from all over the world. A menagerie. Mostly they have been private, but there are a few public ones. In London, England, for instance. Valhalla is going to get a zoo of its own. There will be enormous profit in it. I own the land."

"I don't get it, Norm. What land?"

Norman sighed. Baxter the Weak, Baxter the Fool. It was silly ever to have thought that Baxter could have preceded him anywhere. He may have lain on top of Francine Depew, but he could not possibly have known the gold mine he was tunneling at the time. "The Museum of Western Oddities, Bax. And the surrounding 127 acres. I own them."

"You do, Norm?"

197

"Well, we own them. Same thing."

"Oh. I dint know that."

Again Norman gave his sharp and special look, but Baxter was grinning again, his open honest teeth showing through his beard. Norman smiled back, and they were a pair or mirror images, smiling at one another.

"How would you like to be married to Mrs. Rasmussen for a while, Bax?" Norman asked suddenly. It had never occurred to him before to use his twin in this particular way, but he, Norman Rasmussen, was going to have a new wife, and this seemed like one way to get rid of the old one. Of course, they would have to exchange names.

"Gee, I don't know, Norm. I mean, she's your wife."

So Baxter was going to require some convincing. Norman began to whistle as he removed his wet overcoat.

"Will you want dinner now, honey?" Mrs. Rasmussen asked, still in the kitchen, still invisible.

"No. I have to go back out again soon. You could go ahead and feed the brat, though."

"Yes, honey."

"Now," Norman briskly rubbed his hands together. "We have a lot to do, but day after tomorrow will be a new day in Valhalla, won't it?"

"If you say so, Norm."

"I say so. The Mayor will be re-elected by a wide margin. However, he will have formed some new alliances for better government. I am going to be Commissioner of Public Works, for instance. There are a considerable number of patronage jobs associated with that office. A very considerable number. We are going to have our own people installed in important positions. These are not mere sinecures, though, Bax."

"Huh?"

"These are working jobs. You are going to have one of them. How would you like that? I know you failed to convince the Mayor, but it doesn't matter. He's convinced now. So for you there will be a small job in city government, but perhaps if you take my name, Norman, that would look pretty good, eh? My name, my job, my wife."

"Cornelius," Mrs. Rasmussen called from the kitchen. "Supper's ready." Cornelius blasted his uncle Baxter with a soggy raspberry and trotted off to the kitchen.

"Gee," Baxter said. "I don't know, Norm. I don't know."

But perhaps he did know. Perhaps this would be his way out.

Chapter 6. In Which a Pulse is Observed to be Beating

"They are, on the whole, a bunch of illiterate semi-barbarians, foul with superstition, who regard the inculcation of progressive civilization into their education (with commensurate elevation in their humanity) — not to mention the introduction of good Christian morality — as an encroachment on their superior rights, independence and personal liberties."

Dudley was speaking to the policeman beside him; the subject was the voters. That is, people of the policeman's social, economic and ethnic class.

The policeman, an Albanian Tosk, swarthy, short and sturdy, with a broad, cheerful, uncomprehending face, held a shotgun at the ready in his capacity as the Mayor's bodyguard, but it was the other man in the room who chuckled richly at the Mayor's words. The other man was Arthur Lucklaster, a Civic Leader. As such, he knew the importance of appreciating Dudley's orotund wit.

Dudley Worthington Depew III was known in the inner circles as "The Life of the Party," a phrase of some ambiguity. He resembled a congested knot of cardiac muscle, and provided a steady, life-giving beat to the body politic. He also provided the party with its most colorful epithets for those citizens of Valhalla not of the inner circle: the Catholics, particularly the Irish, or the Albanians and other even more recent immigrants, or, lastly, the dark people who lived under the Cliffside bluffs near the waterfront and worked on the riverboats which still plied the Ohio's sluggish currents.

Thus it was the Life of the Party fermented in the congested tissues of his mind various terms of approbation which quickly gained currency among the better classes, not so much because they were witty and intelligent as because he was the Leading Citizen, the Mayor of Valhalla, related to people in High Places — Washington, D. C. for example: senators, cabinet members and such. It was a good idea to laugh audibly at Dudley's jokes, especially when within his earshot.

So on this election day in 1890 Dudley smiled a late autumn smile, and spoke his election day thoughts, and the Civic Leader beside him, giving a hand, as it were, to the round representative of his party's platform, laughed appreciatively, and this, in turn, caused Dudley to smile despite his secret sorrows.

The most desperate of his secret sorrows swept in to the Mayoral offices just then.

"Good morning, Your Honor," Norman said. "A fine, fine morning it is, too." He took off his hat and smacked it against his leg with a sharp sound. A blustery wind was blowing off the river through chill rainless clouds that moved like globs of cholesterol through vast arteries of sky. It was, Norman considered, a perfect day for an election of this importance.

Art Lucklaster was surprised to see a person of such unsavory notoriety as Norman Rasmussen on familiar terms with the Mayor, but he quickly reflected that politics, as they so often said, made strange bedfellows, and besides, Norman really was a Civic Leader too, although of a different persuasion. So although there clung about Norman Rasmussen a somewhat unpleasant reputation, really, when one considered it carefully, it consisted mainly of rumors. So Art kept his own council.

Dudley managed to conceal his distress. "Hullo," he said with a sour grin. All his steamy rhetoric had whistled away. But his own bad mood could not dampen Norman's enthusiasm. Norman rubbed gloved palms together vigorously, and the sound they made was the sound of large denomination paper money being counted. Even the Civic Leader recognized that sound, and was reassured by it.

"It's going well, very well," Norman assured him.

"The wards are coming in on schedule. We are going to have a bit of trouble with the Salvation Army, but that too is under control."

"The Salvation Army!" Art exclaimed. It was involuntary; he hadn't intended to speak.

Norman nodded without looking at him. "They seem to think they are on the side of Reform. But it is we who are on the side of reform. Don't worry about it."

"I'm not worried," Dudley lied.

The Mayor's office was close and very hot. The potted palm on the large round table seemed to flourish in such a tropical atmosphere and today glistened with robust good health, as wind whistled around the cornices and balustrades of the City Hall. Norman was very pleased about this wind, and hoped it would keep up through the evening hours. "Of course you're not," he said. "I did want to make sure that you were going to be at the victory banquet this afternoon. At five sharp, at the Valhalla Club up on Midgard Avenue."

"I know where it is," Dudley said peevishly. "My grandfather founded the Valhalla Club."

"Of course," Norman soothed. "Of course he did. But it happens to be on that piece of property we discussed yesterday. Where the zoological gardens are going to go."

"Zoological gardens?" Art Lucklaster exclaimed, but no one answered him.

Dudley reddened; perhaps he was embarrassed to have business discussed in front of a Civic Leader, or a policeman. But he said nothing. Instead he rested his plump hand on top of a bronze horse and sulky which trotted forever briskly across the table beneath the potted palm.

"What are zoological gardens?" Art asked, somewhat querulously.

"I have a bit of business to attend," Norman turned to go, leaving his overcoat and hat hanging on the Mayor's coat rack. His business was in this building. Dudley frowned at the overcoat, but thoughts of Mrs. Depew drifted through the fatty deposits in his brain. Last night she had snored louder than usual, her nose had grown more red, her manner more offhand and distant. But she had called out the name "Norman" in her sleep, and dark suspicions had gathered like the increasingly bilious clouds blown before cold winds outside.

Norman whistled as he strolled down the stairs. He went to the Election Records division where Baxter sat on an empty crate with an empty smile on his face. "Hi, Norman," Baxter greeted him.

"Jesus and Jehovah," Norman said. "Have you been here all night?"

Baxter nodded. "Sure, Norman. After I left your house I came right here. I found it all."

Norman nodded. "There's no one here besides you?"

"No, Norm. We dint need anyone, and the people who work here are all Depew's, so I sent them home. All the papers are ready."

"Good." Norman went back upstairs.

The Mayor was talking horses, hand still on his sculpture, when Norman got back. "She's the finest mare I ever saw," Dudley was telling the Civic Leader. "She'll win for sure, with the new sulky I've developed."

"Well," Art agreed, "she'll certainly know the track." He said it without irony. Valhalla Downs was sometimes called "Dudley Downs" because Dudley owned the track, and won so often there.

"Let me tell you," Dudley warmed to his topic; while he had little understanding of government, he was thoroughly grounded in matters of sulky racing. "My new sulky is narrower, with a slightly shorter wheelbase. Consequently it has advantages: it is rigged lighter and is considerably faster, especially on a slow track."

"Ah." The Civic Leader nodded. "Is it consistent with the rules? After all, there are standards — size and so on."

"I'm on the Rules Committee," Dudley assured him. "If you want my advice, a little money on my new mare would not go astray."

"What's she called?" Norman asked from the door.

He was shrugging into his coat.

"Sleipnir. After the eight-legged horse of Odin." Dudley apparently had forgotten his woes.

But they would return, those woes. They would certainly return.

Norman called him from the doorway. "By the way, Dudley. There is another small matter I would like to discuss with you." He gestured Dudley into the anteroom, and there informed him of his plan.

Dudley hadn't expected his woes to return quite so rapidly, but really, he had no choice.

"Adopt?" he squeaked. "Adopt? What do you mean, adopt?"

Norman explained it all patiently, to the beat of that knotted vein in Dudley's temple.

Chapter 7. In Which Events Get Out of Hand

Blustery wind and election fever loosed a madness in the city. Everyone said so, the cop walking his beat up Blood Gully, the butcher in Rat Row near the river, the saloonkeeper at McCauley's Tavern, unofficial headquarters for the party of reform. Especially they said it at Salvation Army headquarters, where the troops were assembled in ranks and rows, tambourines at the ready.

They — the makers of teeth, the cutters of beef, the busy morticians, the mad musicians who strolled the thronging streets in search of lost chords and found notes amid the clatter of laundry swashing on the lines or the clank and rollick of trolleys trudging up hill and down — they said that it all began with a small eddy of adverse votes from the outlying precincts, a ripple of democracy that brought out the rage. The outrage gathered momentum in Depew Concert Hall, where the symphony orchestra was scheduled to "do a little Mozart," and where, instead, substantial numbers of angry people from Schachter's Landing, and the outer fringes of Mount Worthy, had gathered to discuss matters this windy election day.

No clear idea had emerged concerning the agenda of this meeting, but everyone had already voted, and it seemed a good idea to protest the wave of crime and violence which had swept the city of Valhalla since sometime during the summer of '84, six years ago. Alonzo Schmitzer, neck bulging above wing collars, waved over his head a copy of today's Commercial Gazette, newspaper of the better classes, and recited for the benefit of approximately 10,000 well-to-do citizens a litany of social disorganization. The incumbent party, even though it was their party, the party of Dudley Depew, had failed to meet these problems head on. Why did even now forty-seven murderers languish in jail? Why were the courts clogged, and why, as recently as yesterday, were a pair convicted of brutality, robbery, mayhem, sodomy and murder given suspiciously light sentences?

It was noted later that many citizens had brought ropes, hammers, axes and other tools of the building trades to the meeting at Concert Hall. These items were later employed during the riots. It was also noted that the symphony orchestra had been tuning up in the basement in preparation for having a go at the fugue which ends the Mozart Symphony Number 41 (the *Jupiter*, K. 551) when the shouting upstairs became too loud and disorderly to continue. Many of the musicians, particularly the woodwinds and most of the horns, abandoned Mozart to participate in the discussions upstairs and the ensuing violence.

Alonzo announced that the incumbent party was the party of those present here tonight, and really all it needed was a renewed franchise to combat this social decay. More police were needed. A number of second generation Albanians in the crowd, who had moved relatively recently to Mount Worthy's better neighborhoods, nodded and murmured assent. A few cries of "Hear, hear" were heard.

There were more speeches from those representing various citizens' groups, speeches which praised, speeches which assaulted, and speeches which cajoled. Most were extraordinarily tedious, even soporific; a certain restlessness began to grow in the rear of the balcony where the acoustics were particularly bad, and the logic of the speaker's arguments, never very firm, grew increasingly unclear. Yet in the aftermath, even Alonzo Schmitzer was not sure what had actually happened. Whatever it was, it far surpassed his wildest expectations.

It was an unnaturally dark night outside, with a wind more bitter than anyone remembered. Alonzo told Norman later it was as if the cholera plague were sweeping the city again, as it had back in '79, when it took Norman's mother Henry among the 12,385 who perished. It was, in other words, perfect riot weather. The effects of the wind, the strange darkness, the close heat of Depew Hall, the crowding and the endless incoherent speeches, the small swirls of rage and confusion which moved around the vast space at random, seizing one group here, another group there, all were similar to the effects of that cholera epidemic, still vivid in most memories.

"You could feel it, Norm," Alonzo said the following day, when the excitement was cooling along with City Hall. "You weren't there, so you can't know, but it was a living thing, quite wonderful, really. We never could have planned it."

"You were lucky, Alonzo. The victory banquet with Dudley Depew was some chore, I'll tell you. You were very lucky to be in on it — what they call history in the making."

Alonzo nodded, and his chin was drowned in his neck; when it came up for air again, it slathered peculiar sweats.

It began in earnest when someone shouted, "Hang 'em! Hang the little bastards!" That was the official explanation, but no one could pin down either the source of those words or who in fact the "Little bastards" might be. Whoever it was should have been brought to trial for inciting to riot, but of course he never was. Substantial citizens do not do such things, so it most likely was a lowlife snuck into the meeting.

When the crowd spilled out into Central Avenue, small groups had already formed. At the center of one of those groups were three or four off-duty coppers, Albanian immigrants whose command of English was not sufficient for a satisfactory understanding of the issues, but whose talent for violence was undeniable, St. Credula notwithstanding.

By the time the crowd arrived at the courthouse, it had, according to the official militia report, grown to over two thousand. A few rocks were thrown, and from Salvation Army headquarters in Blood Gully a battalion of troops marched forth, banging tambourines and singing a spirited rendition of "Faint Not Nor Fear (for He is Near)." The crowd rushed first toward the police headquarters doors, and when repulsed there by a small contingent of armed officers, turned on the soldiers of the Salvation Army.

The results were, from that moment on, predictable. The crowd was apparently maddened by the sight of uniforms. There could not have been any substantial citizens present; it was presumed the crowd was made up mostly of rowdies from various street gangs, the Blood Gully Hog Cutters, the Feathered Serpents, and others.

When the Salvation Army troops met the vigilantes and street gangs, the carnage was, in the description of one witness, an employee of the Rasmussen Dental Fabrication Works, "like the inmates of the Valhalla Asylum for the Criminally Insane doing the last act of *The Pirates of Penzance*." It was worse. In the first hour alone, twelve people were killed in ways described variously as "gruesome" (the *Commercial Gazette*), "butchery" (*The Post-Dispatch Ledger*), and "on a scale which surpasses even the late Civil War which so tore our Great Nation" (the *Valhalla Clarion*).

That was just the first hour, though. Later Norman would have even more reason to be pleased with the night's events.

Chapter 8. Some Election Night Events

At first the flames along the waterfront were small, fitful and uncertain. This was not because the men in charge did not know what they were doing; it was because they did.

Baxter lounged at the side entrance to City Hall. While he waited, he thought hard about his immediate future, as uncertain as those tiny flames even now sprouting deep inside the Court Records carefully stacked in open rows down in the basement.

Norman was the strong one. Norman was the fast one. Norman was first: first off the starting line, first around the far bend, first into home stretch. Norman was the winner in life's big race.

Norman, Baxter thought, was the hare. He, Baxter, was therefore the tortoise. He plodded along behind, he plodded atop Francine Depew, for after all, he, Baxter Rasmussen, had his needs, too, and later he had developed a more serious interest in Francine who, despite her appetite for white powder, gave him the closest thing to love he had had since Mother Henry died, leaving them both baffled about their mother's precise sexual definition. The mortician had been more than a little startled to discover the Rasmussen twins' mother was decidedly male. But Norman and Baxter had been confused as well as surprised, and had made a tacit decision to bury that knowledge with Henry.

Now Norman had discovered his tortoise twin on his tail, and suggested the switch. Baxter was not entirely certain he liked the switch: it meant giving up Francine for Mrs. Rasmussen, whose image wavered and vanished in his memory even as he thought about it.

The tumult in Heimdall Square grew louder, and Baxter strolled to the end of the alley to watch a gang of

Albanians armed with clubs burst from Central Avenue into the square to clash with the street gangs, already swinging at the Salvation Army. The sound of tambourines collapsing underfoot could be picked out from the din.

"The poor people have been organized," Norman had told him. "Particularly the Albanians. The Albanians don't like anyone, which is fine. If only there weren't so many of them, some might say. But what will be will be."

Norman was right. The Albanians didn't like anyone. Baxter had to look away. He moved down the alley. Wind blew election day newspapers around his feet. BIG REPUBLICAN VICTORY, one of them screamed at him. DEMOS SWEEP CITY, another assured him. REFORM PARTY ON RUN, a third insisted. VOTER APATHY; DEPEW RE-ELECTED; DEPEW DEFEAT PREDICTED. The news tumbled down the narrow street before a blustery wind. It was a madness that swept the city, right on schedule.

Thick Albanian curses came to him on that wind. Tatters and fragments of "Onward Christian Soldiers" flew against guttural expletives. The sounds of gunfire erupted as Republicans, now armed to the teeth, joined the fray. The crowd from Depew Hall had long since scattered. The fire crackling down on the waterfront began to light up the ornate facade of City Hall. Even Baxter, from this side alley, could see the red glow. It was almost time.

The weather was cooperating perfectly. A chill wind blew off the river, though not so chill that large crowds were kept indoors. Yesterday's rain had ceased during the previous night, and the wind had dried all the wooden buildings in town. There were even reports from some senior members of the Fire Brigade that the straw filler in the soft, porous Valhalla brick would burn if the fire was hot enough. Gazing on the reddish glow from the river, Baxter had to acknowledge that those reports must have been correct.

The Republicans with guns were out looking for poor people, particularly the Irish and the Negroes. The

210

Salvation army was on the lookout for sinners, the Albanians were searching for anyone not Albanian, the Negroes were looking for a good time. The gods would punish everyone by giving them what they wanted.

The bell in the steeple of the Church of St. Brigit of the Bloody Sorrows across Heimdall Square struck ten. That was Baxter's signal. He opened the door and stepped inside City Hall.

The building had that peculiar empty sound of public buildings on holiday, the echoing marble, the lost dark vistas, despite the Slyville pyromaniacs concealed in that muffled dark. Baxter walked slowly to the stairwell and looked down into the ebony night.

Could he see the glows of watchfires in those dim recesses, or was it reflected glow from the waterfront blazes which had already claimed three lives? He could not say. He paused a moment to listen, but from the basement there came only silence. Abruptly he decided to check the preparations once more, so he descended the stairs, boots echoing on the metal treads. From far away the sounds of battle came, adrift inside this vast and empty building. He smiled.

It wasn't until he had gone some distance down the corridor toward the Records Department that he saw the first man. He nodded, and the man nodded back.

"Everything ready?" Baxter asked him.

"Yop," he said. He was tall and thin and pale. In this peculiar light it appeared he had no eyebrows and no hair on his head. Baxter looked closer and saw that his hair was as pale as his skin, and that his eyes appeared pink in the dimness. Behind him Baxter could see the dark flames contained in metal drums, ready for release.

"The other's in place?" he asked.

"Yop," the man said again.

"I'm going to check the papers. Wait here for the signal."

"Yop."

Baxter went into he huge room where row upon row

211

of shelving held voting records, birth records, marriage and adoption records, arrest and conviction records, employment and law suit records. He gazed down the rows at the piles of loose papers. He went to the aisle devoted to adoptions and ran his hand along the shelves, looking for the proper section. He riffled through the files in search of the right ones.

"Wot chew doing?" Baxter turned, and saw what must be a brother to the man in the corridor — white fishbelly skin, pink glowing eyes.

"Just checking," Baxter said.

"Oh. Moch longah?"

"No. Just a few minutes. Go back to your post. We wouldn't want any unauthorized persons appearing here."

"Wot?"

"Never mind. Just keep an eye out for strangers."

"Shewah." The pale man melted into the shadows. Baxter returned to work.

The sound of glass shattering flew down the stairwell and lit on Baxter's shoulder like a fat arthritic crow. It lent certain urgency to his motions as he worked his way through the files. A dull explosion was followed by shouting at the front doors. On the other side of the central courtyard a mob appeared to be gathering outside the jail. Shouts of "Lynch 'em" and "Hang de bastids" rose above the background din of the rioting.

His hands were shaking when he found the files, but he tucked them under his arm without reading them. Then he nodded to the shadowy figure in the aisles. As he jogged up the stairs he heard the soft whoosh of paper igniting.

The courthouse fire was one of the most exciting events in that exciting autumn of 1890. Not only did 56 people die in fires, riots and lynchings, but City Hall itself burned to the ground. The militia came in, and the prisoners were moved in time, but Baxter's work with what was called the Dead Vote brought a resounding election day victory to Mayor Depew, and with it the curious alliance called the Reform Movement which put Norman

Rasmussen, history has said, firmly in control of the city and county of Valhalla.

Of the records Baxter had salvaged from the basement, however, no trace was ever found.

Chapter 9. In Which There is a Spontaneous Occurrence

Dudley Worthington Depew III sat alone at his enormous desk in his Mount Worthy home. On the gleaming surface before him were a decanter of smoky and particularly virulent liquor, and two sheets of legal paper. One paper was the official appointment of Norman Rasmussen to the position of Commissioner of Public Works, a position which commanded 1,485 patronage jobs.

The other paper was more private in nature, but equally abhorrent.

In his hand was a large crystal glass one-third full of the liquor. The rest, and three or four prior glasses, had vanished into his capacious bowel. With the breakdown of the alcohol into sugars, other byproducts and energy, the vein which beat in his temple increased its tempo and dynamic, from piano andante to scherzo forte. Such a range could only result from the effects of the Romantic nineteenth century on music.

That rapid, alarming beat was the result of a concern more immediate than the history of music, however. Dudley was waiting for the subject of these documents before him, and his reluctance to sign was at war with the pressures to do so immediately. For example — and the very thought caused him to gulp the remainder of his glass and reach stiffly for a refill — there was his uncle, Senator Frederick Depew, whose telegram had arrived last night urging no more delays.

And then, gulping once more, there was grand-uncle Roger, who lived in bitter semi-retirement at his hog and horse farm across the Little Hawking River beyond Schachter's Landing; his brief note on the subject brooked no argument whatsoever.

Dudley's eyes sank in fatty deposits; only a small red gleam would greet his visitor when he arrived. The thought of the visitor caused a quantum jump in his arterial tempo. Layers of fat around his heart, drenched in the esters of alcohol, echoed with the labor of that organ's pounding. Dudley drank again.

He thought of Francine, previously a secret embarrassment, now gone over to his nemesis, lost without farewell in such a way that he, Dudley Depew, had been forced to co-conspire in her defection. This was the second document on his desk.

A large tear, iridescent in the gaslight, squeezed from between his lids to roll down the terraced terrain of his face. It hit the corner of his mouth, and his tongue delicately probed out to taste it, redolent with the flavor of alcohol esters. For some reason the thought that even his tears tasted of alcohol amused Dudley and he emitted a snorty whimper.

He didn't know whether the man coming to see him was going to be Norman Rasmussen, the Norman Rasmussen with whom he had presumably dined only two, or was it three? nights ago at the celebration banquet while the lovely old baroque City Hall was burning to the ground during the riots, or whether it was going to be the other one, the twin. Dudley would never know Baxter had taken over Norman's identity and wife and position as Commissioner of Public Works so that Norman could retire to a comfortable job as Boss of Valhalla behind his twin, and that with it he was going to get Dudley's name and Dudley's wife Francine. He would know, however, that she was going to be comforted by a lifetime supply of the opiates so necessary to her continued happiness, guaranteed by Senator Frederick Depew through certain connections he maintained with elements which must be kept secret though they were an indispensable part of the economic fabric of American Society. Senator Depew was a conservative, and so had immediate and useful access to the criminal classes. He knew certain tasks could not be left to

215

official government agencies.

Another tear trickled from Dudley's other eye. It bobbled to the rhythm of that pulsing vein just above. He looked sideways at the gas flame of his lamp, and through the iridescence of the tear it was strangely beautiful, as though its loveliness were heightened by his misery.

A quiet knock on the door interrupted his meditations. "Yarf," he barked, his articulation slurred. A butler on silent feet announced Mr. Norman Rasmussen, who followed close on his heels.

"Good day, Your Honor," Norman said cheerily, shaking rainwater from his cloak.

"Are you him or the other one?"

"Oh? Ah, yes. I'm him. I couldn't really trust Baxter with this particular chore. He seems to resent me, although I can't imagine why." Norman shook his head in mock bewilderment. The thought of Francine's languorous body, his as long as he fancied it, was too delicious to conceal.

Dudley, however, chose not to notice. "Is it raining out?" he asked instead, although the evidence was pooling at his visitor's feet as he sat with a sigh in the Morris chair opposite the desk.

Norman didn't answer. Instead he clasped his hands before his stomach and smiled. Dudley shifted uncomfortably. He started to speak, thought better of it, began again. "I suppose...."

Norman nodded, smiling. "I suppose," he said.

"Would you like a drink?" Dudley muttered with evident lack of sincerity.

To his relief Norman shook his head. "I won't be staying long, Your Honor. Not long at all." He continued to stare at the fat Mayor. Francine's husband. A twitch of disgust traveled across his upper lip, vanished into his beard.

Dudley sighed. He reached for the papers on his desk, dropped his hand, lifted it and grasped the decanter instead. He poured himself yet another glass. The vein in his temple was pulsing so rapidly and strongly that one beat seemed to

216

follow another on its heels, giving the impression of small rodents running one after another through an even-smaller flexible tunnel. A tiny alarm sighed through Norman when he noticed that vein, for he could see that there was, as yet, no signature on the documents on the desk. It would complicate things greatly if Dudley failed to sign.

Norman forced himself to relax. Dudley would sign. Norman had exchanged telegrams with the Senator. He had taken the train to Schachter's Landing, and a coach from there to old man Depew's hog and horse farm, and spoken with him face to face. Dudley would sign.

"Valhalla needs a new City Hall," Norman said casually. "It's a big contract. Lucrative. Us Depews would want a hand in it."

A strange sputtering snort came from Dudley. Norman was going too far.

"Perhaps if you just sign those papers," Norman suggested. "I could be getting along and not trouble you further."

With an ominous glare, darkened by a flush of blood in his oily face, Dudley Worthington Depew III reached for the papers. He moved his pen above the paper. He sputtered. Dudley was good at sputtering. He had, as members of his immediate family would testify, sputtered his way through childhood, a series of Eastern preparatory schools, Yale '56, Valhalla University Law School (founded by his father Dudley Worthington Depew II), and finally he had sputtered his way into public office. Only last summer he had sputtered his way through the opening ceremonies of the Bifrost Bridge which spanned the River and connected Valhalla with the town of Roseville, in Ohio.

"Go away," he sputtered.

Norman nodded. "Certainly," he said, pointing at the pages. "As soon as you sign."

The vein pulsed. Dudley bent to his task. His pen point trembled above the page. Some kind of fit was upon him. Norman reached out and helped. The pen scratched

217

over the page, ran dry. Together they dipped it again, finished the signature, first on one page, then the other.

Norman stood with a sigh. "I am now," he said, "a Depew. With rights and privileges pertaining thereto and etcetera, etcetera."

Dudley Depew, scion of the Depews of Valhalla, original settlers of the western slopes of Mount Worthy overlooking the Little Hawking and the Ohio Rivers, serene high above the waterways' mephitic vapors, planters of vast if diseased vineyards, tramplers of bad grapes and vintners of sour wines, owners of vast orchards of shriveled walnuts, politicians and public servants, arbiters of good taste, righteous patriarchs of the city, an ancient family which included among its ancestors a signatory to the Declaration of Independence, two Secretaries of War, Senators beyond counting, donors to the art museum and other civic institutions, military heroes and generals, founders of the Depew Opera House (which unfortunately burned to the ground the day after completion, resulting in a tidy profit from Valhalla Life and Property Assurance, a closely-held Depew family corporation), Dudley, heir to it all, was apoplectic.

He wanted to speak, to make as cutting retort, to produce the bon mot which would put this upstart, this usurper in his place.

But he could only sputter. "Gnk gnk gnk," he said.

A particularly colorful flush painted the broad emptiness between his two wings of upright and distinguished hair; he became a robust sunset behind the vast walnut ocean of his desk.

"Knnh," he said. "Get...out."

"That's an awful noise, Dudley. Are you all right?"

The fatty pouches beneath the Mayor's eyes fill with some kind of fluid; the noise continued, nasal, ichorous and disturbing.

"Well, I won't bother you any more today." Norman went to the door. "So long."

He left the door open. A couple of steps down the

218

corridor he stopped.

It was a muffled thump he had heard, as if something dense and oily had exploded. Norman returned to the room.

Something dense and oily had exploded: Dudley Worthington Depew III was gone. The room was dark with a dreadful smoke rising from his chair. Footsteps pounded up the hallway behind Norman. A small group gathered at the entrance to Dudley's study. Its members stared in awe at the chair. When Doctor Hauser examined it later, he found nothing but the still-smoking shells of Dudley's high-buttoned shoes, pink unscorched feet still in them. On the floor around the desk were a few charred buttons and scraps of clothing.

"What is that stuff he was drinking?" Norman asked the butler.

"I believe it is called Sinker Sauce, sir," he replied in a dazed voice.

Doctor Hauser said later that it was the only recorded instance of the spontaneous combustion of a human being in Valhalla history. He speculated that it might have been the cellulose base for his false teeth which were torched by his cigar. "That stuff burns dirty," he said.

Chapter 10. In Which the City Changes Hands

It was bad, but not too bad.

Really, he thought it would be worse, more difficult, more embarrassing. Naturally, he hadn't anticipated facing all the other members of the family quite so soon, but two days ago Dudley had combusted and not only as the newest member of the family but as an official of the city of Valhalla as well Norman was called upon to participate. So it was that Norman trudged across the infield green.

Mayor Depew sat, rotund and calm, atop a marble column erected beneath a satin tent on the center of the starting line especially for this occasion. Resting now. Quiet as dust, quiet as ash.

Ha ha, Norman laughed inside, careful to maintain his solemn face. Dudley, he thought, has really made an ash of himself this time.

Norman sported a carnation in his buttonhole, white with crimson streaks radiating outward from its heart. He had picked it out himself, from the vendor down on Front Street near the levee. Just down from the ruins of City Hall. His silk top hat was freshly brushed.

He was president of the Rasmussen Dental Fabrication Works, the power behind the new Commissioner of Public Works (Baxter, posed as Norman, as he, Norman, was now posing as Baxter), Founder of the Valhalla Zoological Garden. And he was an adopted Depew, related to the ancient Depews who were so active in disseminating Good Works.

Only a slight concern over Francine marred his affability. Francine was here, and while she had been supplied with plenty of cocaine to ease her through this trial, she had been rather cool toward him the past couple of days. A tiny vertical line creased between his brows. Francine was just up ahead, swathed in black crepe. He would have to console the widow.

Low clouds gathered over the race track, threatening rain. He reflected on that, too.

"Damn," he said softly.

"Excuse me?" Francine turned. She was as one of the Depew matrons, severe and elegant. She gave no sign of recognition. "What did you say?"

"Nothing," Norman assured her. "I didn't say nothing."

Francine sniffed. Well, she'll get rained on too, Norman thought. Some satisfaction in that. He lagged behind, just in case he spoke aloud again, his somber mask slipping.

I am the most powerful man in Valhalla, and no one knows it. Since he had swapped identities with his twin Baxter so he could spend time with Francine, she seemed so indifferent. Furthermore the colorless Mrs. Rasmussen seemed to be on to that trick as well. Did she know Baxter too well, or was his twin not playing his part? The colorless Mrs. Rasmussen never said a word, but the quality of her silent suffering had subtly altered, and when she spoke with lowered eyes and head, her voice held a new element of reproach Norman found insufferable. So he stayed away.

Thirty-three years old, he thought, and no one knows I own the city. I have no choice, I can't even come in out of the rain.

Two or three people turned to stare at him. He had laughed aloud. It was not appropriate to laugh, not here, not today. After all, this was his adopted father's funeral.

An American flag snapped crisply in the breeze fleeing before the dark clouds moving over the river. They would be here soon, those clouds, he could already feel moisture on his face, a cool sting to it, numbing his nose and the exposed tops of his ears. The flag looked very grand fluttering there before the stands where the Senators and Secretaries and Philanthropists would sit after the cortege.

Norman dipped his head to the marble column as he

221

passed it. Dudley's fat face smiled serenely. His torso was wrapped in the toga of a Roman Senator. Did Mayor's have togas then? At any rate, Dudley was not sputtering. Dudley would never sputter again.

The urn was bronze, fashioned with high Victorian elegance, on a scale that befit the most prominent family in Valhalla, the lords of the gods themselves. A yard high, round, chased, inlaid. Heavy. It looked heavy, and Norman knew it was heavy. He had to help carry it, and there had been a rehearsal yesterday.

It weighed seven hundred pounds, very few of them Dudley's. There had been little of him left to scrape off the chair. The undertaker had been forced to leave the feet in the boots, so the amateur cremation Dudley had begun had to be finished professionally. What remained of Dudley was burned along with his boots and buttons. Norman had been pleased that the three Depews who were pall bearers along with him had also grunted when they lifted the thing.

For the cortege they carried the urn around the entire racetrack, slowly and with great effort, followed in silence by an enormous and very appreciative crowd.

The satin roof built over the finish line had no sides; there would be little protection from the rain when it did arrive. Precious little. Norman tried to maneuver his way as near the center as possible, just in case.

He found himself beside Dr. Hauser, who had pronounced Dudley dead at the scene. Dead, dead, dead. It was, he said later, the easiest chore of that type he had ever been called upon to perform. There wasn't even enough of Dudley left to look for a pulse, much less take it. For once Dudley left behind no doubts.

To Norman's left Francine bowed her head, swathed in thick veils. Mourning, possibly. Or disguised. Norman knew her pupils would most likely be near the size of the mouth of Dudley's urn.

He took her elbow sympathetically and murmured something. She appeared to take no notice. She was thinking about Baxter, damn him.

Dr. Hauser nodded soberly to Norman. He was a young man, Dr. Hauser was, grandly mustachioed; the scent of lavender wafted from him, mingling with the odors of real flowers, including Norman's carnation. Norman nodded back, dropping Francine's elbow. Later, later.

The services began.

"Ashes to ashes," the Right Reverend Archibald Ovandrill intoned. He was smooth and round and aglow with the prosperity that comes with good fellowship. The First Universal Church of Jesus Christ, Gentleman. His service would be precisely the most tolerable length. His sense of timing was uncanny. "Dust to dust."

It was an inspiring eulogy he delivered. "In the race of life," Reverend Ovandrill began, "Dudley Worthington Depew III was a winner."

With effort Norman suppressed a snicker.

"It is here, on the track he built, and where so many of his victories were won, and where so much popular amusement for the gentry of Valhalla has been freely given, that Dudley Worthington Depew III will rest. Forever. Dudley Downs, where Dudley has come down at last to his rest."

Reverend Ovandrill dipped a silver spatula into the bronze urn. He pulled forth a mound of gray ash.

"It was here," Reverend Ovandrill continued, "that Dudley developed a new narrow-wheeled sulky." He waved the spatula around at the race track, at the brilliant greens, the dirt, the stands with a roof of graceful domes and rotundas so reminiscent to some of the Museum of Western Oddities. "He gave so much of his time to the ancient sport of harness racing, and so much of his time in harness as Mayor of Valhalla. Now the race is ended. Here is the finish line."

Reverend Ovandrill dusted the ashes gently along the white line in the dirt.

"It was across this very line that Dudley Worthington Depew III trotted his finest horses, pulling his narrow-wheeled sulky to victory time after time."

223

It was true. Dudley, over the course of twenty-three years in harness racing, had cleared nearly a million dollars in prize money. After expenses, bribes and payoffs.

Reverend Ovandrill was tossing the meager ashes Dudley had left along the finish line, but the wind was picking up now in earnest, bringing the first scattered drops of rain, and gray ash began to spume from the silver spatula like spindrift.

Norman retreated a bit beneath the satin roof of the tent, but it did no good. The satin, not meant to repel water, was instantly drenched. Drops began to seep through the roof onto Norman's silk hat.

"And so we commend Dudley Worthington Depew III to the finish line of life," Archibald Ovandrill concluded hastily, scattering the last of the ashes with a swift, inaccurate gesture.

The satin began to snap in the wind as the hard, brittle drops of rain smacked against the wet material. While most of the mourners began to scurry back toward their carriage, Norman watched for a moment. The ashes turned dark and soggy, and spread into the mud of the track. The ruts left by the narrow-wheeled sulkies filled with water, smeared and vanished. A crack of thunder rolled across Valhalla Downs, farewell to Dudley.

Norman smiled. Everything was going his way. Soon he would join Francine in wedded bliss. After a suitable period of mourning, of course. Say, a month. And everyone would think he was Baxter.

He caught a glimpse of something large and white at the far end of the racetrack. It looked like some kind of animal, a wolf perhaps, or a dog, but larger.

It was, in fact, an enormous pig, watching the proceedings. Norman shrugged. Nothing to do with him. No. Norman was a confident man, certain of who he was: a man in charge of his own destiny, immune to omens.

BOOK THE FIFTH:
CORY, 1957

Chapter 1. In Which Cory Becomes a Personage of Note

"Name."

"Wernher von Braun."

"Address."

"Number 2, Peenemunde Drive."

"Where the hell's that?"

"Slyville."

"Yeah? You don't look like a hillbilly. Spell it."

Cory spelled it. Withrow had already vanished, escorted down to the cells reserved for "knee-grows."

"Occupation."

"Refugee."

"What kinda occupation is that?" The officer looked up.

"Injuries suffered during the war," Cory said, tapping his bandages. "Never healed properly. I'm a scientist. Rockets."

"What were you doing in that beatnik hangout? Never mind." The officer wrote it all down. "Next."

Cory shuffled away.

Hackamore and Peggy and the chalk-white girl and Godzilla's owner were all gone to Women's Detention. Cory found himself in the drunk tank with the windswept old man, the physics genius and the Dead Man.

"What's your name?" the pop-eyed physics wizard asked Cory.

"Cory."

"That what you told the police?"

Cory shook a head that resembled a rotating cumulus cloud. "I told them I was Wernher Von Braun."

The kid smiled. "That's a good one. You must have been thinking fast. I told them my real name, and now my parents are going to be extremely ticked off. I only go to play chess. I was winning, too. Ten moves, eleven at the most. The Diego response."

"Nonsense," said the man with windswept hair. "The Maksutov opening is unbeatable."

The physics wizard laughed. "He always loses," he said.

"O-o-oh the wayward wind," a drunk began to sing.

"I beat you last week," the man with the windswept hair protested.

"Is a restless-s-s-s wind."

"That's cause I had to be home early."

"Do you realize we are in jail?" Cory asked.

"And tonight," the windswept hair said, "I was setting a trap. You were falling for it. There is a counter to the Diego response. I read about it."

"A trap," Cory said quietly.

The drunk who was singing Wayward Wind began to vomit profusely near the basin. Quite near.

"You thinking about the classic Standish Variation on the Castiglione Defense?" the junior high student asked.

The man with windswept hair nodded.

"Well, your bishop was in the wrong place for Standish," the kid informed him.

"Hah," the man with windswept hair crowed. "That's just the point. This was a new variation. Queen's pawn on king five, right?"

The kid nodded. They were off. Apparently they needed neither board nor pieces, and the game continued.

"A trap," Cory repeated. His face hurt, but the colors of the cell were so brilliant and lovely, the windswept man's hair was so intricate and delicate, the eyes of the physics wizard so intent and blue that Cory fell into a rapture of contemplation and forgot where he was.

His face lay in a satin-lined casket under a drowsy bank of blossoms. In the background solemn strings were dense and mournful. Mozart, surely, but he could not place the piece itself. One of the quintets, perhaps. It was strange

227

he could not place it, though. Usually he recognized Mozart immediately.

Hackamore Ovandrill was beside him, her plump pink face swathed in black veils like those his mother Belle wore when she dressed up for an Occasion and wore one of those tiny hats trimmed with funeral gauze. Hackamore was weeping.

Cory looked down at his face. It wasn't strange his face was having a funeral here in jail. His face looked back up at him, and it too was weeping. Beside him Hackamore's sobs syncopated with his own.

He put his arm around her. "Don't," he said. "Don't. It was time. It had a good life, a full life, a rich and rewarding life." He sounded like Eleanor Roosevelt.

"A good life, ooooh," she wailed. Her wail turned into a strangled series of sobs, almost like retching.

A halo formed around her head. Perhaps it was the ceiling light, which was round also, with a wire grill over it. But it seemed to be a halo. She was holding out her hands. In supplication, or benediction. The hands had spots on them. She was St. Credula. The Ulcerated Martyr of Shköder. Someone had told him that Shköder was a city in Albania, although this seemed unlikely. Albania was such a small country. Yet if he walked the streets of Mount Worthy he could hear its hard flat syllables descended from ancient Illyrian. Most of the immigrants to Valhalla, he knew, were Ghegs from the north of Albania, where the city of Shköder perched on the shores of Lake Scutari: the Ghegs were drenched in superstition, hardy and fierce, predatory and sullen. The officer who took his name and address had been Albanian. And here was Hackamore Ovandrill, poised in his cell, the Ulcerated Martyr of Shköder, with a halo around her head.

"Oh," he said to her. "Help me."

"What's that? Help? Help?"

Was that really the scent of funeral flowers all around? It didn't seem quite right. And yet there was his face, lying amid the satin and blossoms, smiling at him.

Smiling? Laughing. Ha ha.

"The queen is pinned," said the physics wizard.

"Queen spinned?" Cory asked. "Do you know anything about rockets?"

"There, there," Hackamore Ovandrill said, hands stretched out toward him, the ulcers in her palms squirming with maggots and worms. Her halo had grown intolerably bright. "There, there."

"You know, if you stare at the light like that, you're going to go blind," someone said. Perhaps the man with windswept hair.

"Blind," Cory repeated. "Yes." He nodded vigorously, then stopped abruptly because his face had slipped inside his bandages. A tight pain clutched his chest, too, and he began once more to cry, softly and silently.

"There, there," said the physics wizard. "There, there."

"Where?" shouted the drunk from the basin. "Where?"

"Never mind," Cory said. "Never mind. She wrote a poem. For me."

"Which one was that? Oh, I bet I know." The physics wizard was holding an imaginary chess piece in the air. "The one that started, 'I saw the face of my friend falling off.' I thought it was kind of disgusting."

"So's that drunk over there. He just threw up on the floor." The man with windswept hair made a wry face.

Cory blinked. He thought this was real. Certainly Hackamore could not be in the cell with him. Certainly there had been a raid, and the moon-faced man was dead, and now he was in jail. But he was not drunk.

"I smoked some kind of stuff," he said.

"What's that?" the man with windswept hair said. "No. Don't put it down yet," he told the boy.

"Some kind of stuff," Cory said. "Muggles."

"Oh. Musicians," he said contemptuously. "Are you a musician."

"No. But I do know a little bit about Mozart. Kind of

229

accidentally."

"Mozart? The cave down near Slyville. You can go in it, you know. There's a woman in there." The man with windswept hair shook his hand loosely, whee-oo.

"A woman? What are you talking about?" Cory was confused again.

Certainly it was dark in the cave, and deep, and damp and cool. What was the woman doing there, deep in the dark, the cool dark so similar to this cell, where the sounds of trickling water came from far away? Would she be humming the duet in A from Don Giovanni which began *La ci darem la mano*, 'Here with our hands entwining, Let our designs agree...'?

"Oh, the wayward wind," the drunk said in Cory's ear. "Is a restless wind." His voice ran down and he dribbled on his shirt for a moment. Then he looked up hopefully.

"A restless wind?" he asked. "Born to wander?"

Chapter 2. In Which Cory Bails Out

Cory dreamed he was Alice, visiting Wonderland. A bottle said, Drink Me, and he was about to drink in the faint hope his face would return to him. His face was far away, lost in the woods. Cory was sad and afraid.

"Brown," a policeman called out.

Cory's eyes had been sewed shut, and when he tried to open them, he felt the stitches tear.

"Van Brown," the voice of authority called again.

"Von Braun?" he croaked. He could see the dim outlines of other figures sprawled on the wooden benches in the cell. The man with windswept hair lay with an open mouth from which large gargling noises emerged with each breath. The physics genius sat with his back against the wall. His bulging eyes were open, but he appeared to be lost in a mental landscape of his own, and gave no sign he had heard the voice outside the door.

The drunk had finally finished singing Gogi Grant's greatest hit, The Wayward Wind, and was seated quietly in a puddle of his very own, drawing with a blunt, filthy finger on the wall beside the basin.

"You Van Brown?" the policeman asked.

Cory nodded. His dusky swathes of bandage were dim ghosts in the cell. "Yes," he rasped. The muggles seemed to have worn off. He had a sore throat.

"You can go," the policeman said, opening the door. The hinges made a grating noise.

"Go?"

"You've been bailed."

"Bailed?"

"You beatnik punk refugees ask too many questions. Get out."

He shoved Cory up the stairs, out the front door and into the street.

A terrible quiet was out there, a desolation quiet, as if the world had ended with a whimper while Cory languished. The street lamps threw pools of light. Two empty patrol cars were parked in front, and he felt a stab of remorse. Once he had been the Lone Ranger with a car of his own, a red light and a siren. Now he was an ex-prisoner alone on the empty street.

It was a lovely night with a soft, warm breeze, unusual for November.

"Cory!"

She waved to him from beside a car across the street.

"Hah?"

"Over here," Hackamore Ovandrill called. "Come on." She was gesturing. He blinked twice. Perhaps the world had not ended after all.

He crossed the street and climbed in the passenger seat. "Do you mean me?" he asked.

She climbed in the driver's side before answering. "Of course I mean you. Who else is there?"

He looked around. "I see what you mean. I thought it was the end of the world. What time is it? I had a dream."

Before she could reply, he fell asleep.

Light threw shadows across his face as she drove through the night's swollen darkness, its vast bland evil, and he blinked against it in his sleep. Yet it seemed that it was the light he liked, that in fact there was light in a world grown very dark. Even though the strains of Mozart's so-called "tragic" A minor piano sonata, K. 310, drifted through his head, he felt something near to happiness.

In his sleep he began to hum the melody from the piano sonata, a soft drone barely recognizable as music, but it reminded Hackamore that Cory had been about to tell her something about Thule, Greenland, and Mozart, same as the cave down near Slyville, so she woke him up to ask him about it. He thought he was still dreaming of alternations of light and shade, of tiny pools of light in the inexhaustible darkness of the universe, the infinite interstellar cold against which his personal warmth was smaller than the

232

tiniest candle in Valhalla Stadium just after a night game the Warriors had lost again.

So he said, "Hah?" again.

"You were going to tell me about Mozart. You didn't mean the cave."

"No, not the cave. The composer."

"Yes. How do you know so much about him?"

"Ah." He opened his eyes. They were traveling through the dark. There was no other traffic in all the world. "In Thule, Greenland, where I was stationed in the army, there had been a commanding officer named Colonel Omar L. Detroit. Colonel Detroit was a man who loved Mozart. He had a whole room filled with albums, those thick folders with old 78 recordings of everything Mozart wrote. Everything that was recorded, anyway, which was almost everything. There wasn't much to do in Thule, Greenland, so I spent most of my two and a half years there in that room listening to Mozart. And he had a whole lot of books about Mozart, too, and there wasn't really anything else to read there in Thule, so I read all the books about Mozart. Some of them twice. Colonel Detroit left me Mozart."

"Why did he leave it there, his collection, I mean?"

"Too heavy to carry with him, I suppose. He walked off one day across the glacier and was never seen again. Personally I think the wind got to him, and the cold, and all that white snow and fog. I never met Colonel Detroit; nobody who was stationed there had met Colonel Detroit. He disappeared in 1949. How did you get me out of jail?"

Hackamore smiled her sweet sad smile. Her teeth in the streetlight alternations were large and white and slightly protruding and nothing at all like Marsha Willoughby's perfect small teeth. Her lips were plump ripe plums, or as plump as Cory imagined ripe plums to be, and there was something about the sadness of her smile that made his heart leap into his throat and stop his voice.

"It was easy. All I really had to do was give Daddums a call. The hard part was convincing the cops I was allowed a call. They found 'Navel Lint,' you see. And there were a few words in it that they thought might be on the books. But it seems that you are allowed to say penis but not cock, which has four letters and thus is obscene. You can say screw, which has five letters, but not fuck. Stuff like that."

"Makes sense," Cory said doubtfully; she had shocked him again.

"Not much, if you ask me. But then if there weren't obscene words, I wouldn't be able to get the effects I want, so I suppose I should be grateful. Anyway, I didn't use cock or fuck or cunt or piss or any words with four letters, so they had to give me my phone call and I called Daddums."

"Well, that explains it, I suppose."

"Of course. All Daddums had to do was make a little phone call of his own and they dropped the charges. Against me, anyway, obscenity and such. And then I imagine Daddums made some other calls, you know, and then it turned out that the whole thing was a big mistake of some kind."

"A big mistake," Cory repeated, thinking of the small round hole in the moon-faced man's smooth forehead, the hole meant for his forehead.

She drove on through downtown Valhalla, and as she crossed the broad avenue that stretched from one end of town to the other, she said, "Hey, is this street named after your grandfather or something?" and he looked up at the sign: Depew Avenue.

"I don't know. There was a mayor once named Depew."

"Sure." She looked over at him with a smile. He tried to smile back, but a strange pain twisted his mouth, and it came out a grimace. Fortunately she couldn't see him very well so swathed in bandage was he.

"How did you know I was Wernher von Braun, and why did you bail me out?"

"Mystic wisdom of ancient India," she said seriously, and he didn't laugh. "Insight. In fact, I tried Cory Depew

234

and they didn't have you, so it was obvious. They had set bail so I bailed you out. I had to take a taxi to get my car and some money at home, and then I came back. I bailed you out because you are suffering, and because I like you."

He didn't know what to say. "Thanks," he said. It sounded puny.

"Oh, it's nothing. It'll be refunded. They didn't have a warrant for the raid, and Daddums knows a whole lot of good lawyers."

"Oh. But I arrested him in August. He might not be so pleased to help me out."

She reached over and held his kneecap gently. "Don't worry," she said. "I'll take care of Daddums."

"OK. What did you mean, wisdom of ancient India?"

"Yoga. It's something the Beats are into. Gabriel Flagg taught me some. I do Kundilini, or Laya Yoga. I am striving for Kundilini Shakti, or Inner Woman. My guru tells me I am on my way. Tantric sex, too."

Cory stared. Did he think Hackamore Ovandrill was a virgin, saved for him? Of course not; she had been to Dr. Thanatopoulos. "Tantric sex?" he asked. "Guru?"

"An old man over on the west side. He teaches me the positions, the possibilities. I practice. I'm very limber."

Cory was to find that out.

"Where are we going?" he asked.

"My place."

"Oh." Cory thought about the big mistake that had been made this very night, the moon-faced man, and Hackamore Ovandrill. "A big mistake," he said softly to himself, nodding his white head. "A big mistake." Was he Wernher von Braun nodding at the failure of yet another American rocket?

Chapter 3. In Which We Find Cornelius in Dreamland

Cory was in Hackamore Ovandrill's bed. It was a big bed, a soft bed, a comfortable and comforting bed which cradled Cory as he drowsed. He desperately wanted to stay awake, to rise to the occasion, to hold this soft sad comfortable woman in his arms. His desperation wavered in and out of dream, of hypnagogic reverie in which his face was a latex pancake under chilly water, rippling with old movie effects.

"Hello," he said.

"Hello," his face answered.

"Hello," Hackamore Ovandrill breathed into the bandages over his ear. "Why has your face fallen off, Cornelius?"

No one ever called him Cornelius. "No one," he said, "ever calls me that."

He moved away. "Don't you like it?"

"I think I like it. From you."

"Oh." He could hear her smile.

His eyes were closed, but he began a list. "Sin," he suggested. "I have sinned. But I was raised a Protestant of some kind, and Protestants don't sin. It's in bad taste." He folded down the first finger. "A family curse. Withrow says it is a family curse. Some ancestor's sin, that means. But I don't know who my ancestors are. There appear to be Rasmussens in my family tree, because my Uncle Cornelius is a Rasmussen and not a Depew, which I don't understand because he is my father's stepbrother. I think. But because a curse is based on sin, we are back to the same objection as number one. Protestants don't sin. Belle wouldn't allow it."

"Belle?"

"My mother."

"Ah. Yes. Go on."

A third finger folded to join the others. "Disease. Some social disease. I consider that unlikely, and Dr. Thanatopoulos says it is impossible."

"Dr. Thanatopoulos," she said sadly; it was not a question. "I saw him too."

"I know." They were both sad. He went on. "Congenital disease, I thought. Some flaw in the family genes. A history of falling faces. Now I'm back to the same problem as with number two. I don't know enough."

He was so sleepy he could not open his eyes.

"Don't know enough," she said, stroking his upper arm in small delicate circles. "Know enough."

"Yes," he said. "No."

"Why did you pick Wernher von Braun?" she asked, tracing the circles.

"Rockets," Cory said. "They get away."

He could hear her smile again. Her eyes were closed now too.

"I always thought I looked like Wernher von Braun, anyway."

"Yes?"

"We met," he told her, or a vision of her, or a dream of a vision of her.

"You met," she said to the faint outline of his bandaged head inside her own closed eyes. "You and Wernher von Braun."

"No. We met, you and I. At the Silver Spoon."

"We what?" She was on her elbow staring at him, and he had to open his eyes against the full weight of a terrible gravity.

"The Silver Spoon. In August. One hot night. You came in. It was the night my face fell off, early in the evening. Marsha Willoughby was there. And a dwarf. Oh, God." He groaned. He put his hands to his forehead, swathed in bandages. Faintly tan, they were, from the dried tea Hackamore had put there.

"I remember," she said. "That was you? Sitting at the bar? Drinking Odrerir and mumbling? I was very sad that night. That was the day I went to Dr. Thanatopoulos for a D and C. Abortion. My name is still written on your forehead. And my phone number. And now you're here." She hugged his arm. "Are you tired?" she asked.

He snored.

"You're tired," she said softly. She was still wearing her black leotard, her black turtleneck sweater, her black slacks. She had written a poem, had read to the crowd, had witnessed a killing and been arrested, had done time in jail. Earlier she had smoked a fair mess of ganja, and now, she was quite sure, she was sweet on this stringy pathetic child beside her. Something about him brought out the mom in her soft breast. She put her head back against her pillow and stretched her legs out straight before her. She bent her toes back, spread her hands out to either side of her hips and lifted her legs oh so slowly into a modified *halasana* or plow posture until her toes touched the wall at the head of the bed. Beside her Cory Depew snored on and on.

Slowly she lowered her legs again. She looked at her naked toes where they emerged from the leotard. They were plump and white. Gabriel Flagg, in his sweeter moments, had loved to suck on those toes. If only he hadn't enjoyed slapping her so much.

A tear squeezed from between her lids and rolled across her cheek to the pillow. She made a small sound in her throat.

Cory stirred but did not wake. Hack chewed on her lower lip. Cory was dreaming of teeth. Her teeth. How could she know that?

"Cory," she said softly. "Cornelius."

"Mmm?" he murmured. Her mouth was open and he was at the entrance which echoed like marble and gleamed.

"Cory."

"When I was in kindergarten," he said, turning slightly. "I was bad. I must have been bad, because all I can remember is standing in the hall."

"Cory," she repeated. "Oh, Cory."

"There was frosted glass on the door. Miss Buford's door," he went on. "All fractured. I think I was crying." He began to cry. Hackamore Ovandrill began to cry.

"You had Miss Buford too," Hackamore sobbed.

"You had Miss Buford?" Cory asked. Then he realized he was awake and his bandages were wet. "Oh, God," he said, turning away.

"There, there," Hack soothed. "It's all right. This has been some night."

"Some night. I don't understand. What did I do?"

"We could ask Miss Buford," she suggested, and Cory almost did smile.

"Where is Miss Buford?" he asked. And he did smile.

"In the Widows' home. Every May they give this sort of festival to raise money, and all the old people come out in the sun and look around. Miss Buford smiles a lot. She sits there and smiles and smiles and smiles. It's the saddest thing I've ever seen."

"I don't remember what Miss Buford looked like. All I remember is the outside of her classroom, the frosted glass in the door through my tears. I'm so tired."

"Of course you are. You wouldn't recognize Miss Buford any more. She's very very old, and all she can do is smile. Go to sleep." She held his head and rocked him, and he went to sleep almost as fast as she did. He did not dream of Miss Buford.

He dreamed of the Dead Man's ancient face.

Chapter 4. In Which Cory Learns About the Worm, and Other Items

The Dead Man was walking through a palace of endless corridors, passageways, doors and arches, colonnades and porticoes, fairy-tale courtyards deserted and overgrown, fountains tangled with brambles, dry and thorny. The Dead Man was Grouper Depew; yet he was not. His eyes were unhappy. He paused beside one of the empty fountains and set fire to the brambles. Smoke closed in around him and obscured the world. Then he rose into the air through the smoke, his hands spread out. He was Cory's father's airplane, a lovely V-tail Beechcraft Bonanza, which roared as it dove toward him. Cory tried to run, but his feet were mired and he couldn't move.

The alarm buzzed. He stared into an unfamiliar ceiling and could not understand why the gorilla no longer stared down at him. Then he remembered that they had replastered his ceiling, and he was not at home at 1001 Celestial Street anyway.

Hackamore Ovandrill was gone; there was an enormous empty space around him.

"Hello," he said quietly. There was no reply. Already the small quick images and fragments of desolation were evaporating. He sat up.

A piece of paper flopped before his eyes, a message from Hack taped to his bandage.

"Dear Cornelius," it said. "The alarm is set for noon in case you are not awake. Not to alarm you. Juice in the fridge, and there is a radio, too. Have gone to Serpent Mound to see Daddums and the mater, who will be riding her stallion Merriweather. Otherwise my home is yours. Affectionately."

He walked around touching her furniture. She had a

240

bed, and clothes all over the floor, jeans and sweaters. She had a closet with nothing in it but empty hangers. She had a dresser with drawers full of sweaters. Black sweaters. Nothing but black sweaters. She had dozens of black sweaters, mostly turtlenecks. Some of them felt very soft. He sat hunched in a chair in her bedroom with one of her soft sweaters pressed against the bandages on his cheek.

He listed his liabilities. He had ignorance. Ignorance of family, ignorance of first causes, ignorance of metaphysics, epistemology, eschatology and ontology. He had pain around the perimeter of his face. He had existential dread, and with dread he had the dilemma of existence, the terror of being a self-conscious animal who dies, the awful necessity of living with Absurdity, as Withrow had assured him more than once. A family curse, too, he had, along with no prospects, few interests outside animal husbandry and Mozart, and even fewer ambitions.

All in all he was not a good bet for a round and lovely minister's daughter who was a Beat poet and the owner of a hundred soft black sweaters. Who had talent and grace and ambition, who had influence and money and more education than he. After all, while he had been in Thule, Greenland, listening to Mozart, she had become a junior at Valhalla University. Did that matter?

At last he rose, wandered to her refrigerator and found a small bottle of apple juice. He drank it all; it did nothing to quench his thirst. Carefully he replaced her sweater in its drawer with the others, and used her telephone.

He listened without hearing as the ringing went on and on. He did not know where he was or why he was here.

"Heh-wo," a small voice said.

"Heh-wo," Cory said. "Buster? Is that you?"

"Who dis?"

"Uncle Cory. This is your Uncle Cory. Is your mom there, Buster? I have to talk to your mom."

"Mommy!" Buster shouted into the receiver. Cory winced.

The phone clattered on the wooden floor of Peggy's apartment. Then silence. During the silence Cory forgot once again where he was or what he was doing; he was startled when Peggy came on the line.

"Hello. Who's this?" she said.

Before he thought about it, he said, "I don't know."

"Oh. Cory. You're out. Are you all right?"

"I'm out," he said. "I dreamed about the Dead Man. Peggy, what happened?"

"You sound funny. Are you all right? Cory?"

"Yes."

Finally she spoke again. "Where are you. We tried calling this morning and there was no answer at your place. We called the police and they said you weren't there."

"I don't know."

Peggy was puzzled. "You don't know what?"

"I don't know where I am. Exactly. I'm at Hackamore Ovandrill's. She bailed me out."

"Oh ho!" Peggy said.

"No," Cory told her. "I fell asleep."

"Sure."

"Really. How did you get out?"

"She bailed us out too. Where is she?"

"Gone. To see Daddums. And something named Merriweather. A horse."

"Her apartment's near V.U. Withrow can come up and get you. He has some news for you."

He stared out the window at the quiet Sunday street. The rows of houses had asphalt siding, front stoops and tiny lawns. But the houses were painted cheerful colors, the tiny lawns were green, and the air was filled with the lovely smell of burning leaves. The elms and sycamores still had yellow leaves, and some of the maples had red leaves sprinkled among the yellow, and when they fell they were swept into neat piles by the curb and burned. This street was very different from Celestial Street, which climbed a hill toward the spire of St. Credula. This street was straight and flat. Both directions were mirrors of each other:

242

identical houses, lawns, stoops; only the colors were different. The houses were small, many of them rented to college students. Hackamore Ovandrill was a college student.

He avoided thinking about last night, of death so vividly presented. He thought instead about his future.

It provided him little to contemplate.

When Withrow pulled up, Cory was seated on the stoop, feet up on the low railing. His clothes smelled of smoke and tea and marijuana. His eyes were red and his head was swathed in bandages grown increasingly foul.

"Schachter's Worm," Withrow said.

"Eh?"

"Schachter's Worm. It's a borer. Very interesting. Also I have a job for you."

Cory groaned. His feet slipped off the railing and clattered on the boards of the stoop. "What about this worm?"

"Ah," Withrow held up a long guitar player's finger. "The worm. The worm is turning. It goes through a number of stages which may interest you. Free swimming. Then it bores into dead wood, whatever is drifting in the Little Hawking River. From there it is free swimming again until swallowed, when moves into the kidneys. It likes mammal kidneys, including people. Bores out a small nest for itself inside the flesh of the organ, and there lays its eggs. Fascinating, isn't it?"

"Why do you tell me all this? I don't have any interest in this thing at all."

"It attacks pigs."

"Pigs?"

"Sometimes, yes. And there is Diabolus. A huge white boar that roams the forests between here and Slyville."

"Surely you jest."

"Yes. And no. The diary dates from around 1890. This Diabolus is in it, though I couldn't make out why since the next page is gone. The diary stops there. Then there is the fact that your mother used to be a Theosophist with a strong interest in various forms of divination. Most likely you did not know that, since she gave it up."

"Divination," Cory said without interest.

"Yes. Pig livers, chicken guts, things like that. Very popular up in Slyville."

"Oh, great."

"Well, enough of this chitchat. About your new job."

Cory groaned again.

"What's the matter? Don't you want a job? Listen, boy, they gonna get you anyway. The Absurd. Two years ago our man Albert Camus published his essay on the Myth of Sysiphus. Now Sysiphus, he pushes a rock up a hill, you see, as a punishment for some crime: 'a certain levity toward the gods,' as Camus puts it. The rock rolls back down the hill, every time he gets it to the top. Futile, arduous labor, endlessly repeated. 'One sees the face screwed up, the cheek tight against the stone, the shoulder bracing the clay-covered mass, the foot wedging it.'"

"The face screwed up," Cory echoed.

Withrow smiled. "Right. I have a job for you. Just like that."

"It sounds wonderful," Cory said. "What is it, rolling a rock up Mount Worthy?"

"Good training for your college major. Same job as me, boy. Same job as me. Cleaning up in the zoo."

Chapter 5. In Which Uncle Cornelius Talks Existentialism

"It's not so bad." Withrow was trying to reassure him. Everyone was trying to reassure him. Vincent Black Shadow had tried to reassure him, and for about three hours he was the Lone Ranger, lost in fog. Now Withrow.

"Not so bad?" Cory echoed. His head was a mess. His face hurt, his bandages stank, he was filthy. "Cleaning up animal shit is not so bad?"

"Not so bad," Withrow repeated. They were zipping along through Valhalla's November as if this were just another month in heaven. The sky was an aching blue up there above the yellowing leaves aswirl in the auto's windy passage.

"Lions?" Cory asked. "Tigers? Elephants and aardvarks?"

Withrow nodded. "Also hoofed animals..."

"Hoofed?"

"Like pigs. Wart hogs. And camels and giraffes. Hippopotamus. Also deer, elk, wildebeests and springboks with cute curly horns."

"Horns."

"Horns. Also ostriches, parrots, flamingos and condors."

"Birds?" Cory shuddered. He didn't think he cared for birds.

"Lots of exotic animals in the zoo, Cory. You'll learn a lot. Bears and bats, elephants and eagles. Bugs and badgers."

"You're a poet, too, Withrow," Cory said in terrible gloom.

The radio announced that Don and Phil Everly had risen to number one on the top forty. *Wake Up, Little Suzy* had arrived, but *Bye Bye, Love* had dropped off. For the sake of nostalgia, the DJ played *Bye Bye, Love*, already a couple of months old, a moldy, or perhaps a golden oldy. Back in September it had been the number ten song for the month.

"Bye Bye, love," they sang. "Hello, emptiness."

Cory and Withrow listened in silence as Don and Phil said it all.

"That's it, Core. That's the whole thing." Withrow turned the radio off. They were crossing Dudley Worthington Depew Avenue. The day was golden. A golden oldie.

"What whole thing?" Cory asked without interest.

"Hello, emptiness. Don't you see? Don and Phil are America's Existentialists. The Jean-Paul Sartre and Albert Camus of the United States. Bye bye, love. Bye bye, happiness. Man's fate, to be alone in an absurd universe, and to die at the end. Emptiness. The void. True heroes, they are, in the face of such terrible news."

"You're kidding. Don and Phil?"

"Sure, Don and Phil. Why not? Hello, emptiness. Embracing the void, aware of its absurdity. True philosophers, the achievement of American thought in 1957. They should be at Harvard."

"The Everly Brothers?" Cory was incredulous. Wolfgang, Wolfgang, where were you now? Withrow Duquesne was seriously considering the Everly Brothers in the same breath as Sartre and Camus. Cory tried to think about the C minor mass, but he kept hearing Don and Phil taking their leave of happiness.

Withrow nodded and smiled. The day was nodding and smiling too, a gentle breeze tossing the last golden leaves from their branches and making them dance to the ground in happy spirals.

Cory could barely lift his head, burdened with bandages. His eyes were heavy and fell to his shoes. His shoes had stood in his jail cell the night before where the drunk had thrown up singing Gogi Grant's greatest hit. The

246

Wayward Wind. Born to wander.

"Where are we going?" he asked.

"Ah, that is the question, isn't it?"

"What kind of answer is that? That was a question. 'That is the question, isn't it?'"

"Yes."

"Ah, a direct and firm answer. Yes. Shit."

"That too," Withrow nodded.

Cory tried again. "Where are we going? Now. In the car."

"Enjoy the day, Core. Sunlight on the autumn trees, the whisper of tires on the road, swishing through the fallen and drifted leaves. Reflect on the evanescence of life, the transitory nature of existence. Don't worry so much about where you're going. You won't get there any sooner."

"Sometimes, Withrow, I think philosophy has done you a world of harm. It was a simple question, really: Where are we going? Nothing metaphysical about it. I don't really want to know what Jean-Paul, or even Don and Phil, have to say about it."

"Stoop's Grocery. We're going to Stoop's."

"Oh." Cory was nodding his bandaged head vigorously. "Swell. Great. Stoop's Grocery. Home of the ghetto Existentialists. Grocery Dog is going to lecture me on Martin Buber and Karl Jaspers."

"You know a lot of names, Core, but you are one ignorant dude when it comes right down." Withrow was smiling again. They entered the Cliffside Ghetto where the buildings grew tall and narrow and red and the streets grew skinny and crowded.

"The Warriors ended the season in eighth place. They did better when they were called the Berserkers," Withrow said. "In 1908. They led the league in 1908, the Valhalla Berserkers did. In '09 they fell to last place as the Valhalla Warriors. Boss Rasmussen wanted to clean up their name, give it more dignity. He took all the soul away."

"Boss Rasmussen? Who was Boss Rasmussen? Not uncle Cornelius, surely."

"No, not your Uncle Cornelius." Withrow's face gleamed in the slanting sunlight astride the ghetto buildings reflected from the facades of all those tenements. "But there is a surprise or two for you."

"I've had enough surprises the past few days."

"Ha ha and he he," Withrow chuckled. Cory did not believe he had ever heard anyone chuckle before, even though he grew up with radio and *Inner Sanctum* and *The Shadow*.

He stared out the window at kids playing stickball though there was a chill in the air; at women leaning across their sills passing advice and shouts of laughter; at teenagers listening at those same windows to the sounds of rhythm and blues from the heart of Cliffside: neoteric, underground, Skid Row radio they called it; at men standing in the doorways of haberdasheries and liquor stores, pool halls and groceries. There, for instance, was his Uncle Cornelius standing in the doorway of Stoop's Grocery right next to Grocery Dog. He was unquestionably the last person Cory expected to see standing in the doorway of a ghetto store next to a person of color. What would Grouper say, not to mention Belle?

"Ho ho," Uncle Cornelius laughed, sticking out his hand. "You're wondering what Grouper would say, aren't you boy? Well, I wonder myself, don't I? You and I should discuss your problem, though, shouldn't we?"

"Problem?"

"The curse, boy. The curse. Your face."

Grocery Dog handed Cory a cold Coke straight from the big red box, and Cory drank it down. "My face. What do you know about my face?"

"Easy, son, easy. Come on in back. They have a kind of meeting room back there, a club or something. Study philosophy or some such foolishness. Never saw much in philosophy, boy. OK for priests or other depressed people, but not for us men of the world, eh?"

"I don't know. I just started college. How's Bow Keep coming along?"

Cornelius collapsed into hoots and gales of laughter. "Terrific. Really had you going on that one, didn't I? Well, it's a lot of damn foolishness, but the fact is, it's going great guns. Busby and Conrad's Department Store ordered two hundred. Now I'll have to go ahead and make 'em. Damn nuisance, but they're headquarters of a chain, and if Bow Keep goes in there, the whole chain will have to have them. Bow Keeps all over the country! I'll make thousands. Maybe more. Hell, millions! Why not?" He wiped a tear of merriment from his eye. "Totally unexpected. Well, you're probably wondering why I had Withrow bring you down here."

Cory did not think this could be Uncle Cornelius Rasmussen. Cornelius Rasmussen was a buffoon, an idiot, a moron. A senile fool.

"I didn't know you had Withrow bring me here." Cory was stalling. Uncle Cornelius had always been a little dotty. Belle called him eccentric in a tone that reminded Cory of the one she used to refer to Rebecca when she looked down her nose at a plate of smoldering veal birds.

Uncle Cornelius collapsed onto the sofa in the Existentialist's Meeting Room under a huge portrait of Georg Wilhelm Friedrich Hegel, the father of Existentialism, a young man of twenty-one the day Mozart died at 36 in Vienna. Uncle Cornelius again wiped the merry corners of his greatly wrinkled eyes and grinned at his nephew.

"You didn't know," he repeated, laughing delightedly. He clapped his hands together. "Didn't know. Of course not. Nobody knows much about your Uncle Cornelius. Just as nobody knows much about Norman and Baxter and what really happened to Dudley Depew, or who Boss Rasmussen was. Or where my own uncle Norman got his new name. Oh, I was just a little kid then, but I found out. I found out, and brother Grigory did too. Who told Brother Grigory? I'm not sure. Nobody is sure. Another mystery. But Brother Grigory has the information, some of it. Then there is what might have happened to your great

249

grandfather. His name was Peabody, did you know that? Where did that name go? Oh, well, I found out a thing or two. I don't know who told Brother Grigory. Momma told me. Nobody ever knew much about her either. Well, well."

He was very happy, Uncle Cornelius was. As if he had put something over on everyone. And he had, too. He fooled them all.

Chapter 6. In Which the Dead Man Meets Hegel

"I feel a sense of duty to you, boy," Uncle Cornelius told Cory. "After all, you're the one on the receiving end of the family's bad business. You're the one losing face."

He was sprawled on the sofa under Hegel's portrait, grinning foolishly. Cory, looking at him, felt a rush of gratitude. He was the only member of his immediate family to take his troubles seriously. Except, perhaps, for Peggy, and he wasn't sure she counted.

"A sense of duty," he echoed wonderingly. "Really?"

"Ho ho, really, boy. You come from quite a family, I hope you know. Quite a family, yes. Complicated. Your father, for instance, bless him. Did you know he set me up in business? A generous man, your father. He didn't have to do that, not really. He came to me one day and he said, Cornelius, why don't we start a new division of the Rasmussen Dental Fabrication Works? I said, are you kidding, Grouper, a new division? And he said Yes, I thought perhaps we should add a line of dental supplies. Brilliant, I told him. Absolutely brilliant. Here I was, Captain Cornelius Rasmussen, U. S. Army, Retired, out of the Quartermaster Corps, certainly qualified to deal in supplies, but what did I know about dentists? Grouper knew I didn't know anything about the family business. Now we have salesmen all over the Tristate area. Every dentist from Pittsburgh to St. Louis, from Chicago to Memphis buys from Rasmussen." He fell into a kindly, inward reminiscence.

"You were talking about the family's bad business, not its good business," Cory reminded him.

"Ha. So I was, so I was. Well, now. Eventually, of course, you are going to have to talk to the Dead Man. You know that, I suppose. I imagine Brother Grigory passed that on, did he? Lives upstairs, the Dead Man does." Cornelius pointed at the ceiling and gave a secret little smile.

"Upstairs? Here?"

"Sure, why not? Nobody knows who he is, though I have my suspicions, I do."

"Who do you think he is?"

Cornelius sat up and looked around. He lowered his voice to a conspiratorial whisper. "Don't tell anyone."

"OK."

"My father."

"Oh. Your father. Right." Cory was nodding. "Your father, sure."

"You don't believe me," Cornelius said with a smile. "But I believe it's true. He's Boss Rasmussen. Used to be, anyway."

"Boss Rasmussen? Withrow was talking about Boss Rasmussen. He changed the name of the Warriors. In '08."

"Right. He was Boss of the city for years. He fell on tough times, eh?"

"Uncle Cornelius, you're going a bit too far. If Boss Rasmussen was the most powerful man in Valhalla at the turn of the century, the Dead Man couldn't be him."

"No? Well, never mind. It doesn't matter. Withrow!" he shouted suddenly.

"Hi." Withrow stuck his head through the doorway from the front. He grinned and winked at Cory.

"Do you still have the diary?"

Withrow nodded.

"Whose diary is it?"

Withrow smiled. "Francine Depew."

Cory frowned so intensely that his bandages wrinkled and a ring of fire shot around his face. "Grandmother Francine?"

"That's right," Withrow agreed.

"What was her diary doing in my ceiling?"

"As I said, the building where you live did not have a good reputation. In the 1890s 1001 Celestial Street was the most famous cat-house in Valhalla."

"Ha ha," Cory laughed without humor. "And ha ha. Withrow, what is this? That's ridiculous. It implies that my grandmother was a prostitute. That's absurd. Grouper would never allow it. Belle would never marry the son of a p-p-prostitute!"

Withrow shrugged. "She was very beautiful," Uncle Cornelius assured him. "I remember her."

"This is too much. Too damn much. Last night I saw a man killed in front of my eyes. The Dead Man was there. The police..."

The door at the back of the room swung open and the Dead Man shuffled in. His breath whistled in his large nose. His steps were very tiny and careful, and his head wagged back and forth as if he were saying No to the universe. When he saw the group in the room he stopped.

"Don't talk to me," he said. "I'm a dead man." He fell into a sorrowful stance, leaning slightly to one side. "A dead man," he repeated softly.

"Of course you are, father," Cornelius said.

The Dead Man looked up. "Father? Whose father? I ain't your father, sonny. Not me. I'm nobody's father. You're not talking to me, no. I'm a dead man."

Cory did not expect much from him. "I wish Hackamore were here," he told Withrow. "She can talk to him."

"But you're Norman Rasmussen," Cornelius told the Dead Man. "Boss Rasmussen."

The Dead Man shook his head. "Nope," he said. "Not me. Not me. I can't be him. I'm just a dead man. In charge of the dead vote, I was, but I remember, I remember." He fell into a slough of remembering.

"What do you remember?" Withrow asked gently.

"Eh? What's that? No, it wasn't in the spring, it was in the fall. November. As if it was yesterday. The flames! The whole waterfront was burning. And shots, too. A colonel in the Salvation Army right in front of me, he fell down. A tiny hole in his forehead, so small. You wouldn't

253

think a hole that small could kill a man. One minute he's standing there singing *Onward Christian Soldiers*, swinging a club, the next minute lying in the street, his face lit up by City Hall. City Hall was burning, too. He was smiling, but he looked surprised. I remember. Baxter told me." He looked up. "Didn't he?"

"Baxter who?" Cornelius asked.

"Baxter Who. I don't know Baxter Who. No, his mother was Henrietta, just like Norman's. And then she died. It was awful. Disease everywhere, even on Mount Worthy. People filled the church, a new church it was, with a monastery. Full of foreigners, Albanians. The church was crowded, I remember that, crowded with sick people. They said, don't go in there, it's the plague, people are dying in there, and the screams, awful, they were, the screams, I was a young man then, a young man. Once I was young, not like now. I was alive once." He looked around hopefully. "Wasn't I?"

Withrow nodded. "Sure you were. Who were you?"

But the Dead Man didn't answer. He was staring at Hegel's portrait over the couch.

"That's him," he said.

He sat down on a plain wooden chair beside the table.

"Who?" Cornelius asked.

"Baxter Who?" the Dead Man said. "Not him again. I don't know him."

"I don't think he's your father, Uncle Cornelius."

"Perhaps not. He does seem confused, doesn't he? Well, never mind."

The Dead Man was staring at Hegel as if he were a member of the family who had disappointed everyone. He no longer answered when spoken to.

The others shifted uncomfortably. The presence of the Dead Man was dampening conversation. Finally Cory cleared his throat. "Um," he said.

"Uncle Cornelius. What about the, uh, the curse. You mentioned bad business." He glanced at the Dead Man, who was sunk into contemplation of the poster, but whose

254

eyes were turned inward. As he watched, the eyes dropped shut, and the Dead Man seemed to fall asleep. His mouth dropped open a little, exposing perfect dentures. Cory looked away.

"Yes," Uncle Cornelius said vaguely. He appeared to be sunk into the same gloomy contemplation as the Dead Man. "Bad business. Betrayal, and revenge. Oh yes, they're going to get revenge. They're after us, you know."

Cornelius looked into the silence of his lap.

Cory waited, but it appeared nothing further was forthcoming from either his uncle or the Dead Man. They had settled into a silence which gathered a kind of negative momentum moment by moment. Cory felt they might vanish into that silence before his eyes.

Uncle Cornelius sighed and climbed to his feet. "Well, Cory," he said. "It's been nice having this chat. We don't get a chance to talk much, do we? We must do it again sometime. Soon." He patted Cory on the shoulder and left with Grocery Dog.

Cory watched him move from the gloom of the store to the brilliant sunshine in the street. It was hard to believe that 560 miles overhead a 184-pound Russian basketball twenty-two inches in diameter called Sputnik was orbiting the earth at 18,000 miles per hour. Cory found it as impossible to understand as what was happening to him down here. He looked back at the Dead Man.

The Dead Man was seated at the table with a litter of books on Existentialism before him. His eyes were swallowed up in a network of tiny wrinkles, his chin was on his chest, and his gnarled hands were clutching each other as though they were two different people locked in mortal combat.

Chapter 7. In Which Cory Has a Religious Experience

"Hi. Can I come in?" he asked.

Hackamore Ovandrill stood in the door of her apartment and frowned. It was a pretty frown, a symmetrical mix of uncertainty, puzzlement and curiosity. "Who are you?" she asked.

"You don't recognize me?"

"I can't say I do. You look a little like Snooky Lanson. Or Wernher von Braun. Oh, Cory!"

"Can I come in?"

"No." She closed the door.

Cory sighed and knocked again.

The door opened. "Why," Hack said, "if it isn't Wernher von Braun. Come on in. I've been expecting you."

Cory turned to go. "I'm in the wrong place."

She laughed and grabbed his arm. "No, no, this is the right place. Now, where have you been? I haven't seen you in a week. Not that I care, of course, but I was a little curious."

"You don't care?"

"Cory, you are such an ass. Of course I care."

"Then what did you do to your apartment? I was here by myself a week ago, and it did not look like this. This looks like a tent or something."

"It is a tent. This is material from India. I find it inspirational."

"Inspirational?"

"For my yoga."

"And what's that you're wearing?" He wandered around the room touching the billowing walls, earthy reds and yellows glowing where they were backlit by a window. Material covered every surface of the room but the floor, which was scattered with satin cushions. The bed was gone. All the furniture was gone.

"It's called a djellabah. From Tangier. Do you like it?" She swirled around, and the material billowed up. Cory caught a glimpse of plump white thigh, and sighed.

"Yes," he croaked. She took his hand and pulled him down onto a pillow. She touched his face in wonder. "It's rubber," he told her. "I got it at one of those theatrical costume stores."

"It looks real," she assured him. "But it doesn't feel real. I suppose it does look better than those bandages. How are you? And seriously, where have you been?"

He frowned, but the mask did not convey much of the expression. The mask remained relatively cool, disinterested, aloof, casual. The mask gave Cory everything he might ever want. The mask made him a Subterranean, "hip," as Kerouac was to say the following year, "without being slick...very quiet, very Christlike." Was Wernher von Braun hip? Was he quiet? Was he Christlike? Cory did not know. He did not really know very much about Wernher von Braun.

"I've been around," he said. "I'm fine," he said.

Hackamore didn't believe him. "I don't believe you," she said.

"No. Really. I'm fine."

"Bullshit, Cory. You're terrible. Your voice is terrible, hollow and empty; your posture is terrible, bent, sagging and unhappy. You have a deep spiritual sickness. I know, for I am a minister's daughter and spirit is my Daddums' business, though I think he may not really be very good at it, but still, I can spot that kind of thing a mile away; you should take up yoga."

"No thanks." It was true. Cory was depressed. Of course, his voice was empty and hollow because it was trapped in this rubber mask, which had a sweet damp smell to it, a rubbery Halloween flavor. He just wanted to be Wernher von Braun, famous rocket scientist, a man with a mission.

"I will not, I think, take no for an answer. Lie down."

"No," Cory said, lying down.

She took his hands and slowly massaged his palms with her thumbs. He sighed. She took off his shirt. He said, "What?" and she said, "Shh."

She took off his pants. He did not protest. She massaged his feet. His feet curled with pleasure. She sat back and looked at him, her white djellabah billowed around her. "You're skinny but beautiful," she said.

He opened his eyes. His lashes curled up through the eyeholes of his mask. He looked at her, and asked with his eyes whether she was kidding. She must be kidding.

"Are you a virgin?" she asked.

"Not exactly," he said.

"Good. That means you nearly are. Marsha Willoughby doesn't count."

"How do you know about Marsha Willoughby?"

"Ha ha," she laughed gently.

"The only woman in Thule, Greenland, was the dietitian. She was a major, and wouldn't sleep with any rank below warrant officer. I was a corporal until I left. She was beyond my reach."

Hackamore smiled, stood up, and in one sinuous gesture pulled the robe over her head. She was naked.

"And now I want you to watch. I am going to demonstrate some basic postures. First the *halasana*, or plow position. You have been in the presence of this position before, but do not remember. You were asleep; but then, as the Master says, nearly everyone's asleep."

Lying on her back, she lifted her legs very slowly straight into the air. Slowly she lowered them over her head until her toes touched the floor behind her. "It's helpful," she said with some difficulty, "to the back, effective in increasing blood flow to the legs and in reducing fatigue. And now," she lowered her knees, "I am going to demonstrate the *yoganidrasana* posture, or Vishnu's sleep as it's called — extremely effective in balancing internal disharmony and stimulating sexuality."

258

She reached out with her hands and clasped the soles of her feet; then, very slowly, she lowered her knees all the way, until they rested beside her elbows. Blood suffused her head, and a slight giddiness visibly lifted her spirits. Cory was entranced by this demonstration.

She wrapped her hands around her ankles, so that her armpits rested against the insides of her knees. Her fingers lay along the outsides of her ankles now, draped around the soles of her feet. Her lovely large breasts cupped her chin, and she gazed between them through her dainty pubic shrub at naked Cory leaning on one elbow with a visible erection and an invisible smile.

"As you can see," she grunted, "this opens up the *yoni*, allowing energy to flow through the genital chakra. That son of a bitch Gabriel Flagg at least left me with an understanding of the importance of energy flows and a goodly supply of muggles. Not to mention an unwanted pregnancy."

Cory saw a momentary sadness flick across her face, but she was flushed and her breathing labored, so he could not be sure. But she was right, her posture certainly did open up the yoni. And it was, as she told him then, the doorway into this world, a fountain and a receptacle or container worthy of veneration.

Then she taught him the proper ways to venerate. He learned quickly.

Chapter 8. What the Pappers Said

Cory did not understand the calculus. The little letters and numbers were meaningless. *Calculus for the Liberal Arts*. He did not know what that meant. The professor was asking him a question, certain Cory could not or would not answer the question.

The professor was right. Cory stammered. His face slipped, sagged, melted, became someone else's. Wernher von Braun. Wernher would know the answer, he was good a mathematics. As soon as he became Wernher von Braun, he answered the question. The professor looked surprised. He took out a gun. He was tall and pale and bald and his head glittered as he aimed his gun.

"Yes," the professor said. "But I asked Mr. Depew that question. Where is Mr. Depew?"

"I'm sorry," Cory said. "I apologize." Then he said it again. And again.

Then he woke up. Across the street someone was saying, slowly and with great effort, over and over, "I'm sorry. I apologize."

Each repetition of the sentence was punctuated with a slow, solemn thump. Cory yawned as he walked over to his window. Across the street Wilmer Dougherty was straddling his house guest in the gutter. He was banging his house guest's head on the curb. His guest was apologizing, but Wilmer followed each apology with another bang of the man's head against the curb.

Cory watched for a while. The repetitions were monotonous, even-toned, and loud. He looked at his clock, ticking loudly on his night stand. It was 2:45. Wilmer and his friend were directly beneath a street light.

"It's quarter to three," Cory said softly. "Don't mess with Wilmer. He's a martial artist."

Yawning, Cory pulled on his clothes. He pulled on his

rubber mask. Then he looked at himself in the mirror. The mask was very lifelike, especially in the dim, scattered light from the street. He could fool anyone into thinking he was not a Depew, and that he knew the calculus.

His chinos were slick with dirt. He hadn't been to the laundromat for a long time. Perhaps he should do his laundry? He gathered a bundle together without looking it over, just some dirty clothes from the floor, and stumbled out his door.

Suzy from upstairs was just coming through the entrance of the building.

"That guy Wilmer's crazy," she assured Cory as if this were a perfectly normal time to have a conversation. "He's gonna kill that guy."

Cory nodded. His breath was loud against the rubber lip of his mask. Condensation was already beginning to form inside the forehead, but it did not seem to hurt as much as it had.

"Wernher," Suzy said, "I've been meaning to ask you, do you know what happened to that nice kid who fixed my sink?"

Cory nodded again. Was this really happening?

"What?" she asked, looking at him. Cory pointed at himself.

"That was me. What are they fighting about, do you know?"

"That was you!" Suzy snapped her fingers. "Of course. You know, you look older. Wilmer's house guest threatened to throw Wilmer's hi-fi out the window. I could hear him as I got out of the car. My boy friend just dropped me off."

"How'd he like the whip you got him?" Cory felt foolish standing in the dim entryway of the former brothel at 1001 Celestial Street holding an armful of dirty clothes at three in the morning discussing whips with his upstairs neighbor, but Belle had always told him it was important to be polite and ask people about themselves.

She smiled. "He loves it." she said. "You wanna

261

see?" Without waiting for an answer, she turned around and pulled the back of her slacks down, exposing her buttocks. They were delicately striped with pink welts.

"Very nice," Cory told her. "I have to do my laundry."

"Look," she said, pulling them down further. "On the thighs too."

"I already have a girl friend," Cory mumbled, moving toward the door. Suzy pulled her pants up, disappointed.

"I'm sorry. I apologize." The phrase followed Cory up the street until the door to the laundromat had closed behind him. Cory pushed his clothes into a machine and fed it quarters. "It's my quarters to three," he sang.

"Chew!" A voice commanded. Cory jumped.

"Me?"

Brother Grigory emerged from the shadows by the dryers. "Chew! Follow me!"

"But my clothes?" Cory protested.

The monk crooked his gnarled forefinger. Cory followed.

They trudged in silence up the deserted street toward the dark mass of St. Credula, her hands outstretched in silhouette against dark autumn clouds fat with rain. He was sure to be asked some tough questions about the calculus now. This dream was certainly taking some peculiar twists. And it was funny; it felt so real, not like a dream at all.

The church was even darker than the street. At the far end, candles flickered and guttered around the altar. A series of linguistic associations went through his mind as they walked in single file up the aisle, footsteps echoing too loudly. The word gutter, he thought. It means sewer. Why do candles gutter, then? Because the melted wax makes channels in the sides, through which the melt flows, like a sewer. His father was part owner of the Depew Sewage Treatment Plant. Of course. And his life, his very existence, seemed to be in the gutter. Wilmer was killing his house guest in the gutter. His clothes were dirty. But he was washing them. At three in the morning again. Brother

262

Grigory vanished behind a screen. Cory sat down on a small bench a few inches high. His hands dangled between his splayed knees.

"I'm not really Wernher von Braun," he confessed. "I just get him to do my math for me."

"Shoddap," Brother Grigory said from behind the screen. He lowered his voice. "I have pappers," he said.

Cory nodded, apparently unaware that Brother Grigory could not see him.

"Pappers!" the monk hissed.

"Yes," Cory repeated. "Papers."

"Thirty-four yarss ago a man maked confession," the monk said. "He gave me pappers. The Dead Man." There was a long pause. Then Brother Grigory said, very distinctly, "Awntralss. Refench!"

"What? Refench? What's that?" Cory's voice shot around the huge empty stone room a dozen times, colliding with itself on the way back.

"Pappers," the monk said again, in a different voice. He crept around the corner of the ornately decorated screen on which Cory now saw were graphic depictions in gold and red of St. Credula's terrible ulcerations. Brother Grigory was holding in his hands a folder tied with maroon ribbon and stuffed with papers. Cory reached, and the monk snatched it back. "*Okhi*! No. Thiss pappers are some, not all. One pappers iss pig awntralss. I read over and over thousand timess. Max naw senses. Crossed fortunes and loss of face."

He seemed to lose his dense accent when he recited, as if he had been carefully coached in the correct pronunciation. The effect on Cory was uncanny.

Loss of face!

"The time line of the esophagus is twisted three times, each twist a generation....In the stomach we find a human tooth...the presence of twins in the family."

The echoes died away. Candles hissed as they guttered, little sewers of waxy meltdown flowing onto the gold cloth.

263

Suddenly Brother Grigory said in a very loud voice: "The Lord who made thy teeth shall give thee bread!"

Cory shuddered violently.

"Chore dastiny," Brother Grigory hissed, "iss to discover yoursalf." His voice changed from the mantic declamatory style; it became abruptly matter-of-fact. "Not moch, such dastiny." Cory could hear a shrug in the monk's voice.

"I suppose not," Cory said softly. He was looking at the papers Brother Grigory had pressed on him, but the light was dim, and nothing was clear.

"Chess, sarr!" the monk said. "A small dastiny. Very tiny. Goodbye."

"What?"

Cory heard a faint scurrying sound as the monk swished out of the cathedral, hidden by the iconostasis. He stuck his head around it when he realized that Brother Grigory had left him, but it was too late.

Cory returned to the laundromat; his wash cycle was completed. His clothes were compressed against the sides of the washer in a random spray, and it occurred to him that his life was like that, compressed, random and disorderly.

It was time to dry, to fluff, to give body and shape back to his clothes. As they tumbled in the drier behind the little round window, lifeless and dull, he reflected on the night's events.

Wilmer might be down the street still, banging his house guest's head on the curb. Suzy would be caressing her welts, admiring them in the mirror, twisted awkwardly so she could see. Vincent Black Shadow Lavere would be roaring through the dark, dark wind tearing at his spiky hair and filling his white teeth. Marsha Willoughby might have left the Silver Spoon only a few moments ago, with or without her husband, her small pink eyes squinted against the gibbous moon hanging over the horizon. And Withrow, he would be dreaming of Don and Phil and the way they heroically met the dilemma of Existence by embracing the Void in song.

He thought of Hackamore Ovandrill, visiting her parents' mansion once more, out there on the Serpent Mound. Built right over the eye of the Serpent, the Reverend's home was. He was sure of that, for he had checked it on the map. It was there he had been lost in the fog, there he had backed into her father's Cadillac, there he had tried to arrest the solidest, most respectable and important citizen of the entire Schachter's Landing area. He blushed inside his damp mask to think he had actually drawn his gun on that wonderful girl's father.

She was wonderful, too. Her limbs were plump and limber, her mouth was wide and sweet, her teeth uneven and white, her face open and honest, her yoni venerable and warm.

He worshiped her. Her father worshiped Jesus Christ, Gentleman, and he worshiped her father's daughter.

His clothes marched to a halt, bringing meditation to a halt as well. It was nearly four o'clock in the morning. The moon was down, and so, he presumed, was Marsha Willoughby. It was Marsha Willoughby who had led him out of his virginity, and it was Marsha Willoughby who had pushed his face from his skull.

Never mind. The first few sweet measures of the woodwind line of the larghetto of the Mozart Clarinet quintet began to thread through his mind, and he was soothed. Those were haunting notes, solemn notes, mystical notes. He looked at the paper his held in his hand, and wondered how it got there. His clothes were stilled in the drier, invisible below the porthole.

It was an old piece of paper, carefully preserved. He had already heard what it said, and when he read it over again, there was nothing new.

"What the pig said."

It was signed by Dexter Pendragon Willoughby, Sinker Seer. Another Willoughby.

Greed and betrayal in the arrangement of the intestines as they fell. The time line of the esophagus is twisted three times, each twist a generation. In the stomach

265

we find a human tooth. Four generations then. Double branchings of the trachea, rejoining twice—this is a very unusual pig... Cory broke off reading and grinned in his mask without humor.

"This is a very unusual pig," he said aloud. "Where did this paper come from? Whose is it? Why do I have it, and is it about me?"

The laundromat was silent.

"I don't know," he said. "I will find out. It is my dastiny to discover myself. Ha. Greed and betrayal. Twins. Ancient forgotten crimes and a curse. The Lord who made thy teeth shall give thee bread. Over the entrance to the Rasmussen Building." He sighed deeply. He gathered his clothes together and trudged back down Celestial Street through pools of streetlight and shivered as he trudged. The moon, goal of Wernher von Braun's dreams, was gone, leaving a dim glow above the westward horizon, and Cory understood that Wernher von Braun's dreams were not his own.

Chapter 9. A Picnic

Cory staggered under the dead weight in his arms. "What's in here?"

"Lunch," Hack assured him. "Just lunch."

"For how many?" He spoke with effort as he lurched down the steps on her front stoop. "Feels like enough for a regiment."

"Well," she paused to count. "There is you, and me, and Vincent Black Shadow, and Withrow and Peggy and of course Buster. That would be six, but I don't think Buster will eat much. He's only three."

"Everybody is coming on this outing?" In fact Cory was delighted. He felt a rushing wave of good feeling toward everyone sweep through him. They had all been swell through this, his face falling off, and the shooting at the Telltale Heart, and jail and bail and oh, everything. Just swell.

Hack was beaming. "Yes, everyone. The whole gang. I ran into the girl with the lizard and asked her, but she was busy. She had a lot of trouble getting the lizard back from the police, it seems. They impounded him."

"Godzilla?"

She nodded. "It ate one of the policemen's money. Twelve dollars. He wanted it back."

Cory was laughing inside his mask. He staggered on down to his DeSoto and put the huge picnic hamper in the trunk. The rusty hinges creaked miserably when he closed it.

Hack appeared with an armful of blankets and pillows and sheets of colorful Indian material. "There's a place up there to picnic, and it's a lovely day for this time of year, but we might want to put up an awning. Open the trunk again, please."

He nodded seriously as he creaked it open. "Right. An

awning. You're amazing."

Vincent Black Shadow roared up in his bike, spurted a couple of small doughnuts of black smoke from its exhaust, grinned wildly, and handed Cory a paper bag with two bottles of wine in it. "It's local," he shouted, shutting off the motor in the middle so that the word "local" echoed with the sounds of his dying engine.

"Local?"

"Depew Vineyards Estate Bottled Burgundy, Vintage 1954. It is a truly dreadful wine, but it does contain considerable alcohol, all things considered. The Lone Ranger would drink it."

"I'm not the Lone Ranger."

"And I'm not Tonto. Still, it'll do the job. Hey, I hear you start at the zoo tomorrow."

Cory nodded. Cleaning up.

Vincent winked and raised a thumb. He gave a tug on the bottom of his leather jacket, zipped it up tight, and let out a war hoop. "Bee-ootiful day," he said.

"You want to know something?" Vincent leaned forward to Cory's ear. "My ancestors," he whispered, "are buried in the Serpent Mound." He stood back with satisfaction, arms crossed like Tyrone Power in *Pony Soldier*.

The sky was blue and cloudless, the wind was swift and chill, the air was clean and pure, and the street had a Sunday stillness about it. Cory stared at Vincent, and Vincent stared back with a smug expression. Finally Cory said, "Does Hack know?"

Vincent looked horrified. "Does Hack know? No. Think of the guilt, kemosabe. Here her father, a man of God, lives in the old Depew Mansion, a house built right on top of my ancestors. The desecration! It would devastate her. You mustn't breathe a word of it to her. Promise me you won't say a word."

Cory shrugged. "All right."

"What are you two whispering about?" Hack asked, coming down the steps with a pair of folding lawn chairs.

268

"Oh," Cory said, nonchalant. "Nothing."

She smiled. "Sure. By the way, Vincent my friend, I have something rather dreadful to tell you."

He frowned. "Oh?"

Cory pushed the lawn chairs in beside the wicker hamper.

"Yes." Hack was speaking seriously. "I found out, just yesterday. I think perhaps you'd better prepare yourself."

Vincent made a show of preparing himself. "All right," he said. "I can take it."

"Well," she said. "It's about the Serpent Mound. It's your tribal burial ground."

"No!" Vincent exclaimed.

"I'm afraid so. It's a very sacred place for your people. The girl with the lizard is an anthropology major. She told me. I'm very sorry. You see, our house is built right on top of it. It's been there for ages, that house. Since the 1850s, before the Civil War. Of course, it was Depews who built it, so I suppose it's not my fault."

"I would never blame you," Vincent said seriously. Then he winked at Cory. "But to tell you the truth, I was just telling Cory about it. I learned it yesterday from my grandmother, who lives out in Schachter's Landing. Don't worry about it. If you worry about anything, worry about the house. It might be haunted."

Cory was thoughtful through this exchange. He was thinking about Hackamore Ovandrill's house. "Why?" he asked suddenly.

"Why what?" Hack and Vincent both asked.

"Worry about the house."

"Well, if the Serpent Mound is a burial ground, it might be hollow, filled with burial chambers. The ground might not be too, er, stable, you dig?"

Cory smiled at the joke. "Well, the house has been there for over a hundred years. Nothing has happened. As for being haunted, though, that's a different story."

"What do you mean?" Hack asked.

269

"They used to have seances or something like that out there. Your grandfather, I think. Did you ever hear of Dexter Pendragon Willoughby?"

Both of the others shrugged, No.

"He was something called a Sinker Seer. I have a document, given me by Brother Grigory, called 'What the Pig Said.'"

A pretty little furrow appeared between Hack's brows. "Who's Brother Grigory."

Cory told them about his two meetings with the monk at the laundromat. "This paper seems to be a piece of fortune telling, taken from pig entrails, or, as Brother Grigory called it, awntralss. Anyway, it seems to apply to my family, although there are a lot of things in it I don't understand yet."

"You don't actually believe in that stuff, do you?" Hack asked. "Because there's something else I think we might really have to worry about."

"What?" Vincent Black Shadow asked.

"My father is putting in a bomb shelter. Below the basement."

"I see what you mean," Cory said.

A yellow VW bug clattered up, and Withrow, Peggy and Buster tumbled out.

"Well, if it isn't the Existentialists," Cory said, and they smiled, and Peggy gave him a little sympathetic squeeze for his fallen face, and Buster jumped up and down making car noises, and it was several moments before Cory realized Buster was making noises like Cory's DeSoto, which did, he felt, have a rather distinctive voice.

Then Cory slammed the trunk lid, and they all climbed into the DeSoto, which screeched into life of sorts, and clanked down Hackamore Ovandrill's street away from the University south toward the countryside and the hills all colors of red and orange and yellow and tumbled with fallen leaves, so that the twiggy branches of all the trees were sometimes bare and sometimes not, and clouds of many colors danced in their passage, and the summer

270

meadows had turned tan and stubbly with cut corn, their furrows filled with last night's rainwater reflecting the deep cobalt blue of a faultless sky.

During that drive out into the country where Cory did, indeed, recognize the name of the Mozart Cave because it was his beloved composer's name, but not the cave itself, for it was one of the lesser-known attractions of the Valhalla area, Cory forgot who he was and what his pain, and laughed with the rest of them, oblivious to ominous clouds gathering just beyond the western horizon, and to the darkness coming behind it, as he had forgotten the darkness which had preceded this very day, the death and violence at the Telltale Heart when a pale balding man had tried to kill him for reasons Cory could not understand although he knew it was true. He had forgotten also his hideous night in jail, and the sick sensations he felt whenever he thought of his evening with Marsha Willoughby. Her pink rodent eyes. Her pale skin, her peculiar speech, her relationship with Dexter Pendragon Willoughby whose prediction seemed to involve some kind of doom.

It was a lovely Sunday afternoon, after all.

Chapter 10. The Mozart Cave

The afternoon had been a great success. The picnic was a delight, Cory felt better than he had in weeks. He was surrounded by friends. Peggy and Withrow brought their guitars and sang soft songs, and after they sang and drank some wine, and smoked up a bit of Hackamore's muggles, they all hiked to the Mozart Cave.

An old woman took a dollar apiece from Hack and Cory, who pretended they wanted to go down into the dark earth, while the others laughed and jeered. The old lady worked in a small building that looked like a gingerbread house fallen hard on stale times.

"Is this place safe?" Cory asked. If she recognized Wernher von Braun, she gave no sign.

"Hah hah," laughed the old woman. "I been here near thirty years. I seen 'em come and I seen 'em go."

"What does she mean by that?" he asked Hack, who shrugged with a laugh. Her laugh was a package of lime and lemon Necco wafers at a special Sunday afternoon matinee.

The old woman shoved a grimy mimeographed page across the worn counter to him. MOST AMAZING WONDERS OF NATURE EVER SEEN! the page announced. THE PLACE WHERE MOZART WAS MURDERED! it said. !!!SEE BLIND FLESH-EATING FISH!!! !!!KILLER DINOSAUR BONES!!! !!!UNBELIEVABLE FOOTPRINTS OF PREHISTORIC GIANTS!!!

"Prehistoric giants?" Cory asked.

"Sure," she said. "Big shambling brutes twenty feet tall." She cocked her ancient head and blinked at him with eyes that glittered wickedly. "Sure as my name's Gertie Sly you'll run into 'em. Footprints this big!" She held her hands a yard apart. "Look careful, you can see they had

272

toes."

"Toes."

"Damn right. Toes. Horrible misshapen toes, with evil hooks on 'em. Probably still some of the brutes in there, way down where no one's ever been. People hear 'em down there, sometimes. The Mozart Caves go on forever underground, they say. Forever. Ain't no end to it all, just tunnels and galleries and holes in the earth where the damned souls wander, lost as punishment for doin bad. You could get lost in there. Science fellers say they were all filled with rivers, oncet, but now they's just the underground crick. And the fish. Don't stick your fingers in. Tear the flesh off in seconds, those fish will."

"You're kidding," Cory assured her, close to laughter. Tiny tears of merriment squeezed between his lids.

"I don't kid, sonny. Ask the Boy Scouts."

"Boy Scouts?"

"Sure. If you see 'em. Been in there more'n a month, they have." She burst into an extended bout of a kind of wheezing cackle which it took Cory a long moment to realize was laughter. "Lost, heh heh," she gasped. "A whole goddam troop of them, lost, oh, my God, hahhah." Finally the merriment subsided and she blinked again.

"Wonderful," Cory said doubtfully. Outside, He turned to Hack. "I don't like it," he told her. "It's dark."

"Oh, Cory," she said irritably. "Don't be an ass. I have a flashlight."

The Indian summer sun slanted across the dark opening of the cave and gave a sharp preternatural clarity to every bare branch around it.

"I just don't like it," he repeated, but more softly than before.

She held a flashlight in one hand, and led him with the other into the darkness. It was high enough for them to stand, but too narrow for them to walk abreast, so she pulled him through a series of curves until the honey light of all outdoors, of sun and of life, was gone, replaced by a palpable dark as thick and dense as hot tar. The path, which

273

Cory could not see since Hackamore Ovandrill was in front holding the light, felt as if it were descending. He thought he could hear the scrape of Prehistoric Giant toes on the rough limestone of the floor.

Abruptly the cave opened out, and he could stand beside her. His breath was short and he felt a little dizzy, in part from the muggles and in part from the fear. The room they were in was so huge the light from her torch could not reach the far wall; it could only reveal an endless series of smoothly undulating mineral draperies, thick, half-melted columns, the sparkle of spear-points depended from the ceiling and the broken trunks of tan stone scattered across the jumbled floor. A man-made path wound among the shattered trunks and waxy columns. A spill of mining tailings sloped up the wall. "Where they used to dig out the feldspar," Hack told him. Far away they could hear a dripping, an occasional creaking, a bell-pure splash.

"I don't like it at all," he said, too loudly, and a crashing series of echoes thundered back at him, "At all, at all, atall, atallatallatallatall." When they had died away, there was a momentary pause, a sharp crack as some fragile mineral growth gave way and fell, and then, after an intolerable wait, a terrifically loud crash as it splintered on the floor.

"Damn," he whispered.

"Shh," she shushed him, whispering too. "Come on. I want to show you where Mozart was killed."

"Why?" he asked, but she was already moving and did not hear.

As they walked along the path, the flash revealed only circles and ellipses of the cave, which began, in some obscure and extremely unpleasant manner, to resemble the insides of a living organism, an intestinal sequence of cilia and looping peristaltic contractile muscles. It was, Cory told himself, an illusion born of the bad illustrations in his freshman biology text and bred by his too-active imagination. But he couldn't help thinking that the Prehistoric Giant was all around him, preparing to digest.

They found the river.

"Look," Hack said, and the cave answered back, "Look, Look, Looklooklook."

She pointed at the water.

A pure white fish hung in it as if suspended in air. The water was invisible it was so clear and free of mineral or motion.

The fish was three inches long. It had no eyes.

"I wonder what it eats," Cory said.

"Boy Scouts," Hack assured him. "Don't stick your finger in."

"Ha ha. That fish isn't big enough to eat a Boy Scout."

She shrugged. "You're probably right. They do get bigger lower down, where the Killer Dinosaur bones are."

"Right," Cory whispered. "But higher up than where the Prehistoric Giants still live, shambling around in the darkness looking for blood to drink. And etcetera."

"Probably," she agreed, offering him another Necco wafer of her laughter: chocolate.

She led on, across a series of stepping stones in the shallow river, and through another series of rooms and galleries and open cathedral spaces.

"I wonder if that old woman owns all this?" Cory asked, and she stopped so suddenly he bumped into her.

"Don't you know?" she asked, staring at him.

"Know what?"

"Your Uncle Cornelius owns this place. It used to supply the Rasmussen Dental Fabrication Works with feldspar back when they still made teeth out of porcelain."

"You kid me."

"Nope. Come on, the room we want is next. It's where Mozart and Manfred Hauser died."

"Hauser is my mother's maiden name."

"Sure. It's common name around Valhalla. German."

They were working their way through a small passageway when she stopped.

"Now," she said. "Take off your mask."

275

"What?"

"Go on, take it off. There's no one else here."

"No."

"All right. Goodbye. I'll just leave you here." She had the flashlight. He was plunged in instant darkness deep as a sock.

"OK, OK," he shouted into the dark. The passageway muffled the sound. "I'll take it off!." He pulled off the mask. Hack's hand touched his in the dark. She took the rubber thing, deflated now and without form.

The light came back on. She led him through the twisting passage until it opened into a vast cathedral of reddish rock streaked with yellow, which in places seemed to mix to a fleshy tone.

Once they were in the huge room, her torch revealed what it was that had startled Augustus Mozart when he first saw it.

Some mineral had turned most of the stone of the walls jet black; the chamber appeared to be decked in mourning crepe. All except the Prehistoric Giant.

She was a flesh color so real she was alive. And she was twenty feet tall, or would have been if she were standing.

But she was not standing. She was reclining on a bed of black cloth, and she was naked, and her posture was utterly obscene and inviting, one crude stone hand placed near her crotch with an unmistakable gesture.

She looked very familiar.

"Wow," Cory breathed.

At the same moment he realized it was an illusion. There was no naked Maja there, no woman: the configuration of mineral deposits gathered over the centuries had formed a vaguely human shape which, from this angle and in this light somewhat resembled a reclining woman. There could be no denying the eerie shiver that went though him as he gazed across the cavern into the darkness of that tunnel toward which the hand was pointing, a narrow canal out of which unspeakable things would be born.

"Mozart probably said something similar," Hack whispered. "Eerie, isn't it?"

"I know," Cory said. "It's Saint Credula."

She smiled, beckoning.

They walked forward, hand in hand, to the giant's feet. Her vaginal tunnel was dark, dark. They bent down to look. Hackamore Ovandrill held the light.

Cory gave a sharp gasp of surprise. "There's a face in there," he said aloud, and the cave gave it back to him, "Face in there, in there, inthere, face in there, there."

It was his — his own pink, unformed face gazing back at him, about to be born for a second time. How, he wondered, had he managed to get himself born the first time?

BOOK THE SIXTH: GROUPER, 1923

Chapter 1. Grouper Aloft

As usual, Grouper was lost.

It didn't bother him, much; the afternoon was too fine, with light cumulus clouds that seemed born to wander over the green patchwork of Indiana.

Back at the grass field in Chicago he'd fallen into conversation with another student pilot named Charlie Limburger or some such, and lost track of time, so he was running a bit late returning to Valhalla. It didn't matter; wind whined in the wires, the wing spars creaked as he bumped over rising columns of air, his engine roared. He glanced up at the tube that gauged his fuel supply and saw it was still half full. This was one of the finest aeroplanes he had ever owned, not like his old Curtiss JN-4 at all, but a really sweet aircraft, and although he was a superficial pilot, as one of his instructors had put it, he had total confidence in himself. He had crash-landed too many times to be alarmed at the prospect: usually he just ran out of gas.

A certain violet tinge was gathering in the air. It would be dark soon. He began to whistle.

His father Baxter Depew, an erratic man who gave a disturbing impression of schizophrenia, had given him his first plane, a clumsy biplane of mongrel origins, part Curtiss Golden Flyer, built in 1911, but with a heavy water-cooled 8-cylinder Tetrazzini engine which produced 76 horsepower on a good day. Almost immediately he had driven it across the grass field they called an airport and plowed through the white fence at the end, a good day for the Tetrazzini, but a bad day for the plane. The mongrel never flew again.

His mama Francine doted on him and gave a little cry of alarm when he wrecked the plane; his father appeared to have forgotten that he had, in fact, presented him with the machine, and expressed indifference to its destruction.

He got another, a Standard E-1 fighter-trainer built in 1918 with a Le Rhone 9-cylinder 80 horsepower air-cooled rotary engine and fabric skin which now decayed quietly into the soil of a Tennessee cornfield where he had dropped it one inclement afternoon in the summer of '19. So he got another. And another. Francine could refuse him nothing. But this one, this was a sweetheart, a nearly-new 1922 Curtiss-Cox Cactus Kitten, the last of four ever built, a racing triplane with a top speed of 196 miles per hour.

Up ahead the river was winding sluggishly through the low hills: his only problem now was to decide whether to fly upstream or down. Navigation was not his strongest talent as a pilot, but he wouldn't have to go far either way: he would hit Louisville if he went west and Cincinnati if he went east; Valhalla lay in between.

Quite by accident it seemed he arrived precisely on target: the succulent outlines of Valhalla from the air looked considerably like a naked woman lying slightly on her side, her buttocks jutting into the air, curved into the bend of the river, with the furrow of the Little Hawking Valley dividing them. Mount Worthy made one lovely hip, and the hills above the Cliffside area where the Negroes were beginning to move were breasts, drooping one over the other gently down to the soft blanket of green elms beside the river. It is true he had to squint for the illusion to be credible, and the light had be just right (as it was at this moment, slanting across Indiana and the river, dappled with cumulus shadow), and his altitude and position had to be correct (he steered a bit to the southeast in order to see her at her most open, vulnerable and inviting). But if he did these things, and approached over Schachter's Landing from the south it looked as if her vast green legs were spread a little and the fuzzy brown patch of buildings and dusty streets beside the Little Hawking formed an inviting pubic triangle.

The truth was that Farley Rasmussen Depew roiled with lubricious juices of a frustrated erotomania. Only in the air, where columns of heated atmosphere rising beneath

281

cumulus clouds lifted him and smacked him down again when he emerged, was he safe with his unspeakable lusts; and so he flew on and on, hour after hour, neglecting his main concerns at the Rasmussen Dental Fabrication Works, where he was head of the business, a business about which he knew practically nothing, and in which he had no interest. His real interest was flying around the body of Valhalla, exploring all its imagined secrets and dark mysteries. This, he told himself, showed he was in control of his glands.

He circled Schachter's Landing in a frenzy of fantasy lust, squinting to soften the crudities of her outline, to turn the buildings and dust into soft curly hair, the V-incision of the boat club into labial folds, the slow curve of the Little Hawking into the gentle buttock-furrow of her supine form, and darkness gathered and for a time aided "Grouper" Depew's imaginary coitus. And then his Curtiss C-12, 12 cylinder V, liquid-cooled 435 horsepower engine began to cough. It was time to forsake this peculiar passion and land. He looked around for a field.

He shrugged. There was an airport of sorts in the small of his beloved's back, and while that was not ideal, it would have to do. He would crash if he tried to land on the gentle mons of the Serpent Mound: too many trees.

So he approached the meadow beside the Silver Spoon, a speakeasy and gambling spot near the Louisville highway. He'd been there before, and as usual he cut it a little too close and had to glide in the last couple of miles, making a cross-wind landing that had him bounding and veering across the grass in one of the worst successful landings of his career.

Which was how he met Belle.

"That was the worst landing I've ever seen," she said when he climbed down into the growing gloom. "And I've seen a lot."

"Really?" he asked indifferently, preoccupied as he was with a badly twisted wheel, result of a buried rock, invisible in the grass and evening gloom.

She was leaning on the fence at the edge of the meadow a few yards from the Silver Spoon, which at times doubled as the terminal building. Inside a radio blared out some scrawky jazz from WVVA, the Voice of Valhalla. She had bobbed hair and red lips, a sullen smile and a dangerous air. At least it looked dangerous to Grouper, but to him all flesh and blood women were dangerous.

"Farley Depew," he said, extending his hand. There was little he could do about the wheel until daylight.

"Oh," she gave a little Southern curtsy. "Belle Hauser. I like to watch the planes."

"Why is that? Do you fly?"

"Oh no. I would never do that. But they do seem to be, I don't know — powerful. I like that."

"You like big machines?" Grouper's curiosity arose and stiffened. Belle seized his hand, gave it a perfunctory shake and dropped it.

"Oh, ah just lo-ove them."

His imagination took a swerving then; she liked big machines! The broad naked body of Valhalla's environs faded, replaced by a dim Gibson Girl of the imagination, patterned on the even dimmer vision of his doting mother Francine, whose red nose was always proudly asniff, and whose clothing harkened back to a more sedate era, with long tailored shirtwaists and leg-of-mutton sleeves, an ivory cameo broach at her throat. Yet here was Belle Hauser, with crimson lips and swelling hips. Grouper forgot his enormous earthy bride. Here was one of flesh and blood, dangerous perhaps, but as enamored of big machines as Grouper himself.

"Would you like to have a drink?" He gestured to the Silver Spoon. Belle gave a little nod, and they went inside.

The Voice of Valhalla was informing the world around just then of the discovery, earlier that year, of Tut-Ankh-Amen's tomb near Luxor, Egypt. The Voice of Valhalla was the most powerful radio station in the world in its day, and felt it fitting to concern itself with the opening of the 3400-year-old tomb of what had once been

283

the most powerful voice in the world of its day. The public relations minds at the radio station thought that way.

Grouper, known at the Silver Spoon for his hearty "Come on group" when he bought a round of drinks, had no trouble gaining both entry and service. The bartender had, on the spot as it were, invented a new drink called "The Toot Uncommon."

It tasted awful, but Grouper was delighted. Mixology was sort of a hobby of his; his competitive spirits were aroused.

Chapter 2. In Which There is a Courtship Only Moderately Successful

"Oh, the rockets red glare, bombs bursting in air, oh hell."

Belle and Grouper were singing off key when Grouper forgot the words. The crowd had grown with the darkness outside, and a brisk traffic in Toot Uncommons had developed; the bartender had replaced his bathtub gin with straight grain. No one complained.

Belle's crimson lips grew brighter, too, and Grouper found himself unable to take his eyes off them: behind their bright crimson her teeth flashed when she sang. For the first time in his life Grouper was attracted to teeth. All those long days when he actually bothered to go down to the Rasmussen Dental Fabrication Works he saw teeth, row upon row of teeth. Never before had he paid attention. Now he did. Her teeth had qualities: a strength and power, a square determination, a subtle intelligence, an incisive keenness, a canine devotion. He failed to notice the perspiration which marred the powder on her cheeks, nor was he aware of minor imperfections in the shape of her legs, a slight thickness in the ankles, concealed by silk stockings. All he noticed were teeth.

He tried to make her laugh. When she laughed, he could see her teeth, and looking at her teeth produced in his muzzy bosom sensations as close to those of flying he had ever had on land. A slight giddiness, a closeness of breath, an exhilaration.

His "Oh hell" produced the laughter he had hoped, and Belle's mouth opened wide. He leaned slightly forward to peer into the depths of her mouth and slid from his stool, stumbling against her. She leaped back in alarm, and he placed his head against the gardenia pinned to her dress.

285

She reached uncertainly to stroke his hair, half disgusted and half intrigued. Her father the good physician had never given her quite the same kind of admiration this man seemed to be giving, and she felt perhaps there was something a little wrong in it.

So she stroked Grouper's dark hair for a brief moment and then pushed him away. "Don't," she said, not unkindly.

He moved away, and banged the small of his back against the corner of the bar. A wince of pain passed over his honest, empty face. For a tiny moment, quickly forgotten, that pain was premonition.

She put her hand to her mouth, and gave a little cry, "Oh!"

"Sall right," he said, waving away her concern. After all, he was a pilot, and she liked big machines. "Wanna dance?"

Was that a hot Charleston the band was playing? The absolute latest? It? "Oh," said Belle. "Oh, twenty-three skidoo!"

"I haven't heard that since I was a kid," Grouper told her as they began to bang their knees together and kick out their heels. "Oh, twenty-three skidoo." They were having a good time. He could tell.

Later, on the trolley into town he thought perhaps he should get Francine to buy him a car. She liked big machines. She liked drinking. She liked everything he did. She had wondrous glowing teeth. Her only defect was a certain shyness, perhaps. A reluctance. Grouper was not sure; he lacked experience in these matters. Francine, to the extent she could, had always managed his affairs. Grouper had no idea that Francine's extent was not far, that the quantities of charlie she hauled into her nose increasingly impaired her faculties, that she lived in another country, a land far from the one her son, Grouper Depew, inhabited. All he knew was that Francine was the most beautiful, most intelligent, most sophisticated woman in the world, and that he would never be worthy of her.

Perhaps, though, he might be worthy of this radiant

doctor's daughter; after all, she liked big machines.

The trolley was a big machine. Perhaps he should buy a trolley. Then he realized that he already owned a trolley. This trolley, in fact. After all, he had considerable stock in the trolley company. At least he thought he had stock in the trolley company. Tomorrow he could ask his business manager if he had stock in it. And if he didn't, why not?

"I have stock in the trolley company," he said. Instantly he regretted it. Did it sound like showing off? He looked carefully at Belle's swimming face, but her expression would not stay still long enough for him to read it.

Overhead the wires hummed. Grouper's complex alcohol-drenched erotomania hummed as well. He reached into his pocket to readjust himself on the pretext of getting out some gum. "Gum?" He asked, offering her a stick of Juicy Fruit.

Belle sniffed. "No, thank you," she said; disapproval was an electric sign flashing on and off on the Times Square of her face. Grouper had visited New York between colleges and had seen what everyone called the eighth wonder of the world. Now he considered Belle's face to be that wonder. She didn't like gum!

"I don't care for it myself," he assured her. "Never have. I carry it to offer people. How about a cheroot?"

She averted her eyes.

He was lighting one. He loved smoking these cigars with square-cut ends almost as much as he loved flying. His head was soon wreathed in smoke. Ashes dropped on his shirtfront. The night was warm and close. The trolley wheels clattered and clanked in a soothing rhythm. Grouper sighed.

"Ahh," he said. Belle did not reply. His eyes drooped. His cheroot dangled from his lips. He was a powerful young man, a wealthy man, a significant figure on the face of the earth, a citizen of Valhalla. He had beside him a woman. Tomorrow he would buy an automobile, and they would take drives in the country. Later they would be married, and he would fly over the contours of her body looking for succulent places to land.

The landscape slithered past them, corn and meadows, farms and fields. Small woods tossed like coins onto the dark emptiness. Grouper stared at it all. The trolley squeaked to a halt for a moment at a railroad crossing, and in the light from the train passing Grouper saw a huge animal standing beside the tracks, staring into the trolley directly at him. A beast with lowered head, small eyes and huge tusks. A beast of the whitest white, covered with bristles.

A pig.

He was never sure later whether it was Belle's cry or the smell of smoke that awoke him. All he really knew was that his shirt was on fire, and that he would carry a tiny irregular burn scar on his left breast for the rest of his life.

A scar that was nothing to the one he would carry on his soul. Belle was doubled over with laughter. "Oh, my God," she said, over and over. "Oh, my God. You're on fire! Oh, God!" Her hand was on her mouth, concealing her lovely teeth. When she took her hand away to slap her knee in delight, Grouper saw that her teeth were stained crimson by lipstick. She looked as if she had been eating something freshly killed and her mouth was full of blood.

He wanted desperately to take her to bed.

Chapter 3. In Which the Chicken Escapes

Belle took Grouper with her to a *session*, as it was called. It began badly; the chicken made a terrific mess.

The event was at the Reverend Archibald Ovandrill's house in Serpent Mound. Archibald had officiated at Mayor Dudley Worthington Depew's funeral thirty-odd years before; since then his metaphysics had grown increasingly eccentric. Now, at the age of 82, he was some kind of occult crypto-Theosophist who had adopted as his protegé a young man from Slyville named Dexter Pendragon Willoughby, a nephew of his wife's. Dexter had brought the chicken.

Grouper and Belle drove out to Reverend Ovandrill's in his brand new Hispano-Suiza touring car. Even Grouper was impressed by the size of Reverend Ovandrill's estate. He gave a shrill whistle when he saw the house. "This guy does pigs? Pigs and chickens?" He pulled the handle of the emergency brake, and all four chrome-plated wire wheels locked in place, spewing gravel against the underside of the car.

"I'm sure I don't know what you mean by that," Belle sniffed. "Does pigs and chickens, indeed. This is serious exploration of areas as yet poorly understood, but the reading of entrails in an ancient art."

"I don't know much about art," Grouper admitted. "But it sounds fairly disgusting."

Foxworth met them at the door. "Good evening," he said politely. But Foxworth was always polite. He was paid to be polite.

"Good evening, Foxworth," Belle said. "This is Mr. Depew."

"Good evening, sir," Foxworth said.

"Good evening, Foxworth."

"A pleasure to meet you, sir."

"A pleasure to meet you, too, Foxworth."

"Please come in, sir. And Miss Hauser. Reverend Ovandrill is expecting you."

"Thank you, Foxworth."

"Thank you, Miss."

"Come on, group, this could go on all night," Grouper muttered.

The entryway was roughly the same size as the nave of the Cathedral of St. Credula. Foxworth took Grouper's hat and coat and hung them in a closet. He took Belle's wrap of dead foxes and placed it in another closet. He led them through a series of arches, room after room, to a salon at the far end of the west wing.

Grouper was there introduced to Dexter Pendragon Willoughby. Dexter was extraordinarily tall, extremely pale, with sprouts of vigorous blond whiskers like small misplaced goatees growing from the points of his cheeks. The cheeks themselves were sharp, and the overall effect was eerie in the extreme. He looked like an apprentice devil.

"Dexter's one of the blessed," Belle told Grouper. "An angel."

"Really?" Grouper asked.

Foxworth appeared with drinks. "Ah," said Grouper with enthusiasm. "Drinks."

"The Reverend does not approve of alcohol, sir," Foxworth informed Grouper. "These beverages are non-alcoholic."

If Grouper was disappointed he managed to conceal it. He did, however, make frequent trips to the lavatory during the evening where he was well served by a silver flask. He felt quite benign by the time the chicken appeared.

Reverend Ovandrill was seated in a wheelchair. A soft gray afghan covered his legs, and his watery eyes peered myopically around the room. Belle brought Grouper quite close, so the Reverend could see him. "This is Farley Depew," she said in a loud voice.

"Farley who?"

"Depew, Reverend Ovandrill. Farley Depew."

"Depew? Did you say Depew?"

Grouper could not tell whether Reverend Ovandrill was hard of hearing or merely a bad conversationalist.

"Yes, Reverend Ovandrill. Depew."

"Oh, sorry. I thought you said Depew."

Grouper nodded, his hand outstretched for shaking. Reverend Ovandrill ignored it. He seized, instead, on Belle's soft hand and buried his mouth in her palm. Then he rubbed her hand over his face and sighed deeply.

"How's Wally?" Belle asked the Reverend sweetly. Grouper wondered who Wally was.

"Wally? Wally? Wally is fine. I believe he's at Yale now. Yes, I'm sure of it. Isn't Wally at Yale, Foxworth?"

"Yes, sir, your son is at Yale Divinity School, sir."

"There, you see?" Reverend Ovandrill said smugly. "I knew it. He was always sweet on you, Belle. Wally always liked you. Who's this?"

"Farley Depew, Reverend. You just met him."

"Of course, of course. Never mind."

"Well, if we're all ready, perhaps we should get started." Dexter stood beside the fireplace. The rich carving on the marble mantle providing a fitting backdrop to Dexter's stature and pale complexion. The mantle was seven feet high; so was Dexter. The marble was white; so was Dexter. They had been made for one another.

"He's from Slyville," Belle repeated. "They're all Sinkers up there. That's where he gets the Gift."

"What gift?" Grouper asked in a husky whisper. He had just made a trip to the lavatory, and was feeling tolerant and sociable.

"The Gift. Prophecy."

"Oh." Grouper nodded vigorously.

"He's almost never wrong," she assured him. "It's quite wonderful, really."

"I'm sure it is," Grouper said. Covertly he looked more closely at Dexter Willoughby and the mantle. The

291

carving on the mantle and around the fireplace represented life in the city of Gomorrah in Biblical times. Gomorrah was once a real city west of the Euphrates, and life there was not all that different from life in other cities of the period. The mantle had picked out some of the more interesting, some might say lurid, aspects of urban life to dwell upon; Dexter's left hand was brushing the smooth, rounded buttocks of a man engaged in breaking the Biblical Commandment against coveting things belonging to one's neighbor. In this case, several things belonging to one's neighbor.

"You can stop nodding," Belle told Grouper.

"Oh. Yes." Grouper stopped nodding.

Foxworth appeared bearing a large speckled hen with wild eyes. "Here is the chicken, sir," the butler told Dexter. Dexter frowned. The expression pinched the points of his cheek goatees toward one another so they almost met in front of his nose. Grouper found himself nodding again.

"Stop that," Belle whispered sharply. "You're embarrassing me."

Grouper did not want to embarrass her. He wanted to embrace her. He stopped nodding.

"Thank you, Foxworth," Dexter said, taking the chicken.

"You're quite welcome, sir," Foxworth replied. He left the room.

"Hah!" Reverend Ovandrill cleared his throat. The sound, in the silence which had followed the entrance of the chicken, was startlingly loud, and occurred at the same time Dexter had reached to the mantle to bring down a large ritual carving knife, presumably for purposes of sacrificing the chicken, though the candles had not yet been lit.

"No pig?" Reverend Ovandrill sounded disappointed.

"Not tonight," Dexter answered. "Too messy for the living room, wouldn't you say?"

"Harh!" the Reverend said. "I want a pig! Get a pig."

"Are we the only ones here?" Grouper started to ask

Belle, but at that moment the pullet panicked, fluttered violently in Dexter's arms, and because he had one hand reaching up for the knife, she got away.

"Foxworth!" Reverend Ovandrill shouted in an unexpectedly loud voice, wheeling his chair violently toward the crimson ottoman where the chicken had momentarily roosted.

"Do something," Belle hissed at Grouper. He started uncertainly toward the hen, but she scrawked viciously and fluttered off the ottoman toward the open door. Dexter interposed himself, waving the knife, his other hand out in a shooing gesture. The hen backpedaled, reversed course, and deposited an archipelago of panic droppings in a broad semi-circle on the Persian carpeting.

"Get a pig," the Reverend shouted. "This chicken is no good!"

Grouper found himself, some moments later, standing in one of the islands with a crazed chicken in his arms.

For a moment he locked eyes with Dexter, who had his knife raised over his head for a downward stroke. Then Dexter lowered the knife and looked away.

Grouper handed the hen to Foxworth, who had finally appeared.

"Thank your, sir," said the butler.

"Thank you, Foxworth," Grouper replied.

"Foxworth," Dexter said. "Let us go do the pig, shall we?"

"Certainly, sir. The pig."

Grouper retired to the lavatory. When he returned, Dexter was bent intently over a silver platter spattered with guts.

When it dawned upon Grouper what had happened and what he was looking at so curiously, he could not help himself.

He vomited. Profusely. Onto the Persian rug beside one of the little gray islands of the archipelago. It was the beginning of a chronic problem.

The whole evening turned out badly.

293

Chapter 4. What the Entrails Said

Cornelius is such a sad sack, Grouper was thinking; colorless issue of a colorless woman. As soon as he left a room in which Cornelius' mother was sitting (and she was nearly always sitting) Grouper forgot the shape of her face, the size of her body, the color of her hair. He could hardly believe that she was the wife of the mysterious man who had been called Boss Rasmussen.

"A penny for your thoughts, Honey," Belle said. She didn't really mean it; she was, in fact, distracted by the paper in her hands and really wanted to tell Grouper her own thoughts, but she had been brought up properly.

"Uh," Grouper grunted. He must do something about Cornelius. It was only fair that Cornelius have a place in the family business. He knew that. Grouper wanted to be fair. After all, Cornelius was Grouper's close relative. But what could Grouper give him to do? Grouper himself didn't know what to do. Old Alonzo Schmitzer ran the company without any help from Grouper Depew.

Belle looked up at the grunt. "What did y'all say, Dear?" she inquired in her sweet southern voice.

"Eh? Oh, I think I said, 'Uh.'"

"Uh? You said Uh? That doesn't seem like much of a thought, Grouper."

"Thought? Why would that be a thought?" Perhaps he could create a division of the Rasmussen Dental Fabrication Works for Cornelius. Now that was a thought. A whole new division. Give Cornelius the responsibility. Most likely he would botch it completely, the division would sink without a trace, the company could take a tax write-off. Those new tax laws were so complicated. Grouper got a headache just thinking about them. Now that Cornelius was out of the army, he would have to have something to do, and this could just be it. Then, when he failed, Grouper could reluctantly ask him to go, and RDFW would be entirely his.

"It's quite amazing, isn't it, Honey?" Belle switched the subject over to the one she intended to discuss in the first place, this paper in front of her.

"What's that, Dear?" Grouper assumed Belle was referring to sex. They were on their honeymoon, after all, billing and cooing like a pair of white doves at this new resort hotel on Lake Drowning Sow in the hills south of Valhalla. It was spring, and they were seated in wicker rocking chairs on a huge veranda which stretched the length of the white wooden building. An old-fashioned carriage clopped down the dirt street before them. No automobiles were allowed within the resort confines.

It was a romantic spot, perfect for the mutual exploration of this peculiar new human activity called sex.

Belle didn't care for it.

For that matter, Grouper didn't care for it either. Not nearly as much as he thought he would. But perhaps in time they might get used to it.

"This paper, Honeybuckets. Dexter's augury. 'What the Entrails Said.'"

"What the entrails said?" Belle had been carrying that paper with her ever since his humiliating experience at Reverend Ovandrill's house last year. Now that he thought about it, he realized she had referred to this augury more than once in the intervening months.

Grouper was so distracted these days, Belle thought. His business was doing so well, but with his father Baxter drifting in and out of some mysterious disease, Grouper worried constantly. The last time she saw her father-in-law, though, he had appeared in the best of health. "Yes, Pumpkin, What the Entrails Said. Dexter sees such interesting things, don't you agree?"

She was tormenting him. That was it, her sweet southern voice was in fact dripping sweet southern venom. Constantly reminding him of his humiliation that night when he threw up on the Reverend's rug. So he grunted again, "Uh."

Another carriage clopped by. Dust rose from the street, flies rose from the horses' droppings. The trees all around were flushed with new green, rising sap, reproductive juices oozing all over the place. Not far away was the Mozart Cave. Cornelius had acquired title to the Cave, and controlled the flow of feldspar to RDFW. This thought made Grouper grind his teeth even as it had helped him decide to offer Cornelius a place in the business.

In the distance yellow sunlight danced off the ripples on the surface of the lake.

"Did you say 'Uh' again, Marshmallow?" It was so difficult to keep his attention sometimes, business affairs, or his father's health, preoccupied him so. He was a very important person in Valhalla, though, and he was dashing, and he did love aeroplanes.

"Yes, Cupcake, I believe I did." Why couldn't she leave him alone? He had forgotten his desperation to bed her. It just hadn't been what he expected it to be. Perhaps they were doing it wrong? And again, he had forgotten her perfect teeth. But he remembered them when he glanced over at her, and she was smiling at him, and that lovely translucent dentition gleamed in the afternoon sun of Springtime. He basked briefly in their glow.

"I am going to tell you what the entrails said, Buttercup." She smoothed the paper in her lap. The very lap in which Grouper had been trying to find his way these past few days. Belle had held out for marriage, and he had finally succumbed. After all, her father was a prominent physician, and Francine had blessed the union in her absent, doting way.

"Uh," he said, sinking once more into the problem of Cornelius. Dental supplies? Cornelius had been in the Quartermaster Corps during the Great War (later known as World War I, to distinguish it from the other great wars that followed). Dental supplies would be perfect for Cornelius. Expand their line of false teeth with a separate division. Grouper felt a flush of pride at his business acumen, then. It was, he thought, the first idea he had ever had.

Belle was reading. "Crossed fortunes and loss of face are evident in the shape of the liver. There is confusion written there, a result of crimes committed in ignorance; greed and betrayal in the arrangement of the intestines as they fell."

Grouper felt ill again. Her reading brought the sensations of that evening back to him. "Uh," he grunted. "Nonsense. It's all nonsense. Chickens, pigs, pah!"

Belle smiled sweetly. "Wishful thinking, Grouper. Wishful thinking." She went back to reading. "'The time line of the esophagus is twisted three times, each twist a generation. The twists are unusual. In the stomach we find a human tooth. This too is significant, though the meaning is not clear.' But of course that is your business, isn't it, Dear Heart? Teeth. So this augury must be about you. I confess I can't really make out what it all means, though, and it seems I've been thinking about it forever."

Grouper rolled his eyes. The white boards of the balcony over his head contained no meanings either. He looked out at the lake, but the light was bright and glaring and insanely dancing. Just when he had an idea, too. He wished he were up in the air, in his plane, banking through the vast seductive body of Valhalla. Now that he had been exposed to the real thing, he thought the landscape, on the whole, was more attractive. Belle's ankles were thick.

"Well," she continued. "'Four generations, then. Double branchings of the trachea, rejoining twice — this is a very unusual pig — indicate the presence of twins in this family. It is not clear whether there are two or three sets of them.' Do you think we will have twins, Grouper?"

He knew how to distract her from this terrible litany. It required sacrifice on his part, though. Great sacrifice, just to do his husbandly duty. He looked deeply into her teeth. "Come on, group," he said in a husky voice. "Let's go up to our room."

"Must we?" she asked. Grouper thought the expression before him might represent eager anticipation.

297

"Yes," he rasped. "We must."
"Very well," she said, bright with forced cheer.

Chapter 5. In Which There is a Visit to the Cave

The hostility between Grouper Depew and Cornelius Rasmussen was intense, mutual and absolutely *never* mentioned. In each other's presence they maintained a hearty civility. This was a façade as elaborate and false as that on the Rasmussen Building in downtown Valhalla; it fooled nearly everyone. But for his part Cornelius felt that he was the true heir to the Rasmussen Dental Fabrication Works; after all, he was Norman's son; his name was Rasmussen. Yet his father alternately ignored him and doted on him. His colorless mother had retired into a brittle somnolence from which she awoke only to perorate, in a drab voice, on injustices inflicted upon her by her husband, who suddenly, on the eve of becoming acknowledged Boss of Valhalla, appeared to lose, if such were possible, what small interest in her might have remained.

True, Farley was younger, but his mother was older. Francine was 43 when her son was born. Grouper represented the tenth of Francine's pregnancies, the only one who survived to term. This failure rate didn't appear to concern her; she doted on her only misbegotten son with a single-mindedness powered by cocaine. The world was quite unclear to her, but it was also not particularly important. Nothing was important except her supply of sniff and her son Farley.

For his part, Grouper grew up detesting Cornelius. He detested him because he was older. He detested him because his own father Baxter Depew looked so much like Cornelius' father that they might be twins, though of course this could not be since they had different last names. Everyone said they were cousins.

Now that Cornelius was out of the military and

apparently ready to go to work, Grouper's dislike intensified. Cornelius' presence meant constant contact. Day-to-day, business and social contact.

Grouper ground his teeth. Somehow, and he could not discover the way of it, but somehow Cornelius had acquired possession of the Mozart Cave. He owned the damned thing. Outright. Grouper's attention was elsewhere. Now it was necessary to give Cornelius a job. Very necessary. So Grouper considered himself the most benevolent of relatives, the kindest, most generous, most gracious. Almost a saint. Belle certainly would approve. So he ground his teeth.

So he suggested this little trip down to the cave to see what wonderful old Cornelius had been doing with it besides ripping feldspar from its bowels, since they were in the neighborhood on their honeymoon anyway.

It was absurd. First they had to take one of these ridiculous carriages out of Lake Drowning Sow Resort; an hour wasted watching an unmatched pair of horses defecate before their very noses. Then they got in his powerful new automobile and discovered that the fuel tank was dry. Another hour wasted. It was high hot noon by they time they emerged from the dense forest of the hillside into the open where the Cave was.

"Oh, look!" Belle exclaimed.

"What?"

"Over there, by the trees."

It was looking straight at him; it appeared when the pig was sure Grouper had made eye contact, it moved leisurely along the tree line, watching the carriage all the time as it rattled along toward the cave. Finally the huge white form drifted silently back into the forest and vanished. They arrived at the cave, and again Grouper gaped.

"Oh," Belle clapped her gloved hands together in delight, the swine forgotten. "How quaint."

"Quaint? Quaint?" His voice squeaked.

"Oh, yes," Belle drawled, not looking at him. "Ah

300

think its chah-min'." She had lapsed into a gushing southernness Grouper found detestable.

"Chah-min'," he muttered. "She finds it chah-min'."

There was a new structure beside the cave, a structure which certainly would have been worthy of Arlene Bethany Rasmussen Wilberforce: a gingerbread house.

"Come on, group, a gingerbread house?" Grouper said. "It looks like a God-damned, son of a bitch, bloody bastard gingerbread house."

"Really, Grouper, you shouldn't curse," Belle told him, entranced before the gingerbread house. "It's not polite."

"Yes, Dear," Grouper said with a sarcasm entirely lost on his bride.

A plump, sunny woman dressed as the wicked old witch was inside the gingerbread house, just waiting for Hansel and Gretel to come tripping along. Like the wicked witch, she was charming and polite.

"Howdy, folks," she said pleasantly. "Nice afternoon, ain't it? Sunny spring days, they do bring up the sap. You folks interested in the cave? Can't say I blame you, it has a fascinating history, truly it does."

"Shut up," Grouper said.

"Haw haw, why Dear, you mustn't say such things," Belle said, slapping his arm. "He doesn't mean it, it's just his little way," she told the wicked witch.

"Honeymooners, are you?" the witch asked with a witchy leer.

"Sho 'nuff," Belle tittered, loud enough to cover the sounds of Grouper's grinding teeth.

"What is this place?" Grouper demanded through his clenched dentition.

The witch looked puzzled. "Why, the Mozart Cave, of course. Quite a famous attraction in these parts. But you know that, that's why you're here, ain't it, now?"

"No," Grouper told her shortly. "It isn't why we're here. We're here because this place supplies me with some kind of rock. Feldspar, I think. For teeth." He grinned wolfishly at the witch.

"Oh, well, of course. You must be Mr. Depew. Mr. Rasmussen told me you'd be along one day. I'm awfully pleased to meet you. My name's Gertie Sly, from up Slyville way."

"Did you see a pig? Over there," Grouper asked.

"Oh, don't you worry about him," she answered with a smile. "That's only old Diabolus. He's a hundred years old at least. Smart devil, he is. My cousin Charlie's been hunting him for years, though I don't think he really wants to get him. Charlie Balshajt, maybe you know him?" She spelled it. "Pronounced Ball-Shy-it." She lowered her voice.

"I don't think he's serious about catching old Diabolus. You know why? Because that old pig is supposed to be on a mission." She laid her forefinger alongside a nose, pointing upward. "From the gods."

"Oh." What was the fear that shot through Farley Depew then, and made his teeth ache?

"Now, here's our little brochure," she said in a normal tone. "You might want to look it over before you go into the Cave."

"I'm not going into any cave," Grouper shouted.

"Oh, I couldn't," Belle said at the same time.

Grouper read the brochure. A man named Wolfgang "Gus" Mozart, an immigrant from Westphalia, no relation to the composer ("What composer?" Grouper asked Belle, who shrugged), had discovered the cave. This Mozart was a man with a talent for turning over a dollar. Once he had operated the very first restaurant on the shores of Lake Drowning Sow, perhaps the first one that sold fast foods in the world. Back in 1783 he sold fried venisonburgers with goat cheese to the Indians.

It was on December 4, 1791, the same night that Mozart the composer lay dying in Vienna, that this Mozart had stumbled upon the cave. He and a companion by the name of Manfred Hauser (a very distant relation of Belle's) were exploring the cave. The demand for venisonburgers

302

had died down somewhat since '83, and he'd taken to a little amateur spelunking.

Around midnight Gus entered one of the deepest rooms of the cave, lifted his torch into the air, and breathed in a loud and wondering voice at the sight before him: "*O du schwanz, du, leck du mich im arsch!*"

The brochure did not mention what it was he saw. It did note that Manfred's German was uncertain, but he clearly understood the implications of the words Gus Mozart had just uttered.

An expression of surprise, perhaps delight, this little detail of interpolated history. How could anyone ever know, really, what Wolfgang had said, or how Manfred took it, except by the results? Manfred took it personally, that much was clear from what happened next. But Manfred took everything personally. He took the miserable winter weather, for instance, very personally (it was snowing fitfully). He took Daniel Boone personally, for that matter. ("A bully," Manfred told everyone, though he had never met the man. Only Prudence Sly (known as 'Mammy' in her later years), of all the inhabitants of Slyville, had ever met Daniel Boone, but then there were unsavory rumors about that relationship Manfred preferred not to dwell upon, especially since he yearned quite hopelessly for Prudence himself.

Manfred took darkness personally, and sunlight, and disease.

Naturally he took Gus's statement personally.

He was holding a coil of climbing rope. Since he was standing behind the expedition's leader, he couldn't see the object of Gus's exclamation; he would have taken it personally anyway.

"Lick your ass, you say?" Manfred exclaimed, slipping the noose of his rope around Gus's neck. "Call me a prick, will you?" he screamed, and yanked the noose tight.

His shout of rage brought down a delicately poised stalactite. When the cave was rediscovered fifty years later,

303

his skeleton was still neatly skewered by a spear of stone. The bones of his hand were still coiled by the rope, which was slipped around the neck of the other skeleton.

"Why," Belle breathed with distaste. "That's a disgustin' story."

"Yes," the witch laughed. "Ain't it just."

"Come on, Sweetie-pie," Belle said. "Let's get out of here."

"Yes, Dear," Grouper replied. "Let's."

Chapter 6. In Which Grouper and Belle Look Over an Investment

Belle was excited. Belle worshiped him. Belle thought Grouper was twenty-three skidoo, the cat's miaow. Grouper was sure of it. After six years of marriage Grouper still lacked insight.

"Where are we going?" she asked, yawning daintily behind her gloved palm. It was early in the morning, their wedding anniversary. Mist hung over the Valley, rose in ghost curtains from the brown wrinkled surface of the river, in ripples, in delicate traceries. Forsythia dazzled the dawn eye. Dogwood bloomed in small explosions all over the place; the sun itself was a yellow dogwood blossom in the pale blue-white sky.

Grouper's roadster growled up the gradient of Mount Worthy along Midgard Avenue. Trolley wires overhead sang in the heat. They passed the corner of Celestial Street, and Belle, looking out the window at the passing scene pointed out the huge baroque building on the corner at 1001. "Now that's an old building," she said, and Grouper grunted in satisfaction. Marriage wasn't going to be so bad, after all.

The building at 1001 Celestial meant nothing to him, though his mother had spent so much of her middle adulthood there. Francine was dead now. A small sigh of grief passed through him. She had sniffed right out of the world shortly after he and Belle had returned from their honeymoon. It was as if she had been waiting patiently for Grouper to get married and settle down, and now that he had done so, she could retire.

It was true, Grouper reflected, that the fire seemed to have gone out of her marriage. The old man was mostly paralyzed with stroke, and stared at her with some kind of mute emotion; reproach, or adoration. He had fallen into a terminal silence out of which no messages emerged.

Finally Francine simply dried up, adored to death, worshiped or blamed into abstraction. She became a huge marble statue of an angel with her hands lifted in supplication to the heavens over her own remains in Valhalla's finest cemetery. The sculpture's bad taste was matched only by its cost. Everyone said it was the most artistic money could buy.

Grouper and Belle growled down the slope of Mount Worthy. Across the ravine Grouper could see the Inclined Railway, clanking noisily in the still air as it climbed toward the restaurant at the top. Beyond the restaurant was the Rasmussen Zoo. The thought of the zoo set Grouper's teeth to grinding again. Rasmussen! The name bothered him more and more lately. Cornelius Rasmussen. The Rasmussen Dental Fabrication Works, located in the Rasmussen Building. Boss Rasmussen. Rasmussen Zoo. Everywhere he turned that unfortunate name appeared, mocking him. He was a Depew, and the Depews were an old, established, secure and significant family.

His father, Baxter, had told him repeatedly when he was young that the Depews were important. So why did the name Rasmussen appear everywhere? He didn't know, and now Baxter would tell him nothing.

"Where are we going?" Belle asked again. The downtown streets were quiet this early. A trolley clattered along under their overhead wires, and a few automobiles plied the highways, but there was a pleasant kind of silence, an atmosphere of somnolence and leisure. The new Busby and Conrad Department Store tower was rising on the west side of Heimdall Square. Grouper continued west, out of the basin along the river on the old Schachter's Landing Road. The orange sun, rising behind them, darkened as it tried to burn away the dense mist on the surface of the river to their right. Belle gazed at the thick white pudding without much curiosity. She was worrying about the new domestic help.

306

"Lovely day," Grouper said.

"It's going to be very hot," she answered.

"Still, lovely. Mist rising from the river, sun shining in the sky."

"Humid, too," she said. "Vapors from the river are very unhealthy."

"Unh." Grouper had learned to grunt when Belle got into this mood. He was about to show her something very special, and he did not want her to sour before they got there.

It wasn't going to be that easy. "Why do you always grunt like that?" she asked sweetly. "It's quite unattractive."

Grouper looked at her and smiled. It was his best smile, his most sincere, conciliatory, placating smile. Unfortunately the smile contained teeth grinding over the growl of his engine. Belle smiled back, but hers was clearly sarcastic.

Maybe marriage wasn't going to work out as well as he had begun to hope. But surely she would be pleased when she saw what he was about to show her.

"Shouldn't you be going to the office today?" she asked a little later. The road swooped alongside the river here, and the water, rising from the winter rains and the snows upstream in Pennsylvania somewhere, lapped right at the edge of the paving.

Grouper grunted again. He hated the office. He was constantly reminded that he knew nothing about business or false teeth, nothing of dental supplies. He was reminded by Alonzo Schmitzer, who, although in his seventies, appeared to know everything. He was reminded by Cornelius, who was at the office every day at seven in the morning, developing the dental supply side of the business into the most profitable department. He had twelve salesmen on the road already, after only a year, and was about to add three more. Dentistry was booming.

Grouper frowned.

Then they came around the final turn, and he said,

307

"Here it is."

Belle frowned. "Here what is?"

A large cement structure stood before them, surrounded by a cyclone fence. There was a guard at the gate who saluted Grouper and waved the car on through.

"Can't you guess?" Grouper asked. Belle shook her head no. "Well," he said, a little disappointed, "the sign isn't up yet. But this has been in the papers every day for months now. Tomorrow is the grand opening, but it's already operating at nearly full capacity. A vital part of the life of the city."

She shook her head again. "I don't know what this place is, Grouper. What's that smell?"

"Ah, that's the beauty of it," he said, inhaling deeply. There was a bad smell, but Grouper relished it as a fine perfume. "You see, here is the confluence of the Ohio and the Little Hawking Rivers. It's the perfect location." He took her arm and guided her into the building.

Belle stood, dazed, on a catwalk. Shafts of sunlight slanted down through skylights in the roof onto the huge square pools where pumps thrummed, huge mechanical arms rotated, pipes poured effluents. The sunlight lit up the swirls of multi-colored liquids which met and mingled. Vivid reds, deep forest greens, cobalt blue, delicate pink, purple and violet swirled together, iridescent browns and greens overlapped and blended, shot through with streaks of deep indigo and midnight black. The smell was overwhelming, but Grouper was grinning broadly.

"Isn't it lovely," he said. It was not a question, for he seemed to be speaking to himself in an aesthetic rapture. "The colors. The patterns as they swirl together. The sunlight as it hits the shapes, lighting them up. Beautiful. You know, I like to think of all these different colors as representing the various groups of the city, all the different nationalities and colors and religions and such, all flowing together like this, mingling and becoming one great flow."

"The smell, Grouper. It's awful."

"Well, of course, Honey. That's sewage." Grouper

308

was puzzled. Sometimes Belle was so dense.

"Sewage?" She was truly shocked. "Sewage? You have brought me out to a sewage plant? My God. I'm going to be sick."

She did look a little pale. He took her arm again, guided her back outside. "You do look pale," he said.

"How could you?"

"But, Sweetums, this is the new Depew Treatment Plant. I invested a lot of money in this plant. I had to swing a lot of complicated deals to do it. Daddy was pleased when I told him about it, I could see it in his eyes. This was a city contract. It was very lucrative. I'm going to make a great deal of money, and it's named after us — Daddy, you, me. I thought you'd be pleased." Grouper was genuinely puzzled. It was very nearly the first thing he had ever done in business, and was going to make him a tidy bundle.

"Never," Belle said in a small, tight voice like the overwound mainspring of an antique clock, "never, ever mention this place to me again. Never, ever suggest that we visit it again, if you wish to remain married to me. I find it difficult to believe you thought that I would be interested or impressed with such a disgusting thing."

Grouper never mentioned it again.

They returned to Valhalla in silence. On the way Grouper drove his year-old roadster at high speed into the floodwaters which had risen over the highway while they were at the Treatment Plant. The automobile sank in four feet of water. Belle had to perch uncomfortably on the back of her seat while Grouper swam and slogged back to a farmhouse to telephone for help. It took their marriage a year to recover from the disaster of this day.

Chapter 7. In Which Belle, After Many Years of Marriage, is Finally Introduced to the Family Business

Belle asked her husband what it meant.

"What does what mean?" he asked her politely. They were standing in the street in front of the Rasmussen Building. All of downtown Depression Valhalla was lit up, the Busby and Conrad Tower was atwinkle with Christmas cheer. Vaudeville night at the Valhalla Eleanor Porter Millenarian Club had suffused them both with good spirits, now that Prohibition was over. If Grouper sensed even a hint of reproach or criticism in Belle's question, he gave no evidence of it. He was polite.

"That," she said, pointing up at the motto carved into the plaque of oak above the front door.

"Oh, that." After twelve infertile years of marriage, this was Belle's first visit to the Rasmussen Dental Fabrication Works.

The lettering was ornate: The Lord Who Made Thy Teeth Shall Give Thee Bread. The gilded scrollwork glowed in the soft Christmas lights from Heimdall Square.

"Yes," said Belle. "That. What does it mean, the Lord who made thy teeth shall give thee bread? Some kind of family motto?"

"Yes. After all, we do make teeth, my Dear. The best in the Tri-state area — probably the best in the country. It's all in the feldspar."

"Don't do that, Honey," she ordered, her sensitive ear attuned to grinding molars. "Or you'll have to go back to that dentist in Slyville." Dr. Balshajt, the dentist in Slyville, was no small joke between them. Grouper still suffered the effects of what he continued to think of as some primitive form of vengeance, although he could not for the life of him comprehend what grudge the dentist could hold against him.

"Ha ha." The keys he pulled from his pocket were attached to a long chain which draped across his stomach. He opened the front door and led her into the dark, silent building.

"We lease out the first five floors," he said. "Our business does not require the ground floor so we moved it to the top two. For instance, we lease most of the second floor to a Dr. Thanatopoulos, a Turk or Greek or something. A foreigner, anyway. You'll like him. Well, here." He ushered her into the brand new Otis elevator which, although the electric elevator had been around for more than a third of a century, had only recently been installed in the Rasmussen Building. This modern cab was a cramped cage with an iron grate for a door which clanged shut like the Gates of Hell.

"My, that's loud," Belle giggled. Grouper hadn't heard her giggle in a long time, and felt heartened. True, she had laughed at the Vaudeville, but that was different, really. This was the girlish sound he'd liked the first night they had gotten drunk together.

The elevator's speed control was the size of a tricycle wheel; ordinarily a man named Jeeps, who had been hired sometime during the Great War, operated it, but Jeeps was not on duty when the offices were closed, so Grouper had to operate the elevator himself.

Grouper stopped with a flourish right on target, thinking that it was piloting skills which made him so deft with the elevator, and Belle clapped with delight at Grouper's way with big machines.

His office had a small but efficient bar. The ice bucket was full, and he now performed his alcoholic alchemy in silver cocktail shakers.

This was a moment of peculiar intimacy for a couple who had been married so long, and who had, only eighteen months before, barely been speaking to one another. The tour of the Depew Sewage Treatment Plant had introduced

311

a certain tension into their relations, and Belle spent most of her waking hours criticizing Rebecca for burning the veal birds, a concoction which Grouper thought highly overrated.

Now though, for the first time since that ill-fated afternoon, they clung to one another and giggled, sipping at the exotic drinks Grouper had, as he called it, "whipped up."

He took her out into the workrooms, snapping on the banks of overhead lights. A mellow but inadequate illumination spilled over the benches where presses and molds, calipers and kilns stood shrouded under Sunday canvas dust covers after the six-day frenzy of porcelain dust. Blazing filaments writhed inside the bare bulbs, and the green tin shades of the lamps grew hot. At the far end of the room a dirty window embedded with chicken wire let some of the light out, but none in. Beneath that window outside was the tar-and-gravel roof of the office building next door. The roof was studded with metal vents and pipes, which constituted the view Grouper had from his own office window. It was a constant source of irritation to him.

Alas, many of those pipes led into this very long and narrow room, where they twined across the ceiling in a complex and seemingly random pattern of additions and conversions. These pipes carried inside them various contaminated substances vital to the business of making false teeth: acids, neutralizers, alkalis, steam.

An enormous radiator under the window gurgled and sighed to itself.

"Sort of spooky, Cupcake," Belle said, leaning against Grouper unsteadily.

He put his finger to his lips and tiptoed down the aisle, leading her. Rows of teeth grinned down at him.

Her silk stockings began to whisper an electric thigh-song as she walked behind him, a subtle whisk-whisk Grouper found intensely erotic. A soft implosion in his gut made him gasp aloud. His fingers curled in anticipation of unsnapping the rubber clasps that held those stockings up.

There was a wood-and-glass cubby beside the radiator. The walls were covered with calendars sent to the Rasmussen Dental Fabrication Works by suppliers of dental equipment, manufacturers of large molding machines, and members in good standing of the insurance industry. These calendars displayed young women with coquettish looks who peered under their lashes at Grouper and Belle. They peered also between their legs, bent double away from them, hands clasped delicately behind their knees. They peeped over the tops of their knees, doubled up against their chests, arms wrapped around them.

None of the women wore anything except perhaps lipstick, and a chemise draped artfully to display more than conceal.

"Spooky," Belle said again. And again she giggled. She was not shocked at the calendars, as Grouper had been certain she would be.

Hope leaped in him. "Yes," he breathed huskily. "It is, isn't it."

The soft, electric sound of silk filled the tiny room.

Belle whimpered a little as Grouper groped. For the first time she reached on her own for his painful erection and thumbed it forth from his Pollyanna pants.

Grouper whimpered.

Her voice grew turgid and husky as she told him she was glad he was a member ho ho of the Valhalla Eleanor Porter Millenarian Club.

His hand was now inside her flapper dress. She leaned on a swivel stool against a calendar, eyes closed, mouth open. Her own little bow of lipstick was round with surprise. Grouper buried his face in the soft sweet smell of her neck and his reply was unintelligible. He leaned back and spun the stool so that Belle rose higher in the air, spinning round and round. "Ooooh," she squealed, delighted. Grouper adjusted her altitude with the same dexterity with which he handled the Otis, or his Curtiss-Cox Cactus Kitten triplane.

Silk foamed at her knees.

His target hove into view, clear in this incandescent office. His hands groped at the soft substance of her breasts as she hauled him shamelessly home, and he began with slow sure strokes to satisfy his marital itch in an altogether new way, one bull's-eye after another.

And so it was Grouper and Belle conceived a pair of fraternal twins who would become known as Cornelius and Peggy.

Down the long aisles of the Rasmussen Dental Fabrication Works teeth gleamed in the shadows, uppers and lowers and complete sets, row upon row of them, delicate porcelain incisors, bluish bicuspids and thick sturdy molars, arcs and arches smiling on and on, smile after smile after smile.

Teeth without faces.

Chapter 8. An Unfortunate Occurrence

Belle slept most of the time, dreaming of her husband's office and what she now carried this September of 1936.

Swollen, her delicate body distorted and bulky, she heaved herself from room to room with deep, distressful sighs, reproach in every quaver of every line she spoke.

Grouper spent more and more time in the air above Depression America contemplating his first love, the landscape of the city and environs arranged languorously beneath him. He devoted the remainder of his ground time to the development of new, exotic alcoholic concoctions. Curious and unlikely recipes drifted through his mind as he gazed down into the pubic sprawl at Schachter's Landing or the soft bosoms of Mount Worthy; bourbon and curacao, gin and rum and guava jelly, vermouth with maple syrup and banana puree. Grouper was gaining a widespread reputation for his cocktails, drinks which were known and consumed from Pittsburgh to Cairo, from Chicago to Baton Rouge. The Flamingo, the Suffering Partridge, the Gray Eminence, all were his inventions, drinks praised in films, drunk in lounges in Louisville and St. Louis, ordered with a flourish in night clubs outside of Cleveland, their originator all but forgotten.

Those who knew Grouper was responsible were filled with awe; they were touched by his genius whenever they drank.

Grouper found, during the difficult period of incipient paternity that flying around thinking about cocktails distracted him from certain responsibilities he would rather not contemplate. Fatherhood, for one, bothered him. It appeared an unnatural state of man. Look at his father.

Cornelius also bothered him. Cornelius, popular with the employees of RDFW, Cornelius whose Midas touch turned his very fancies to gold; Cornelius who had taken Grouper's own idea of a dental supply division and turned it into an empire which rivaled teeth in size and profits.

Grouper thought, Well I have talents, too. I can make things. I can create something new, something that was not there before. And it was true. He was the greatest mixologist of his age and region, perhaps of all ages, of the entire country.

His final responsibility was to his own father, who grew daily more incompetent. The old man had taken to a wheelchair to be rolled around the city waving a cane at strangers, propelled by a burly Albanian Tosk, an immigrant in flight from the continuous civil strife that had come with political freedom in 1920. His only utterance was a sharp, unpredictable cry of "*Zogu!*"

Years ago Francine, a pale, alabaster and almost fleshless body, had sniffed herself away, and from that moment the old man too had dwindled. No sign remained of those strange recurrences of robust good health which had appeared before she died. Now he was confined, speechless and erratic, to his chair, dependent on his Albanian; his "cousin" Boss Rasmussen was seldom seen any more either.

This early September day was one of those peculiar ones, with a strange light, a deep orange-violet. Fat cumulus clouds hung around, not white so much as dirty gray, dark on the undersides, with sheets of rainy virga trailing beneath them, evaporating before reaching the ground, but splattering his goggles as he flew through them, stinging his face with cold moisture. He flew in increasingly wild patterns above the city, on occasion plunging himself into wild spins through the clouds themselves, lost in the enveloping gray, surrounded and disoriented.

Those times he would let go of the stick, kick hard on one of the rudders, and wait to see what would happen, where he would emerge. Usually he popped out the side of the cloud, caught a glimpse of the ground in some unusual configuration, tilted crazily, sometimes overhead, or his little triplane would go into an erratic spiral, and he would plunge out the bottom of the foggy dew with the sexual grotto of Schachter's Landing spinning straight ahead, the nose of his airplane plunging toward it with a rising whine as the engine over-revved, and at the last minute he would ease the stick forward and kick in opposite rudder to pull mercifully out of his spin just in time to graze the treetops of the Serpent Mound, where the huge Ovandrill estate sprawled near the old Depew Farms.

There was something about the danger, the odd shifts of gravity, the alternating pressures on his body, that distracted him from Belle's ugly belly and what it meant, that took breath and mind away from Cornelius' depredations on his territory, from his father's irritable grunts and wasted face with its sparse whiskers.

Grouper thought about his father, a cranky old invalid who loved nothing better than to be wheeled out into the country where his chair left deep grooves and loops and whorls in the soft grasses, a kind of unintelligible script only pilots could see; and as he was pushed around he would hoot loud, demented cackles while the Albanian shouted, "Zogu!"

So it was that Grouper's thoughts had naturally turned to his father as he flew about the skies, throttling back to heave his machine into a stall and spin, pushing the stick forward to build up speed, hauling it back gently to climb into the outside beginnings of a loop, and then, when upside down at the top snap suddenly into a half-roll to complete a lovely maneuver which was named after Max Immelmann, the German aviator who developed it, and who died at 26 in the Great War, 1916. Grouper would spin down again through a cloud, grinding his teeth, mind only half on flying, and as a consequence, as so often happened, he ran his gas tank dry and had to make an emergency landing.

The usual abdominal sinking hit him when the engine coughed, followed by the usual elation when he knew he

317

was going to have to prove his skill once more. Then a sinking when he considered that this beautiful Stampe was likely to become scrap, followed by another bout of elation when he thought that this would be an opportunity to get another aeroplane, this time, he thought on his way down, a Macchi MC.72, perhaps, the classic Italian competition seaplane that had set the world all-time seaplane speed record of 440.698 mph, the last racing seaplane designed by Mario Castoldi. It had a 3000 horsepower Fiat AS.66, 24-cylinder V, liquid-cooled engine.

That aeroplane was fast as hell, it was true, and he could land it on the river! He was tired of this biplane anyway, with its relatively underpowered Renault 120 horsepower engine. The Macchi was very fast. But then, it might not be very maneuverable. Perhaps the Stampe was a better plane, really. After all, it was an improved version of the De Haviland Tiger Moth by Jean Stampe, the Belgian De Haviland agent. He'd put ailerons on both wings for greater maneuverability. Yes, he should try to land gently.

Meanwhile up there, a new drink, his greatest yet, had come to him: a subtle blend of Angostura bitters from the bark of a Brazilian tree, Japanese rice wine and French cognac. He thought perhaps he might call it the Gloria Mundi.

Wind whispered through the wires, flowed swiftly along the fabric surfaces of his three wings, hissed over the cowls and burbled through the row of exhaust outlets on each side of the engine housing. The wind sang a song to him, the Song of the Crash.

Ahead was a field. He was west of Valhalla. He must have strayed while he was spinning through that last fat cloud, for he had attempted pulling out of the spin into a barrel roll while flying blind in there, and perhaps he had miscalculated. As he emerged the field was canted at an eighty degree angle, which he quickly corrected. Once into an approach glide, he felt free. There would be no problem. The grass was scribed with curling lines like writing.

He was not certain where he was, though it had to be

close to Serpent Mound somewhere. Perhaps near the old Depew Farms. The sun was in front of him, setting beneath the clouds. When his altitude was low enough the sun came out and blinded him.

It certainly looked like a farm. Dark shapes which at first he thought might be shrubs, and then realized were not. They were, it couldn't be, but they were: Pigs. This could be serious.

It was one of those peculiar coincidences, this intersection of two completely separate events. But down there on the open field the taciturn Albanian was wheeling the old man around the old Depew horse farm. Perhaps the old man had memories shrouded somewhere in that decaying mind of glorious days past when Boss Rasmussen ran the town and had applied pressure to Dudley Worthington Depew, who adopted him, and appointed him Commissioner of Public Works, and gave him his wife, and exploded.

The papers described what happened then as a terrible calamity. "Tragic," a news reporter on WVVA called it. "An event so strange, so preternatural, so uncanny as to be the unmistakable Hand of Fate," said a prominent national news magazine.

Grouper knew none of this, though. For the first time in his life the labyrinth of his origins interested him, and he was trying to read the curlicues of script pressed into the grass of the field as he glided in.

The Stampe was out of gas. The sun was in the pilot's eyes. The wheelchair at the end of that bizarre writing was in the wrong place, at the wrong time. There was no way to avoid what happened.

He was only a few feet above the ground, fifteen or twenty, when the enormous white boar loomed ahead just underneath the setting sun, a white shape which must have weighed over 800 pounds, a shape with small eyes glittering malevolently in the backlit darkness of its lowered face. Grouper reacted instantly, pulling the stick back and kicking hard right rudder. His plane skewed violently, the lower wing brushing within a couple of feet of the swine's back. The startled animal kicked up its trotters and bolted parallel to the plane.

"Rawrk!" the pig shouted loudly. "Wheeeeeiiii!" The sound was of fingernails on a blackboard. The Albanian heard the pig and saw the plane sailing silently toward him at the same moment, for the expression of surprise and horror was later found frozen on his face.

"*Zogu! Zogu! Ahmet!*" he shrieked, pushing hard at the wheelchair; for some reason he kept hold of the handles, and had propelled both himself and the chair directly into the path of Grouper's Stampe, now bounding down the grass in huge leaps.

The final bound almost cleared the wheelchair. Almost.

As he had feared, the plane was wrecked. The main gear caught on the arm of the wheelchair, and the plane went into a vicious ground loop. Her tail skid caught the Albanian under the chin, "Zog...!" It lifted him in an arc and dropped what was left forty yards down the field. The wheelchair was a twisted wreck.

Its occupant was paste.

When told of the accident, the shock propelled Belle into labor.

Chapter 9. The Labors of Love

They were to be the worst two days of Grouper's life. He paced the hospital corridor, his arm in a sling, while unknown horrors took place in the labor room. He fancied he could hear the screams. Agonizing, drawn-out, tortured screams. Bloody screams. Belle was not strong; she was a genteel creature, delicate and high-strung. Grouper felt ill.

Belle was, in fact, in a deep narcotic sleep, sound and tranquil. Her labor was painless. She would awake at the hairdresser's, the children would already be enrolled in school, their first year's wardrobes purchased and the nanny firmly in charge.

Grouper didn't know that. Late yesterday his airplane, tank dry as a Salvation Army turkey dinner, had bobbled smack on top of his ailing father. It was an accident. A terrible accident, unpredictable, impossible, incredible. He still found it incomprehensible that old Baxter had somehow indicated to the mute Albanian that he wanted to go out to that particular farm on that particular fall afternoon to be wheeled about that particular field in the chilly showers which had been falling off and on all afternoon.

In truth, no one understood how the old man communicated with his Albanian. The Albanian had been heard to utter only the word, "Zogu!" It was not clear whether he could read, and anyway, Baxter was paralyzed and could not write. All he could do was sit drooling in his chair and glower. True, on occasion he managed to produce an expression which resembled a smile, in the same way that the droppings left by the horses at Lake Drowning Sow Resort resembled their producers — a metaphysical resemblance, by association, as it were. Baxter had shot him that look when he told him about the Depew Sewage Treatment Plant deal. Grouper had chosen to interpret the

321

look as approval.

But the expression on his face when they extracted what was left of him from the mingled wreckage of the wheelchair and the Cactus Kitten was not approval. Most certainly it was not a smile. It was, Grouper thought, gazing down at the face that topped what was left of his daddy, an expression for which there was no word in his vocabulary. He had sprained his elbow, and saw everything through a pink mist of pain, yet he tried to interpret the look, to sort its contents, though they were as thoroughly mixed as the various effluents at the Depew Sewage Treatment Plant.

Surprise was certainly there in the eyes, wide open and staring. Very little pupil, but an amazing amount of white was visible. The mortician had apologized for being unable to close them. The effect of those bright bands of white sclera showing between the stretched lids was very unpleasant.

There was a strong disapproval in the lines beside the mouth, and a violent resentment in the pinched aspect of the remaining nostril. A pinched, sullen impression between the bushy white brows might have been rage.

Belle was deep in labor, had been swiftly carried away to the hospital, and he looked at the body for a while, unable to describe even to himself what he was seeing, although there was certainly nothing pleasant or supportive or memorable in these remains.

Finally he went to the hospital, and paced for hours in a corridor which smelled just like the funeral home of disinfectant and formaldehyde. When he seized the arm of a nurse who made the serious mistake of taking a route from maternity to intensive care which intersected Grouper's own often-repeated route, he found out that his wife was likely to be some hours in her labor, for the contractions had subsided, and Belle was slumbering contentedly in narcotic nod-land, and he, Mr. Depew, might just as well go out for a drink. Furthermore it appeared that sforswear

he was going to be delivered of twins, so the drink

322

might be doubly helpful, as it were. Grouper paled.

So of all the men who peopled this sweet earth, he called Cornelius, who had never married, although he seemed to have an extremely active social life, and to gain a great deal of fun and satisfaction from it, and to make great deal of money, as Grouper knew all too well from the quarterly board meetings he and Cornelius held for the Rasmussen Dental Fabrication Works, and from his own sporadic examinations of the books. Yet by some obscure family instinct Grouper wanted to huddle with Cornelius for warmth and comfort, and so they met at the Silver Spoon Saloon, where Grouper had first courted his bride, and there he passed on to the bartender the recipe for his new drink, the Gloria Mundi, and he and Cornelius drank Gloria Mundi after Gloria Mundi, toasting one another, and memorializing Baxter Depew himself, God rest his soul after all his suffering, and it wasn't Grouper's fault, really it wasn't, the sun was in his eyes, and he was, after all, making an emergency landing in the only available field having spun down through a cloud, and it was certainly too bad about the Albanian, but his end was swift and mercifully without pain, and Baxter's pain too was over now. And Belle would be fine, just fine, the doctors would take great care of her, she was feeling no pain herself, it would be easy, for Cornelius had heard a great deal about how painless childbirth was these days for women of gentle birth, what with the miracles of modern medicine and anesthetics and all.

Grouper's pain was considerably lessened if not altogether dissipated when he abruptly remembered the moments before his crash.

"White!" he mumbled.

"Eh?" Cornelius said. "What's that? Say, I wanted to tell you about my new invention. A two-sided soup ladle for the breadlines. It'll speed things up considerably."

"It was a pig, Cornelius. Huge and pure white. I thought that was a horse farm."

"You see, you can pour in two directions at once. Just

dip the ladle, and the soup goes out to both sides through these sluices. Two people hold their cups under the sluices..."

"It used to be the Depew Horse Farm. What was that pig doing there?"

"Pig? What pig? What are you talking about?"

"I swerved to avoid a pig. A huge white pig."

"Pigs have forty-four teeth. Some of them are remarkably human in shape and color. We use them as blanks."

"Blanks?"

"Not the tusks, of course. People don't have tusks."

"Father," Grouper assured Cornelius, signaling for another Gloria Mundi, "used to say that his mother Henrietta worried about pigs. Especially a huge white one. Evil, he said. With teeth."

Grouper began to cry. Very quietly. "I saw it on my honeymoon," he said to his Gloria Mundi.

When he returned to the hospital, his wife was sitting up in bed having her hair done.

"Hullo, my dear," he pecked her on the cheek and dropped a double armload of roses in her lap. "'N how're we tonight?"

"We're fine," Belle sniffed sternly. "You're drunk. I have never been through anything so painful in my life. Have you seen the children?"

"Children?" Grouper asked her, momentarily disoriented, having been reassured at length that Belle had felt no pain.

Belle glared at him, and through the haze of pain and Gloria Mundis her expression so closely resembled the expression on Baxter Depew's face that a ripple of utter horror washed through him, giving impetus to a rapid series of repetitions of the flavor of his drinks, rising and falling through his esophagus.

"Our children," she hissed with a rattle and a rapid strike. Grouper leaped back as if he had discovered a venomous reptile at the bottom of his glass.

324

"Children? Oh, the nurse said twins. We have children." He sat abruptly in the only available chair, the energy holding him up suddenly depleted.

"I would appreciate it," Belle said slowly and distinctly, "if you would go and take a look at them. I would like to be reassured that they are acceptable."

"Acceptable?" he mumbled. "Yes." Wearily he climbed to his feet and staggered out into the hall. He took a deep breath outside her room, straightened himself, and strode purposefully off in a random direction. Halfway down the hall he had forgotten his errand.

Some time later he found himself sitting in a waiting room. A nurse approached him then and asked him if he were Mr. Depew. He assured her he was nearly certain that he was, and she led him through labyrinthine corridors to an enormous window.

He looked in. He peered into the faces of his brand new twins, a boy and a girl, and beside him the nurse was beaming with utmost pleasure and delight. She simply loved children, she did.

He stood. He stared. He balanced alternately on his heels and the balls of his feet, swaying gently to and fro.

The two little faces before him had their eyes closed as tightly as their fists. Their faces were red and puckered; they were so utterly ancient, wizened, shriveled and knotted with the foreknowledge of certain death that Grouper, in that absolute instant of time, saw as clearly and distinctly and graphically as if it were Enlightenment itself, that he, Farley Depew, called Grouper, was going to decay and die himself, and that he was never, ever, in the great and glorious world, going to live forever as he had always utterly and wholeheartedly believed.

That knowledge rose in him as though God himself had just unclogged his soul with a Cosmic plumber's helper, and the entire afternoon and evening of Gloria Mundis rose with the sharply limned image of a white pig and his gorge to be projected violently onto the linoleum floor of Valhalla Hospital before the glass window to the newborn nursery where Cornelius Hauser and Margaret Rasmussen Depew gurgled in their new and short-lived innocence.

When he went back to Belle and told what they looked like, she said, "What? Red and wrinkled? I will not have unacceptable babies; I will not have them red and wrinkled! You must say there has been some mistake!" She threw a tantrum. "My babies," she shouted, "will not be *red* and *wrinkled*! *No*! I won't have it."

Chapter 10. In Which Grouper Demonstrates his Affinity for Kierkegaard

Grouper Depew, as he had every morning since his children were born (or, he thought, perhaps it dated from the pig entrails), was throwing up. After twenty-one years he accepted it as a condition of life. Had anyone asked about it, he would have expressed surprise. "Doesn't everyone?" he would have asked.

He heaved, gasped, struggled, constricted; he retched. A wretched retch, painful articulation of fundamental despair, rejection. He lost, tossed, the poisons of the night. Morning snarled outside the banks of window, above the autumnal flower beds, now bare and wet. Morning, and Grouper must needs throw out, reject, repudiate, abjure, foreswear what the light revealed, for it revealed his very soul, its dimension and limit.

Not that he thought, crouched over the bowl of white ceramic, in terms so metaphysical. No, his misery was not meta at all, but quite earthly. Thoughts were scattered and small, frightened creatures accustomed to the darkness of dim, storm-tossed forests in his mind. Thoughts were nearly invisible, nearly voiceless, only the small wink of dawn off eyeshine or toothgleam.

Every morning he improved, rising Phoenixlike from the ashes of his indignity, knees red with the imprint of the tiles. The position before the toilet bowl was akin to prayer, and closely identified with the special pleading, the invocation and benediction of poor Francine's pale religions, or the even paler worships of Slyville, of the Sinkers, or worse, the superstitions of strange howling in mountain forests of Albania, ancient in the moonlight where the human form could not hold to its shape and men would change to wolves or deer or swine.

327

So Grouper felt his relief itself must have an invisible dimension, parallel to the spiritual realm even though his religion was that of the Reverend Ovandrill, emptied of magic. Jesus, Reverend Wallace Ovandrill often said, was a gentleman. Decorum demanded of Grouper devotions that were private and solitary.

Then he would be ready for the day, ready to step forth into the late 1950s to do battle with the forces of commercial chaos and evil competition. It was, he reflected (for perhaps the ten thousandth time) tooth and nail out there. But Eisenhower was in Washington and all was right with the world.

He passed Belle, seated at her dressing table. She was dipping from her tiny bottle the pills that kept her own metaphysical devils at bay: Miltowns, they were, meprobamate 600 mg., and they did relieve her anxiety. Last night the veal birds had burned again.

She assayed a smile. The effect was gruesome at this hour, but Grouper's relief held, his good spirits buoyed him through this brief squall, and he sailed on into the calm waters of the dining room, where soft boiled egg, dry toast and a small deep-fried fish fillet awaited him.

Here his newspaper, propped against the flower vase (empty now, in autumn), informed him of the state of the world. The shakeup in the Kremlin continued. Good. Serve those Russkis right, sending a helpless dog into space like that. All summer there had been shakeups over there. Well, Eisenhower was in the White House and all was right.

Rebecca dropped the coffee pot on the table. He grunted. She grunted. It was the morning ritual. They both felt better. She slouched back into the kitchen with a low growl. Grouper poured his first cup. He ate a bite of fish, a bit of egg. The egg was overdone, the white barely running, the yolk almost solid. The toast, however, was definitely dry. He smiled appreciatively. He could hear Rebecca singing in the kitchen. Negro spirituals. All was right with the world.

He rose sated from the table, the Valhalla Clarion

rifled for satisfactory news. All the headlines rhymed. WOMAN RAPED, PRISONER ESCAPED; VOTERS REGISTERED, DOWAGER INTERRED. There was talk of a big league football team franchise. He considered getting involved with that. There was talk of a new stadium. That, also, he considered.

There was an item: PROBLEMS RAMPANT/AT DEPEW TREATMENT PLANT. The plant was no longer doing its job. Effluents were making their way into the River. Louisville had complained. Tests showed the presence of unwelcome bacteria as far downriver as Cairo, Illinois. Too bad for Cairo. Perhaps he should call for a new bond issue to fund a remodel of the plant. He would have to go to Cornelius about that, though.

A shadow fell at the thought of Cornelius. The old fool was always ahead of him. He decided not to worry about the Sewage Treatment Plant.

To hell with the sewage. He had taken a tidy profit on it thirty years ago. It was no longer his concern.

He brightened. He stood in the front door and gazed out at his lawns, his hedges, his driveway which contained his automobiles. He took a deep breath of the damp November air. He sneezed. The sneeze was almost as satisfying as his earlier regurgitation.

Belle clattered across the hall behind him. She sniffed. "Close the damn door, Grouper," she said. He turned, and saw that she had put herself together. He glanced at his watch, and noted that it had taken her one hour and twenty-five minutes. Possibly it was worth the time; she did look better. Her lips were crimson; her hair was brushed and glossy, its dyes and colors nearly matching the color he remembered (albeit vaguely) from their courtship; her clothing was impeccable, without sin. Her heels were high and pointed, and they hit the marble of the foyer like exclamation points punctuating a series of insults.

He closed the door and covertly watched his wife as she vanished into the pantry. He swelled with something akin to pride. His home, his maid, his wife, his breakfast, his automobile, his city, his business, his lawn and shrubs and flower beds, his furniture and his paintings, his new built-in hi-fi, and at the airport, his airplane. His doctor (Thanatopoulos), his minister (Ovandrill), his lawyer and his accountant. His basement wine cellar and the cedar paneling in his attic storage. The cord of dry, sun-cured oak logs for his fireplaces (two). His age (57) and the accumulated wisdom that came with it. His custom-made shirts and their many sets of gold cuff-links. His suits. His camel hair coat, his silk ties. His charm and sympathy, his standing in the community. His goodness and generosity: his qualities — not brilliant perhaps, but solid, dependable and fair. His bank account, his stock portfolio, his long-term tax-free municipal bonds, his real-estate holdings, all his investments and his values. His safe deposit boxes (three of them). His pigskin wallet, resting inside the Scottish wool of his suit against his hip. His skills — piloting, driving, golfing, mixing, dictating. His children.

Pride fled. His children. His frown came back. He was not proud of his children. His children were a burden. His children had been a burden since the very moment they were born, a moment he preferred not to remember, attendant as it was with accidental death, and with insight so deep and unpleasant he had vomited on the linoleum outside the nursery window, and had done so every morning since. His children, eyesores, renegades, under-achievers, a rebuke to him and everything for which he stands (he put it precisely in his mind, for which he stands, as in "and to the nation for which it stands"). Peggy, gone to folk singing and a Negro! husband. And now Cory, the boy, retired or discharged out of the army as a corporal, and working, for God's sake! at the zoo! Exclamation points clattered across his mind like Belle's stiletto heels.

His children.

The telephone jangled. Once, twice, three times. He paused, considering whether to remain and see who it was, or proceed to his automobile and drive downtown. It was a

November day. Gray sleet smeared the streets.

"It's for you, Mistah Depew," Rebecca informed him in a sour voice. "It yoah son."

"Yes, yes. Him." Grouper felt impatient, a residue of sour thought remaining.

"It's me," Cory said to his father. "I just found out. Did you know that your grandfather was eaten by pigs?"

Grouper remained in the silent grip of November paralysis, the receiver loose in the grip of his left hand.

No, he did not know that.

BOOK THE SEVENTH: FAMILIES, 1957

Chapter 1. In Which Cory Gets Work

Cory waved the yellow slip of paper in the air in front of the gorilla they all called Kierkegaard. "I called him," he said. "I called Grouper and I told him his grandfather was eaten by pigs. I don't think he believed it. He didn't say anything. You're sure that was his grandfather?"

Withrow nodded. "You read the clipping."

"Sure I read it. But it didn't say it was my great-grandfather. It said it was some man named Baxter Peabody."

"Hey. Francine got the clipping from Baxter Rasmussen, who got it from his mother Henrietta Rasmussen, who got it from his mother, who owned the Museum of Western Oddities, and who started the Rasmussen Dental Fabrication Works. Why would she save it unless it was a family matter?"

"I don't know. Why would his name be Peabody?"

Withrow shrugged.

Cory put the paper away and stared at Kierkegaard; Kierkegaard stared back.

"You see what I mean about him?" Withrow asked, nodding toward the ape. He was lounging against the door to the cage, a bunch of bananas dangling from his hand.

"Yes, I see what you mean."

Kierkegaard sat cross-legged on the cement. Over his head the gray clouds sealed the sky with the luster of shellac. His eyes had the same gloss.

"Drugs," Withrow said.

"Really?"

"Miltowns. A new thing. His despair is allayed. The savage beast is tranquil. Very, very tranquil."

Kierkegaard's face was tranquil. His dark lips hung loosely away from large yellowed teeth, his furry cheeks were slack. The sly look was gone. "Why?" Cory asked.

"There were...complaints. Kierkegaard was offending some of the citizens. It's their zoo, after all. If a gorilla is constantly committing suicide in front of visitors, the city does not like it. This is the Rasmussen Zoo. This is the gorilla in the Rasmussen Zoo. He kills himself for show, and people complain. The Director gave a speech along these lines the other day. The Assistant Director gave an order to the Head Zookeeper. He passed it along to the Vet, who passed it along to Land Animals, who passed it along to Primates, who passed it on to me. Along with a bottle of pills."

"And you give Kierkegaard the drug?"

"You said it, brother. In his bananas." He held up the bunch in his hand.

"I don't think I like it. Drugging the gorilla. We'll be next."

Withrow grinned. "Whatchew mean, next? You taken a walk through Cliffside lately?"

"Yeah, a while back, when we went to Stoop's. With Uncle Cornelius; and the Dead Man. Why?"

"Ha. Come on. I'll show you around."

It was Cory's first day at work. He had a new job. A new face. His Wernher von Braun mask sat on a stalagmite in the Mozart Cave and smiled enigmatically, waiting for the Boy Scouts. A thin ache throbbed along his forehead, down his cheeks, beneath his chin, but he had to admit no red line was visible, no evidence of fallen countenance, lost face.

But he had a lot of unanswered questions, including the one he had just asked: Why?

They strolled along the alley behind the cages. Withrow showed him the locks, the feeding doors, the storage rooms. The crew's clean-up cart. "You rake the stuff up, shovel it into buckets, heave it into these carts, wheel it down to the loading dock and into a truck. You get used to it. As for why, we already get drugged. There's a lot of drugs in the ghetto; it's always been big business. Not always in Cliffside, either. For instance, at one time it was pretty big business at the building where you live." Withrow was giving him a curious look, paused at a door. Cory wrinkled his brow.

"The diary again?" Cory said hopelessly.

"The diary."

The sullen sky was low and lusterless, oppressive. Yesterday a dog flew into space, now zipping around the earth every hour and forty-two minutes, sending beeps and tones. The dog's name was Laika. Sputnik was still there, beeping too. Mao was in Moscow. On Saturday Navy beat Notre Dame. The Rangers had routed the Boston Bruins 5-0. Today in Valhalla there might be snow in the air. The temperature hovered around the freezing mark.

"The diary," Withrow went on. "Francine Depew. She wrote down things, about her baby, Farley Depew, her tenth child, the only survivor. She talks about her husband Baxter Depew, and her first husband, Dudley Depew. A brother? I can't find out. Dudley was the mayor, Dudley Worthington Depew III, who exploded..."

"Exploded?"

"And cocaine. She wrote about cocaine. Cocaine, she said, was wonderful stuff."

"She was a drug addict?" Cory didn't believe it. "I don't believe it," he said.

Withrow shrugged. "So she said."

"I mean, I don't believe that's my grandmother. For one thing, that's a pretty big coincidence, wouldn't you say? To move into a building at 1001 Celestial Street which just happened to be the building in which my grandmother lived, and find her diary in my ceiling..."

"Worked. She didn't live there."

"Worked," Cory agreed. "Vincent Black Shadow says no one is going to believe in the address, much less this kind of coincidence."

"Not believing don't change the facts, boy."

"OK."

Withrow opened a door. A small office for the crew. Walls held calendars with enticing women, meticulous

336

drawings. They were bent over, looking out of the picture with enigmatic smiles. They were wearing underpants. A few had visible nipples, very pink. None of them looked like Hackamore Ovandrill, though they all were in excellent physical condition.

Cory got a time card. He learned where the clock was. He got a schedule of feed runs, cleaning times. He learned where to hook up the hoses. His map showed him where the birds were kept, where pachyderm and dromedary, civet and wombat, cat and hoofed stock, peccary and warthog and iguana lived. What they ate. Later, Withrow assured him, he would become more than familiar with the condition of the animals' food once the animals had processed it, and it became, Withrow said, "second-hand."

They went back outside. It was not snowing, it was doing something else, something unpleasant: a half-formed, embryonic, unfinished blizzard, a kind of fetal weather that miscarried overhead. Clammy, indefinite precipitation surrounded them as they hunched back to Kierkegaard's cage.

He was seated in the sleet exactly as before, a cosmic indifference upon him. The hair was plastered with gooey moisture on his low, sloping head. His eyes were a dead end road in yesterday's downtown. When Withrow and Cory approached, his dull eyes lifted and focused like a blurred and badly developed photograph of an abandoned mining town in the desert of zoo existence. Did a flicker of recognition, of sly anticipation, flare briefly there? Cory could not be sure. Pity wept over him, tears from heaven dampening his own lids. Kierkegaard had lost face, hope, soul itself. The darkness in those eyes was interstellar, light-years of emptiness. Sickness unto death. Fear and trembling. The end of the act, too old for show biz, his life a retirement home for indigent actors. A silvery string of drool looped carelessly from his slack lip to his chest, continued to the cement. The Great Chain of Being, floor to lip, a demonstration of cause and effect, gravity at work. There was gravity in his face, in the hanging lip, in the

337

reddened lids beneath his pouchy eyes, which sagged under the weight of experience painfully forgotten.

"I can see why they call it dope," Cory said softly. "But I can't believe my grandmother..." He stared at the gorilla. The gorilla stared back listlessly. But perhaps a spark in the eyes meant the Miltown was fading. Yes, there was a spark in those piggy eyes, a slyness. The oversized head moved a little, cocked slightly to one side. He hadn't entirely forgotten his talent, the meaningful meaninglessness of his life.

Kierkegaard was definitely looking at Cory. Recognition in his eyes? He leaned fractionally forward.

He banged his forehead on the cement: a small, dry, disinterested gesture, barely recognizable, a sad indifferent thump, more a blip, but there, the real thing. Kierkegaard still lurked in the abandoned building of that body. They hadn't gotten to him entirely.

Cory smiled.

Chapter 2. In Which Cory Gets a Message

Cory moaned deep, earthen howls of confusion, despair, frustration. Crypt-creaks, stone and iron. He considered these auditory effects. They were inadequate.

"I don't get it," he said. "I just don't get it. Baxter Peabody, my father's grandfather apparently, was eaten. By pigs, pigs! and now this." He smacked the back of his hand against the diary, producing a crisp report, a pistol shot.

"You worry too much. No wonder you think your face is falling off." Hackamore Ovandrill contemplated her fingernails. They were oval, smooth, clear, hard. She glanced at Cory then, and her look was also smooth, clear and hard, but patience was wearing thin.

"I don't think so any more. It itches, that's all." He scratched. "But this," he waved the letter at her. She yawned. "This."

He threw it down. The yellowed clipping from the March 23, 1858 edition of the Valhalla Clarion fell out: MAN DEVOURED BY PIGS.

"She was a junkie!" he said. "She was a whore!" Hack did not answer. She was out of sorts.

Cory tried a question. "My father's grandfather's name was Peabody," he said. "My grandfather's name was Rasmussen. My father's name is Depew. How can this be?"

She sighed. "How should I know? Where did the name Depew come from?" She stood up, stretched. Her arms quivered over her head, and Cory sighed too.

"A mystery," he said. His clothes smelled of animals — mammals and reptiles and birds, their products. Hack kept her distance. "I'm related to Boss Rasmussen, too, somehow."

"Well," she smiled. It was unpleasant, that smile, toothy and false. "That's nice." She didn't think it was nice at all.

339

"I can't help my relatives," he flared.

"Then quit talking about them so damn much. Sometimes you're such an asshole, Cory!"

"OK," he said. "OK. That does it. That really does it." He did not say what it was, what it does.

She glared at him. She was out of sorts.

He humphed and left the room. He slammed his door and the glass panel shook.

"I love anger." Suzy was sorting through the day's shipment of catalogs at the mailboxes. Equestrian equipment. Hackamore's mother was an equestrienne, jodhpur breeches and riding boots. Big hips. And of course he had once met her father. But perhaps bygones would be. So he was going to meet them Sunday. After church. He and Hack were going to church to hear the Reverend preach. Then they were going to her home for lunch. This was Thanksgiving week. Hack insisted that her father had a short memory. Besides, it was dark out there, and foggy that night. It all had ended well. Cory lost his job. That should have been enough. A thin gruel of snow covered the lawns of Valhalla.

"What?" Cory asked absently.

"You're angry," Suzy pointed out. "I love anger. It excites me."

"You're crazy," Cory told her. She smiled.

"Thanks," she murmured. "I needed that." She was joking.

He pushed past her to the front door. "Your girlfriend giving you trouble?" she asked.

"Yes." He snapped it, like gum.

"I hear you two, sometimes, down there. Bouncing. It's exciting. No whips, though. You ought to try whips, a little punishment."

Cory rolled his eyes and pushed out into the cold slush. Mozart wouldn't have liked whips. He was too busy doing music. Sublime, not ridiculous.

Wilmer stood in his yard. He had boards, a pair of sawhorses. He was breathing through his nose, inhaling loud and deep, once, twice, three times. He raised his hand, lowered its edge onto the board, raised it again, with each breath. The November air sucked reluctantly into his nose, and from there to somewhere else. When it came out, it plumed white in the air. He reminded Cory of a taxi horse from a Sherlock Holmes movie, with Basil Rathbone. Then he remembered that a taxi was called a "hack." He grunted again, soft abdominal explosion.

Wilmer was disturbed by the sound. He stopped inhaling to glare at Cory.

"You," he said very distinctly. "You're cruisin' for a bruisin'."

Cory rolled his eyes again, this time at the empty gray sky. "God," he said.

"Hi, yahhh!" Crack. The board split. Wilmer's muscles were rock. So was his brain.

Cory walked glumly down to the corner of Midgard Avenue. Brown leaves filled the gutters, drifted on the sidewalk. The leaves were edged with white frost; there was damp in the air, a threat. Upstairs at 1001 Celestial Avenue his grandmother Francine Depew had sniffed the white cocaine. She had hidden her diary in the floor; he found it in his ceiling. There was no doubt. She was a whore and an addict; he was living in a former brothel. He was living in, as Belle had told him once, "sin" as well. Shacking up. Sometimes here, sometimes at Hack's apartment. Now they were fighting.

He thought about The Dead Man, who lived above Stoop's Grocery. Near the stadium. But they were going to build a new stadium. The old stadium was too old. The new stadium would be new. They were digging a hole for the new one.

Sleet trickled under his collar. Sleet turned to fire, slithered down his spine, dampened his belt line in back. Physical misery. He welcomed it. He felt like Suzy. Suffering.

He remembered Brother Grigory, then, up the hill. He turned around, and trudged up toward St. Credula's spire.

Brother Grigory had told him some things about suffering. "Von," he'd said, "is soffrin. Two is soffrin has causings." He could still hear Brother Grigory saying that. Slursh, slop, at the laundromat. Little Richard was singing *Keep A Knockin*. Cory believed there was suffering: his great grandfather was eaten by pigs, his grandmother was a junky whore. What else would he learn? It was no wonder he thought his face had fallen off. Those facts entitled him to a certain amount of suffering, on the whole.

Soffrin has causings.

The iron gate to the courtyard at the monastery was closed, a large padlock snapped through the chain. Cory could see the old fountain in there, filled with slush. St. Credula lounged on her bed of pain and suffering. She looked like the giantess in the Mozart Cave. Dead shrubs contributed a desolate ambiance to the yard. The brittle leaves scraped under his feet, around his shoes. No one was around. A small bell button stared Cyclopean at him. He pushed it. It made no sound. He might have been pushing a stone.

There was no response. What had Grouper said when he told him about the pigs. Nothing. The telephone wires were as empty as this yard, this fountain. Grouper thought about something else.

Sleet began to fall, smack the pavement, freeze. Cory too froze. He turned away from the church, walked hunched against the cold.

"Pssst!"

He looked around, but there was no visible source to the sound.

"Psst." Ah, in the door of the laundromat. The mad monk gestured, a peculiar hand-down waving toward himself, as if he wanted to draw warm air from a fireplace into his belly. Cory went in.

"You said suffering has causings, cause. What is the cause of suffering?" he asked.

Brother Grigory cocked his head, peculiar bird-eyes bright in the fluorescents. It wasn't until after he had asked that Cory noticed the laundromat was filled with people. They had paused in their work to look at him. He flushed, felt crimson fire around his face. Metaphysics in the laundromat. Withrow was right, life was absurd.

"I said you, vot chew vhant! Don't know nottink, you. Nottink. Lissen me good, there was man from east, far far east, you say Asia? Come to Epirus when I was young man. Says me truth of soffrin, soffrin has causings, causings is desire, vot chew vhant!"

"Oh." The man was an idiot. The day was idiotic. Hack, and Suzy and Wilmer Dougherty all were idiots. Desire. Vot chew vhant.

Brother Grigory was giving him that look again. Cory stole glances around the room, but the others had gone back to their laundry and were paying him no further attention. The slursh and slop, all next to godliness. He realized he smelled of animals.

So Cory nodded. "Sure," he said. "Sure, I get it. Yes. Desire. Right."

Chapter 3. In Which Grouper Gets a Shot

"Right," Grouper said. He pointed.

"Right," Dr. Thanatopoulos repeated. He was not looking, eyes fixed instead on the hypodermic filled with yellowish fluid.

"You're not looking," Grouper complained. His trousers were around his ankles. His pucky buttocks were marbled liver in this dreadful light. Outside darkness was upon Valhalla.

"No," the doctor agreed. "I'm not. But I do know the difference between right and left. You said right, right?"

"Right."

Dr. Thanatopoulos swabbed vigorously at the left buttock with his alcohol and cotton. Grouper clucked into his crossed arms leaning on the examining table. He barely noticed the cooling evaporation. "That's left," he said.

"I got a weird one last summer, did I tell you?" Dr. Thanatopoulos liked to tell his regular patients about the weird ones. For some reason he had a lot of them.

"No," Grouper started to say, but it turned into a yelp as the needle bit.

"Funny," the doctor said. "It doesn't usually hurt." He peered at the needle as if it had betrayed him.

"Ah," Grouper sighed as the Dexedrine-vitamin complex hit his system. "Ah. Ah."

"Cory Depew," Dr. Thanatopoulos continued, tossing his apparatus into a stainless steel emesis basin filled with soapy water. Bubbles sloshed over the side. "He thought his face was falling off. Your son, I believe."

Grouper would have groaned. He could feel there was a groan down there, deep in the bowels, as it were, of his being. But it was a stillborn groan, a groan died aborning, smothered in amphetamine rush. He simply felt too damn good to groan, despite being reminded of his cross, his

344

burden, his Nemesis.

"*Christos anesti*," Dr. Thanatopculos muttered.

"Come on, group, you always say that," Grouper muttered, thinking about his scn, Cory Depew. What was he doing. He'd called that morning to say something about his grandfather, eaten by pigs. Ridiculous!

"Means Christ is risen. An expression for Easter. Hope. Rebirth. The boy, your son, his face falling off. Pah! Foolishness. Young buck, randy. Gets laid all the time."

"It is convenient to come to you," Grouper mused. "You are in the same building. I am your landlord. Very convenient, for both of us."

Dr. Thanatopoulos did not hear a threat. Dr. Thanatopoulos had a Turkish medical degree, and was, besides, a little hard of hearing. He was leaning back now against the wooden bookcase. Behind him the jars rested, draped in dust. Shachter's Worm in sluggish fluids. And out at Schachter's Landing near his home, the Worm was entering a larval stage again, upriver. By spring the Little Hawking would be swarming, red tide in the creek bed.

He tented his fingers, slid them together. All the Depews were patients of his. Miltowns for the wife, vitamins for the husband. The boy got vitamins, too.

"Your lease is up soon," Grouper mused. Dr. Thanatopoulos made him mad, red fists of tiny rage, curled like the Worm.

Dr. T was nodding. "A strange young man, your son," he continued. "Nothing remarkable about him at all. Ordinary, you might say." His voice was wistful, dreamy. Apparently he hadn't been listening to his patient. "You can pull your pants up now." The doctor's English was impeccable.

"Oh." Grouper's threats were either too veiled, or were falling on the doctor's admittedly deaf ears, filled as they were with white explosions of hair.

"For instance," the doctor continued, "I couldn't describe him to you if you asked. Even his face, ordinary. No evidence of disease. Now, with a D and C, nothing is

345

visible either. Usually I don't even check. We call it a therapeutic dusting and cleaning. Young ladies, they get into trouble, need treatment, a little dilatation, a little curettage. Nothing special, nothing difficult. An amateur could do it. Open up the cervix, stick in the old scraper and clean out the uterus. A snap, you would say. But your boy, ordinary boy with a strange complaint. I hear you bought a new airplane."

"The rent could go way up," Grouper said, before the last sentence sank in. His threats must be working, because the doctor was no longer discussing his children, child. "Yes. Beechcraft Bonanza."

"Ah." Dr. Thanatopoulos laid his finger alongside his nose, as if this were profound news indeed. "I wouldn't recommend flying for a few hours. The vitamins, you know."

"I'm going to the office. Upstairs."

"Yes, yes, of course." The doctor sounded impatient. Grouper smiled. A little pun there, impatient, patient, ha ha. "Business," he said. He was now pressing his finger into the side of his nose, so the word came out bid-diz.

"I'm open at night," the doctor said, taking his finger away to gesture at the darkness outside. "He showed up late. Very late. I was asleep. On the cot. I do that sometimes, when Mrs. T is having one of her socials. Can't stand Mrs. T's socials. Horse people, you know. Mrs. Ovandrill, for instance. Smells like a barn. A nice smell, some people say, but not I. Not I."

"Right." Grouper nodded. "Right. Animals. My son now works with animals."

"Oh? The one whose face fell off? Did I tell you he came in one night. During the summer, it was."

"About your lease," Grouper suggested gently. "You might want to consider an increase in the rent."

"You might want to consider your vitamin shots," the doctor snapped, hearing perfectly well.

Grouper had forgotten his vitamin shots. He nodded again, waving his hands. "Right," he repeated. "Right.

346

Forget it. Of course. vitamins. Very important, vitamins. Wouldn't want to fool around with vitamins, no, ha ha. The rent will remain where it is."

He straightened his tie. He was smiling. His little groan was dusted away, cleaned away. D-ed and C-ed, ha ha.

He forgot the lease. He felt good. He felt marvelous. There were no clouds on his horizons, no blastulas inside. He was in no trouble at all. No. Life was good. He was very, very comfortable in the world.

And why not? He had the doctor, he had the accountant, he had a brisk business in teeth. Everyone needed to chew. And over the door to the Rasmussen Building there was still that lovely plaque: The Lord Who Made Thy Teeth Shall Give Thee Bread, and so He did, so He did.

Even if the founder of the company, the man who carved that plaque, the visionary prophet of false teeth, even if he had been eaten by pigs.

"Right," Grouper said again, aloud. "Right."

347

Chapter 4. In Which There are Crocodiles

Belle telephoned Cory the day after he told his father about Baxter Peabody.

She said, "Cory, dear."

He groaned. It always meant trouble. It meant: "Cory, dear, I'm going to tell your father," or "Cory, dear, wait until your father gets home." And so on.

Now she said, "Cory, dear, your father is very upset." Then she waited. He said nothing. Finally she said, "Well?"

"Well," he said. "Well, what, Mom?"

"Haven't you got anything to say for yourself? Your father had to go to the doctor!"

"The doctor? What, is he sick?"

"Your father had to go to the doctor because he is upset." A southern belligerence was creeping into her accent. What Peggy called her ante-belligerence south.

"Maybe he's upset because his grandfather was eaten by pigs."

She called regularly after that. Sometimes Hack answered the phone, and Belle would sniff, and then she would hang up.

"Your father is upset because he wasn't asked to be on the Commission," she said this particular morning.

He asked her what commission. Hack was glowering at him across the room. Her glower distracted him. She was still out of sorts. She had been out of sorts for two weeks, ever since Belle started calling regularly.

Belle told him what commission. "Investigating that night at the coffee house. They wouldn't let your father be on it," she told him. "They said he might be biased. After all, you were arrested." She did put an odd emphasis, as if the word you had an unpleasant aroma, like his clothes.

"He might be biased," Cory said. "Peggy was arrested too."

348

Belle ignored this. Peggy was not anyone she knew. "Your father said that just because his son was arrested did not mean that he was biased. He is completely impartial."

"Did they think he would be biased for me or against me?"

"We're very disappointed in you," Belle said.

"Mom, they shot a man. Through the head. He was pouring a cup of coffee."

"I'm sure they had their reasons," Cory's mother told him.

"Mom, he ran a coffee house. They served coffee, that's all." Well, he knew that wasn't all. He'd been smoking the tea, grass, muggles, gage, that Mexican shit Gabriel Flagg had given to Hackamore. "Besides, they shot the wrong man. It was a mistake. They wanted to kill someone else."

"The police know what they're doing, Cory, dear. That's why they're the police. I'm sure the police don't shoot the wrong people."

"I'm glad you're not on the commission."

"I'm not biased," she said.

Cory told her he had to go to work.

"God," he said.

"Oh, shut up," Hack said. "You sure let people push you around. Gabriel Flagg wouldn't let his parents push him around. In fact, he pushed them around. He pushed his father out the second story window of their house in Perth Amboy."

"I have to go to work," he said. He had no classes today. Tomorrow was Thanksgiving. "We have new crocodiles arriving at the zoo."

"Oh, goody. Whom do you think they were trying to shoot, anyway?"

"Me," he said.

Hack snorted and went back to her nails.

The new crocodiles were there, in crates. They were all grinning with their eyes closed. Withrow thought they were dead.

349

"They look dead to me, Marvin," he told the Head of Reptiles.

"*Hi*ber-nay-tin."

"They ain't movin, bossman." Withrow put on his ghetto jive. He did not like the Head of Reptiles, a hillbilly named Willoughby from the tiny village of Idd, Kentucky, near Slyville, a man who despised knee-grows with a frenzy which bordered on dementia.

"*Hi*ber-nay-tin. Low meta, meta, something. Them critters's asleep."

"OK."

"You. Depew," Willoughby said with a sneer. "Put 'em in water. Walk 'em around."

"Walk 'em around?"

"Right. Walk 'em around. In water. It'll wake 'em up."

Cory looked at their teeth. All three had many, many teeth. "Do you know what second-hand crocodile feed looks like?" he asked Withrow.

"Nope. These here are the zoo's first alligators.

"Crocodiles."

"Sure." Withrow nodded. "I expect it'd be pellets or balls."

"Heaps or rounds," Cory suggested.

"They's carnivores — probably heaps or mounds."

"Loaves," Cory leered. "Fishes and."

"Loaves," Withrow agreed. "Anyways, them dudes's dead."

Cory and Withrow loaded the crates onto dollies. They rolled the dollies along the paths behind the cages to the reptile house. The crocodiles did not move. There was a kidney-shaped pool. They unloaded the crocodiles, which were stiff as boards, into the water. They floated, as if stuffed with kapok. Cory and Withrow, wearing hip boots, pushed them around. They showed no signs of life.

Withrow shook his head. "Dead," he said. He and Cory sat on the edge of the pool and watched the crocodiles drifting aimlessly. Finally they bumped into the sides of the pool and stopped. "We're never going to find out what used crocodile feed looks like from these things."

"Whadda hell you two doin?" Marvin Willoughby asked.

"Marvin," Cory said, getting back in the water to push the crocodiles around some more, "I've been meaning to ask you. Do you have a sister named Marsha?"

"Married to my cousin Big Mike," Marvin said, frowning. "One mean son of a bitch, Big Mike. His old man's a cop. One mean son of a bitch, his old man. Why?"

"Just wondered."

"Keep pushin them crocs. Wake em up."

At quitting time they rested the crocodiles' chins on the cement at the edge of the pool. Their teeth gleamed in the twilight of the reptile house. They looked, not ready for dinner, but as if they were resting just after.

"Just like the army," Cory said. "Pushing dead crocodiles around."

"I didn't know they had these things in Greenland," Withrow said. "How are you two getting along?"

"Me'n Hack? I don't know. Not too good. Ever since we went up to the cave that day, you know? She seems different. Mad all the time. And my mother! She's disappointed in me, in us, I suppose. I don't know."

He looked at the crocodiles. Teeth. "The Lord Who Made Thy Teeth," he said.

"Yeah," Withrow agreed. "It's a dog eat dog world."

"More like a pig eat pig world."

They went out into the evening. The clouds were gone, there was no snow on the ground, but it was cold. The earth was hard and bleak. Midgard Avenue sloped away toward the riverfront. A gap in the buildings down there, a black place in the twinkling lights, lights of commerce, lights of business, lights of industry and transport. Lights of life, going on, flowing like the river.

"See that black hole there. That there hole is the new stadium. Them crocs is dead."

Night came swift and mean. Hard ground. Cory

turned up he collar of his coat. Down the hill was a ravine; Midgard Avenue was a bridge there, over Dudley Worthington Depew Avenue. Beyond was Valhalla University.

"Night, boys," said the watchman, locking the gate.

"You said it," Withrow answered.

Chapter 5. In Which Grouper Practices His Art

What small thoughts wafted through Grouper's mind? Thoughts that were questions: why? Thoughts with the faces of swine. He watched Belle abustle in the dining room. Preparations for Thanksgiving dinner, were there place cards? Of course there were place cards. Everything had a place in Belle's universe. Belle was an orderly person. Miltown kept her orderly.

It was not snowing outside, not raining. It was nothing. He wasn't invited to be on the commission. He'd failed to get in on the investment group involved in the new stadium. Clearly they were going to do very well. Already the hole down by the waterfront invited comment and speculation. He'd stopped there yesterday. People were talking. Get the games out of the ghetto and into downtown. Make a bundle. And the old stadium? A loss, but the city owned it.

Sure. The Rasmussen Building was a few blocks away from the hole. Cornelius was making a lot of money in dental supplies. Electric drills, big items. Pneumatic chairs. Light fixtures. Large things with huge mark-up. Big profit items. Small, mass-produced items, too. Toothbrushes. Now he was talking about electric toothbrushes. "That's the ticket," Cornelius said. "Everything's gonna be electric. Big bucks." Not like teeth. Teeth required skill, industry, specialized equipment, secret processes and hard-to-obtain ingredients. Labor costs. Salesmen. Skilled workers. Low profits eaten away by rising cost of goods.

Resentment was a palpable quality of Grouper's atmosphere. Cornelius was coming to Thanksgiving dinner. Cornelius' damned magnetic bow tie rack was raking in the dollars. Busby and Conrad's department store had them all over the place. All of a sudden everyone was wearing those clip-on bow ties. Who would have believed it?

Grouper wandered to the bar. He felt more comfortable in the bar. At home. Here was his laboratory, his studio. Here his creative juice could flow; he could stew up something new, something utterly different, something that gave satisfaction. He may not be good at business. He may not be good at investing (in the end the Sewage Treatment Plant barely broke even). He may not be good at politics like his father, or at chemistry like his grandfather (eaten by pigs! Cory had told him; he didn't believe it). Absently, he pulled out a bottle of Calvados. He poured a dram or two into a silver cocktail shaker.

He paused, bottle tilted over the shaker. No, he might not be good at any of those things. But he was a good pilot — he'd never been injured, and it wasn't his fault he had run out of gas a few times — he had no head for figures. And he was a good mixologist. Really, that was what he should have done with his life. He looked down into the cocktail shaker. Grenadine, he thought. Yes, pomegranate flavor would blend well with apple. Sweet, and hard. He smiled. His resentment was beginning to fade. He poured in a dash of grenadine.

It was a pleasing color, this mix. Yellow-green, like spring grass.

Crushed ice. He put cubes in the machine, and metal rods whirred. Chunk, he had a pan full of ice. That too went into the shaker.

He was well into creative trance by the time the doorbell began to ring. He did not hear the bell, did not notice when the guests began to file into the bar. They gathered into a semicircle to watch as he worked. A fine dew had collected on his brow, a brow somewhat furrowed by the years, but a fine one, a noble one, broad, serene and clear. His eyebrows were gray tufts, almost feathery, like the antennae of a moth. His glasses blinked light from the aquarium lamp in which a particularly vicious Siamese fighting fish swam in endless tiny circles. There had been evenings in his past when the fish had had to prove itself. It had been worthy, had met every challenge. He had named a drink after it. That night someone had pointed out that a Grouper was also a fish. That particular someone had never been invited back; a lapse of good taste best forgotten. Grouper could no longer remember the person's name.

This afternoon only close friends, relatives, family were there. They all knew the rules. No smart remarks. Grouper concentrated, aware now of the effect he was creating. All were attentive, curious. Without looking up Grouper knew them all. The impossible old fool Cornelius was there, with his dewlaps and pouchy eyes. He looks awful, Grouper thought, not looking at him but contemplating with half his mind the recipe at hand. There was Calvados and grenadine and crushed ice, of course. He had added Benedictine and lime juice.

Reverend Ovandrill was there, along with his wife. Secretly Grouper felt Reverend Ovandrill was something of a bore. He was, for one thing, almost absurdly stout; for another, his primary topic of conversation was his houseboat, which he kept tied up at the Schachter's Landing Boat Club. The boat seldom did anything like cruise, or even really float. Mostly it stayed tied up. On occasion, the Reverend and his wife would have a small party; cocktails, mainly, of the most pedestrian and boring sort: Scotch and water, Bourbon and soda, gin and tonic. No imagination.

Dr. Thanatopoulos was coming, but not for dinner. He was coming after dinner for drinks. That would be pleasant, for Grouper would be called upon to create a completely different sort of libation after the turkey. His mind raced ahead, trying out various combinations. Something heavy and sweet, no ice. Brandy and champagne? No, it had been done. Besides, that would require ice.

Grouper finished his preparations, and lifted the chilled shaker into the air above the level of the bar. It glistened with condensation. An appreciative "Ah" went up from the audience. Something about the gleaming, well-polished silver and the cold dew on its surface created an impression of great solidity near reverence. Perhaps it was the hieratic way Grouper lifted the chalice, holding it before him and contemplating it before he began to shake it.

The shaking produced another appreciative exhalation, the "Ah" nearly adding the "men" at the end, the chant of the congregation at devotions. Grouper shook the container first at one of his guests, then at another, blessing them all in turn. The Reverend's hands were clasped across his belly, a smile almost belly-sized on his broad, sunny, engaging face. He nodded when the silver shaker moved his way, a small bow as he received the benediction.

Belle entered, a holiday smile on her own well-prepared face. She stood at the back while Grouper shook, waiting patiently. He shook at her. She, too, bowed slightly, wearing a festive coral dress in exquisite taste.

Grouper put a strainer top, also silver, with a spring wound around the underneath to hold back the crushed ice on the shaker. He placed a long-stemmed glass on the bar. He positioned the glass carefully, in the precise center. He looked at the glass for a moment, holding the shaker. It was a dramatic moment. The effect was going to be very special. There would be various aspects of his creation for the guests to contemplate: its color, its consistency (was it grainy or smooth?), its temperature, its subtle blend of flavors; its viscosity (would it pour slowly or fast?). There was a palpable suspension of breath in the small room. Even the Siamese fighting fish stopped its incessant circling of the round aquarium lamp to watch.

He lifted the chalice.

He tilted it.

The substance within began to move, slowly at first, but gathering momentum. Ice hit the restraining springs, and pure fluid emerged, hung on the chilled silver lip of the shaker, began to pour. There was a vast exhalation in the room. The effect was electric.

The color, too, was electric. A dazzling, utterly limpid

blue, like a deep mountain lake in the north woods when the sun hit it just right. The guests sighed as one.

"Hi, folks," Cory said from the door to the bar. He had not as yet seen the Reverend Ovandrill.

They all turned as one, shocked by this intrusion on their sacred ritual.

"You!" Reverend Ovandrill said. He began to choke.

His large wife, weathered a deep rich tan, smacked him soundly on the back. He staggered, sputtering, and fell heavily against the bar. The bar, which was on rollers, shot away from him, and hit Grouper in the solar plexus.

The silver shaker flew out of his hands, over the bar into the aquarium lamp, which shattered with a deafening report.

All the guests watched the Siamese fighting fish drown in the electric blue beverage Grouper had not yet named.

Chapter 6. Thanksgiving

Belle's horror was electric, too.

Her initial impulse was to go for Miltown, but
Miltown was upstairs, and upstairs meant a long broad
sweep of stair, a corridor of empty walls, foamy pale carpet
across the bedroom, the narrow cedar spaces of the dressing
room, and the white ceramic dazzle of the bathroom where
the mirrored medicine cabinet would reflect to her the
aging face she had before she could reach down the tiny
white oblong tablets. And all that was horror, too.

So she stared instead at the dying fish, and through
her shot all the existential agonies of embarrassment, the
deadly faux pas, the gaffe. These were fine people here.
The finest in Valhalla. Nearly. Not quite the finest, of
course. There was the Randolph Scott Depew family, for
example. Well, the Depews, all the other Depews, had
fallen on hard times. Their station in society had been
eroded. Still, she was disappointed her husband was not
intimate with the R. S. Depews. They were the oldest if not
the wealthiest, and once had been the most important
Depews in the area. They owned a farm near Schachter's
Landing. Her father had told her they once raised the finest
thoroughbred horses in the state there. That was long ago.
They raised something else, now. Something more
profitable. Grouper had crashed his plane out there, the day
before the twins were born, the day of the terrible accident
from which Grouper had never recovered. The R. S.
Depews refused to have any dealings with Grouper.

Belle shuddered. It was an awful experience, that
shudder. It moved from the small of her back to her neck,
around the front of her abdomen. Goose bumps rose on her
bare flesh. She flushed the coral of her tasteful dress.
Fortunately everyone was still staring down at the fish,
flopping on the floor in corrosive blue fluid.

358

"Dinnerzerved," Rebecca anncunced to the guests' backs.

"Hah?" Grouper gave a start. "Not now," he muttered.

"Yassah." Rebecca turned to go.

"Wait." Belle roused herself, spoke through horror. "We will eat, Rebecca."

"Yass'm." She turned again to go.

"I was going to name it the Velvet Ragnarok," Grouper said sadly.

Rebecca turned back again, under the impression he had addressed her. "Whassat, sah?"

"I was going to name it the Velvet Ragnarok."

"Oh." She left, shaking her head.

Belle gave a difficult laugh, took Mrs. Ovandrill's arm. "Come," she said. "Let us dine."

The Reverend stared at her as if she were unspeakably stupid, and she lowered her eyes. For some reason he always made her feel that way, but never so keenly as now. His eyes were nearly lost in their pink pockets, but they twinkled in there with righteousness. Again she thought of Miltowns, nestled together in their bottle upstairs, a temptation nearly irresistible. It had been so long, so many years of disappointment. Then she lifted her chin and swept into the dining room, trailed by her guests.

The meal was a disaster. Reverend Ovandrill refused to look at Cory opposite him. As a result his eyes darted around inside their fat like rabid rodents trapped in suet. No exit.

Cory in turn stared intently at Reverend Ovandrill. He glared. His eyes were wide; he was a snake, a mantis, a basilisk with his stare. No wonder those rodents ran.

Belle suffered Cory's disappointing manners. He chewed. He swallowed. He stared.

Belle suffered.

Grouper grieved for his lost Velvet Ragnarok.

Reverend Ovandrill hated. His wife thought of horses, their high heads and proud feet drumming on the graves of forgotten ancestors with names like Balshajt and

359

Willoughby.

Cornelius gloated. Grouper was sure of that. Cornelius was always gloating. His business was booming. The Dental Fabrication Works was falling on harder times. New methods had developed, new materials like acrylics. New equipment, modern technologies. RDFW had failed to invest in new skills and equipment. Business was falling off. The brisk Christmas season was upon them. It was almost 1958. Business was not brisk.

There was wine with dinner. Grouper had a wine cellar, though he did not care for wine. Too tame. He belonged to Prohibition, a spirited era. The wine was terrible. Frog wine, sweet and heavy, an anemic yellow. Belle's idea.

Belle's bracelets jangled. She listened from time to time as they jangled her nerves. Miltown was out of reach, far away, overhead. So she drank a bit more wine. Cory was beside her at the table. Rebecca slouched through the room with silver serving platters: sweet potatoes, cranberry parsnip ring mold, baked bananas, salad of artichoke hearts and vetch. The Reverend at least was eating, but then, when he wasn't drinking, the Reverend was almost always eating. There were close ties between Belle's family and the Reverend's. Her father had pronounced Mayor Depew dead of spontaneous human combustion. Rasmussen false teeth were implicated as well. Something about the celluloid base and the cigar. She shuddered. The Reverend's father had officiated at the funeral. Close ties. The Inner Circle. Depews, and Hausers, and Ovandrills. Why didn't she feel better?

She didn't feel better because the Randolph Scott Depews had never invited her to their farm. Their parties used to be famous. The Society page of the Clarion covered the parties at the old horse farm thoroughly. Her face never appeared on the same page with the R. S. Depews. Never. And she had had such hopes for her daughter. A big debut at the Club. The R. S. Depews would have had to attend. But her daughter had run off with a knee-grow. No debut.

Her artichoke heart was bitter, bitter. She almost wept. The pain, the terrible pain of childbirth, and then the children, vipers at her very breast. Poison. And bitter. Set her teeth on edge. Her teeth. The children had always been animals, small animals with sharp teeth. Foxes and weasels and rats.

So Grouper mourned; Belle suffered; Cory dreamed a pageant of worries. The turkey lifted its wreckage above the silver platter like an ancient sailing vessel scoured by sea and wind, only bare bones, curved ribs, naked backbone. Dinner limped on, dead as the turkey. Outside, twilight gathered, deepened into gloom. The large house presented a cheery aspect to the passing traffic.

After dinner a small storm developed. Cory sought evasion, Belle sought detention, Grouper sought restitution. Reverend Ovandrill, hearty eater, prevailed on Grouper to mix the after-dinner drinks. Grouper reluctantly agreed, but soon he was humming at his creative play, mixing and shaking, crushing and pouring. Belle prevailed on Cory to apologize to Reverend Ovandrill, who for some reason was unaware that Cory had accepted an invitation to his house to officially meet him this coming Sunday. Cory did not enlighten him. His situation with Hackamore was delicate enough these days.

And where was Hackamore Ovandrill? Belle, who found her disagreeable, asked. Cory, who knew she found her friend the Reverend's daughter disagreeable for no other reason than that he liked her, assured her that she was having Holiday dinner with his very own twin sister Peggy Duquesne in the Existential Room of Stoop's Grocery.

Cornelius overheard this revelation, and saw opportunity. "So," he asked Cory with a wink, "how's the investigation coming along?"

"Investigation?" Reverend Ovandrill asked, turning around. The impression of his turning around was of a great ocean liner approaching a pier. Copious food and plentiful alcohol had rendered unto him a vast, stately dignity, accompanied by an air of solemnity and sanctity. A light

361

dew had formed on his ruddy brow, perhaps from the intensity of his labors.

"Yes," Cornelius answered. The various sagging fleshy plates of his face rose with his smile, like a cluster of holiday balloons ascending into a placid autumn sky. "The investigation."

"You mean, of course, the Commission of Enquiry," Reverend Ovandrill assured Cornelius, who smiled more broadly yet.

"Fine," Cory said, answering the real question, which concerned his investigation into the family past. "How's Bow Keep?"

"Booming," Uncle Cornelius boomed. "Ha ha. Amazing how many people are wearing those ridiculous things."

Reverend Ovandrill was wearing a clip-on bow tie. He fingered it, aware of Bow Keep's economic significance. Cornelius grinned.

Belle, hovering on the edges of this conversation, began to wish she had not invited her son. Grouper appeared at the door with a tray. The tray held a reprise of long-stemmed glasses, foaming with a creamy white substance with what could only be nutmeg sprinkled on top.

"Ah," Reverend Ovandrill breathed, reaching. "Egg nog."

"No," Grouper said modestly. "But similar."

"Delicious," the shepherd said, looking appreciatively at his half-empty glass. "Utterly delicious." A thin line of beige foam lined his upper lip. Belle perceived the first subtle wobble in his stance, and alarm began to grow.

"Of course," Grouper agreed, somewhat less modestly. His spirits, ha ha, were picking up.

The doorbell rang. Dr. Thanatopoulos appeared at the entrance to the living room. Another small social swirl erupted as the guests turned toward him, swept him into a conversational eddy, carried him downstream. Cory wondered how many secrets he knew.

The Reverend's daughter's D. & C., for instance. His own falling face and vitamin treatment. He tried looking intently at his father, his mother, Cornelius. What did the doctor know about them?

This was a lull. Reverend Ovandrill had forgotten the insult to his bow tie, not to mention the insult to his dignity that Cornelius was on the Commission and he was not. Alas, the conversation swerved back that way; the lull was over.

"How's the daughter?" Dr. Thanatopoulos asked Reverend Ovandrill.

"We don't have a daughter," Belle said, misunderstanding.

Cory's suit began to itch. "You do too," he said, a bit too loudly. Conversations halted around the room. Faces turned. Words trembled at the edge of his mouth, hard words, bitter words. They trembled there, waited, leaped into the room. "She is married," he said slowly, distinctly, "to a Negro. He has a doctorate in philosophy from Ohio State University. He is a smart, talented person."

"I don't think..." Belle began, the alarm bells ringing at the back of her head moving frontward to clang at her temple.

"I know you don't," Cory said. Oh, bitter.

Vipers, Belle thought, biting at the breast. That, or indigestion. The turkey was overdone.

"Go to your room," Grouper commanded, forgetting himself.

Cory snorted. Yes, distinctly a snort. "We have some new crocodiles at the zoo," he said. "They are lively compared to this zoo."

Reverend Ovandrill sat down. He said, "Oh, dear," very softly. Mrs. Ovandrill patted his arm. The odor of horse pervaded throughout.

Cory decided to leave.

"Happy Thanksgiving," he said.

"Don't you be snide, young man," Belle snapped. Miltown miles away. Oh and she yearned for it so.

Rebecca appeared at the entrance. "Yall want coffee in heah, Ma'am?"

"What?" Grouper whirled. His drink sloshed, and a thick off-white glue slipped down the side of his glass and over his knuckles.

Rebecca was puzzled. Her question was simple, ritual. "Do you want coffee? In here?"

"No!" said Grouper.

"Yes!" said Belle. Cory snorted again.

"Young man, I'm cutting you out of my will," Grouper said.

"You don't have any will," Cory told him. "Your grandfather was eaten by pigs."

"His grandfather was eaten by pigs?" Cornelius said. "That's interesting. My grandfather was eaten by pigs, too."

"Shut up, you idiot!" Grouper told Cornelius, a lifetime of abiding resentment erupting. "My grandfather was eaten by pigs."

"Why, I know that, Grouper," Cornelius told him mildly.

"'If thou cast us out, suffer us to go away into the herd of swine,'" Reverend Ovandrill murmured. "'And he said unto them, Go.'" He looked up and smiled vacantly. "'And, behold, the whole herd of swine ran violently down a steep place into the sea, and perished in the waters.'"

"Oh, shut up," Grouper said.

"Yes, dear," Mrs. Ovandrill spoke, one of her rare utterances. "Do be quiet. It's none of your business, really."

Rebecca shifted from foot to foot in the entry.

"Oh, what is it?" Belle's own irritation erupted. There was a clear connected chain of volcanoes across the living room, spewing ire crimson enough to match the minister's face. His pouchy eyes were swelling shut.

"Coffee, Ma'am?" Rebecca was chastened, her voice was humble.

"Yes, all right." Belle fretted. The party was going awry. Already Dr. Thanatopoulos was moving toward the door.

"I'd better be..." He spoke softly to the ceiling, which did not reply. "...going."

The door sighed shut. Everyone could hear his automobile start in the silent wake of his departure. He purred away, down the broad sweep of driveway to the quiet suburban street, sticky now from earlier sleet amelt on the asphalt.

Silence persisted. Silence grew teeth and bit. Silence was a terrier after Rat Good Fellowship, brought to ground, hiding deep in burrow.

Rebecca brought in the coffee. She poured thick coffee into tiny blue ceramic demitasse cups. She murmured, "Cream, sugar?" to each of the guests. The guests nodded or did not nod according to their natures.

Rebecca discreetly retired, and still Terrier Silence dug, chewed, persisted.

Cory was caught, one foot nearly lifted in departure. Silence was a trap, his other foot was clamped tight. Silence was a hunter, silence was in ambush, silence gunned down innocence and courtesy in a blaze of utterly soundless bullets. Cory pulled against it; he wanted out, escape, flight.

It was the end of November, and number ten on the Hit Parade was *April Love*, sung by Pat Boone.

Chapter 7. In Which There is a Sermon

"Oh, Lord," Reverend Ovandrill raised his hands to distant springtime in a discrete supplication. "We beseech You, oh Lord, in the spirit of Good Breeding, to sponsor us for membership in Thy Club."

There was a silence after this request, as if a reply were expected. Inside the silence was dripdripdrip.

The dripdripdrip was icicles. Icicles hanging from the church eaves, draped along the roof edge, dangling from tree branches, festooned on lamp posts and ornamental shrubbery. Serpent Mound was swathed in ice. Serpent Mound was shedding a skin of dirty ice, a scaly glaze of rococo stalactites, spirals, helices, glittering crystal daggers, diamond stilettos, poignards and dirks of ice, melting, clear waters running in gutters, falling in the dead flower beds, soaking the brown lawns, gathering dirt and silt into thick roiling mud, torrents of muddy water running along curbs, down storm drains, across the low points of the sidewalks and through intersections, cascades of goo flowing, splashing, turning corners, taking on momentum and force, tearing out fall plantings, eroding the hillsides, smearing the Parkway, seeping through the interstices of earth. Weakening foundations. Dampening underground walls.

Cory was in the back listening to the dripdripdrip. Everyone knew this thaw was temporary. This terrible winter would continue, one of the worst in history.

Hackamore breathed in his ear. The hair on his neck stood up. He was still mad.

"Lord," her father continued from his pulpit. "We are all of good family here." An appreciative murmur rose from the congregation. It was true. They were all of good family there. "We have been to good schools. We have avoided excess."

It was true, looking around Cory could see the smiles.

Reverend Ovandrill's excesses were well know, and entirely visible in the series of chins which tucked themselves into the white clerical collar. But of course he was not referring to that sort of excess. Not at all.

Grouper and Belle were there, too. They were already members, Cory was sure of that. What were the excesses which they had managed to avoid?

Cory leaned to Hack. "The crocodiles were dead," he whispered.

"What?"

"The crocodiles. They were dead. For two weeks now I've been walking them around in the water, but they were dead all along. Not hibernating."

"Oh, for God sakes, Cory."

Reverend Ovandrill was squinting into the dim mellow light of his church, leaning forward with thick hands on the pulpit. His church was slightly episcopal but essentially nondenominational, ecumenical but very Christian. His chins quivered with emotion. No one present could have stipulated exactly what that emotion might have been, but it was intense. In fact, it was confusion. Reverend Ovandrill never really knew whence his sermons came, nor whither they might be tending.

"There are some here this morning, Lord, who suffer. They suffer from confusion." He spoke of himself; it was a good rule to do that when he was confused; it was a practice he followed religiously. "They seek the solace of Your Club, the quiet of Your bar. Time to reflect and to collect." He paused again.

This thaw was odd, a sudden gust of warmth after the blizzards of the last two days. The beginning of December, it was, and weirdly warm. But it would not last. Cory thought about three dead crocodiles and wondered why he was here.

Reverend Ovandrill interrupted his reverie. "There are members," he intoned, riding the wave of inspiration. Once Reverend Ovandrill had hold of a metaphor, he was reluctant to let go. He was a terrier with a metaphor, he was. "And there are non-members. Sometimes we are called upon to make distinctions, to discriminate. To choose. There is Caesar's world, and there is Your world. As it says in Matthew, 7:14, 'Straight is the gate and narrow is the way, which leadeth into life, and few there be that find it.' We are talking here about membership, Lord, in Your club."

He squinted around the chapel again, astonishment on his face. He wondered where this would lead.

"Last summer, Lord, there was violence in our city. Violence." He looked around again for the source of this violence.

There was a murmur of agreement from the congregation, although they did not, for the most part, know what violence exactly their minister was invoking.

"Was this violence the result of excess, Lord? Was this violence a penance for sin? Our club, which is Your club, has a Commission of Inquiry looking into the matter. Some members here today are on that Commission." He leaned back and clasped his hands across the front of his surplice. He smiled. Then he leaned forward again.

"'And few there be that find it,'" he repeated. "'And few there be that find it.' This must tell us, Lord, that not everyone can be a member. Not everyone can join, can dine at Your table, and drink at Your bar. Not everyone can swim in Your pool, play on Your courts, putt on Your green, go eighteen holes with You."

He must have realized then that his metaphor was drifting out of hand, for he changed tack. "But Matthew seven says, and I quote, 'Beware of false prophets, which come to you in sheep's clothing, but inwardly they are ravening wolves,' which can only serve to remind us, Lord, that there are those who appear to have good breeding, but do not."

Cory grinned a long winter wolf grin, toothy and mean. Breeding. Francine back there, devouring cocaine. Baxter Peabody, eaten by pigs. Norman, adopted through blackmail. Excess everywhere he looked. Excess and bad breeding, carefully hidden. His face had fallen off, and now he grinned. Grouper knew. Cory watched him. Cory folded his fingers together inside his palms. This is the church.

But Grouper was good. It didn't bother him at all. Belle was the one squirming. But she had good breeding, her father was Dr. Hauser, a solid man, citizen of Valhalla, important and rich. He had good breeding, and so must she.

She was married to Grouper though.

Reverend Ovandrill was checked momentarily: either his logic was wandering or he was insulting his congregation. Memorized verses left over from seminary came back to him in a flood, currents of inspiration flowed freely as the snows of his intellect, melted by four martinis quaffed before donning surplice, tumbled into the river of words flowing from him; he was in full flood. "For, 'By their fruits ye shall know them.' And so it is written indeed, Lord, that application for membership shall be processed by duly elected members of the Governing Board. 'But the children of the kingdom shall be cast out into outer darkness: there shall be weeping and gnashing of teeth.'"

The stained glass windows portrayed the farmers of Schachter's Landing arming themselves for Civil War, a war in which they never got, in the end, to participate, but the arming itself rendered them heroic in the imagination of the artist. In these days of social change, it was not clear whether they were to be applauded for arming themselves to fight the north, or for failing to fight. A shaft of parti-colored sunlight shot through the farmers and lit up Reverend Ovandrill's white surplice and face with what appeared to be a Technicolor disease.

Cory raised his forefingers tips pointed together. And this is the steeple.

"For the Lord would never do anything in poor taste, nor anything indiscreet, although there are some who are fearful of being like the 'whole herd of swine who ran down a steep place into the sea, and perished in the waters.'" He appeared then to recognize the quote he had trotted out at Thanksgiving, and swerved once more

369

without pause. He flipped at random through the enormous Bible in the lectern, reading from it without looking, "As it says in Nahum 2:10, 'The faces of them all gather blackness.' And while Negroes may go to our schools, Lord, keep them, we beseech You, from our clubs."

That hit home.

"The Commission of Enquiry, what has it found? It has found that members of Your Club, Lord, did not condone that violence, no! Those were not members, they were *Albanians*! They were *hillbillies*! They were *albinos*. Genetic defects, people, Lord, of low inbreeding, bent on *revenge*!

"Revenge for what? You will ask, Lord. We too will ask. We do not know. Perhaps You do. If so, do not tell us! They are not members, how can we understand them? We cannot? We are members!"

It was a socko sermon. Belle reflected. Peggy had run off with a knee-grow, after all. Grouper's bad breeding, some defect in his family tree, must be responsible, responsible for the violence, the Albanians, the defects in her children. Belle filled with hostility. Vipers, she thought again. She had nursed a nest of vipers to her very breast — husband and twins, all vipers. Bad blood.

Cory watched the sermon hit home as he spread his thumbs apart, and thus opened the doors. Reverend Ovandrill wrapped up.

"Oh Lord," Reverend Ovandrill said. "We have paid our dues on time. We have been fruitful and multiplied. We have tilled and reaped. We are not responsible for our past, for our ancestors or their forgotten crimes. Reward us. Let us in."

Oh bitter, bitter, Belle thought. Her life a waste. Been fruitful and multiplied. Paid our dues.

"Amen," Reverend Ovandrill said.

Cory spread his palms upward and wiggled his fingers.

"Amen," said all the people.

Chapter 8. A Man to Man Talk

Time went by, the fat shufflebutt dimly seen through the dark trees of winter, an absent-minded snuffler. Cory passed inspection at the after-church luncheon and was instantly forgotten again. He passed his courses for the fall semester and signed up for Animal Husbandry 102. And then one day in January, Hackamore Ovandrill took him to her ancestral home for the second time, deposited him in the salon with the carved pecan fireplace and left him there with the Reverend, her Daddums.

"Nonsense!"

The Reverend snorted. Clear martini swirled moodily in its frosty glass.

"What?" Cory gave a yelp. The Reverend was drunk.

"All nonsense! I don't know what I'm talking about. My sermons, I don't know where they're from, what they're about. A fraud, it's all a fraud. Young man... What did you say your name was?"

"Cory. Cory Depew. Belle and Grouper's son. I'm dating your daughter."

"Ah. Yes. Now I remember. We've met somewhere before, haven't we?" Reverend Ovandrill peered at Cory through the pouches of his eyes.

"Thanksgiving. I came for dinner the Sunday after Thanksgiving. You gave a sermon."

Wind howled around the cornices, the eaves, the cupolas, the towers. Of course this house was not as large as Cory's first impression. It wasn't a palace. Just a mansion that once belonged to the Depews.

Mrs. Ovandrill clacked through the room, high gloss on her high boots, a swish to her jodhpurs. She was both plump and pinched.

"Oh. I was thinking of someone else, maybe. Thanksgiving. Yes, I remember." The reverend reminisced, sunk in martini. Where was Hack? "A time of thanksgiving. We give thanks. We eat turkey. Do you know what lies next door to us, son, to the south?"

"No, sir."

"Pigs. Yorkshire and Chester Whites mostly. The Depew Hog Farm. They breed 'em over there. Snuffle, grunt, oink. My mother Narcissa bless her soul used to tell me about pigs. A great white boar that roamed the woods. A thousand pounder, at least. A monster. I'll tell you a story, son."

Reverend Ovandrill grew orotund and fulsome. Cory settled himself. Time has passed. Christmas had passed. New Year's had passed. The Silhouettes were saying *Get a Job*, number ten and rising fast. Danny and the Juniors were *At the Hop* (number one, also at the top of the rhythm and blues chart), Ricky Nelson had been *Stood Up* (No. Two). Cory knew them all. Numbers three through nine: *Great Balls of Fire* (Jerry Lee Lewis), *April Love* (Pat Boone), *Peggy Sue* (oh, Buddy Holly, doomed, doomed!), *Jailhouse Rock* (Elvis, of course) and *Raunchy* (Bill Justis). He knew them all.

"Mrs. O would not like to know this, son. I count on you to keep mum. It would upset her. Narcissa, my mother, was from — that way!" He jabbed with his thumb and watched Cory closely.

"The library?"

"No, no, no. South." The Reverend's voice sank to a whisper. "Upstream. Slyville!"

Cory stopped his contemplation of the top ten. "No kidding?"

"Used to be that a great white boar roamed the woods down there, in the hills. A killer, they said. Of sheep, chickens, dogs. Hard to believe stories like that. Pigs root, they don't hunt, they don't do that sort of thing, but for certain he caused a lot of damage, trampled down fences, smashed chicken coops. Broke into my mother's grandfather's pig pen and let all the hogs loose. Lot of people hunted him, went after him with guns, set traps,

372

waited at his favorite spots, or what people thought were his favorite spots. Her granddad Norman Balshajt put out his favorite sow one time, staked her out ready 'n willing. He never saw that boar, not once, but damn if that sow didn't get pregnant. She had a litter, too, thirteen piglets, and one of 'em grew huge and white and mean. He got away, broke loose from the pigpen and left. People said they saw that boar for years, roaming the hills."

He finished his martini and rose to get another. The howling wind brought more snow, more ice. Reverend Ovandrill put ice in his drink and settled into the soft chair again.

"Do you believe in God, son?"

"I don't know. I suppose so," Cory lied.

The minister laid his plump finger alongside his nose. "I don't," he confessed suddenly. "It's the way they look at you. Sometimes I go down past the horse pasture. I walk along the fence. There's one pig watches me, always watching, a white boar. Big. No thousand pounder, but big. No God could make an animal that'll look at you like that. Not a benevolent deity, anyways." He shook his head and his jowls rolled lubriciously. "The pigs," he continued, his voice dropping off, "they're... too... fucking... *intelligent!*"

A fine mist hit Cory's face. "And they're unpredictable, and fast and strong. You can never tell whose side they are on! They know things, things they shouldn't. They know we want to eat them, we're going to eat them. But it's horrible, the teeth, small and sharp and...wicked. Tusks. They want to eat us, you know that? They're over there pretending to play, rooting and snoozing, but they're watching us. God, the dreams I have. Do you know anything about magic, boy?"

"No, sir."

"My father was a Theosophist, a student of the occult. Pah! He was a moron. Christ! He lived to be ninety-three years old! On and on. Wouldn't let go. A fellow named Dexter Pendragon Willoughby used to hang around here. A protege of my mother's. Maybe a relative, a nephew or something, I don't know. I was young then, just a boy. He told stories too. Terrible stories. He knew things about Norman Balshajt. He told me once my mother was illegitimate. A bastard child, borned out of wedlock, spawn of a no-good drifter, a man named Baxter Peabody, a thief and a seducer. A killer. He killed Norman Balshajt and seduced his daughter Pristine at the same time. I can't feature that, son, I really can't. No man could do a thing like that, not in a decent world. I say it in church, but it's a fact, son, I'll say it here and now, God is no gentleman! But I will tell you, Narcissa wouldn't rest. She told me things, just before she died. She wanted revenge something awful. She wanted something terrible to happen to the man who did that to her mother and her grandfather. Something terrible did happen to him, too. Yes, something awful happened to that man."

"What? What happened to him?" Cory whispered, but Reverend Ovandrill was at the wet bar again, freshening his drink. He paused by the windows, shattered with frost.

"A hard winter," he said. He turned back to Cory. "The Russians," he said, very distinctly, "are going to attack us. Soon. With atomic weapons. Radiation, fallout, heat and terrible shock waves will destroy the earth. It's all there in Revelation. 'And the angel took the censer, and filled it with fire of the altar, and cast it into the earth: and there were voices, and thunderings, and lightnings, and an earthquake... And the seven angels sounded and there followed hail and fire mingled with blood, and they were cast upon the earth: and a third part of the trees was burnt up, and all green grass was burnt up....and as it were a great mountain burning with fire was cast into the sea: and a third part of the sea became blood: and a third part of the creatures which were in the sea, and had life, died: and the third part of the ships were destroyed...and there fell a great star from heaven, burning as it were a lamp, and it fell upon the third part of the rivers, and upon the fountains of waters: And the name of the star is called Wormwood: and the third part of the waters became wormwood: and many men died of the waters, because they were made bitter.' And I am so afraid..."

He was looking out the windows again at the wind and blowing snow, through the blurred explosions of frost on the glass.

"Excuse me," Cory whispered. "I thought I heard Hack calling."

"No!" the Reverend thundered. "You think I believe all that nonsense just because it's in the goddam Bible? Don't be silly. That's the kind of crap my father believed. Theosophists, bah! I believe it because it's real, in the world around us. Atomic bombs, boy, that's what we are talking about here. Radiation sickness, fallout. Rotting flesh, Rains of fire from the sky."

He pointed at the floor. "Down there, that's the only place to be when it comes. Down there. I have a shelter."

Cory could see the shelter. He could see the shelves of provisions, the drums of water, the blankets and medical supplies stored in the plain gray cement bunkers. There would be weapons, too, of course, for afterwards, when the survivors came up to confront the mutants, horrible creatures twisted with agony and new, terrible hungers, roaming the hills and valleys and canyon streets of Valhalla. There would be all that and more. There would be Cory Depew and his beloved Hackamore Ovandrill, ready to emerge into the new world, ready to repopulate it all.

Wallace Ovandrill sat abruptly on his couch. He leaned back. He laid his white hair against the back of the sofa and closed his eyes.

He sighed.

"Crime, son. Crimes everywhere. I preach about it. I ask they be forgiven, those crimes. Hell, I ask they be forgotten. I don't want to know about them. But they come in dreams, the crimes. Seduction, torture, and murder and the theft of fire. Her great grandmother Mammy Sly cursed Baxter Peabody. My God, could she curse. A plague of swine. Pursued by that great white boar that wandered in the mountains of the Old Country. She blasted Baxter

Peabody unto the fourth generation.

"That's your generation, son!"

"Do you...?" Cory began to ask. But he knew the answers to that question, and many others.

Besides, Reverend Ovandrill was asleep, his jaw lost in his chins.

Chapter 9. In Which Large Questions are Raised

"What kind of a world is this?" Cory asked Withrow Duquesne. "Atomic bombs and Perry Como singing *Catch a Falling Star*? The McGuire Sisters singing *Sugartime*?"

"Worry about something else."

"What?"

"Well, the river is frozen over solid. You can walk to Indiana or Ohio. Worry about Schachter's Worm."

"Why should I worry about that?"

"The worm is going to turn. The secondary larval stage is a wood-borer. It has an almighty complicated life cycle. Goes through the egg stage, the wood-borer stage, the mammal-kidney stage, the free-floating stage. You can worry about that, because it is about to enter an active part of its forty-year cycle."

Cory put his finger on a page of *Swine Management*, by Bustard and Alamo, Fourth Ed. Icicles fractured the distant sun, but the crew shack was warm. "I have a paper due. Listen to this. 'The Chester White originated in the early nineteenth century. Farmers in Chester County, Pennsylvania, developed the breed from original stock brought over from England by William Penn. Like most stock breeders they were interested in increasing the size of the animals, their adaptability to the particular terrain of Chester County, and of course, their productivity. Chester Whites are not only large, they are extremely prolific. They are, of course, white all over, like Yorkshires, though paler of hue than the latter breed. Usually they are gentle, sensitive and intelligent, but there are occasional reports of the boars "going rogue." In such cases, which are admittedly rare, the animals become destructive and hostile.' How is it you know so much about this Schachter's Worm?"

377

Withrow produced *The Strange Origins and Historical Development of Schachter's Landing, Kentucky*, July, 1856. "This pamphlet," Withrow said, "has written on it in a very faint and nearly illegible script, the name of Baxter Peabody, a man later eaten by pigs. The back flap also has some writing on it which you may want to take a look at, although it too is difficult to read."

"You're right. I can't make it out," Cory said, handing the pamphlet back to his brother-in-law. "Why don't you tell me what it says?"

An icicle broke loose from the eaves of the zoo crew shack and shattered on the frozen walk. Cory could see into the back of Kierkegaard's cage where the ape sat huddled against the bars, shivering. He no longer vomited for the folks, but he had certainly lost his *joie de vivre*.

"'Coach through ashes. Despair, teeth from feldspar and high heat. The paste must have consistency of pig dung. The explosion. Horror. Everywhere I look that white...' (I can't read the next bit) 'I am so afraid, the End is at Hand. Golden tush, the Lord Who Made Thy Teeth. Madness.' My guess is that he wrote this on the coach trip back down from Slyville. There's no date, but best I can place it was fall of 1857. He died the following winter. Eaten."

"That's what Hack's father said. 'I am so afraid.' He thinks the end is at hand, too."

The door banged open and Cory jumped. "Don't do that, Vincent. Jesus."

"Jesus, yourself, kemosabe, I just got to tell you this. It was such a fine day..."

"It must be ten below out there!"

"Like I say, a fine day, sun is shining. So I got on my Black Shadow and I rode down to Idd..."

"But there's nothing down there but Albanians and...oh, Indians."

"Cory," Withrow said gently, "there are times when you lack tact."

"Yeah."

378

Vincent nodded his spiky head. His cheeks were red, more red than ever, and streaks of cold tears tracked back from his eyes, lost in black hair. "Yeah," he echoed. "My grand aunt lives down there in a miserable little shack, but she loves it so, and is she ever full of stories. So, I went down there through the crystals of ice and snow and it was a journey I tell you like a vision quest such as my people used to make. And she told me things."

"Told you things?"

"Told me things."

"About pigs."

"How did you know?" Vincent Black Shadow was genuinely surprised.

"Just the way things are going."

"She told me things about pigs and the Indian Way, and I am going to tell them to you because I know you are interested and you have a paper due in your animal husbandry class and I know things, told me by my great-aunt. On the way back I went by your place. Here's your mail."

Cory shook his head as he took the envelope. "Pigs. There's no end to it, is there?"

"Do I detect a little whine there?"

"No," Cory said. "You detect a big whine. It's not fair. My goddam face fell off! I get attacked by crazed Albanian cops with a private grudge."

"Whadda you mean by that?" Vincent asked.

"I mean they meant to shoot me that night at the Telltale Heart. But my face was covered with bandages. And then at the police station I gave them Wernher Von Braun's name, so they missed me. I thought it was a joke, but it saved my life."

"Wait a minute, here, now, there then," Vincent drawled. "You ain't gonna tell me you're beginning to believe all this crap, are you, Cory? Curses, and crazed albinos and people eaten by pigs. It's all a big joke, right?"

"I'm not so sure." Cory opened his mail. The envelope was embossed on the back with a name and address.

Reverend and Mrs. Wallace Ovandrill
Number Two Asgard Avenue
The Serpent Mound
Schachter's Landing, Ky.
Request the Pleasure of Your Company on the Ides, March
Fifteen,
Nineteen Hundred and Fifty-Eight
At Seven-thirty in the Evening
To Celebrate the Completion of Reverend Ovandrill's Fallout
Shelter and Wine Cellar.
Black Tie.
RSVP: Serpent Mound Three Six Six Six.

"Fallout shelter? That man of God has a fallout shelter?" Vince the Cynic.

Cory defended him. "He's afraid. I mean really afraid. He doesn't even believe in God. Probably he's an alcoholic. His wife rides horses all the time. His daughter smokes marijuana and writes dirty poetry. She's had an abortion. His mother told him he had to get revenge on Baxter Peabody and all his succeeding generations, unto the fourth. He apparently doesn't know that Baxter Peabody's son Norman was named Rasmussen, and that he was adopted by Dudley Depew and changed his name to Depew. He doesn't know I'm the one he's supposed to get. But probably he will find out. So his life may not be all that great, you know?

"The thing is, I'm in love with Hackamore Ovandrill who, whether she knows it or not, is charged with getting me somehow; maybe that's why we're not getting along so well at the moment. And now that I think of it, Dexter Pendragon Willoughby is probably the father of Big Mike Willoughby whose wife is named Marsha and who got my virginity under circumstances I'd rather not remember, oh God damn."

"You talk too much, kemosabe. You have a paper on

380

pigs to write, and later on we are going to meet with that crazy monk of yours, so perhaps right now you should shut up and listen."

So Cory listened to his faithful Indian companion tell him the things he had been told, and the ice cracked on the river, the earth rolled on toward the sun, which only appeared to decline. A little wind picked up across the river. Frost formed on the hairs under Kierkegaard's nostrils; he looked around uneasily, as if aware in some dim way of doom accelerating toward them all.

Chapter 10. In Which, After an Historical Digression, Brother Grigory Hears a Confession

"It wass," Brother Grigory told them, "de ent of August, 1922, vhen Mustapha Kemal Ataturk attacked the city of Smyrna."

He sat beneath Hegel's portrait, and his audience strained forward to hear what he was saying. It was, indeed, difficult to understand his English, but the story unfolded nonetheless.

Within ten days the city had fallen, was sacked and burned, and all Greek survivors escaped by sea. The adventure destroyed both Lloyd George in England and the Sultanate in Turkey, and created thousands upon thousands of Greek refugees.

It was a dismal period for Greece. At the treaty of Lausanne, completed in July of 1923, northern Epirus was returned to Albania, and Smyrna along with its environs was turned over to Turkey, as well as the islands of Tenedos and Imbros. Italy got the Dodecanese, Britain got Cyprus. In all the confusion of the reorganization two insignificant refugees among the thousands were created. The twin sons of Constantine Thanatopoulos, Costa and Grigory, swirled unnoticed in the sweep of history.

They were separated when Constantine went to Smyrna in 1903 to engage in the trading of dates and currents, taking three-year-old Costa with him. Mrs. Thanatopoulos remained behind in northern Epirus, died, and Costa's twin Grigory was offered to the monastery at Permet in the dry dismal mountains there. In 1923 both had to leave their homes, and emigrated separately "to the America" where they settled in Valhalla, City of Light on the brown Ohio, Costa with a Turkish medical degree and Grigory with an Albanian Orthodox religious vocation. Since by this time he spoke Albanian as well as Greek, the monastery of St. Credula the Ulcerated Martyr of Shköder atop Mount Worthy (where, it was said, the "Worthy" retreated during the cholera epidemic of 1879, spreading the disease to those who already lived there, among them, as it happened, Henry Rasmussen, a.k.a. Henrietta, herself in loco parentis to twin boys) was ideal for Grigory to practice monkery. His English, alas, remained rudimentary.

So it was with only the dimmest comprehension that he listened to the rambling confessions of a dazed man one dull afternoon in the fall of 1923, while Grouper Depew was a-courtin' Belle Hauser, and only a few weeks after he, Grigory, had arrived here in the America.

He had been sweeping the inner courtyard of the cathedral of St. Credula on orders of the abbot, a courtyard filled ankle deep with the leaves of elm and sycamore. He swept the leaves into a huge pile beside the cement fountain which commemorated the saint's Final Ulceration, an infamous event long since drained of metaphysical meaning. It did provide an opportunity to Valhalla's older Albanian residents to vent an inarticulate and sullen rage at their oppressors, whoever they may be. No one remembered any longer that St. Crecula's ulcerations were the tertiary result of a routine seduction and subsequent infection by a Turkish pasha with a halitosis as advanced as his pox. Credula herself was, in those days of 1623, a simple girl whose legs parted of their own volition, and whose simple, generous nature had gotten her into trouble twelve times as a matter of record before the pasha gave her syphilis and she entered the convent at Shköder for treatment.

The Final Ulceration depicted in the fountain was aided in its portrayal by the effects of forty years of harsh Ohio Valley winters, which had streaked and corroded the porous cement until only the unpleasant outlines of St. Credula's fatal torments were discernable. On her face, Brother Grigory reflected, was an expression which appeared somewhat less than holy, and her position, recumbent on a draped bed, with her legs in the position they had adopted most readily in life, was not the traditional position of adoration. The fact was that St. Credula always appeared, to Brother Grigory at least, to be in the throes of sexual orgasm, although he had no first hand knowledge of what that condition might be like, for a woman. As for himself, he'd had dreams, and the dreams had led to frequent furtive sinning on his own part, so he did have first (and here he could not suppress a small chuckle) hand knowledge: despite his vocation he knew an orgasm when he had one.

He spent much of his time in the courtyard, and eventually, in the weeks since he had arrived, the abbot had given him responsibility for its maintenance. As a result he was just bending down to ignite the pile of leaves beside St. Credula's fountain when this wild man grabbed his rough brown sleeve and implored him with a dumb and frantic look.

Startled, Brother Grigory dropped the match. St. Credula's eyes were opened wide, bulging in ecstasy — piety, pleasure, or pain. He gave a nod to acknowledge the desperation of the man holding his sleeve, and the leaves beside him flared into fiery life, igniting the hem of his cassock. He was obliged to plunge himself through the thin layer of ice on the water in St. Credula's fountain in order to extinguish the blaze. Then he led his suppliant into the dim cathedral to hear what he presumed was some kind of confession.

The man was distraught, with wild hair, and a beard cluttered with the remains of more than one breakfast. His eyes were shot with blood. He appeared to be in his sixties, possibly older. Brother Grigory was only 23, and quite innocent of most worldly matters, including the accurate gauging of age. He was, however, a good listener, especially when addressed in a foreign language of which he had only the most imperfect understanding, an understanding helped little by three years of English taught by a near-illiterate peasant from Sparta who had once traveled on a freighter to New York City where, while spending three days in a jail cell for excessive public drunkenness, he had acquired his own knowledge of English. Later he fell heir to a couple of grammars, and from them taught English to the children at the monastery in Permet.

There is a grand flow to history: history is a river, vast and implacable, a deep flow which carries small things along with complete indifference. He, Grigory Thanatopoulos, was a small thing, and this moment was a tiny eddy in that huge imponderable current. He felt deep gratitude to God, and to St. Credula, his Voice on Earth, for granting him his eddy in time, his small place in history. Here, in the city of Valhalla in a bend in the Ohio river, in 1926, Brother Grigory heard the confession of a stranger who spoke in a difficult language of sins and deceptions it would take the poor Greek monk a lifetime to untangle.

The voice of confession, cracked and whining, droned on and on, and the empty cathedral echoed until the syllables, even had they been uttered in a language he understood perfectly, would have been overlapped and muffled by their own repetitions.

Brother Grigory heard names among the spray of unintelligible words. Norman and Baxter. He got the impression that Norman was strong and Baxter was weak. It was unclear whether the man before him owned one of these names or not.

He heard other words, words he recognized because they had profound meaning for him personally. Words like "betrayal," and "love," and "deception." Finally, very distinctly, he heard the phrase, "pig entrails."

"Peek awntralss?" he repeated. "Vhats mean peek awntralss?"

The wild man stared at him. He shook his head, and his grizzled hair flew around it like spray on a rock. He had been kneeling in this cold empty place for twenty minutes spilling the corrupt, humid secrets of his soul to this monk, and the monk was responding with gibberish.

Brother Grigory realized he had made a mistake. With

the alacrity of the truly simple he adopted a solemn expression, and uttered the one phrase he could enunciate clearly in English. "Go on, my son," he said.

The man, at least forty years his senior, appeared relieved, and continued to drone out his incomprehensible confession. Brother Grigory began to hope for a swift finish. For one thing the leaves were burning unattended in the courtyard. It was conceivable a stray breeze might toss some embers onto the roof of the cathedral and spark a problem. For another, pressure was beginning to built up in the Grigory's bladder; soon it could overcome his years of discipline and zeal. His mind began to wander, and a small frown of worry appeared between his guileless brown eyes.

The penitent seemed to feel that frown was one of empathy, for he looked up in gratitude, and thrust into the monk's hands a large folder bound with maroon ribbon, sealed with cracked wax. It had an official appearance. Brother Grigory was so surprised that his fingers closed reflexively on it before he could protest, the man gave him a penetrating stare, and then, before he rushed out into the dull afternoon and vanished into the smoke from the burning leaves beside St. Credula's ecstatic fountain, uttered another completely clear and comprehensible phrase.

"I don't know nottin," he said as he turned. "I'm a Dead Man."

"Wait," Brother Grigory called out, but the man was gone. It was some time before he looked down to examine the object in his hands, and many years before he understood what it was. Yet he always felt that there was a luminous glow of Destiny about it, for it had appeared as the result of vast and incomprehensible events which had swept him into a collision with this particular time and place. Surely there was some powerful significance to his life from that moment on. He would devote his life to understanding it and what it all had to do with entrails.

Then he handed Cory the folder of papers, the wax seal broken. "Orichins of Soffrink?" he said hopefully.

386

BOOK THE EIGHTH: THE WHITE PIG, 1958

Chapter 1. On the Whiteness of the Pig

Cornelius Hauser Depew   Vet. Sci. 102

Instructor: Dr. Barrow   March 5, 1958

ON THE WHITENESS OF THE PIG AND THE ORIGINS OF SUFFERING

As the white whale is to Ishmael, so is the white pig to me.

Its size, its heft, its indestructible whiteness which is both all colors and no color at all, the neatness of its step as it moves through the forest and the silence of that tread are things of awe and terror.

Some of the qualities which contribute to my personal pig-dread come from the swine itself without regard to its hue. These qualities are: connection with the earth, rooted, so to speak, in the primal soil from which all life springs; a profound spiritual, and possibly physical, interchangeability between hog and human, as in the story of the Gadarene swine, when Jesus drove the devils out of the young man from Gadara and into the herd of swine, which then "ran violently down a steep place...and were choked in the sea;" a sense of unrealized potential in talent and intelligence many have reported about the hog (Cf. "Some Tentative Correlations Between Cortical Complexity and Adaptive Intelligence in <u>Sus Scrofa</u>," where it

389

is suggested pigs are more intelligent than dolphins, themselves sometimes called 'sea-hogs');[1] a wisdom in the eye accessible only to initiates of certain mystery cults;[2] an existential carelessness toward death; and a nearly neolithic awe of primitive and divine pigdom, a sense that somehow the hog is God.

The Graikoi, pre-Homeric Greeks, for example, worshipped a crone-goddess most often depicted as a sow. Their rituals, according to Harlow and Bacon,[3] were "dark and dreadful, and involved the sacrifice of <u>pigs and human beings</u>." (Italics mine.)

This last, I believe, is what contributes most to the primitive terror pigs inspire — that sense of <u>identification</u> with the pig, the feeling that swine and people are somehow the same, interchangeable in the dark blood-rituals of the inner world! My brother-in-law suggests humans and pigs share self-knowledge — that is, the knowledge of mortality and the feelings of helplessness which arise from that knowledge. The terror before absurdity forces man to attend to existence itself, wherein the risks of life are great and absolute, for the consequences are life or death. Pigs seem to know this.

Further, the awe, and subsequent rejection and disgust many people feel toward swine (their associations with filth and gluttony and greed) are based not on knowledge, but ignorance. Yet the associations are very real, and spring from some hidden horror within the human species. When we delve into the myths about swine, we find that fear expressed.

Boars attacked many of the great heroes of bygone ages. There was the boar Erymanthian and the boar Calydonian; there was the wild sow of Crommyon. Attis, and Zeus and Adonis and Osiris were all gods killed, (and perhaps eaten?) by swine. Some gods were seen riding on enormous pigs. Demeter, the Corn Goddess, was initially depicted as a pig. Pigs, naturally enough, were originally corn gods.

The gods killed by swine were all symbols of rebirth, resurrection. And resurrection itself is a terrifying thought because it implies re-experiencing the agony of birth, the "trauma" as Freud called it.

Add to all this the color white, and you can see why the whiteness of the pig inspires such supernatural dread.

White, as Melville points out in <u>Moby Dick</u>[4] is often associated with goodness, purity and virtue, with radiance and spirituality, with perfection, as in, say, the perfection of a white 1956 Ford Thunderbird. Yet there is another aspect to the color which combines with the hog to create a being that is truly awful: the profound associations of the color white with all that is most evil and despairing within the human soul.

Melville says, for instance: "What is it in the Albino man so peculiarly repels and often shocks the eye, as that sometimes he is loathed by his own kith and kin! It is that whiteness that invests him, a thing expressed by the name he bears. The Albino is as well made as other men — has no substantive deformity — and yet

391

this mere aspect of all-pervading whiteness makes him more strangely hideous than the ugliest abortion. Why should this be so?"[5]

Why <u>should</u> this be so? Perhaps, he suggests later, it is the pallor of death. We look around us, and everywhere we see Death's white sign. In popular films we see it in the pallor of Dracula, in the white shrouds worn by his brides, in the ghost-pale presence of the Frankenstein monster or in the icy wastes where <u>The Thing</u> wanders. It is present in the glacier and fogs of Thule, Greenland, where I spent almost three years. It is present in the mists that rise on summer nights in Schachter's Landing as on the Serpent Mound itself. White is the color of mourning in Japan. White is the color of the Saint's image sprawled in the fountain in the courtyard of the Church of St. Credula, the Ulcerated Martyr of Shköder, as she exhales her final agonized breath into the steamy Valhalla air.

White of course is the color of ghosts, of things leached of life. It is the color of snow, "Winter kept us warm, covering/Earth in forgetful snow..."[6]

It is the color of Fear itself.

The White Hog finds a place in the symbolism of Indian, Albanian, and the local Sinker cultures. The Illyrians, from whom the Albanians of the Valhalla region are descended, believed the world was formed by, and they were descended from, an enormous white sow larger than heaven, who separated her litter into black piglets and white piglets. Of the white, one, named Abhehu, was a potent magician, able to change into a human being and back into a pig at will. He can be called upon in times of great need to inflict dire punishments on one's enemies, provided that the curser is Albanian and a believer.

The word Albania itself comes from the Indo-European root albho — which has related meanings of "white ghostlike apparitions," and, in Greek, the word alphos refers to the dull white of leprosy. The great white pig Abhehu was everywhere, but could only be seen by a priestess of the Pig Cult, or, for ordinary people, out of the corner of the eye as it drifted silently among the trees.

This legend is still very strong among the Sinkers of Slyville, and was the origin of the primary Sinker ritual of dropping the bride down a well. If she sinks and drowns, she is saved, and is carried off by the White Boar Abhehu to heaven, where she will be suckled forever by the Mother Sow. If she floats, she is a sinner, and must stay in this world and be subjected to the carnal appetites of her husband, a terrible fate for Sinkers. Sometimes, apparently, the White Boar is still seen, and is the source of much superstitious fear.

Among the Indian cultures of northern Kentucky, particularly those of the Little Hawking, or Mumaway, Valley, the north became associated some time in the seventeenth century with a great white Boar. By this time the pigs imported from the Caribbean by Ponce de Leon had spread as far north as Michigan, and had somehow bred themselves into a ghastly pale white color. It is no wonder then that they are associated with the north and its snows. Further, though, the White Pig holds powers not possessed by animals of other directions and colors, magical powers. They have wisdom; they are remote from men's concerns, and most of all, the quality of their wisdom is ambivalent. They know things, the Indians say, things which they will reveal if asked, but they are things most men would prefer not to know, things which, when learned, drive them mad.

Wild pigs in general are to be feared. They have tusks; they are very fierce and willing to protect their territories. Thus the boars of Greek mythology were the most difficult quarry on a hunt.

But the truly awful thing about the hog is that he will eat anything! The pig is omnivorous, and while we may comfortably feel that the pig is only interested in swill, or slops, or corn, he will, in fact, eat meat, and do so with teeth very like those of a human, although he does have more of them (forty-four, to be precise). This is more than merely another point of identification between man and pig; it is a horror. Men have consumed swine meat for thousands of years, but behind this careless consumption is a secret knowledge that the tables, as it were, could be turned, and have been turned. Pigs have eaten people. My own great grandfather was eaten by the sanitation swine which once roamed at will through the streets of Valhalla.

The legend in Slyville and surrounding
areas that the Great White Hog Abhehu wanders
those woods holds that this awesome pig harbors
a deep-seated and inexplicable hatred of
mankind. This is not true. I know for a fact
that this hog hates only me and members of my
family.

This is why I feel such deep dread of the
white pig, and find therein the origins of
suffering. Not only is there a universal
uneasiness on the presence of swine and the
color white, but there is also an active
malevolence abroad in the land. And of all these
things the Albino Pig is the symbol. "Wonder ye
then at the fiery hunt?"

FOOTNOTES

1. Stock Breeder's Quarterly, Fall, 1957,
p. 146.

2. Bacon, Lloyd, The Mythic Pig, Trotter &
Co., New York, 1932, Ch. 3.

3. Ibid., page 273.

4. Harpers, New York, 1851, Ch. 42.

5. Ibid., p. 166.

6. T. S. Eliot, The Waste Land, line 5.

Chapter 2. On Pigs and Existentialism

"How'd you do?" Hack asked him on the way to the party.

Cory read from the paper in his lap. "Professor Barrow says the following: 'While this is all very poetic, and shows substantial research, your paranoid imaginings are of little concern to the Veterinary Science Department of this University. Where are the lists of swine breeds? Where are the lists of parasites, infestations and infections? Where is the analysis of the proper feed mixtures for healthy rapid growth, the proper combinations of bone meal, ground sorghum, phosphoric acid, activated animal sterol, oxides of zinc, copper, manganese compounds, magnesium, the iodides and the phosphates, carbonates, acids, chlorides and vitamins? Where is the discussion of new artificial insemination techniques? Where is any mention of the newer breeds of swine, the new American Landrace, the Maryland 1, the Beltsville 3 and so forth? This paper has nothing to do with hog husbandry. C minus.' Professor Barrow did not care for my term paper."

Hack had to agree. She pulled in her lower lip as she drove Cory's DeSoto out Louisa May Alcott Pike. March was filled with strange lights, shifting shadows, cold wet, wind and gathering darkness. Cory thought there were portents in the heavens. A cloud shaped like a pig floated overhead, fat with snow.

The same pig-cloud floated over Cliffside, where a pickup truck loaded with armaments idled at the street corner not far from Stoop's Grocery. Inside, the Existentialists were meeting in Emergency Session.

"Already the stadium is gone," Withrow was saying. "There's a hole down by the river where the new one is going to be. Maybe. Someday. Two people have already jumped in that hole and drowned. Two suicides, right through the ice. Camus says that the question of suicide is the only significant question man can ask himself. Be that as it may, our friend Cory is not asking himself that question. Vincent, is that truck still out there?"

Vincent Black Shadow Lavere moved with his stealthy Indian tread through the curtain hanging over the doorway, through the canned goods and boxes of pasta and jars of pickled pigs feet and chitterlings, to the front door. His engineer boots thudded away on the wooden floor. They thudded back.

"Yup," he said. "It's Big Mike, all right. Marsha's with him. And at the other end of the street is a patrol car. I think it's the same cop that did the shooting at the Telltale Heart."

Withrow nodded. "From Slyville. What do they have against us? Aside from the fact that Cory screwed Marsha? That shouldn't be a big deal — so have most of the regulars of the Silver Spoon."

"The curse," Peggy suggested.

"According to this," Withrow waved a sheet of paper in the air, "the curse was on all the descendents of Baxter Peabody unto the fourth generation."

"Maybe it took them all this time to figure out who we were. After all, Baxter Peabody died. The twins were named Rasmussen, and one of them changed his name to Depew. Perhaps they were confused by all the name changes?"

Withrow grunted. "'I call upon the Great Swine of Diabolus, whose whiteness is Terror and whose Golden Tushes reek of Blood, to root him out, to trample him beneath his hooves, to crack his bones, and the bones of all who follow.' She was not without a certain vindictiveness, that old lady."

"Kemosabe, you gotta gift. Litotes."

"What," Peggy wanted to know, "is litotes?"

"A kind of understatement." Withrow, who had a PhD in philosophy and who had studied logic and rhetoric, knew.

397

"And how did you know, Vincent?"

"Not only am I the world's greatest motorcycle mechanic, I am also, as it happens, an Intellectual. What are we going to do about those palefaces, and I do mean pale, out in the street? They're coming this way."

The bell at the front door jingled then. A soft inquiring voice addressed Grocery Dog up there behind the counter. "Carry Depot, gootcher farkletits?"

"How's that?" Grocery Dog asked in his lazy drawl.

"Corey Depew," Marsha Willoughby asked distinctly. "Where is the son of a bitch?"

"Wall, now," the Existentialists could hear Grocery Dog gazing up at the ancient flypaper which dangled from his distant ceiling. "I believe he gone out to the Landing foah a party. I b'leeve that."

"Come on, Mike," Marsha said. "I know where he's gone. To our cousin's. That slut. Let's go."

"Cousin's?" Peggy mouthed.

"Vincent," Withrow said. "You go upstairs and get The Dead Man. We can get out the back. Then we should follow them." He put his finger to his lips, and they tiptoed to the back door. Vincent returned down the stairs, leading The Dead Man, who had his usual dazed look.

"I don't know nothing," he whispered conspiratorially. "I'm a Dead Man."

"Sure, kemosabe," Vincent said.

The fat pig cloud hung its belly over Cliffside, darkening the streets. The four of them climbed into Withrow's ancient VW and they nosed around the corner. Big Mike and Marsha were pulling out. Withrow was about to follow, when the squad car from the other end of the block started up. He paused long enough to let the black and white go by.

The Dead Man spoke suddenly. "Reverend Ovandrill. Out in Serpent Mound. They'll be going there."

"That would mean that Hackamore is our cousin," Peggy said. "I don't believe it."

"What's her grandmother's maiden name?" Withrow

398

asked.

"Narcissa something. I don't know."

He shrugged. "Whatever it is, I think maybe we should go straight there. It looks like there might be a little trouble at the party."

The pickup truck and the squad car were gone.

"They have a head start," Vincent pointed out.

"This is true," Withrow agreed. He gunned his tiny motor. On the VW radio The Four Preps were about to launch into Number Six, *26 Miles*, when there was a knock on the driver's window.

"Yes?" Withrow said, rolling it down.

"Important messaches I haff for Depew," Brother Grigory announced. "Must with you go."

"Sure. Hop in."

The monk mashed himself into the back seat in a clatter of beads, pushing The Dead Man and Vincent against one another. Brother Grigory looked closely at the Dead Man for a moment.

"Knowing you I am," he stated, pronouncing the 'k' in 'knowing.'

The Dead Man did not reply.

Withrow popped the clutch, throwing everyone against their seat backs. Job done, the fat pig cloud moved on.

They drove in swift silence. It grew darker. Buildings grew scarce, then nearly vanished, replaced by white fences and snow-spread fields showing brown stubble like a wino's cheek. Connie Francis sang Number Nine: *Who's Sorry Now*. Withrow turned on his headlights.

"We're gonna be too late," Peggy said.

"Soffrink," said Brother Grigory suddenly.

The Dead Man nodded. It might have been in agreement.

They left Louisa May Alcott Pike, drove up the flanks of the Serpent. There was no other traffic. A white fence wound along the road. Behind the fence were hogs, rooting in forgetful snow, seeking a little life with dried tubers.

Withrow was fond of T. S. Eliot, closet Existentialist.

"Cory's on the wrong track," he said aloud. "Eliot says, 'If all time is eternally present, All time is unredeemable.'"

"Huh?" Peggy said.

The Dead Man nodded again. He was all time, eternally present. "I'm ninety-nine years old," he said. "Maybe a hundred, I think my birthday's soon. What month is this?"

"March," Brother Grigory said.

The Dead Man nodded. "March. Yup."

"Where are we?" Vincent asked.

"Asgard Avenue. Serpent Mound."

"I thought I sensed the powerful presence of my ancestors. Look."

He was pointing outside. Through ragged clouds a shooting star showered sparks into the mist. "'And graves have yawned and yielded up their dead. Fierce fiery warriors fight upon the clouds...Which drizzled blood upon the Capitol. The noise of battle hurtled in the air, Horses did neigh and dying men did groan, And ghosts did shriek and squeal about the streets.'"

"Yuk," Peggy said.

"*Julius Caesar*, by William Shakespeare," Vincent said modestly. "Today is the Ides of March. The fifteenth. The portents. Can't you feel it, though? There's something in the air."

"Yes. I'm worried about those crazy albinos." Peggy said. "You missed the driveway."

"Damn." Withrow braked. Perry Como sang Number Five. *Catch a Falling Star.*

Chapter 3. In Which the Characters Descend

"Now then, everybody, let us move to the shelter," Reverend Ovandrill called the revelers to order. Uncle Cornelius, and Dr. Thanatopoulos strolled, deep in conversation, to the head of the cellar stairs.

"You must be Foxworth's son," Belle was saying to the butler.

"Yes, Madame. My family has served the Ovandrills for many years now. My grandfather started with Reverend Archibald back in the eighties, Madame."

"It's wonderful to be here again, after all these years, Foxworth."

"Yes, Madame. Would you care for another mushroom cap paté?"

Cory, beside the mantle in the sitting room, was lost in the intricate carving. "Say, Hack. This is Sodom and Gomorrah, isn't it? I mean, it's hard to tell what these people are doing, but it involves a whole lot of them. Besides. I think that's Lot's wife there."

"This is a minister's home, Core."

"Your grandfather built it? I thought it was, well, older."

"He bought. Cheap. From Dudley Worthington Depew's estate, back in 1890. Dudley's widow didn't want it, and it seems she needed cash."

"That would have been Francine, I think. My grandmother."

"Come on, everybody, let's not hold up the show. To the shelter!" The Reverend was bursting with pride.

"It is unusual to have such beautiful stairs going to a basement, isn't it?" the Dr Thanatopoulos remarked to Cornelius, looking at the elaborately carved cherrywood banister and lintel. The stairs themselves were covered with oriental carpeting, the predominant color of which was a

401

pale blue. Mellow light rose from the cellar, deep, dim, rich and woody.

"Mm." Cornelius seemed to expect exquisite taste from the Reverend and his wife, who was a woman of abundant Eastern establishment funds and total dependence on Robert and William, one of the finest decorating teams in the city.

Cory and Hackamore paused at the French doors leading to a small garden, where a decorative fountain pretended to splash into an ice-choked basin. They leaned against one another. Beyond the garden, through a gate in the brick wall, they could see a curve of the driveway, and beyond that the broad rolling fields of Depew Farms.

"How long have my parents known yours," Cory whispered.

"In the old days Belle was a Theosophist. She used to come out here to visit my grandfather who had a man named Dexter Pendragon Willoughby read entrails. Sometimes a chicken, sometimes a pig."

"Awntralls."

"What?"

"Awntralls. Brother Grigory calls them awntralls. That's what he meant. His name was Willoughby?"

"Yes. Well, it's called 'haruspication,' telling the future from pig entrails."

"No shit?"

"No, entrails."

"Ha ha. Dexter Willoughby? Well, well."

A silence fell upon them as they watched the darkness deepen over the fields. The clouds were scattered and pale and through them the stars were chilly points that glittered.

Hack sighed. "Oh, Cory," she said softly.

"Mmm?"

"I don't know how to say this," she began.

"Say what?"

"Well. I think I want to apologize."

"What for?"

"I guess I thought I knew what was good for you. See,

402

I wanted to save you. I couldn't save my... I mean, I had an abortion, and I was looking for a cause."

"I was a cause? That's what I was? A cause? Like Communism?"

"Well," she smiled, "not exactly like Communism."

"Huh. Capitalism, then. Or golf."

"Don't be silly. I planted the mirror in the Cave. I thought if you saw your face in there, being born, it would give you back your, well, lost face. I didn't realize all this persecution was real."

"Look," he said, pointing. Headlights were working their way slowly up the drive. Suddenly, beyond the vehicle, the sky flared with a strange smoky light the color of ripe tangerines.

"What is it?" she asked.

"Northern lights," he suggested, remembering Thule.

"Except for one thing."

"What's that."

"That's south. They'd have to be southern lights."

"No such thing," he said doubtfully. "I don't think."

"Then what is that?"

"It's the goddam war, that's what it is," Reverend Ovandrill said behind them. "The goddam Russians have done it, they've started World War Three, they've hit us with everything they've got. First that sputnik, then that dog, now this. That'd be Lexington they hit there, those lights. The A-bombs are going off. Armageddon, make no mistake about it. Come with me."

"That's funny," Cory said.

"What's funny?" Hack's voice shook.

"That out there looks an awful lot like Big Mike's truck. And it's stopped. There's another car coming, too."

"Let's get moving, boy. We don't have room downstairs for any more people. They'll have to take their chances. This is it, this is Doomsday. I only hope to God we're members." He turned briskly for the cellar stairs. He gave off a jaunty, cheerful air.

They started down; the others were already there. The

403

hi-fi offered a selection of Mozart Divertimenti, a medley shocking in its disregard for the spirit of the composer: Lawrence Welk, with the Lemon sisters humming melody. He had paused on the stairs, so the sound of the basement door clacking shut was louder to him than to the others.

Reverend Ovandrill was pocketing the key as Cory turned.

"You've locked us in," Cory said.

"You're damned tootin," Reverend Ovandrill assured him cheerfully. "This is the End of the World, son, and don't you forget it. I mean for us to be survivors."

"You can't really be serious, Reverend," Grouper protested from the foot of the stair. "There hasn't been anything in the papers about this. The Russians wouldn't do anything like that. I mean, Ike..."

"Oh, do be quiet, Grouper," Belle said.

"You didn't see the lights, Grouper," Wallace Ovandrill said. "Eerie. Weird glowing from Lexington, from Louisville. Hell, Cincinnati's undoubtedly ashes by now. We'll be next. There are vital industries in the Valhalla area."

Cory said, "The lights were pretty strange, dad. Kind of blue. I suppose it could have been bombs."

"You bet your booties they were bombs, son. Come on, folks, you'd better get acquainted with the shelter. We're going to be here quite a while."

It was certainly not the cement bunkers Cory had imagined when Reverend Ovandrill had told him about his shelter. No plain gray walls. No iron framed cots, no drums of drinking water, shelves filled with canned goods and Ritz crackers.

There was a saloon bar along one wall with brass fittings and etched glass mirrors. The bar was hardwood, and had been taken from an English pub, possibly by Dudley Depew himself. The bar was extremely well stocked, and Grouper was already at work.

"I don't think I can do anything original tonight," he said. "How about a plain Independence Day Punch — two quarts of this fine Snapdragon Bourbon here, some pineapple juice, lime juice, a lot of club soda, and I'll throw in a little orange bitters?"

"Bitters," Mrs. Ovandrill echoed. "My horses will die." She began, very quietly, to cry.

Five small but exquisitely furnished bedrooms surrounded the bar and kitchen areas. A comfortable sitting room, not as elaborate or large as the one upstairs, but tastefully done, seated the group comfortably. They sipped in silence at their Independence Day Punches and stared moodily at the lighted dial of the hi-fi.

"I don't understand it," Belle said at last.

"Understand what?" Cornelius asked. Conversation had died long ago, and fear had moved in, a ninth unwelcome guest, unless one counted Foxworth, who was preparing their first underground meal.

"I don't understand why Reverend Ovandrill doesn't have a radio down here. I declare, I have read the Civil Defense brochures, and they absolutely insist that you have a radio in your shelter. He's got this lovely music, but there is no radio."

"Honestly, Belle, it did not seem necessary. A useless luxury." Reverend Ovandrill was changing the record. "There will be no stations operating. Later we will get out the short wave, and see if there are any survivors elsewhere. But for now, we might as well make the best of it."

"There couldn't really be a war, could there?" Cornelius asked Dr. Thanatopoulos.

"*Christos anesti*," the doctor muttered. "I have seen plenty of war in my time. Why not?"

"It was a weird light," Cory said.

"Two weeks," Wallace was assuring Belle and Mrs. Ovandrill. "Three at the outside. These bombs are dirty, but the fallout's got a short half-life. We have provisions down here for months. Water, power, food, everything. We'll be quite comfortable. Hell, come look at the wine cellar!"

Everybody followed him. It was a beautiful wine

405

cellar. The temperature was precisely controlled and all the wines were vintage.

"We are thirty feet underground here," he said. "We are perfectly safe."

The walls began to shake, and all the vintage wines chattered in their bins.

Chapter 4. In Which the World Ends

The bombs fell all night.

"Cory. Honey," Belle whispered. "I'm scared."

Cory didn't know what to say.

"You two," she said. "You and Peggy. So small, so very small, such tiny wrinkled little things. You were animals, do you remember? the two of you. Always small animals, foxes and mice and wolves and bears. Pigs too, sometimes, grunting and oinking. It was cute, really. You two, together on the floor of the sun room on all fours, squealing."

The walls shook, and the sofa trembled under them. Cory could hear his father throwing up in the bathroom, even though it wasn't morning yet. "Squealing," he urged.

Belle sighed. "Squealing, little piggies. Or squeaking like mice. You had sounds for all the animals. I used to sit for hours, watching you two. I couldn't understand how you did it. I didn't understand children — so small and helpless, I think I hated you. So much responsibility."

There was no trace of that gushing South in her voice other than a minor harmonic overtone, a blurred softness to the vowels. She was talking to someone lost inside herself, her eyes blind.

The toilet flushed. The plumbing system was self-contained, cunningly cycled through itself according to the latest scientific Civil Defense procedures. The bomb shelter had cost the Ovandrill's over one hundred thousand dollars, even though they already had many of the furnishings. The Reverend had pointed out, though, that it doubled as a family entertainment center, so it really had two uses, and was not simply an expensive luxury dedicated to one unlikely use.

There was a pause after the gurgle of the toilet. Cory could hear his father climb shakily to his feet.

The sounds of retching began again with a fresh assault on the walls. Plaster dust sifted down the corners.

Belle continued. "You two were born. I was so happy it was over at last. I'd felt so heavy and ugly, so awkward and sick all the time. Now I didn't throw up any more; that was when Farley started, the day you two were born. He'd had that horrible accident, so strange. A coincidence, I told him. How could he know his father was out there in that field."

She nodded toward the south. The Depew Farm. "It was a white pig, he said. A huge pig loomed up in front. He didn't have any power left, no gas, but he yanked back and swerved the plane to avoid the animal and there was his father in his wheelchair. And that Albanian too. Grouper heard the Albanian shout '*Zogu! Zogu!*' The king he was, King Zog. It was like killing the king. I told him, I said Grouper, Farley, you killed the king's man. To think that Grouper's father, Baxter Depew, was being served by a servant of a real king! And your father killed him. Baxter was the good brother, not like that Norman. Oh, it was an accident of course. It couldn't be helped. But think. Royalty. We were so close to royalty, and didn't even know it. Why is this happening?"

"I don't know, mom. I'm not even sure it is."

She looked at him sharply. "What's that?"

"I'm not sure it is. Bombs, I mean. It doesn't make any sense."

"Of course it doesn't make any sense. Nothing makes any sense and more. Why were you and Peggy animals all the time? I wanted you to be people. To talk to me. Your father, gone all the time, down there at the company. He worried so much. He worried about Cornelius. Cornelius owned the Cave. They get something from the Cave. Used to anyway. Something important, I forget what it is."

"Feldspar," Cory said. The toilet was flushing again. Cory worried there might not be enough water to last three weeks if his father kept flushing it like that. But he was getting rid of all that Independence Day Punch.

408

"Whatever," Belle said softly. "Whatever. You two would hide. You were, oh I don't know, three, four? I worried so, my God, the panicky feeling I'd get. 'Rebecca,' I'd say. 'Where are those kids?' 'I dunno, ma'am,' she'd say, so insolent, she didn't care at all. I have to look for them, those twins. So much work and responsibility, and they wouldn't even be people! Little piggies, little foxes, little wolves, gnawing at my heart. A pain, here, sharp, like teeth. Sometimes I hated you kids. So much. My life. I thought it was going to be beautiful. When I first saw your father. He had an airplane, he was fun. Handsome too. He was a handsome man, your father." Belle sat up suddenly. "Where is she?"

"Who, mom?"

Belle looked around, a white wildness in her eye. "Oh." She slumped again. "Peggy. I thought Peggy was lost. Of course. She is lost. Ran off with that..."

"Withrow, mom. He has a degree in philosophy."

"There! You see? Useless nonsense. Besides he's a...Negro. A folk singer. He works at the zoo!"

"So do I, mom. I work at the zoo."

"Certainly. You were always animals, you and Peggy. I lost her, you know. She became an animal. She lives like an animal, with that Negro."

"They're married, mom. They have a little boy. He's cute and smart. They're a nice couple, mom."

"Really?" she said without curiosity. "A nice couple. Hm. She was a fox most of the time. A fox with a name. I forget the name."

"Secret."

"What?"

"The fox's name was Secret. Or Seek, for short. Peggy always wanted to hide, to be secret. The pig's name was Monster, I remember now. He was very big, not a little piggie at all. Huge, and quick."

"Monster? Your name was Monster? I didn't know that."

"We were real little. We helped each other, Secret and

Monster. Secret could get in places Monster couldn't. Monster could protect Secret from the lizards. The lizards were the bad guys. They were always after us, cause they ate foxes and pigs."

Secret and Monster were free. They could root and burrow, they could run, and they had a special friend: Rebecca would give them treats, little cakes and cookies, the kind foxes and pigs loved. They could see in the dark, too, and speak a special language only they knew. The lizards couldn't understand their language, the huge green lizards that were always angry, always hunting for them, digging for them, scratching at the entries to their hiding places, ready to snap and eat. Monster could turn, he had sharp tusks, sharp hoofs, fierce eyes. Secret had little teeth like needles and could see far and deep, could hear the tiniest forest sounds, the distant footsteps of the huge slow lizards. It was a game, hiding from the lizards. And it was not a game. "You and dad were..."

She didn't hear the rest of the sentence, for the walls were shaking again, and her hand reached out to Cory's arm, the fingers hooked deeply into his biceps.

"We're going to die, Cory. All of us. We can't survive. I don't know how. Foxworth isn't going to prepare dinner forever. How can we repay Reverend Ovandrill? There won't be anything left. All gone. No city, the river dead. Everything will glow, they say, with an awful blue light, a sickness. Will we change? Will we be different? Horrible sores, vomiting? I've read those pamphlets." She started to cry.

The hi-fi was off. The others were trying to sleep, retired to the guest bedrooms. The bedrooms had beds, closets, wardrobes with warm clothes. Grouper left the bathroom at last and walked blindly into one of the empty bedrooms. Cory could hear the bed creak as he lay down in the terrible silence of the bomb shelter.

He didn't see Hackamore standing in the doorway to the sitting room looking at him. After a moment she turned and disappeared.

"It can't be," he said. "I don't believe it."

"Then why are the walls shaking?" his mother shouted. "Why is the world falling down around us?"

More quietly she said, "Why did you two always hide? Small animals burrowed in the earth, buried in the earth, hiding. Dead, damp, clammy earth all around us. We're going to die, all of us, down here in this awful place. There is no air. Fire is stealing all the air!"

Outside the night was bright with swelling domes of hideous light, shot through with bands and arcs of purple and red.

411

Chapter 5. In Which Grouper Is Unexpectedly Candid

"Dad." Cory could see the whites of his father's eyes in the dim light of the bedroom. "Dad? Are you all right?"

"All right." The whites moved, vanished, reappeared.

"You were sick. I thought maybe...you needed something?"

"No. Nothing. I don't need anything."

Cory hesitated. Belle was lost to him, sunk in private grief. Hack was in a room somewhere with the door closed. Rev. and Mrs. Ovandrill were likewise gone. Uncle Cornelius and Dr. Thanatopoulos, who had been giving him strange looks all night, were in the library, emptying another bottle of some incredibly rare vintage, their third. "What the hell," Uncle Cornelius had said. "It's the end of the world."

It didn't really seem like the end of the world. For one thing, it was very quiet. From time to time dust would sift down the corners to white mounds. A large crack had opened up along the wall between the wine cellar and the half bath off the pantry, but it appeared to have stabilized. Other than that the bombing seemed to have stopped. Oddly, the panel of Geiger counters and barometric readings gave no clues to what was occurring outside. Nothing unusual registered there. Radiation, Reverend Ovandrill stated, had not reached Valhalla yet. The prevailing winds were westerly, and St. Louis, no doubt obliterated, was too far away.

"What about Louisville?" Cory had asked.

"Gone," Reverend Ovandrill said with every appearance of pleasure.

"Shouldn't the radiation be here by now?"

"Well, not necessarily. A slight southerly course in the winds." He pointed at the wind gauge. "Radiation

412

bypassed us for now. I would say our chances of survival are excellent, all things considered. I believe we are, in fact, members."

Members or not, the night was quiet, but everyone in the shelter seemed to have sunk into a marshy stretch of psyche, no longer available for comment.

At some time shortly before midnight a frantic pounding was barely audible on the cellar door. Hackamore's father had requested everyone to ignore the sounds, assuring them that the door was perfectly capable of withstanding the effects of a near-miss from a seven megaton bomb, and was not likely to succumb to the feeble onslaughts of frantic atomic victims. Eventually the pounding stopped.

It was four in the morning.

A sharp crack brought Grouper upright. "What was that?"

His words were drowned in a long, jagged series of creaks, as if a 1952 Henry J automobile were being remorselessly pressed beneath an enormous mountain of basalt. Dust fell in curtains onto the bed. Cory froze in place, his hands out before him, palms up. They filled with little mounds of dust. When it stopped falling, he saw his father's hair turned pure white with the plaster.

From the outer rooms voices murmured. "What was that...Oh, my God, it's the End!"

The following silence went on and on. Cory began once more to breathe. Grouper stirred, and the dust fell around his face.

"What's that I hear?" Grouper asked. Very far away, a small snuffling sound.

"The grunting of pigs?" Cory said softly.

Grouper shook his head. White powder flew around his head. He sighed.

"I'm afraid, Cory." His voice was soft, almost inaudible. "Since the day you two were born I've been afraid. I wake up early in the morning. Panic and pain. Every morning I throw up. I'm used to it now. Gravity, you see. Every year, every day, it pulls at you, it pulls you down. Harder and harder to stand up straight, harder and harder to hold up your head. Each day it pulls, shoulders slump over. Old age waits, nothing to do but shuffle along, bent. Gravity, and so much experience, you see. Time goes faster and faster. Children bring that on. Faster and faster, more and more memories. Memories that weigh, did you know that? Memory has mass. Memory pulls me down too. At the end of memory is Death. Death has a face, you see. A terrible face, a face with a snout and small mean eyes. And teeth. My God, the teeth. They are wicked, death's teeth, so long and sharp. When you told me about Baxter... I looked at your faces, you and Peggy. So small. So old. Faces a thousand years old, Cory, the two of you, lying there in the nursery, wrinkled and red and blind. I saw death in those faces. They're supposed to be innocent, babies' faces. All innocence and possibility, but I didn't see that, not innocence at all, but awful wisdom, awful knowledge. Pain, and suffering and death. My father, paralyzed for years, couldn't move in that silence. Horrible, Cory. I wanted to ask, but he couldn't speak. He didn't say anything. Not one word. Who was I? I didn't know, I would never know. My mother...so quiet and pale. She loved me. She changed me. Cooked my favorite foods. She was a terrible cook. She didn't understand food. But we had servants. People had lots of servants in those days. She had lots of servants, but she always cooked for me, ham, pork chops, knuckles. I liked pork so much she used to say I'd turn into a pig. A little laugh. So pale, that laugh, so small and weak, I don't know, a sort of hnh hnh sound, far back in her throat. She was so pale, she got paler and paler, weaker and weaker. Some kind of wasting disease, she always had a white powdery mark around her

nose, the corners of her mouth. What was it? She died, you know, and father was so silent by then. He was a powerful man, I saw very little of him, and then he just...stopped. One day he was in that chair and he never left it. That man. 'Zogu!' He always shouted that. King

Zog, he was, I looked it up. King of Albania, but not for long. Not for long. I crash-landed you know. I think I heard him shout that. Just before I.... Hit. There was the animal, huge and so white, white as a cloud, as the cloud I was in before the engine stopped. Of course I never checked the fuel, it was so beautiful, so clean and pale. Francine was like that, clean and pale, but something monstrous, too, looked out of her eyes. And then I went to the hospital, and there you were, the two of you, and I saw your faces, those tiny wrinkled faces, exactly alike. There was death in them, you see, those two faces, your faces. Death, monstrous, misshapen, white. That pig was so big, I could see his teeth. I swerved, he screamed like death, a sharp sound that cut, that squeal, the squeal of death. I fear paralysis, I fear pain, I wake up in fear, age, years, decay, the long dying my father, my father, God Cory, my father wasting like that, forever, frozen in that horrible silence, he shook his cane at the world and now it's going to happen, we're down here under the earth, if we come up our skin will rot away, the pain will reach into our bones and pull them out of us, through the flesh, blisters and blood, our eyes will explode. Dudley Depew exploded. I heard that. Father used to say, Dudley exploded, he seemed pleased, then he got sick. Sometimes he was better, sometimes not, sometimes he was fine, just fine, like nothing was wrong at all, then he would be weak and so tired, especially after Mother died, she just got paler and paler until there was nothing left, I didn't know what to say to her, the skull showed through her skin, she trembled all the time, her hands shaking, shaking you could see she was dying, and Dr. Hauser said there was nothing wrong, she was just fine, fine, she would be fine and she died one day, I found her on her bed as if she had no skin left at all only the alabaster bone of her skull, her teeth grinning through those lips, I will never forget I see it all the time, I saw it in your faces, the two of you looked so much like her, except you were red like my father paralyzed, I kept thinking what did I do to suffer like this, what did I do? I don't know, Cory, but those shapes,

415

that awful white boar on the open meadow, it was so green, though there were clouds and darkness around, but I spun down, leveled out, it would have been a perfect landing, then there it was, that white shape before me, screaming, I swerved, I swerved, God I tried, what could I do? I killed my father."

Grouper's head was bowed, his face in deepest shadow. Cory stood painfully, frozen himself in a position of dread. He felt the cold fear of death itself, brushing through him, ghost wings fluttering in his heart.

"Do you know," Grouper continued, so softly, his voice ghost wings too. "Do you know the terror when the heart flaps, jumps, irregular. My God, I'm dying, what did I do? I know that terror every day, Cory. The heart, so steady and invisible, suddenly jumps, leaps out of your body, shouts at you. I can't breathe then. I know death, the terrible face of death, its bony cold hand and the fear of rotting in the earth, of suffocating, dying inside a face that cannot speak, inside a face that is going away, freezing, numb, just a mask on the skull, ready to fall off, be lost. I saw Francine like that. My mother. I saw Father looking out through that frozen face, so empty, the eyes full of sorrow, of pain, of horror. I can never forget. I wake up in the morning and the nausea takes me. I throw it all up, over and over and over."

Grouper lay back. He turned away from Cory onto his side. He pulled his knees up onto his chest. He put his arms around his knees and hugged himself into absolute silence.

Chapter 6. Love at the End

Cory tried five doors. Behind door number one the Reverend and Mrs. Ovandrill were heaped and moving under the covers. As he softly closed the door, Cory heard Mrs. Ovandrill cry out.

"Canter, Wally. Post at the canter. Oh, yes, yes, post. Up and down, Wally, up and down, that's good."

Door number two revealed Foxworth, chin in his wing collar. An empty bottle of five star Napoleon Brandy, vintage 1866, was tipped precariously against the leg of his chair. When it fell, Foxworth should awaken.

Door number three allowed Cornelius and Dr. Thanatopoulos to look blearily at Cory. "C'mon in, laddie," Cornelius suggested, and hiccoughed.

"Neh, neh," Dr. Thanatopoulos affirmed. "Iss thuh harrowing, boy. Hell. Thuh harrowing time. 'N this's Chateau Lafite Rothschild 1933. No'a very good jeer 'm 'fraid."

The fourth door was the wine cellar. The dim bottles rested, rested, ranked and glimmering in the dim light with deep reds. Dark and cool in the wine cellar, but Cory saw the gap in the wall was wider, revealing only a deeper darkness, a darker black beyond. The earth, it would be, underground where his father feared to go. Cory feared it too, and so the fifth door showed him his beloved and estranged Hackamore. She was on the bed, holding the *matsyasana*, or fish posture, in full lotus with her head back, crown resting on the mattress. Her full breasts fell to either side of her arched body, the pink tips seeming to wink at the darkness. It took Cory a long moment to realize there were tears rolling from the corners of her eyes across her forehead and down her temples into her hair.

"What is it?"

"Come here," she ordered. Her voice was strange, but

it could have been the arched position of her neck.

They did the thirteen positions of the *Chandamaharosana*, the Tantric Path, the Great Moon Elixir, which symbolizes the full moon in both the macrocosm and the microcosm. They moved through Taoist positions, the Nine Positions of the Dark Girl called Turning Dragon, Tiger's Tread, Monkey's Attack, Splitting the Cicada, Mounting Tortoise, Fluttering Phoenix, Rabbit Sucking Its Hair, Overlapping Fish Scales, and ending with Cranes with Joined Necks, in which Cory sat comfortably while Hack sat on his lap, his Jade Stalk deep in her Wheat-shaped Cave. He aided her movement with his hands under her buttocks until she came to climax and her moist secretions flowed copiously, as the manual insisted. For a lad whose knowledge of female reproductive anatomy came from Tampax brochures passed on to him in high school by Vincent Black Shadow Lavere, Cory had come a long way. They finished with a variation of the position called Reeling-off Silk. In the West it was referred to as the missionary position, the only one acceptable in Eisenhower America.

"I used to swear," Hack said later as her tears dried, "that I would never die a virgin. If I knew the world was going to end, I would've grabbed the first man I could find."

"The world is going to end. Probably it has already ended. Our world. I used to think it would be the most wonderful thing in the world for the world to end, for me to be in a bomb shelter with a beautiful girl. To survive, to, well, repopulate the world. Adam and Eve."

"I might not be able to have children. I had an abortion."

"It's not as nice as I thought it would be. We're down here with Cornelius and Dr. Thanatopoulos and Foxworth and my parents."

"And mine."

"They are not the best people in the world. Not the most capable of living under primitive conditions. Not real

418

wilderness survivors. All I did was survive three years in Thule, Greenland."

"You know a lot about Mozart. You have a lovely Jade Stalk. You don't feel sorry for yourself any more. You have your own face back. You're all right." She started crying again.

He held her. "Why aren't you happy?" he asked. A foolish question. It was the end of the world. No more Nash Ramblers. No more hula hoops. No more movies in three dimensions. No more Captain Video. No more Herb Philbrick, who led three lives as a Communist for the FBI. They were all radioactive clinkers now, political affiliations forgotten in the universal Ragnarok.

"I am happy," she said and the world exploded.

The bed tilted sideways and they fell to the floor, pinned together under calico and mattress ticking. A button pushed into Cory's backside; he pushed back. Dust fell in swathes and curtains, the creaking sounds loud in his ears. Far away he could hear the clatter of bottles, the groans of the war victims, the screams of the wounded. He and Hack pushed back at the bed, and it suddenly scooted along the wall, leaving them exposed. Fortunately Reverend Ovandrill was not there to witness the aftermath of his daughter's most recent debauch.

They struggled into clothing, Hack and Cory, without a word between them. His breath was harsh. He could hear them grunting. "Do you hear?" he asked at last. "Do you hear them? They're coming."

"Who? Who's coming?" She struggled with her black turtleneck. Her lovely breasts disappeared into soft darkness.

"The pigs." He crawled across the tilted floor to the doorway. She followed. The floor trembled underneath their hands and knees. Sharp cracks, high-pitched, terrible tearing sounds and low rumbles, dust and noise filled the air.

The others were in the big central room, crouched on the Persian carpets bunched against the downhill wall.

419

They were looking into the wine cellar.

Cory and Hack crawled to the door and looked in.

Something looked back.

It was a face.

No. It wasn't a face. Not really. It was a skull with empty eye sockets and grinning teeth. The light was bad.

"What is it?" Belle asked softly.

"It looks like a skull," Mrs. Ovandrill answered. Fear had numbed her voice.

"Why is it talking?" Cornelius asked. It was a reasonable question.

"What's he saying?" Belle wanted to know. It was not clear whether she was referring to the skull or to Cornelius. Nobody responded.

"What happened to my wine cellar?" the minister demanded. The soft mixture of vintage esters filled the air, exhaled from the darkness along with pungent and only vaguely identifiable odors — damp earth, decay, death. The skull stared for a long moment and then, with another tremor of the earth, toppled forward toward the crouching group of survivors, who scurried backward out of the way.

The skeleton shattered against the door sill. The skull exploded into fragments and dust. Feathers flew. Foxworth appeared with a torch.

The lamp's beam moved into the darkness. It was like a tongue exploring its own mouth. The darkness was vast. Light touched against more bone faces, more grinning yellow teeth. They crawled as a group to the edge. The wine cellar was gone, the shattered wall tilted at angles inside the chamber in the earth where the Indians had buried their dead so many centuries ago. The Indians had claimed revenge; they had seized Reverend Wallace Ovandrill's wine cellar. Heaps of bottles, shattered and gurgling, were scattered on the uneven floor. Fumes rose, mingled with the earth. Someone coughed. Mrs. Ovandrill giggled. Cory was sure the giggle was pure hysteria.

The sound of earth sliding downslope came to them. There was movement there in the darkness, grunting, the

420

sounds of breathing. The atomic survivors held their collective breath.

"What the..." Grouper began.

Shapes moved; obscure gleams as the lamp passed over them. A new and growing source of light appeared. Foxworth snapped off his torch and the shelter was plunged into a darkness so sudden that Belle screamed. Scrabbling sounds came from the burial chamber. The floor under them shifted again, and one by one they slid through the yawning doorway, dimly outlined now as their eyes adjusted, and on into the cavern beneath the Ovandrill mansion. Far above them an irregular gray opening had appeared, and in it the shapes were moving. Many shapes, pale and obscene, shapes that made sounds.

Grunting and rooting sounds.

Pigs.

A figure appeared among them.

"My wine," Hackamore Ovandrill's father said sadly. "My vintage wine. All I was going to carry into the future. Gone. Look. It's gone."

The figure was sliding down a slope toward them. It seemed to be wrapped in a cape or robe of some kind. The first questing snouts appeared, quizzical and rubbery. A white hog sniffed at Belle, who screamed again, backing frantically. Grouper held her.

"Iss nottink to be fearing," said Brother Grigory. He was surrounded by pigs, the rescuing saint of hogs. "Quack iss all," he said. "Quack."

More faces appeared above him. Some of them were very pale.

Chapter 7. In Which Pigs Drink Wine

"Get back," thundered the Reverend. "He's radioactive!" Belle screamed again and began to sob.

"Whattid he mean, quack?" Cornelius asked Dr. Thanatopoulos.

The figures at the top of the slope where a gray dawnlight was brightening began to move down it.

"Look," Cory said. "It's Peggy and Withrow. And Vincent. Vincent, what are you doing dressed like that."

"My people!" Vincent Black Shadow Lavere said, looking around the chamber. His face was creased with red streaks of war paint, his head haloed with enormous eagle feathers. He held a rattle of skin and bone in one hand, and a kind of whisk in the other. Over his forearm was a hide shield, painted with dream images. His buckskins were richly worked with beads and colored quills. He looked around the chamber. On stone shelves in the roughly circular cavern skeletons sat cross-legged dressed in soft doeskins, as if attending a tribal meeting. Their skulls were smiling. They held weapons, woven baskets, tools.

"This is the Serpent Mound. Of course they're your people," Withrow said. He was carrying the old folder stuffed with papers, trailing maroon ribbon. Peggy came down the slope. Others were following.

"Whattid you mean, quack?" Cornelius asked Brother Grigory.

"Not quack," Dr. Thanatopoulos said. "He didn't mean quack."

The pigs were everywhere, huge and white. Their tough rubbery snouts were nosing through the bodies, through the damp loose earth and plaster and cement debris of the cellar, through the wine bottles heaped and scattered. TheyThe c were slurping at puddles of Chablis and Côte de Nuits, Maconnais and beaujolais; they were gulping down rivers of heady vintages from the Valley of the Loire, of Pouilly-fumé and Sancerre and Vouvray, Saumur and Anjou; they waded through pools of Bordeaux, Pomerol, Grâves and St. Emilion; they swam and drank oceans of Verdicchio and Frascati, Valpolicella and Soave Bardolino, tides of Lacryma Christi and Cote Rôtie, Rheinpfalz and Neuchatel; they swilled down burgundies from the former Depew estates when they were the major wine producers of Middle Western America.

They grunted and squealed, whinnied and gasped, rumbled and belched. A hundred white swine of all sizes waded through the treacly mud. "Snrrr, ghank ghank, whooo-i-i-iooo, garf garf," they said.

A big man sauntered down the widening slope from the upper world, a man broad in the shoulders, mighty of thew, and God-ghostly pale. He had a floppy hat and a great big gun. His wife was with him.

"Carny," his wife said to Cory. "This'z Big Mike, yaller gonna getchup, sucker."

"Marsha!" Cory gulped. Hack hugged his upper arm and held him close. Big Mike was accompanied, and when his companion filled the opening to the dawn world without, all the questions flying around the cavern faltered and fell away. Heads turned.

He was huge, that much was certain. As his bulk moved down, and light returned, some details of his bulk emerged. His face was seamed, deeply indented, wreathed in fissures. The eyes, nested in a thousand crags, were small and brown and warm, but they were also wise and remote. They were eyes that saw for a mind that could not be fooled. His mouth held a smile, tolerant and superior, and showed teeth that were ancient when the world was new: yellowed, worn but each in its place, all there and ready for business.

He weighed a thousand pounds at least, and his tusks were fiercely curled. He moved his jaw, and they clashed together, grinding with a sound that seemed to echo in this suddenly small space. His bulk moved slowly but with

423

apparent grace down the slope. All the other pigs left off their rooting to look at him, for here was the King of Hogs, the Swine God Himself. His low head swiveled from side to side, as if looking for someone. He had no neck, so the front of his torso moved with the motion of his head. The soft small eyes came at last to rest on Cory Depew, and he paused. He stared.

Cory tried to stare back, but the pig-fear buried deep in his genes was upon him, and he could not lift his eyes above the razor edges of the Boar's front trotters where they rested on the edge of fallen earth and plaster where the slide had heaped against the side of a toppled wine rack.

The Boar grunted once, "Grfpt." Then he moved silently and slowly toward Cory, the fourth generation, the last male of his line, the ultimate goal of a curse pronounced a hundred years before. He didn't even stop for Peggy, the female twin. The curse was not for her. He stepped daintily around the skirts of Reverend Ovandrill's dressing gown. The minister stood as one bemused, his own plump palm extended toward his horsy wife, dressed in a bathrobe and jodhpurs and pink slippers with fluffy pom-poms. She was dazed herself and said nothing. An adolescent pig had been munching at Wallace's gown, but had left off when the Boar entered. He now went back to work, tossing the light satin material up with his snout, catching the hem in his mouth, chewing for a moment, before tossing it into the air again. Reverend Ovandrill did not appear to notice.

Cory was paralyzed. The Boar moved toward him. His mottled ivory tusks gleamed in the confused farrago of lights — interior lights from the shelter, Foxworth's torch, now on once more, the brightening dawn light from the world above. They curved out and back, and clashed together as he walked, working his jaw. The mouth was long, deep, and as Cory well knew, richly toothed, forty-four multi-purpose teeth, the teeth of an omnivore. Like man, his cousin, his double, his image. The Boar was white. A leprous white, the white of apparition and nightmare, of ghost and death. His sides were round and smooth, his bristles dark and stiff and long. His tail was straight, and had a full brush at the end. His hooves were black and shone in the glimmering light as though lacquered. He was Vengeance afoot. He would root out guilt, and punish what he found. He wanted Cory, who felt only an intolerable itch around his face again where once he had lost it, and got it back, and now was scarlet with fear and guilt and was going to lose it once more. The pig would clean his skull, the tusks would tear, the teeth would chew, and Cory would take his place among the ancient bones buried here so long.

Belle whimpered, a mewing sound deep in her throat, beyond tears. Peggy moved to her, put a hand on her mother's shoulder without thinking, and Belle turned slowly, wordlessly, to her daughter who had married a Negro. The vast shape moved past.

Cory lifted his eyes. The Boar was large. It grew in size as it approached. It was ten feet from him, five. The jaws were working. Cory paralyzed, hand outstretched, face aflame, tried to speak. He wanted to say Stop.

A precariously poised skeleton fell from its niche. The body toppled forward, the skull detached from the neck and rolled across the dirt floor to stop at Belle's feet. She whimpered in horror and drew back, but the skull grinned up at her for a moment, before the jaw bone, overtaxed, fell from the skull entirely, leaving a disturbing grin with a bite larger than the world itself. Belle clutched her daughter to her.

When she looked up, she saw that the skeleton had fallen away from an opening in the earth, a cavern that receded beyond the limits of their light, a tunnel that went, so far as she could tell, as far as the Mozart Cave.

The hog moved the final steps to Cory until the breath wheezing through his gaping nostrils blew warm and damp on Cory's hands. The small brown eyes looked quizzically up at Cornelius Hauser Depew. The mouth worked, the teeth clashed, the tusks ground against one another, and

Cory could see all too well that the tusks did indeed have a golden color, mottled by brown spots, the ancient ivory color of mythic gold, the dragon hoard.

He summoned up the courage to look back into those small eyes. The pig squinted at him. The look was mild and curious. Yet their eyes were locked together, boy and swine. Hack had retreated a step, her own arm stretched a little to keep her hold on Cory's upper arm. In the rapt tension of the moment, Cornelius, too, had paused.

Cory backed against the wall, surrounded by skeletons, ivory grins, the naked dead.

Cory and the Boar, Diabolus, the Great White Hog Abhehu, were nearly eye to eye, the beast was that tall. His chest was deep and rich and his haunches bulged with power. He gleamed white.

He was Wrath.

Chapter 8. In Which Some Other Things Also End

The light increased in the burial chamber. Suddenly a weird figure uttered a cry that shivered through two octaves, rising and dying. Vincent Black Shadow Lavere was on his hands and knees, crawling grotesquely through the mud, writhing. His face was hidden behind an enormous wooden mask fringed by long black horsehair. The face of the mask was distorted and horrific, with wide distended lips, a tongue extruded to the chin, a red beaked nose, deeply furrowed brow, bulging eyes that stared. The cheekbones had prominent blades curved sharply upward. The face itself was painted black.

"False Face Society," Withrow murmured.

"Eh?" Cornelius asked. But Vincent was crawling toward Cory and the Boar, which watched curiously. As Vincent crawled, he made strange muttering noises and grunts. The pigs left off their alcoholic rooting to stare at this apparition in their midst. Vincent, the mask covering his head, held a staff before him in one hand, and with the other shook a rattle made of tortoise shell, scraped it on the ground. He moved toward Cory in a hierophantic trance, twitching and groaning, uttering his weird cry.

"False Face Society. Indian healers," Withrow said.

"Oh."

Vincent crouched in front of Cory. He shook his rattle. He reached into a pouch at his waist and withdrew a handful of ashes. He stood to his full height, taller than Cory, and rubbed the ashes on Cory's head. He traced the outline of Cory's lost face with ash. He bent to moisten his hand from a pool of spilled wine, dipped ashes again, and smeared Cory with the paste, streaking his face with black and gray, still muttering and shrieking. He shook the rattle over Cory's head, pressing him back.

427

Cory, backed to one of the shelves, was pushed against the corpse of a long-dead Indian. This body was better preserved than the one which still grinned up at Belle and Grouper, and did not fall apart, but Cory, backed into it, was cheek to cheek, his own living and the Indian's dead face side by side.

"Yaaa-a-a, hey!" Vincent chanted, shaking his rattle. He seemed to see something detach from Cory or the body, and he drove it back, along the irregular black wall of the burial chamber toward the light, some vague form in the air, dark and evil, nearly invisible, possibly imaginary so that those down there in the remains of Reverend Ovandrill's wine cellar and bomb shelter blinked their eyes to clear the clinging gray vision from them. By then Vincent was moving up the slope of dirt to the surface driving whatever evil spirit it might have been before him. His voice faded and disappeared as he also moved out of the cavern.

Cory, back to the wall, cheek to bone, stared into the small dark eye of the boar and trembled. It was the fear-flood sweeping down on him again, all he had said, all he had feared of pigs and teeth and death.

"I know you," he said.

The boar lowered his massive head. His breath moved through his throat and nose, a deep hot whuff into the dust at his feet.

"I know you," Cory said again.

The boar looked up. "Yes," he said. "You do know me. And I know you."

The boar's flank quivered. His small eyes looked at Cory directly. The eyes were deep with malice. One hundred years of malice, of intent, or wrath, gathered in the eyes that stared out at small Cory trembling.

"You know me," Cory repeated in a raw whisper, knowing that all his obscure guilt, his small rebellion, his lost face and innocence, his troubled love, all were collected into this moment, eye to eye with the White Pig that had hovered at the edges of all his fathers' lives,

428

glimpsed dim and menacing in the forest margin, drifting through the fogged autumn wood of the past century of his family's history. The Boar before him now had long haunted his own dreams as well.

The chamber receded, vanished. Cory stood alone with the beast in a primal forest. They faced one another a few feet apart. Cory's hands had risen, as if to fend off what could not be denied.

"I am the origin of suffering." The beast's voice was muffled and deep. "I have moved through your life, and your father's life, and his father's, and yet his father's before him. Four generations have passed since I was charged with this task: to prod and allow no rest, to let my hot breath pursue, to keep the tread of my feet falling always behind and coming closer. To puncture your desire. You pretend you are innocent, a victim of circumstance, an accident of birth. But you are not innocent, not a victim, not an accident. You want, like all people."

Cory tried to look away from those now terrible eyes, and found he could not.

"You have deceived," the pig continued. "You have seduced. You have shown cowardice and fear. You have been weak when you could have shown strength, hidden when you could have given light."

"It's true," Cory whispered. He wanted to hide now, wanted to flee and hide. He wanted Secret with him; he wanted to be Monster once more, yet in front of him now was the true Monster, the real beast he had only tried to imitate.

The boar shook his massive head, rippling the thick folds of skin behind his neck. "You are the last," he said. "You are the end."

The silence was long between them then.

"No," Cory answered at last, surprised that his voice was a little stronger, a little louder in the deadened air of this forest glade. There were no sounds, no breeze in the thick summer leaves. The light from above fell in thick shafts to the bare earth. Each leaf, each stone, each wrinkle of bark stood out in clear relief. "No," he repeated.

The boar tilted his head.

"I am not the end," Cory said. "I'm the beginning. I've been running long enough. I've lost face and found it again. I've been reborn. I'm not the same person. You don't need me any more. I don't need you any more."

"Ah." The boar breathed out again. He took a step toward Cory, then another.

So Cory stared at the Boar, eye to eye. He turned his hands, palms out, a gesture of peace after a hundred years of war and fear.

"Stop," he said, softly but with sudden great authority.

The huge boar stared back.

Then, quite abruptly he sat down and with a slow, corkscrew motion on his haunches, he lifted his left rear trotter, and scratched, with incredible delicacy, at his ear, his tiny eyes screwed up in pure delight.

Slowly the pigs turned back to their work, but it was clear by now that most of them were drunk, unsteady and sated. A few snuffles and grunts, and one by one they lay down, or turned in two or three circles, chasing their own tails for a spot to snooze, settled, snored, heads lolled to one side, tongues here and there out, eyes closed.

The group stirred, blinking. They looked at one another.

"I still don't know what he meant by that," Cornelius said. A querulous edge crept through his words as he watched Cory, who was squatting beside the enormous boar scratching at the tender place in his tough skin behind the large expressive ears.

"He means, my dear Cornelius," Dr. Thanatopoulos said carefully, navigating carefully the oceans of vintage now flooding his circulatory system, "it was a 'quake. An earthquake, you see. There was an earthquake. He grew up in Albania, where the mountains shake all the time. Did you know he is my twin brother? We were separated when very young."

430

"Don't be ridiculous. There are no earthquakes here. This is the Midwest!"

"Oh they are rare, it is true. But the bedrock is riddled with faults under here. Get away from me!" He spoke sternly to an adolescent porker which had begun to nibble in earnest on his trouser leg. The pig squealed and trotted a few paces, to look back with a hurt, reproachful expression.

"What about the lights?" Reverend Ovandrill asked. "We saw lights in the sky, bombs going off." His disappointment in the failure of World War III was a cigarette snuffed in his morning coffee.

The doctor shrugged, a gesture which nearly toppled him.

"Sometimes," Withrow offered, "large earthquakes are associated with eerie lights — glowing beams and columns of light in the sky. I suppose they could look like atomic bombs going off. So that's why you all locked yourselves in the shelter. We couldn't figure out why you wouldn't come up. We pounded on the door. The 'quake had opened up all kinds of subterranean caverns — this area is riddled with them, you know, all the way over to here from the Mozart Cave. And the pigs were loose. These Slyville people," he gestured toward the group of gun-toting albinos which included Marsha Willoughby, "seemed to be coming after Cory, and since I had concluded my researches, it seemed we should get out here before any further harm was done."

"I don't know," said a quavering voice. Cory looked up from his engagement with the Boar. "I don't know nothing. I'm a Dead Man."

The Dead Man was shuffling down the muddy slope, hanging tightly to Big Mike's arm.

"We know who you are," Big Mike said. His voice was soft although edged with the Slyville twang.

"Who?" Cory asked, standing.

"Iss knowed now," Brother Grigory said, moving closer. "Dead Man iss Baxter. Baxter Rasmussen. He chanched places wiss brodder Norman. Chanched name

431

too. Become Norman, he did. And Norman becomes Baxter Depew. He it wass wass Valhalla boss one time. Dead, now."

"What?" Grouper shouted.

The Dead Man looked up. "Baxter?" he said.

The Boar sat and watched attentively, his soft brown eyes shifting from one to another.

"This can't be Baxter," Grouper whispered. "I... Baxter. No, it can't be Father. Baxter was my father."

"I told you I finished my researches," Withrow said, opening the folder. "I have two items here. First, this folder, which Cory got from Brother Grigory. These are old records — birth and death certificates. They have helped us to trace this strange and tangled family, which I, I am almost proud to say, have married into."

He produced some sheets of paper. "From this information I have prepared some genealogies. One is a genealogy of the Depew family. It is a very confused story, but perhaps this will help. You can see that although he was called Baxter, he was, in fact, really Norman who was adopted by Dudley Depew just before he died. The man you killed, sir, may really have been your father (about which more later), but he was *in truth* Norman Rasmussen, Boss of Valhalla." He put his lean brown finger on the chart, and traced the lines of fathering and mothering, of substitution and reversal. They all bent close to look.

A GENEOLOGY OF THE DEPEWS OF VALHALLA

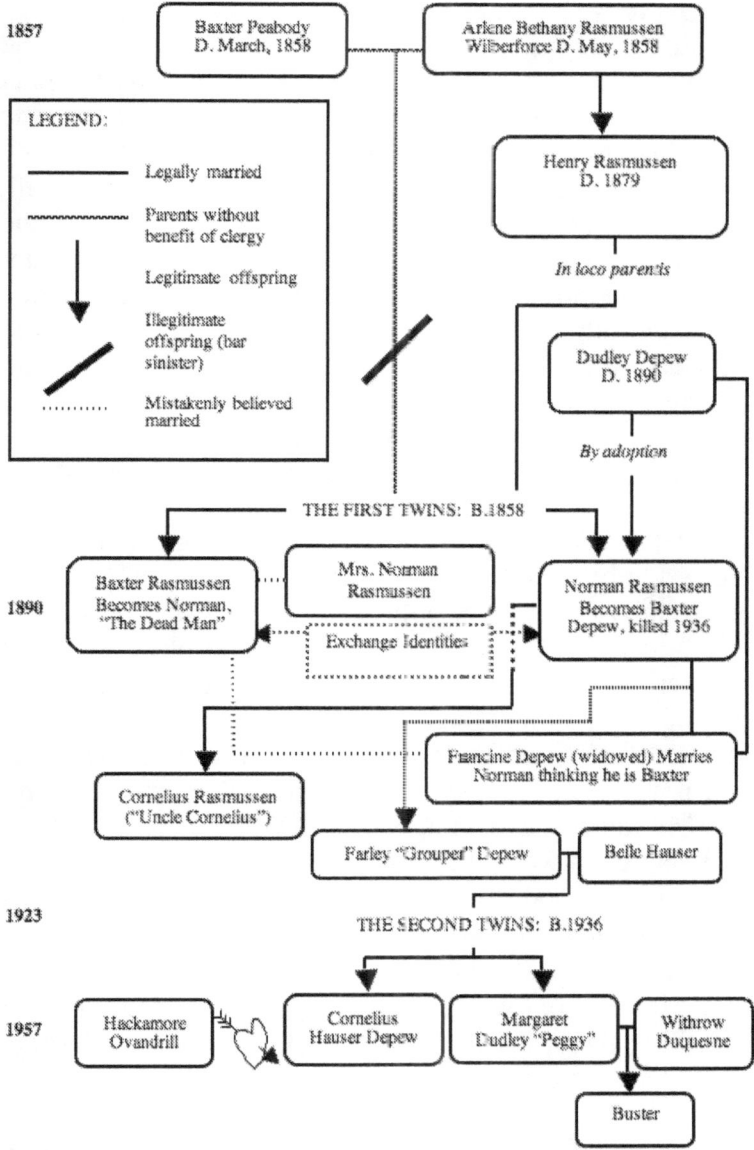

Cory smiled and shook his head. He reached out and Hackamore Ovandrill took his hand. They moved together.

"I don't understand," Grouper was saying. "I just don't understand it. What are those funny arrows pointing

433

at me?"

Withrow laid his long dark finger on the page. "Ah," he said. "Francine's diary. We can't say for sure, but she may have suspected that your father was not really the man she married, whom she thought was Baxter. You see, she loved Baxter and thought she had married him after Dudley died. But that was after they had switched identities. Still, she began to suspect that the man she married was not the man she thought he was. So she met secretly with the other twin, the one now known to her as Norman. We know that he was in truth born as Baxter Rasmussen. We know him as The Dead Man, and he's your father, not the real Norman, the man you accidentally killed."

Grouper sat on the ground, looking at his feet.

Reverend Ovandrill was gazing sadly at the spilled wine. Beside him Dr. Thanatopoulos said gently, "A libation. Think of it as a libation. For the gods, you see. This is a holy place."

"Huh? Oh, yes. A holy place. I'll have it restored. I had no idea this house was built on such a place. A burial chamber. There were stories, of course. About the house, why the Depews lost their power in Valhalla. Desecration. Ghosts. Who would believe in ghosts? I'm a man of God, but I never believed. My mother was a Sinker who didn't sink. My father was a man of God. Did he believe? I don't know. Narcissa wanted revenge, it was all she talked about. I never understood her. Cory? Grouper? Innocent people, I would have said. Why? What does such a God want?" he gestured to his daughter, holding Cory Depew's hand. "That Indian or whatever he was. Did you see it? Something there, an evil spirit? God. I don't know. There are too many religions here, too many heathens. Are they *all* right?"

Reverend Ovandrill shook his head, his expression both baffled and sorrowful.

"It happens I have also prepared an Ovandrill family genealogy," Withrow said. "You are all, it would seem, related, if somewhat distantly, to Mammy Sly, the woman

434

who cast the curse."

A GENEOLOGY OF THE OVANDRILL FAMILY

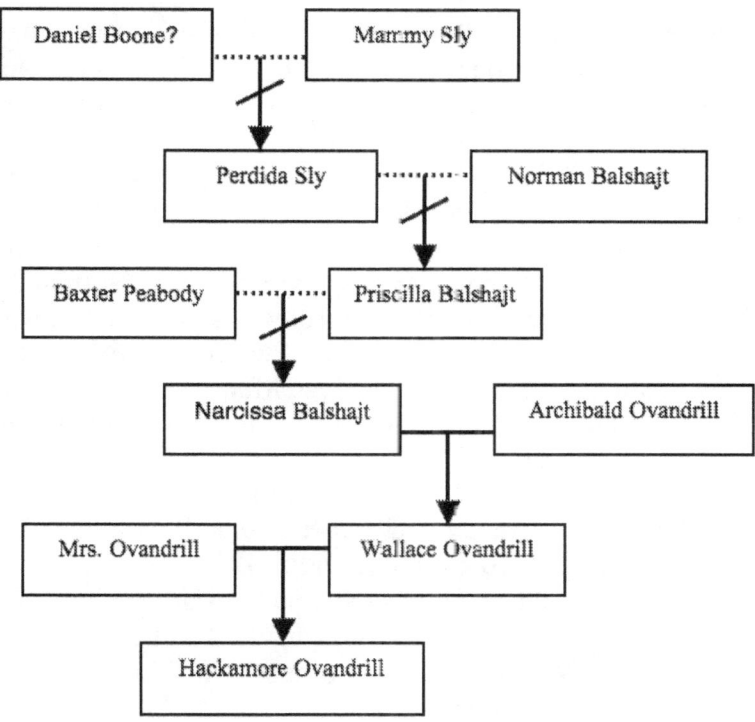

"I suppose that explains a lot," Hackamore said thoughtfully, hugging Cory's arm again. "But maybe it doesn't matter any more."

Dr. Thanatopoulos suggested to Grouper that he might want a shot.

"Thanks, perhaps I do," Grouper answered. He didn't know whether this was for a shot of vitamins or a shot of whiskey, and was beyond caring.

"No," Cory said to Hack. "I feel fine. I haven't felt this fine in a long time. You know something? I get along with animals. I thought this beast was going to eat me, but then something happened. I...spoke to him." He tapped the boar on top of his head, and the animal grumbled deep in his throat with pleasure.

"But what happened?" she asked.

"There was an earthquake," Cornelius was telling Grouper and Belle. "Everybody thought we were crazy down here, locking ourselves into a hole in the ground. Not a good place to be in an earthquake, you know. Ruined the wine cellar. We could've been killed!"

"Killed?" Grouper asked. "Killed? I killed my uncle, not my father. An accident."

The Dead Man spoke again. "That was Norman," he said in wonder. "That was my twin brother. Norman. I thought I was him. All this time. He was sick, Norman was so sick. An evil man. So long ago." He looked up. "I don't know nothing," he said. "I'm a Dead Man."

"It's all right," Cornelius said softly. "You really are Baxter. It's all right."

The Dead Man's eye was glistening with moisture.

"He was my father?" Grouper said, still looking at his feet. "Baxter? I killed Norman? Didn't I?"

"Half brodders are," the monk said softly. "Or cousins? Baxter to me confession made. I not understood, but now iss clear. Chew and Cornelius half brothers are. Haff same fadder. Maybe," he added doubtfully.

Grouper sat on the ground. He picked up the paper and stared at it. "So much fear," he said. "So much fear."

The huge boar stood suddenly, and turned, presenting his side to Cory, who was for a moment indecisive; then he nodded and placed both palms on the boar's back. He swung his leg over, holding tight the rolls of thick hide at the beast's shoulder in his hands and looked around. The boar snuffed softly. Then he turned and walked slowly up the slope, carrying the man Cory Depew on his back. The other pigs, one by one, rose and joined in the procession as it marched out of the earth into the light.

Chapter 9. In Which There is an Improvement in the Weather

It was a clear day. The wind's breath was warm across the land. The towers of Valhalla glimmered on the far horizons; the Little Hawking gleamed in the morning sun.

"It was the Ides of March," Withrow said. "Portents and change."

Cory did not answer. Marsha Willoughby stood across a green patch of meadow looking at him. She licked her lips with a gesture cruel and lascivious, small perfect rodent teeth peeking behind her pink tongue. He couldn't see her eyes, but he knew they were smiling behind those dark lenses. Then she shrugged and turned away. Big Mike also turned, and behind him, after a brief pause to gaze at Cory, the huge white Boar followed.

"I don't get it all," Hack said.

"Does it matter?" Cory asked. "It's over now. The curse, the crimes."

"Really?" Withrow asked, and winked. He was looking over at Peggy talking to her mother.

The sun was a growing yellow balloon expanding above the larches and buckeyes at the eastern edge of the Depew Farm. Connie Francis had number seven: *Who's Sorry Now.*

"You don't think it's over?" Hack asked.

Withrow shrugged. "I don't suppose anything is ever really over, you know. Not until you're dead, anyway. And even then, who knows? I've been thinking of going into the Church."

"What?" Cory didn't believe him.

"Sure, why not. This is the land of opportunity. Perhaps I could become the first black Pope."

"Oh. You're kidding."

"Yeah. My man Camus won the Nobel, as you know; he always said the question of suicide was the most important of all, and it seems to me that since you have just..."

"Spent the night in a bomb shelter in fear of world suicide?"

Withrow nodded. "Spent the night cowering in the cellar while the planet fell apart. I thought perhaps you might have some thoughts on these major Existential issues."

"I do have some thoughts. One, I'm glad to be alive. Suicide is silly. I suppose that's number two. Cowering in a fallout shelter is not a good way to take up the slack between birth and death, any more than worrying about whether you're losing face or not is a good way to get on with things. If I do anything with the rest of my life, it'll be, besides working with animals, to get rid of this ridiculous notion the world needs a lot of atomic bombs. Look at our fear, Withrow. Peggy. Hack. Look. We spent the night in a bomb shelter. That's a dumb way to spend our time! We're afraid of gigantic cockroaches and tarantulas roaming the earth eating people like gumdrops. Ugly mutations and progressive wasting diseases; we lumber around through the desolation of our movies looking for love. The end of the world? Horror? It's stupid. Hack, I don't know where your father got the idea we would be safe down there in the cellar, but in fact we were in more danger than if we'd stayed in the living room. We desecrated Vincent's ancestors. We have to learn something from all this."

"That was a speech," Peggy said.

"You noticed."

The sky was clear. The pigs emerged from the yawning hole. The enormous Ovandrill mansion, once the Depews', loomed behind them all. They stood, scattered in small groups, around the snow-covered lawns, the flower beds and fountains. The snow on the ground was melting, and green lawn was beginning to peep through. Spring was on its way. Perhaps.

"You never know with spring around Valhalla," The Dead Man said. "I remember the spring of '91. It was after the elections. Very late spring was that year, very late. Not like the year that Henrietta died. Terrible heat that year, and the cholera. Thousands died, even our mother. Poor Baxter Peabody. He was our father. We never knew our father, did you know that?"

He addressed Cory, who nodded. "He was eaten by pigs," Cory said.

"How's that?" the Dead Man asked. "Eaten you say?" he cupped his hand to his ear. Then he smiled. Then he began to laugh. He staggered away from the little group, cackling hysterically. There was something very funny there somewhere, and the laugh was infectious. Peggy smiled and rotated her index finger around her temple.

"He's a dear old man, anyway," Hack said. "I used to talk to him all the time. He was a good listener, and I was very sad."

Big Mike's white Ford pickup truck started. They all turned to watch it drive away. Marsha waved.

"She screws everybody, you know," Hack said.
Withrow shook his hand and grinned a white grin. "That's what they say. But here's a copy of the genealogies all together. You can see that in fact Cory and Hackamore are cousins, since they both have Baxter Peabody as great-grandfather; and Big Mike and Marsha, who are, by the way, first cousins, have the same great grandmother as Hack..."

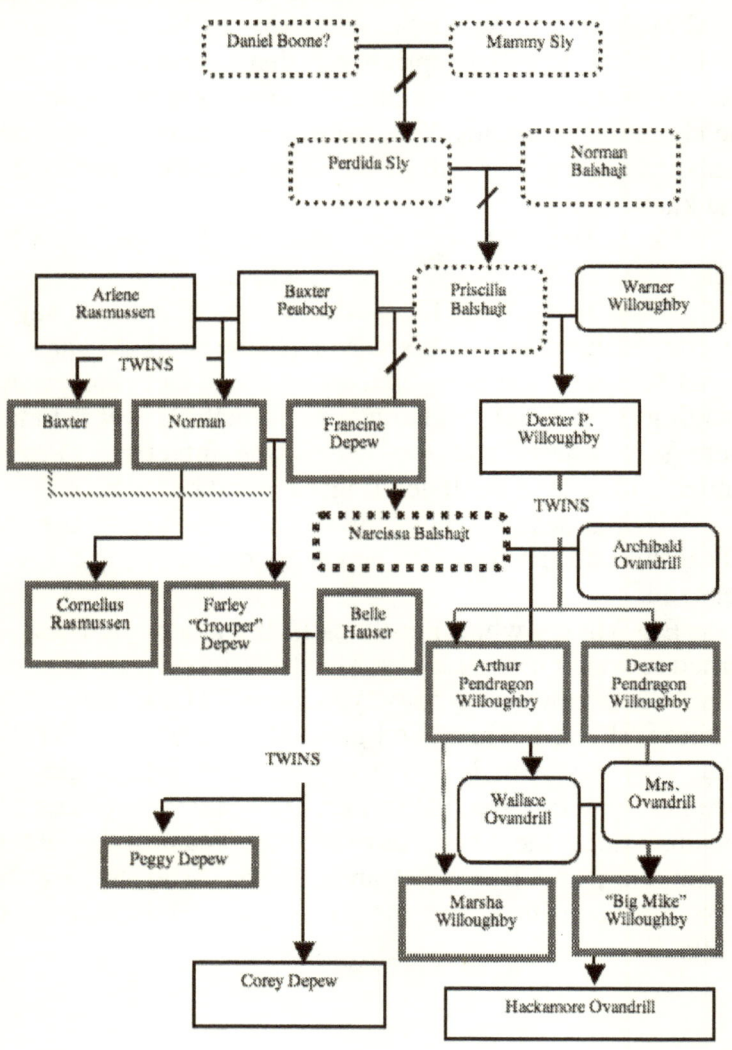

"I've added this little line of doubt from Baxter to Grouper," Withrow pointed out, tracing the dashes on the paper.

"Hmph," Belle grunted with infinite disgust.

Hack whispered in Cory's ear. "I don't care if you did

screw her," she said.

"It wasn't so great," he said gallantly, but with great sincerity. "After all, she did it for revenge. I don't think it was supposed to be fun."

The great white boar was seated in the back of Big Mike's truck, looking back at them all with a vast dignity. His small expressive eyes seemed to twinkle with good humor.

"He knows something," Cory said. "Something we don't know."

People approached from the farm. The pigs themselves, still reeling from the wine, grunted and trotted toward them. "Sooo-eee," a farmer called. More pigs appeared from underground. "Ahhh-oooo-eeiii-hah-hah-hah!" His hands were cupped around his mouth, and the call ululated as though mourning the loss of innocence and life and earth itself.

"Some quake, hah?" he asked when he arrived. "Phew, ain't never seen nothin like that in these parts. 'Cordin' to the radio there was a quake around here back in 1811, but nobody knows why. Maybe the Mississippi shifting around or something. Nobody knows. Hell of a show, though. All them hawgs got loose, come romping around over hereabouts. Soo-eeeii!"

The drove gamboled around the farmer, squeaking delightedly. The young ones with smooth faces and eyes still limpid with innocence, the adolescents swaying with newly discovered authority, the adults who had avoided the trip to the slaughterhouses of Cincinnati and Valhalla moving with a stately dignity which suddenly broke as they burst into ecstatic frolicking on the now trampled snow, their trotters cutting runes into the crusty surface as the warm breath of spring blew across them all. They turned upon themselves, and learned Withrow, watching, quoted:

"'For he is the servant of the Living God, duly and daily serving him. For at the first glance of the glory of God in the East he worships in his way. For is this done by wreathing his body seven times round with elegant

441

quickness.'"

"Couldn't'a said it better mahsef," the cheeky farmer said. "Them hawgs is something else. C'mon, Soooo-o-o-eyyy, pee-yug!"

A hundred happy hogs were gathered around now, ready to head for home after their night out, their excursion into the underworld, their social ramble. As they turned to go the farmer said, "Mighty happy to've metch'all. Specially considerin you're friends of my cousin, Big Mike."

"How's that?" Cory asked, but the herd was on its way, and his words were lost in the general hubbub of departure, the grunts and cries of "Rawrk," and "Wheenk," the "woof woof," barking and "Baawwrp," and "Ronk," and "Howwruff," as all the shapely white bodies moved away.

"I didn't know you were friends with Big Mike," Vincent said. His headdress and grotesque mask were gone now, but streaks of warpaint still zagged across his cheeks.

"I didn't either," Cory said.

"How're you feeling?" the Indian asked.

"Terrific."

Vincent nodded. "Powerful medicine," he said.

"Why did they leave?" Hack asked. "I thought they wanted revenge."

"It was the Boar," Withrow told her. "The Boar was the curse. When Cory faced the Boar the curse was ended. The generations were blasted. After all, Core did believe he'd lost face, that his face really fell off. It's all over now, though. The Hundred Years are up."

"Hem," said Reverend Ovandrill.

They turned. Foxworth was standing at the doorway to the solarium. There was no great visible damage to the house, only a slightly skewed look to the north wing where the cellar had collapsed. Foxworth suggested that everyone might want to have a bite of breakfast now.

As they moved toward the house, Reverend Ovandrill shyly tapped Vincent on the shoulder.

442

"I'm, uh, well, sorry," he began. "About my shelter falling into the, uh, burial grounds. I mean, well, I'll have it sealed up. You understand. It wasn't intentional, you understand."

"Oh, I understand," Vincent assured him. "These hills are riddled with caves anyway. You are probably connected with the Mozart Cave through this accident. Besides, they're all dead. I'm sure you will be forgiven. But of course my people would be grateful if you could take care of the Mound."

"Yes. Hem." Reverend Ovandrill moved briskly into the house, followed by the others, each according to his or her own nature.

Chapter 10. In Which Another Voyage Begins

Comes the first of May, and the river's ice is breaking up at last. Cory and Hackamore walked along the levee watching the big chunks swirl away. The floods were subsiding too, and the fat brown river is just another big bunch of water going down, finding its way according to gravity to the Mississippi and the Gulf of Mexico, unconcerned about the New Madrid Fault Zone or any other doom. It was, after all, spring in the Midwest.

They came to the board fence around the new stadium. The boards were weathered gray and warped, and behind them the hole was deep.

"Looks like a crater," Hack said.

"The war is over," he answered. "This is all that's left." The bottom of the hole was filled with dark water. "The earthquake caved in the sides. The caves opened up."

"The Warriors will have to play in four feet of water," she said.

"A new sport? Water baseball? Someone jumped in here last month, but they fished her out. Should we get married, do you think?" he asked.

They got into Cory's DeSoto and drove through the clean streets, past the blazing dogwood flowers and the thick bright green of new leaves, past the Rasmussen Building where the family motto carved in oak still quoted Zoroaster though few remembered whence those strange words came, and where the teeth were cast and shipped, and Dr. Thanatopoulos was even then injecting Grouper Depew with his weekly vitamins to keep away the dread. It was a sunny Thursday in Valhalla. Ragnarök was over. Heimdall Square was washed clean of winter's memories. The tower of Busby and Conrad was still the tallest building in town, but was being threatened by newer, more ambitious structures. Within, however, Bow Keep was

444

moving well. Clip on bow-ties adorned a half a million necks in Valhalla alone.

They cruised Midgard Avenue, and passed 1001 Celestial Street on the corner. The Slyville Sinker hex sign still protected the entrance, but already the maintenance man was setting up his ladder to paint it over. The artist had been evicted. A week ago he had nailed himself into his apartment and broken every available piece of glass inside, and the landlord suggested he might want to move to San Francisco where nuts like him were more likely to be tolerated.

"Hi-yaaah!" Crack. Yes, Wilmer was still cracking boards in front of his little cottage. His house guest was long gone. Cory waved as he drove by, and Wilmer paused long enough to wave back.

He drove up Celestial toward the spire of St. Credula the Ulcerated Martyr of Shköder. She still leaned back in painful ecstasy in the courtyard. The laundromat whirred and slurped. All was right with the world.

Only a few miles away, however, Schachter's Worm was turning. As Cory and Hack drove along the gently winding streets of Pecan Heights and greeted the foliage which concealed his parents' home, a legion of pupae were moving through metamorphosis to a new stage, a spiral form with a taste for wood. The sluggish, swollen waters of the Little Hawking backwater by the Schachter's Landing Boat Club were aswirm with tiny borers.

But is was a lovely day and the air was mellow. Cory was in love. Hackamore Ovandrill was in love. The DeSoto's engine purred for a change.

WVUU announced the results of the Commission's investigation into the shooting last fall at the Telltale Heart, a coffee house which used to be located near the University. The policemen involved in the affair had been censured and suspended for two weeks without pay.

"Two weeks," Hack said. "Without pay. That'll show them."

"I got my face back," Cory said. "I don't have to

pretend I'm Wernher von Braun. Nothing is going to give that guy his life back. This is 1958. You can't expect things to be perfect."

"No, no. Right. Of course."

"It doesn't mean we shouldn't work on it. Those ridiculous bomb shelters, for instance. That's not the way to take care of it. We need to stop the crazies from building the bombs. Like Ginsberg said. 'Go fuck yourself with your atom bomb.'"

"You've been reading Ginsberg?"

Cory nodded modestly. "I read *Moby Dick*, didn't I?"

"Yup."

"I'm worried about the animals, too, Hack. We aren't being nice enough to the animals. Take pigs, for instance..."

"Not now, Core, please. I know your thoughts on that subject. I read your paper. I heard you got the grade changed, too."

"Heh. I challenged the C minus. Even one or two medical schools are looking for people interested in humanities. We're going to make some changes in the Veterinary Sciences Department at VU. We're going to make them care."

"Oh, Cory."

Schachter's Landing drowsed in the sun. Chasen Mason sat on the porch of Ranger Headquarters and cleaned his gun. He had never fired his gun, a fact he found depressing, a secret shame. The fact is, the noise terrified him. So he cleaned it. Often. In public. The activity earned him a great deal of respect in the community. He was in a positively jolly mood when the DeSoto hummed past, and waved cheerfully. Cory stopped the car, and Hack leaned across him.

"Do you know where Daddums is?" she called.

"Down to the Boat Club, I suspect," Chasen Mason answered. He clacked the gun back together and sighted down the barrel at the white corner post of the porch.

The gun went off, and splinters flew.

"Je-sus!" Cory exclaimed. It was nothing to what

Chasen would say later. For now he was silent and apparently lethargic, as if transported by a sudden vision of vacation paradise. He failed to answer when Hack, after recovering from her surprise, asked him how long Daddums had been down at the boat.

They walked along the river bank and watched the waters flow. Spring in Valhalla and environs. Baseball season. Those American Existentialists the Everly Brothers had number one, *All I Have to Do Is Dream*. The world was filled with change and innocence.

The boats bobbed at their moorings. It was Thursday, of course, and not everyone was out. Dr. Thanatopoulos would have finished injecting Grouper Depew with the next week's courage and health, but his waiting room was still full. Mrs. Ovandrill was galloping to hounds, in hot pursuit of fox. The fox darted from cover, sat a moment to watch the approaching riders and their loudly baying hounds. Then he turned and sauntered along the edge of the Serpent Mound, tail twitching in the bright sunlight. He showed his teeth in a pensive fox-grin as he listened to the distant hoofbeats. Fox knew a thing or two, he did. He liked this game with Mrs. Ovandrill, although he had never met her personally. His tail swished and was gone, undergrowth closing over the place he disappeared.

The *Holy Cow* was stretched tight against its mooring line as the sweet spring currents tugged at her hull. Reverend Ovandrill was seated on his poop, his comfortable body comfortably seated beside a deeply chilled silver pitcher of martinis, prepared according to none other than Grouper Depew's secret formula by an attentive and taciturn Foxworth. When he saw his daughter and Cory, he raised his glass and held it before his face, so that his left eye vanished behind the olive bobbing in the drink.

"Cupcake," he called to Hack. "Want a drinkie?"

"No, thanks, Daddums," she shouted back from the shore. She and Cory started along the dock as Mrs. Ovandrill's dog Beckett set up a strident clamor. When

Beckett saw who was approaching, though, he subsided quietly, looked around, noticed the minister's white-socked ankle poised before him, and mistaking it, as he often did, for the object of his own obscure lusts, fired as they were by this balmy spring, clamped his forelegs to Reverend Ovandrill's foot and began to arch his back. Daddums, however, had been inured by his martinis, and failed to notice.

"We're in love," Hack told her father. "Cory and I. We're in love. I thought you might want to know."

Daddums raised his glass again. Beckett worked in silence. "Congratulationsss," he murmured. The rope holding him to the pier snapped quietly and the *Holy Cow* turned twice in the current as it majestically receded from the dock. The cocktail flag fluttered above the poop.

Daddums stood, his glass raised. The Worm turned one final time, and water began to seep through the wooden hull. As the houseboat approached the bend in the Little Hawking River which would hide it from sight, it began to slowly settle in the water. Perhaps it would make it all the way to the broad Ohio. Perhaps.

Whatever happened, it was clear that the Lord had approved his application for membership. He was going to join the Club.